Bone Chimes

CASCADE SAGA

By
M.A. Kastle

M.A. Kastle
PO Box 812
Helendale, Ca 92342

Publisher's note: The stories within are works of fiction, names,
characters, places, and incidents either are the product of the author's
imagination or are used factiously. Any resemblance to actual persons,
living or dead, events, or locals are entirely coincidental. Any
trademarks, service marks, product names, or named features are
assumed to be the property of their respective owners and are used
only for reference. There is no implied endorsement if any of these
terms are used.

Bone Chimes/ M.A. Kastle. -- 1st ed.
ISBN 978-0-692-19834-6

This is for Mr. K and my Minions
"Fortune favors the bold."

My sanctuary-

"Hazy gold of dusk mixed with soft ruby hues cast their glow across the mountaintops. Catching the shadows from the boats anchored near the shoreline, their reflections got lost in the ripples and broke the colors of golds and pinks reflected on the water."

CHAPTER ONE

With the rustling brush and snapping twigs, he twisted and blindly fired two shots into the dark. After the echoes died, Rutger listened to the eerie silence settling around him, and waited. He wanted to hear cries or whimpers, anything telling him he hit his target.

Suspect.

Rutger used his heightened werewolf senses to search the area. A void slammed into him. Nothing. No blood. No heartbeat. No essence of human or paranormal.

Nothing.

With his senses failing him, he opened his mouth and prayed the taste of tangy iron and torn skin of a fresh gunshot wound found his tongue. Denied. Bites of frustration ate at him as his patience faded. With his Smith and Wesson 4006 aimed into the woods, he recklessly fired three more shots, their sharp blasts slicing through the air and breaking the silence. He hoped the gunshots would force his target to move and give up her position.

In his current form his senses were better than a human's, but in his wolf form, they were stronger. Bringing his wolf to the surface, Rutger tried searching. He growled with his failure. Out of frustration, because he knew she was mocking his attempts, he shot two more times.

"Come on," he mumbled. *Make some noise.* Rutger drew another breath to have the musty taste of gun smoke wrapped in disappointment fill his mouth. "Move."

He froze, his breath held in his lungs, when footsteps crunching leaves gave away the woman's easy jog. He quickly holstered his gun and chased the sound. His boots slamming into the ground created more noise than the light steps of the fleeing target. Suspect.

The crescent moon cast a weak glow through trees limbs, forcing Rutger to use his heightened sight combined with his senses to race through the thick woods. He ducked limbs and branches, as reaching twigs tugged at his T-shirt and thorns from buckbrush snagged his cotton tactical pants. Ahead of him, he saw a shadow weaving through the thicket of shrubs, the moonlight catching her body as she ran. His energy spiked, his heart pounded, and his drive overflowed with anticipation of catching the person responsible for the murders.

He closed in as the first feel of awareness crawled over him. Her presence, hitting his skin, igniting his instincts, and working into his mind, created a surge of adrenaline racing through his veins. Rutger covered over fifty feet when a darkness descended inside of him, pushing his wolf to fight and his human features to fade.

She wasn't a werewolf. She wasn't a paranormal.

She was human.

And evil.

An energy slid over his skin, thick as oil and felt like it might never wash off. He felt her evil digging deeper and the fight forced him to slow down, his control to slip, and his wolf to rise. Fighting himself, he pushed harder, needing to stay focused on his prey. *Suspect*, he corrected. *Prey*. The line between wolf and man blurred and twisted his insides while corrupting his thoughts. He didn't want to lose her. So close.

One breath, two, and the sound of her breathing nearly curved his lips with a smile and created a growl of victory in his chest. A splinter of concentration returned when he saw her red hair and black shirt. It made her real. She wasn't a phantom. He pushed harder as he ducked under a limb and jumped over the remains of a fallen tree. He knew the terrain and knew in twenty yards the woods opened to a clearing where she would be exposed.

Before leaving the protection of the woods, Rutger pulled his gun from its holster. His instincts screamed a warning and he readied to face the suspect. With no cover, he searched through the silver white light and in to the clearing. Anger took over as the maddening truth glared at him. He was alone. Using his senses, he searched for the woman and her evil. Like a spook, a being capable of turning their crux into splinters, her trail scattered in a million directions.

So close.

"I am Rutger Kanin. You are trespassing on Cascade territory. If you give yourself up, you won't be harmed." *My ass,* he thought. *I'm going to make her pay.*

Stillness answered his bargain. Silence took the forest, and it felt as if someone sucked the life from it. A dull breeze caressed his heated skin, bringing an evil, which saturated the air, turning it thick. The feel resembled the first murder. The sheriff's department hadn't officially classified it as a murder, and they didn't have to. Rutger was going to prove it had been. He exhaled the breath he had been holding when the threads of the woman let go and his wolf calmed. She was gone. *Damn it.*

"Kanin!" Ansel yelled.

"Over here," he replied. After holstering his gun, Rutger took his flashlight from his pocket. He shifted his weight and inhaled, tasting the woods and the dirt beneath his boots but not the fleeing woman's scent.

Ansel Wolt, second in command with the enforcers, and Rutger's trusted partner, approached. His royal blue T-shirt, with the Cascade pack's emblem on the left side, was dark from sweat and dusted with dirt. His jeans showed signs of having battled thorns, and dust turned his black boots gray. He took the bottom of his shirt and wiped his face, and when he finished, he looked at Rutger with yellow wolf eyes. "Did you see her?"

"I did. And lost her." Rutger nearly growled the words. He moved the beam across the area, doing a sweep, its barren land glaring at him.

"I found the body. We have a problem," Ansel reported.

"Besides the body?" Rutger asked. The darkness was protecting the killer and guaranteeing her escape. Off the mountain? How? With irritation growing like an electric charge, he raised his flashlight, and turning in a circle, checked again. The beam brightened the same empty scenery. There were no indentations, and no trace of someone having walked or run through them. It's not possible for a human to disappear.

"Sir, it's missing its entire upper half. There's blood, but not a lot, like it was dumped here."

"Missing the upper half?" Sweat slid down his spine as Rutger placed his flashlight in the side pocket of his black tactical pants. He met Ansel's stare. "What's left?"

"A waist and legs. It's male," he replied.

"How do you know?" Rutger continued watching the woodline and the grasses for movement.

"He is naked." Ansel's voice lowered like he was going to whisper when the faintest feel of energy teased their werewolf senses. "Did you feel that?"

"I couldn't sense a paranormal, thought she was human. That energy is from a magic born. I'm guessing witches." Rutger shook his head. As if trying to find a murderer wasn't a challenge, he had to battle against magic. He hated witches. "Killing isn't enough for them, and they're getting braver. One dead rogue on our territory is one thing, but a dismembered body is going to cause the pack trouble. I'll call emergency services and Sheriff Dayton. Update the baron and explain why I'm calling human law enforcement."

As the Director of Enforcers for the Cascade pack, it was Rutger's job to organize patrols for their properties, work with the soldiers to protect the members of the pack, and the baron and baroness. It meant keeping the territory free from intruders, the pack safe from threats, and local law enforcement on his side. With two murders and the suspects coming and going, the security breach was keenly putting his relationship with the law in jeopardy.

"Yes, sir," Ansel replied, nodding. He stood beside Rutger searching the same empty land for clues. His deep inhales giving away his attempts to catch the suspect's scent and taste. Ansel waited for another second, gave up, and disappeared into the night.

After paranormals and the magic born gained the right to buy real estate, the Cascade pack began purchasing land. To date, they owned over thirty thousand acres in and around the Trinity area inside of Paradise County. The largest parcel of land was the Summit Sanctuary where they held their meetings, pack runs, and the inclusion of new members. The uninhabited areas of land, mostly forest, meant they went unpatrolled. But after the first victim, Rutger wasn't taking any chances. He ordered teams of two and the enforcers began patrolling all of the Cascade lands.

Rutger walked a grid, retracing his path hoping to find a shred of fabric, hair, and blood. He wanted to find blood. If he had one drop, the sheriff's forensic team would be able to test the DNA and they might have an identity. One damn drop. If there was blood, he would use his werewolf senses to know for sure what set her apart.

His search turned up nothing. With frustration playing with

his patience, Rutger marched where Ansel waited and called the sheriff and emergency services. He waited twenty minutes and turned his truck's headlights on using them as a signal. Another ten minutes and two sets of headlights glowed in the distance. "That didn't take long."

"No, it did not," Ansel replied as he drew his fingers through his thick, auburn hair and rubbed the back of his neck. The state of the body fused the air with a nervous energy and amped up his wolf's instincts. "I wonder where she was."

"You think, we're about twenty minutes from the main road, forty from town?" Rutger was glad it didn't take long. It had been a long day, turned longer night, and he wanted to go home. But the quick response had his suspicions working overtime.

"About."

The white SUV with the Paradise County seal on the side, black hood and top, slowly crept up to the scene. Its tires crunched over rocks, sticks, and clumps of foxtails, while its headlights cut through the hanging darkness. Rutger recognized Deputy Harley, her blonde hair, back and braided, and her always present scowl as she passed them to park beside his truck.

"Mr. Kanin, Mr. Wolt," Deputy Harley greeted. Her right hand rested on the butt of her Beretta 9mm pistol, holstered at her waist. Her narrowed crystal blue eyes resembled ice in the pewter light of the waxing crescent moon.

"Deputy Harley, glad you could make it here as quickly as you did," Rutger replied.

"I was in the area. You reported you found a body." She scanned the area. "You were up here and stumbled across it?"

Deputy Harley had yet to accept the Director of Enforcers as a legitimate position and the fact the Cascade pack's enforcer agency possessed the authority to patrol its lands. As a state regulated private security company, enforcers received tactical training, completed a physical fitness boot camp, fulfilled patrolling hours, and passed a criminal justice class, in addition to a paranormal history class. Rutger received more training and possessed more certificates than Deputy Harley, but she had a badge. Rutger was like a mall cop for the pack and the lack of rank kept him from going into detail.

"I received complaints of people camping along Lights Creek, and they're mining. Since this is Cascade territory, they're trespassing. It's illegal for them to be here," he explained.

"At this hour? Don't you think it would be better … safer to call the sheriff's department?" Deputy Harley asked, meeting his gaze. "During normal working hours."

"I have the authority to investigate the complaints," Rutger answered, calmly. There were snags in his black cotton T-shirt, dirt dusting his pants, and his boots were no longer black.

She gave him an obvious once over, her eyes lingering on the Cascade pack's emblem on his shirt. "You weren't up here taking the law into your own hands?"

"No," Rutger answered. Questioned like a child. By a human. He hated it.

"Show me the body."

"Yes, ma'am," Rutger mumbled as he walked. "I should warn you, it's not in good condition."

"Dead things usually aren't."

Rutger shook his head. "There are only legs." He stopped a couple feet away and took his flashlight from his pocket. Before he could click the LED bulbs to life, a bright beam lit up the pale legs.

Deputy Harley drew a quick breath. "This is Delta 8." She held the mic with her left hand while the beam moved down the length of the legs, stopping at the pair of bare feet, and slowly back to the waist.

"Go ahead, Delta 8," a female voice replied.

"I need Sergeant Shaw, another unit, the homicide team, and the medical examiner. The coordinates are in my GPS, upload it from my vehicle," Deputy Harley ordered. She turned the light and her narrowed gaze to Rutger. "You have no idea how it got here?"

"No."

Deputy Harley seemed to consider him, like she always did—part of her believing him and the other part dismissing the lycan. "I know you're not leaving town, so you can go home, but I need you to come into the substation tomorrow, answer some questions, and fill out a report. Both of you."

"Of course." The night, early morning grew darker, evading the coming sunrise and adding to the death.

"Delta 8, a unit is en route. Homicide and the medical examiner have been alerted." The male voice crackled and ended.

"Affirmative. Sergeant Shaw?"

"Notifying him now." The grumbled voice cut off.

"I'm going to assume you searched the area?" Deputy Harley asked, turning away from the body. Her hesitation told Rutger all he needed to know. She didn't like the sight of the legs, naked body, and truth behind the remains. It looked deliberate and deliberately brutal.

"Yes. I saw a woman, red hair, black shirt and pants," Rutger answered.

"You couldn't catch her?" Deputy Harley asked.

Questioning his werewolf speed. "No. She went into the woods and disappeared. I think she was a witch."

"A witch? Non-human, is that why you lost her?" The mocking tone in her voice was undeniable.

"Yes, on both counts." Rutger tried keeping his frustration out of his voice and stopped himself before explaining the witch was using magic, felt evil, and he sounded like a *non-human* loon.

"You can go," Deputy Harley advised as she turned and started toward her SUV.

"We can stay until your backup arrives," Rutger offered. Not out of good grace, no, he might not be able to sense the woman, but it didn't mean she wasn't there. He hadn't heard a car, an engine, off road vehicle, nothing giving away a retreating murderer.

"That's unnecessary. I expect to see you first thing in the morning. You need to include everything you saw, and everything you did, in your report, Mr. Kanin. I stress, everything you did."

Rutger didn't have a chance to respond when flashing red and blue lights accompanied a set of headlights, their beams cutting across their bodies. He looked at his watch, saw it was two in the morning, and it had taken fifteen minutes for the second deputy to arrive. Rutger had the feeling the sheriff's department was watching them. *Figures*. He shook his head, and his mind went straight to his early morning meeting. It was going to be cut short, if it happened at all, and would add another problem to his growing list.

"You can go," Deputy Harley repeated. She waited beside her SUV for the white truck with matching county seal on the side to park.

Rutger waved to Deputy Elm, as he left Deputy Harley and walked to his own truck, baring the Cascade pack's emblem. Ansel stood by the passenger door, watching the deputies. "Do you think they'll take the witch angle seriously?"

"Non-human, you mean. I don't know." Rutger sat behind the steering wheel, started the engine, and waited for Ansel. "I'll talk to the sheriff tomorrow so he understands we're serious. I know the first one was murder, despite it looking like a drug overdose.

This one is dangerous. The pack can't afford to have this continue."

"Agreed." Ansel sat back and continued to watch the deputies. "The baron isn't going to like this with the upcoming wedding. There are going to be old families, elders from powerful clans and colonies, and representatives from the Highguard in attendance. If they don't feel safe, they won't attend, making their absence a show of disrespect and will bring disgrace to the Cascade pack. Not to mention, the Highguard will question his authority as baron."

Rutger grunted; he knew what would happen. When he stepped down as second to alpha, and became the Director of Enforcers, his father, the baron, dealt with backlash from the Highguard. The Highguard demanded a show of power and control. In response, the baron took away Rutger's birthright. "We need to keep this as quiet as possible. The threat to the wedding ceremony and those attending will be another subject I'll discuss with the sheriff." Rutger backed up, turned his truck around, and started down the dirt road and back to Trinity.

A small city nestled in the mountains of Northern California, Trinity was named after the three encampments built as prisons for the paranormals, the magic born, and their family members during the late 1800's. Miles of steel walls held thousands of prisoners labeled non-human, for sixty years. His grandfather had died inside one of the encampments while his father, the baron, had never known life outside. With the non-human prisons becoming impossible to finance, and fact taking over where superstition had ruled, the United States government created United Force. An agency specifically designed to deal with non-humans. UF implemented laws, sanctions, and restrictions to their rights and believing the population was under control the non-humans were released. In turn, the non-humans created Resolution through Sedulity and fought the UF and the United

States to gain back their rights. Their equal rights. After years of court battles, non-humans finally regained the freedom and life they had known and their rights.

Rutger's parents and others didn't leave the area after their release, nor did they run from the torture they had endured and the horrors they witnessed. No, they stayed on the blood-soaked land, proving to the humans they weren't going to back down. To take control of their lives, Healey Kanin, a pureblood werewolf, with the help of several other pureblood families, gained possession of the three encampments, and after tearing down the structures and clearing the land, they built homes, businesses, and created the Cascade pack.

Rutger stopped in front of the lone two-story cabin surrounded by forest. "First thing, we have to go to the substation."

"Can't wait. See you then." Ansel got out of the truck and closed the door.

"The Crimson Years lasted ten years. You could argue they lasted five, the last five years being the beginning of the roundups. Today, though, you would think they were ongoing, the way the non-human community talks about them. I had someone blame the Crimson Years for the loss of their cultural heritage, their identity. As if the traditions of non-humans, specifically shapeshifters, living like animals constitutes as a cultural past." Louis kept talking, his laptop sitting on his thighs as he flipped through pages and spread folders out on the coffee table. "The loudest opposition are the lycanthropes, as if they have a stand."

She cast him a shielded gaze. *I hate this conversation*, she thought, and grabbed the bottle of wine. Jordyn walked to the living room and stood in front of him. "Wine?"

"Please."

"Don't you have shapeshifters in your class?" Jordyn asked. She poured, met his gaze, saw his disdain for all things paranormal, and walked back to the kitchen. She knew he did, he taught the 'Paranormal history' class at the university. A required class if you wanted a career in law enforcement. She had taken the class when she became a soldier for her pack. To keep her temper under control, Jordyn thought about her day and walked to the living room, her bare feet peeking out from the cuffs of her red lounge pants.

"Yes. I'm not going to argue with them. One day we're all human, the next day we're animals and magic born. The term non-human became a legal and recognized description. The shapeshifters lied to the world for centuries, started a war, a bloody war, I might add. The only saving grace to humans were the encampments."

They fought back. "The encampments were death camps, nothing more," she countered and sat down. *Shut up.*

He gave her a sideways glance, his azure eyes glittering with humor. "The way you standup for the underdog, no pun intended, always brings a smile to my face. You know as well as I do, it was in their best interest. The encampments kept them safe from future deaths while the United States, we the humans, decided how to deal with them. Their presence changed the direction of the entire nation."

Safe from death. Her grandmother died in an encampment, and since werewolves are immortal, how the hell did that happen? "Shapeshifters weren't the only prisoners. They imprisoned the magic born, and family members of those being held, human or not." Half the population of paranormals had been exposed during the Crimson Years, but there were those called the *Cloaked*, vampires, demons, fairies, and elves to name a few, choosing to remain in the shadows. How would the world change if they knew nightwalkers were real?

"They have enhanced senses and can wield magic. It created panic and a time of uncertainty. Their abilities changed everything from neighborhoods to the military, and our relationship with other countries," he argued. Louis turned to face her, his face drawn in confusion with a hint of challenge.

Jordyn knew she wasn't going to win, she would dig a hole, jump in, and bury herself in her defense. Eventually he was going to ask why she cared about shapeshifters and the magic born, and she didn't want to answer the question with a lie. Rather than pushing him, she drank deep and hoped the soft tannins and chocolate would drown her instant fury with his comments.

"Thank God for the United Forces agency. Someone has to control them."

Ignore him.

Jordyn's temper was inching toward saying something callous about humans, and it wouldn't end the conversation. It would propel it into an argument. Her mind wandered, her thoughts circling the anger she was trying to control, when the sharp ring of her cell phone made her jump. Picking it up, she looked at the screen. *Out of the frying pan and into the fire.* "It's my mom." Jordyn stood, grabbed her wine, and went to her bedroom. "Hello."

"Jordyn, this is your mother, how was your day?" Mia's cool voice asked.

Jordyn rolled her eyes. "Business is slow, it's the time of year, but it's going," she replied as she sat down in a rocking chair.

"That's nice. Listen, the plans have been updated. We'll meet you at the house, and once you're ready we're going to the

Timber House."

"Why the change in plans?" Jordyn asked. She watched Louis' shadow move across the living room while fear snaked through her. A public appearance.

"Your sister invited several friends, of prominent families, who are unable to attend the wedding. This way I don't have a crowd at the house, right before the wedding. The Timber House is perfect for drinks and light appetizers."

"All right," Jordyn said slowly. She half listened as she pinched the bridge of her nose. A slight ache started across her forehead and was quickly spreading into her eyes. She hated her next question. "Will everyone be there?"

"For drinks, no. Like I said, it's a casual get together for those unable to attend the wedding, and family."

That's good news. "Sounds like fun."

"Jordyn, you've missed so much. Your father and I want this to be special for the family. It's an incredible occasion for the entire pack."

She sat back in the rocking chair, wanting nothing more than to hang up. "I know. And it will be. Bailey is going to be a beautiful bride." Jordyn let the comment about the pack go unnoticed.

"I'm concerned about you."

Her conversation with Louis added to her inability to deal with her mother. Jordyn leaned forward to look in the direction of her bedroom door. She couldn't see Louis, his shadow, and she couldn't hear him. She lost track of him. In fear of him hearing any part of the conversation, she whispered, "Mom, there is nothing to worry about. I will be there and it'll be fine."

"Yes, of course, dear," her mother responded. "Have a good night and I'll see you in two days."

"I'll call you when I'm on my way."

"Be careful." Her mother hung up.

Leaning back in the rocking chair, Jordyn set her cell phone on the table. She could hear the doubt in her mother's voice and sensed the concern. *Concern.* It was controlled irritation. Mia didn't care what Jordyn was doing. As pureblood werewolves, and elders in the Cascade pack, the Langston family held status and it came with expectations. With Bailey marrying the third son of the baron and baroness, Mia was reminding Jordyn not to bring embarrassment to the family. Or the monumental occasion.

She took a drink of her wine, and then a second. Jordyn was surprised her mother hadn't said anything about dating a human, having to leave him in Butterfly Valley, and depending on humans for job security, like Mia did every time she called.

"Must be busy with the wedding," Jordyn mumbled.

"Babe, is everything all right?"

Jordyn's head jerked up. *Don't call me that.* "Just family stuff before the wedding." She cringed at her thought, it had to be the threat of having to go home. She hated going home.

"I'm sorry about our conversation, I get carried away after I've spent the day talking to shapeshifters about their rights. Is there anything I can do?" Louis asked, standing in the doorway. The light from the living room masked his face with a shadow.

"Fill my wine glass." She ignored him. She had to.

"Your wish is my command. Babe, the offer stands, I can go with you." He shifted to lean against the door jam, and she saw he had loosened his tie, unbuttoned the first three buttons of his white dress shirt. He stuck his hands in the pockets of his pressed beige trousers, and crossed his ankles.

With his face shielded, Jordyn imagined him as a werewolf and the image fell flat, closely followed by guilt. "It's a wedding and there's stress over seating and the reception. No one wants a bridezilla." She tried a smile and it felt fake. Like her lies.

"I don't like you having to go to Lakeview when Trinity is

right there. I know an hour separates them, but Trinity is a lycanthrope city. I understand it's getting worse, and they have a population of non-humans. My God, they have a baron who rules over them. The idea is antediluvian. Not to mention, the absurdity. It's becoming a tourist attraction. I know it's old fashioned, but you'll be alone, and it makes me uncomfortable." His eyes narrowed, his lips curving. "I can be there for you."

Antediluvian? "I think I'll manage," Jordyn responded dryly. She wasn't going to Lakeview, and Trinity had less crime than Butterfly Valley, she wanted to point out. "You have classes before summer break. Anyway, I don't want to see my family, let alone subject someone else."

"They can't be all that bad. I like you … a little," Louis teased.

Laughing, Jordyn stood. "A little?"

"Okay, maybe a lot. Come here, I have fire and wine." Louis smiled and stood straight.

"Well, if you insist." Jordyn turned the volume on her cell phone off and left it on the table. She took her glass, inhaled to calm her nerves, and followed Louis to the living room.

He had turned the overhead light off, removed his laptop, paperwork, and books from the coffee table, and replaced them with a bottle of wine. Golds and reds lit the room; the flames reached up the chimney, their shadows dancing on the walls.

"Very romantic, Professor."

"I do try. Come here." Louis took her hand and brought her close. "I know you have to go, but I want you to know, I'll miss you. I miss you and you haven't left."

"I'll miss you. I'll miss this." The privacy of her own house.

Louis leaned down, his lips tasting of human tangled with wine as he lightly kissed her and holding her hips brought her closer. With their bodies touching, she kissed him back, and tried to ignore her mind wanting to pick apart the conversations with

Louis and her mother. As Jordyn worked to stop her thoughts, she took a step backwards, and his fingers feathered her waist. Louis watched her with questions playing in his eyes. When her fingers worked to unravel his tie, he smiled, a confident grin. The fire sparked. While the shadows and flames chased one another, Jordyn held one end of his tie in her hand. Her lips curved, and lightly tugging the silk, she let it slide from around his neck. She lifted it in mock triumph, and after tossing it to the couch, started on his shirt.

CHAPTER TWO

The baron and baroness called Foxwood estate, a six thousand square foot mansion, sitting on twenty acres within Nearctic Valley, home. Across from the house, a two thousand square foot office building served as headquarters for the enforcers. Rutger sat at his desk, drinking coffee, and picking through photos of the scenes. Both victims had been werewolves and both had been moved to the woods, on Cascade territory.

"You can't imagine my surprise when Ansel called last night about the murder. What are those?" Healey asked. His short, coffee brown hair was combed back and complemented his tawny eyes and angular face, giving him an air of authority. He wore a white T-shirt under a rust-colored pullover sweater, three buttons leaving the collar open and folded over, and his dark denim jeans ended at soft leather loafers. From his modern clothing, speech, and demeanor, every detail concealed his one hundred years.

"Photos of the bodies and the scenes. Sheriff Dayton had Detective Russell, with the homicide unit, give me copies," Rutger replied. The baron sat down in the dark hickory wingback chair across the desk from Rutger. "I talked to him this morning."

"You're working with them?"

"This case involves werewolves, and we suspect witches. Since a magic born is involved, I'm working as a liaison. Plus, the sheriff doesn't want this to get any worse. His county won't be a tourist destination if lycanthropes are being dismembered. It would scare away the humans."

"Humans or not, I want this taken care of, Rutger. The wedding is in three days. Trinity is Cascade pack territory. I can't have mutilated bodies, an investigation, and deputies harassing guests when they arrive. I absolutely cannot have the deputies thinking one of my pack has turned rogue and is responsible."

His attention focused on the word rogue. "Their understanding of rogue and the dynamics of a pack borders on ignorant. Detective Russell said they aren't ruling out a *rogue*, but are trusting me, that it isn't anyone belonging to Cascade. Like I said, we think whoever is doing the murders has connections to witches. Deputy Elm and Detective Russell have talked to the homicide detective and it has been recommended to bring in the regional task force, Organized Paranormal Investigations. They handle paranormal crimes and have better resources and manpower."

"Excellent. I need you to keep me updated. And if you think we need more soldiers for the festivities, summit the report to Torin. If you were at the substation, I'm going to assume you didn't have any problems explaining why you were near Lights Creek?"

"Yes. The reports are all in order. Again, they assured me they don't believe anyone from the Cascade pack is responsible. To be safe, I warned them of the incoming guests," Rutger answered, frustrated because he needed to get back to work.

"Just so you clarified your presence. What else do you have to do today?" Healey asked.

"I'm meeting with Detective Russell as soon as he has the medical examiner's report. The first body showed no signs of a struggle and looked like a drug overdose. It is the polar opposite of the second."

"A body without a torso would be opposite," Healey commented. "The baroness tells me she hasn't been able to get a hold of you. The family is having dinner together, you have been officially invited," Healey stated as he stood.

"I'll see what I can do." Rutger wasn't committing to dinner. His phone buzzed, the vibration making clinking noises as it did micro bounces on the dark cherry wood desktop. He looked at the screen hoping it was Detective Russell and was disappointed when he saw Kory's name. He touched the ignore button and looked at the baron.

"The baroness talked to her when she couldn't get a hold of you, and told Kory about dinner. You should have taken the baroness' call." Healey tapped the desk with his finger. "You'll make it. That's an order." After giving Rutger a stern glare, he walked out of the office.

Rutger stared at the open door, heard him greet Ansel and ask a question, when another voice joined the conversation. Jason. He must have escorted the baron. The man couldn't walk fifty yards from his house to the enforcer's office—the Director of Enforcer's office; his son's office—without his sentinel. Rutger shook his head, thought about the rogue, the dead werewolves, shoved the pictures around, and waited for Ansel.

"The baron," Ansel said as he entered. He never wore the standard enforcer uniform of black on black BDUs. His black T-shirt, jeans, and boots being his chosen uniform.

"Usual report. And he reminded me my youngest brother is getting married." Rutger stood, stepped around his desk, and looked out the window to see the baron walking toward the house. Right behind him, Jason followed, and at the same time he watched their surroundings. Rutger's nerves grated when he saw Lord Langston's luxury sedan.

"What will you do?" Ansel asked as he sat down. He turned

to see Rutger staring out the window. His broad shoulders visibly tightened under his black BDU blouse and his hand rested on the butt his gun.

"I'm going to call the homicide detective and check if the medical examiner's report has come in on the first victim," Rutger answered. He watched Lord Langston and the baron greet each other in the tradition of the elders. Lifelong friends. Family. They held each other's forearms, repeated a blessing between brothers, and exchanged pleasantries. "Hopefully, they have worked on the second. I need evidence, anything telling me I'm right and it's witches. And I wasn't chasing a ghost." *Ghost. Rogue.*

"No. I mean what are you going to do when she arrives? Word is, she is expected tomorrow. That comes directly from Jason." Ansel raised his eyebrows as if he had divulged secret information. "She'll be at the Timber House. Her first public appearance in three years."

I know. When Sadie—the baroness' personal sentinel— greeted both men, they entered the house with Jason and Sousa, the baron's second personal sentinel, following. Rutger turned away from the window and with drawn brows met Ansel's gaze. "Jason is giving away intel?"

"To an enforcer. Shall I shoot him?"

Affirmative. "I have a possible double murder, my brother is getting married, there are a dozen dignitaries and their families arriving in town. The baron is in my office every couple of hours questioning my decisions. It's my job to have the personnel to secure everyone's safety and cover the perimeters. There cannot be security issues. One person doesn't get my attention," Rutger replied and sat in his chair.

"Right. Do you want me to schedule a meeting with Torin?" Ansel asked with a smile.

Rutger ignored him. "Affirmative. We'll meet after I talk to the detective."

"Yes, sir." Ansel stood and walked to the doorway. "As a pureblood, and Lord Langston's eldest daughter, and the bride's sister, Miss Langston will be part of the wedding party." Before Rutger could say anything, Ansel continued. "There's more. The baron is withdrawing two soldiers from Torin to serve as his escorts."

The baron couldn't ask me? "The baron requires four sentinels. That's excessive even for him. Who told you?" Rutger asked.

"No one. I overheard Jason talking to Torin. Jason said he has been temporarily reassigned and he needed backup," Ansel explained.

Keeps getting better. "Where is Jason going?" Rutger sat back in his chair and looked at the screen of his phone. He didn't need any more surprises turned problems.

"When Miss Langston arrives, Jason will serve as her shadow."

Shadows were specially trained soldiers and enforcers—their purpose was to get close to a specific person, watch that person, and report back to the baron. Why would the baron assign one of his personal sentinels as a shadow for Jo? "Why?"

"You can ask the baron tonight at dinner. I'm sure the question won't spark a heated conversation." Ansel was clearly struggling to stop himself from laughing.

Heated. More like a war. The thought made his head ache. "We have business."

"I'm meeting Luke at the church and we're going over the security points. When I'm finished with my report, I'll catch you up. If there's anything we need to modify, we'll meet with Torin. I'm told the wedding is gaining popularity among the tourists, humans, and the paranormals living in Trinity."

"The threats associated with spectators needs to be addressed, as well as traffic control. While you're there, keep your eyes open for anything that looks out place, and if you sense anything let me know ASAP."

"Yes, sir," Ansel replied, and left.

Picking a pen up, Rutger tossed it to the desk in annoyance and sat back. The wedding was going to be the end of him.

"Headed back home," Lizzie teased. As the receptionist for Epic Sights, the photography gallery, she sat at a desk answering phone calls, incoming and outgoing shipments, and managing day-to-day business. She straightened, and Jordyn could see her dark red hair and black rimmed glasses over the computer monitor.

"Not home. To my parents' house, and don't get me started." Jordyn stared at a display of four landscapes framed in matte black. "Which one did you say Mr. Cassady purchased?"

"Snow Peak. I'll ship it out today or tomorrow," Lizzie answered.

With a bright caerulean sky as a backdrop, snow-covered peaks glittered in the silken rays of the early morning sun. The mountains moved when Jordyn took the picture from the wall and carried it to the reception desk. "I don't want to leave the space empty. What would you suggest?"

"Something summery, and yes, that serves as a technical term." Lizzie grinned.

"Very savvy." Jordyn rolled her eyes, smiled, and started toward the back to search for something *summery*.

"Jordyn," Lizzie called. Her hushed voice sounded urgent.

Jordyn stopped and turned around. "What's wrong?"

"There's a woman by your Morning Glory landscape."

"Really?"

"Please," Lizzie pleaded. "I'll owe you a coffee."

Jordyn laughed. "Fine. I'll talk to her."

Ocean views, sunsets, and desert scenery photographs sat around her when she met green eyes. "Hello, I'm Miss Langston. Can I help you?"

The woman turned bringing the faint scent of lavender to the air around her. Raising her pale hand, she moved stray strands of red hair from her cheek. "Andrea. I was admiring this photo."

Roasted aromas of coffee had drifted in the SUV, when Jordyn risked driving into the mountains near Trinity to catch the sunrise. Golden hues tangled with pinks and plums, highlighting the twisted trees and casting spider web shadows across a patch of yellow wildflowers. "The high altitude and extreme differences of summer and winter cause the trees to twist. I've always thought they were gorgeous. And in early spring the sunrises are spectacular," Jordyn explained with the memory playing through her thoughts. A bittersweet feeling swept over her as each picture was a window into her life and reminded her of what she gave up.

"I know the Belle Ridge area well. The picture captures its beauty," Andrea said with a smile. "Have you been there recently?"

"Sadly, it's been a while." Jordyn's gaze left the print, her memories drifting, and she looked at the woman. Her shabby blouse, the ragged seams of her slacks, and the holes in her dated shoes, covered by leather dye, felt out of place. "I know the area as Butte Springs." A sliver of awareness skated across her skin, pushing her wolf's instincts into motion, and Jordyn quickly shut them down. Dangerous. She mentally counted the days since she shifted into her wolf form. Too many. Jordyn inhaled, smiled, and gained a sliver of control.

"I heard it from an old miner, it's most likely a fable from his imagination, but I like it." Andrea laughed, an uneasy sound.

"Old stories. Are you interested in the print?" Jordyn asked, holding her gaze.

"No, thank you. I'll be on my way." Andrea smiled, waited a moment as she looked at the print, and after several seconds turned and walked toward the reception area.

Jordyn watched and listened to her heels clicking on the floor. Awareness tugged on her, and using her senses, Jordyn tried and get an impression and the reason the woman alerted her instincts. There was nothing, just human. "It's stress," she whispered and checked her watch. Thankfully, in a couple of hours she would be headed home.

When the woman was out of sight, Jordyn turned to another print. Her favorite print.

Hazy gold of dusk mixed with soft ruby hues cast their glow across the mountaintops. Its reflection got lost in the ripples as she left the soft sand and, picking her steps carefully, entered the water. With a firm grip on her camera, she searched the mountains and the shore for the perfect shot. The cool, evening water was lapping around her thighs nearly touching her shorts as she stared at the sunset.

'Babe, you going to take the picture or what?' his rough voice teased from the shore.

'Yes,' she mumbled absently.

'You picked a perfect evening. The sunset is gorgeous tonight.' His low voice rumbled over the sound of the water splashing against rocks. 'Jo?'

"Jo?" Her name drifted on the breeze and faded. "Jordyn, did you hear me?"

"Sorry. What did you call me?" she asked. She knew she wore her memories on her face.

"Your name, Jordyn," Louis answered. "You were gone there

for a minute." He closed the space between them and wrapped his arms around her.

Jordyn smiled, ignoring the tinge of regret, looked up and met his gaze. "Sorry. My mind is everywhere but where it should be." Jordyn hooked her fingers in his suit pockets while covering her unease with a weak smile. She knew it barely curved her lips let alone reached her eyes.

While the print was a constant reminder of Trinity and her past, it helped her land her partnership at the gallery. Placed in several magazines and commercials, it had given her respect and recognition amongst her peers. Jordyn caught the shadows from the boats anchored near the shoreline, breaking the colors of golds and pinks reflected on the water while Rutger waited for her. Wearing worn jeans, slung low on his hips, and his bare feet buried in a mix of smooth pebbles and sand, the water turned the cuffs dark. She had turned to see him staring at her, his eyes gold with his wolf, and the sun kissing his bare chest.

"A wedding is a stressful time, encompassing emotions and excitement," Louis explained and drew her closer.

It wasn't the wedding. Jordyn fought to escape her memories and the need to get away from Louis. "I can't wait for it to be over."

"It's not too late. I can go with you."

"For reasons I have already explained, you know it isn't going to happen." She was tired of repeating herself. Instead of letting her frustration out on Louis, she reminded herself of her reality. Wrapping her arms around him, Jordyn gazed up at him. His strawberry blond hair looked like he had hastily run his fingers through it, ruffling his usual perfect style. It meant his day had been stressful. To confirm her thought, his azure eyes darkened to deep blue and narrowed on her. "How was your day?"

"Shapeshifters." He inhaled. "Since I don't get to go, I want you by the fire tonight. I'll spoil you so there's no chance of you running away to Lakeview and staying."

Her breath caught and she forced herself to breathe. Running away. "Not a chance. And I would love that. I'll tell Lizzie I'm leaving, and I'll meet you at my place."

"Deal. Want me to pick up something for dinner?"

"I have a craving for Italian," Jordyn responded and backed away from him.

"Pasta it is, my lady," Louis answered with a mock bow. "And no doubt, a robust red."

"No doubt." She laughed, trying to cover her unease.

Louis leaned in, lightly kissed her lips, and taking her hand, they walked from the main part of the gallery to the reception area. Jordyn's heels clicked on the rustic wood floor, the hem of her black skirt grazing her knees while Louis' human feel sank into her skin. She let go of his hand when they reached the reception desk, and he kept walking. At the door, he stopped, and turned around. "See you at home. Bye, Lizzie."

"Bye, Louis," Lizzie said from behind her monitor.

Louis opened the door and walked out of the gallery. The familiar jingle from the chimes stopped as the glass door closed behind him. She watched him cross the narrow street, flanked by shops, boutiques, and her gallery, and get in his luxury crossover.

"He's a sweet thing, girl," Lizzie said, scooting her chair away from the desk.

"Yes, he is." The usual feeling of guilt stabbed her and plummeted her heart into the pool of her lies. "I'm calling it a day," Jordyn told her, attempting for normal. She wouldn't dare leave before six in the evening during the summer months. The tourists were known to take walks after dinner to enjoy the cooler temperatures and less crowded streets. When they walked, they window shopped. Spring wasn't as busy even with the first day of summer days away. "Did Andrea say anything to you about the landscape?" she asked.

"No. Said thank you, and left. She was kinda strange."

"How do you mean?" Jordyn faced Lizzie, her own concerns rising again.

"She kept watching you. And there was a guy outside watching her."

Did Andrea know she was a werewolf? "Maybe they were in awe of my greatness," Jordyn remarked, attempting to let go of the uneasy feeling. She did her best to stop from smiling and laughing. It didn't do any good, and Lizzie joined her. "I tried to say that with a straight face."

Lizzie's laugh echoed in the empty gallery. "That was it, oh great one."

"You're welcome," Jordyn joked as she left the reception area.

After receiving the partnership with the gallery, Jordyn left Trinity for Butterfly Valley, and let three years pass. No one knew what drove her to leave, or about the deal she made with the baron. He set the rules and she followed every single one of them as if her life depended on them. And it did. Allowed one trip a year, she made sure she spent Christmas with her family. When the arrangements had been set for Bailey's wedding, the baron called to give her permission to attend the ceremony. Jordyn found herself heading back to take part in the events.

"Get a grip," she mumbled. "I'm not going to Trinity to see him. I'm going to see my sister. My family," she said aloud as if it was going to help. Jordyn entered her office, and after going through her routine of shutting down her computer and checking her calendar, she grabbed her coat, her messenger bag, purse, and locked the door behind her.

"Have a great evening." Lizzie stood and stretched. "I think I'll check the supplies, then close up. The print will ship tomorrow."

"Perfect. Thank you. If anything comes up, call me," Jordyn replied. *Please, call me*, she wanted to add as the thoughts of her sister, her mother, and the baron's family crowded her mind. *Let it go*, she told herself. She had one night and she wasn't going to allow her worries to change her mood. Not when she was going to see Louis. He would ask her what was wrong and she wasn't going to add another lie. "Have a good night."

"You too," Lizzie said over her shoulder.

Outside, ashen clouds began building into thick clusters and hiding the late afternoon sun. She felt the humidity in the air and the wind picked up with the threat of a thunder storm. It explained the deserted stores and street. Jordyn walked down the sidewalk, passing several shops that sat quiet. At the parking lot, Jordyn hit the unlock on the key fob, opened the SUV door, and tossed her bags to the passenger seat. Behind the steering wheel, she stared out the windshield.

Secrets. They plagued her. No one knew why she left. Louis didn't know he was dating a werewolf. Or in his words 'the underdog'. And there was no end to her lies in sight.

Jordyn started the car, and driving out of the parking lot, she stopped, checked for traffic, and turned left, headed home. Within minutes the downtown area sat behind her, and she focused on making a mental list of things she needed to pack. Clothes, camera gear, and the wedding gifts. *Easy*.

The baron created a set of rules when he allowed her to leave but didn't give her a time limit. It made making plans difficult and made housing more difficult. Jordyn eased her SUV down the dirt road and parked her car. She had rented the isolated house from an elderly woman, who hadn't asked if she was a non-human. The small two bedroom, two bath rental fit her perfectly. The kitchen was decent size, sported new appliances, and opened to the living room. The backyard, under the cover of darkness, allowed her to shift and run. Her grace was the fireplace. She loved the way the flames danced on the walls and the warmth calmed her wolf. The homey feeling made living away from her pack tolerable.

Jordyn entered the house, placed her bags on the dark-stained table beside the door, and walked through the living room to her bedroom. Running on auto, she kicked off her heels, stretched her aching feet, and took a pair of lounge pants and a tank-top from a drawer. With comfortable clothes in hand, she headed to the bathroom. After tossing her blouse to the counter, she picked up her tank-top. Trinity was going to be a test. Friends she hadn't seen in three years were going to have questions. Jordyn had her own. Why the hell did the photograph instantly mean Rutger?

"Hey, you in there?" Louis asked.

Jordyn glanced at the door, her nerves jumping, her guilt expanding. "Yes, bathroom."

"I have food and wine."

Jordyn peeked around the edge of the door so he would hear her. "My hero."

Louis stood inside the bedroom, smiling. "My day is complete."

Jordyn laughed, closed the door, looked in the mirror at the face staring back and cringed. *Lying is killing me.* By the time she changed and walked into the living room, Louis had set the table and poured wine.

"Thank you. This looks delicious."

"You can thank Anthony next time we're in there," he replied. "I know I've been busy with my classes and begging you to take me with you. I haven't thought about what you're facing. Are you prepared to go back after all of this time?"

"I was there for Christmas. And it's my sister's wedding." Jordyn took a sip of her wine.

"Your sister is marrying your ex-boyfriend's brother and that's bizarre. Not as ridiculous as you having to be around your ex and his family."

Ex. If leaving and hoping three years of silence could be used as a break up. "I'm sure my family will run interference for me." The entire pack would run interference for her. Not to protect her from him—she wanted to laugh—but to make sure Rutger kept his perfect steady, strong, and important life. She was a runaway. A rogue. A submissive who was hiding.

"You're sure?" Louis asked.

Genuine concern sat in his eyes, as he stared at her. Guilt. "I'm positive. Don't worry." Jordyn took another sip of her wine and placed the glass on the table. Taking her fork, she absently pushed noodles covered in a rich cream sauce from one side of the plate to the other. She had been starving but the conversation and leaving in the morning was destroying her appetite.

"Yeah, you look like you have it all together." Louis stared at her with worry in his eyes. "This is getting serious."

He needed to stop. To change the subject, she could start defending shapeshifters. Jordyn smiled, putting her best 'don't worry about me' look on. "I'm sorry. Everyone is under pressure for the wedding to be perfect. I know it will be, and it'll be stressful for the next couple of days."

"Don't think about it right now. Since you are playing with your food, let's retire to the living room."

"That's a grand idea." Jordyn stood, and with her approach, Louis met her and wrapped his arms around her waist.

"I like this."

"Me too." She smiled and kissed his lips.

"Come with me." Louis' lips curved into a grin as he led them to the couch. Jordyn sat down and watched him walk over to the fire. Taking the poker, he stabbed at the blackened wood, and added more. When flames reached up and the wood crackled, he turned, gave her a heated gaze, and made his way to the side table to click the light off.

"Preliminary?" Rutger asked as he took the file. He flipped open the cover with the county emblem on it and worked his way through the subpages stating it wasn't a complete report. "Asphyxiation. He didn't have a mark on him."

"Waiting on the toxicology report," Detective Russell explained. "I disagreed with you about the overdose."

"It's hard for a lycanthrope to overdose. Their metabolism is quicker than a human's and they can shapeshift to purge the drugs. I don't understand why there isn't a mark on him," Rutger replied.

"He was a lycan, could that be the reason? He healed before he died?" Detective Russell asked.

Rutger shook his head. "No. To heal he would have had to shapeshift. If he shapeshifted, he wouldn't have died."

"I'm considering contacting someone at Celestial and requesting assistance. The medical examiner knows about as much about lycans as I do. And the blood tests are proving tricky," Detective Russell said.

Celestial, a non-human hospital, with a staff consisting of paranormals served Paradise County. Clio Hyde, one of Rutger's enforcers, was an emergency room doctor at Celestial. "I know Dr. Hyde, who is a trauma physician and would be happy to direct you to someone who could help. What about the new murder?" Rutger asked.

"I read your statement. I'm waiting for the same reports to come back. If there are similarities, and victim one is connected to victim two, then I'll entertain the idea there is more than one person, and witches are involved. That will escalate the case, clearly changing it to a non-human serial killer and we will have a much bigger problem."

"Yes, we will," Rutger agreed. He closed the file, set it on the desk, and picked up a picture. Pale skin stood out from dirt and rocks, and at the angle the picture had been taken, he could see there were no organs around the waist. The muscles of the thighs and legs had been left untouched.

"I have entered the second victim in the Citizen Base and missing persons. I haven't gotten a hit with the missing persons data base concerning the first victim. I've also entered both of their descriptions in the National Crime Log. I have a call into a representative from United Force, maybe I'll get a response."

The Citizen Base, or CB, was a data base of all shapeshifters, magic born, and paranormals throughout the nation. NCL worked the same as the CB, but was a complete system including humans and their criminal records and linked to every government agency. UF would have connections throughout the nation and have accurate information. Rutger didn't think it was going to be any better when one of the victims didn't have a torso, and they didn't have names, or a city of record to narrow the search. He met Detective Russell's gaze, his thoughts going to the baron and telling him the status of the investigation. Stalled. No answers.

"As soon as I'm in contact with the detective from OPI, I'll let you know. Do what you can to keep the specifics of the second murder under wraps. One word about murdered lycanthropes, or missing body parts, and the news will report devil worshipers, shapeshifters gone wild, and who knows what else. You know, whatever they start will spread like a wild fire. Not to mention the general population, they'll panic."

"I'll make sure my people don't say anything," Rutger replied.

"I hear there's a big wedding happening. Congratulations,"

Detective Russell offered.

"Thank you."

"A marriage involving the baron's family has created quite the buzz. I can only imagine the logistics and security headache the events create." He leaned back in his chair, his hands clasped over his pale blue button-down shirt. "When I knew I was going to be working this case, I did my homework. So, I know how complex your pack is and you're the director for security. It's the only reason I'm sharing information. That and your help is appreciated."

Security. Rutger wasn't going to correct him. "I understand. If you need anything let me know." He stood and put his hand out at the same time Detective Russell stood. They shook hands and Rutger left the sheriff's department and headed back to the enforcer's office without answers.

CHAPTER THREE

Jordyn finished her coffee, rinsed the mug out, and placed it on the drying rack. She thought about doing some laundry, washing her car, grocery shopping, anything to delay the inevitable, and maybe miss drinks altogether. What the hell was she thinking? She shook her head. How could she be selfish, when every message from her sister read 'Can't wait to see you.'? There was hiding from her past and there was being a coward. She couldn't live with herself if she disappointed her sister.

"It's my sister's day," Jordyn mumbled as she headed outside. The cloudless sky blazed with spring while the humidity teased rain. At her red SUV, she opened the door, and pushing her duffle bag of extra clothing out of the way, shoved her suitcase inside. After two trips, Jordyn stood in the doorway making sure she had everything.

It's a wedding, not an execution, she reminded herself, and locked the door.

Once behind the steering wheel, with her seatbelt buckled, she stared at her house. Damn, she didn't want to go. Grudgingly, she started the engine, picked a radio station, and messaged Louis. As she backed out of the driveway, she couldn't stop herself from thinking about Rutger. "It's my sister's wedding. People will be too busy to notice I'm there. He most certainly won't," she mumbled. He'd moved on.

Jordyn feared the week ahead of her. Not to mention being alone, seeing everyone, and knowing they would have questions.

Three years ago ... hell, two years ago, she would have explained herself, anger and betrayal included, but now, it was embarrassing. Heartbroken and jealous wasn't a good enough reason to leave your family. Let alone your pack. It had been a decision based in hurt and uncontrolled emotions and without considering the consequences.

One thought lead to another and the memories captured her and played like she was watching them together all over again. "I was running." *Admitting it is half the battle*, she thought. The real battle would be seeing them together, like she was alone and pining for him, because her human boyfriend was three hours away. Out of range. She could already hear her mother and the ridicule.

At the halfway mark, Jordyn stopped for fuel and sent her mother a message. Jordyn refused to talk to Mia and hear about how she hadn't left when she said she would or the lecture about responsibility and the wedding. Back on the road—and her mind easily focused on the mountains, the trees, dogwood flowers, and the emerald green only spring could create—she drove. Her thoughts paused when a sign announcing the turn to Lakeview came and went. She kept driving. It had her thinking of Louis and the web of lies surrounding her and their life together. She did what she had to. One word of a werewolf living away from a pack and they would label her a rogue. The pack in Butterfly Valley, Big Bend pack, already watched her. If her real identity was exposed, it put Alpha Howard at risk and would bring shame to the baron and the Cascade pack. She imagined Alpha Howard's security questioning her while Louis sat beside her. Jordyn would have to explain why she lied and continued to lie. She didn't know if she could face Louis and watch him walk out of her life. Her life was a charade created from a web of deceit, and she put two packs at risk, and trapped herself. "Way to go, Jo."

Several miles later the signs warning drivers there was a shapeshifter community began and started a mileage countdown. The other signs warned drivers not to stop and pick up hitchhikers. Mile one and the sign for Trinity welcomed her. The next sign welcomed her to the Cascade Territory, overseen by the Baron Healey Kanin. He wasn't just the alpha of the pack but the Baron of Trinity. He ruled the entire county, the non-humans living within the Cascade territory, and her life.

"Welcome Home, Jo," she whispered.

"Your family is expecting you at the Timber House, and in case you forgot, the baroness called … twice," Mandy reported. She stood in the doorway, leaning against the frame. "Neither the baroness nor your brother will like it if you're late. I can't imagine what the baron will say."

Mandy, with her strawberry blonde hair pulled back in a ponytail, wore the enforcer's uniform of black BDUs, boots, and thigh holster. Her dark blue almost violet eyes glittered in the warm lights. She should have been with Aydian, verifying security at the Timber House.

"Why are you here?" Rutger asked, ignoring her.

"The baron felt it best if an enforcer stayed at the office. He didn't want CJ here by herself. And between Aydian and I, he chose me."

Rutger didn't like the baron interfering with his enforcers. *He could have told me*, he thought. Then he pictured Aydian taking phone calls, dispatching enforcers and soldiers, and trying to help the poor soul on the other end. On the outside, his tanned skin, sandy blond hair styled into a military cut, ice blue eyes, and muscled build gave him the appearance of military personal. Aydian's build was from hours in the gym as a coping mechanism while he tried to exhaust the demons whispering in his ears. After Aydian was infected, as part of an experiment testing the strength and healing power of werewolves, he had been imprisoned and tortured for over two years. As a result, he dealt with a high level of post-traumatic stress. Aydian did not need to talk to anyone.

Still. "That's true. Have there been any problems?"

"None. If you're late the baron isn't going to like it," Mandy added.

"The baron hasn't liked anything in years," Rutger mumbled. After stepping down as second to the alpha, his father had taken privileges away from him, but not his responsibilities as the oldest son.

Mandy laughed. "Remind me to never get married."

Mate. "Agreed. I'll be fifteen minutes." Rutger ran his fingers through his hair.

"Yes, sir." Mandy left the doorway.

The door closed and he stared at it, imagining the evening, and his thoughts went straight to Jo. Damn he didn't want to go. He needed to find out who was killing werewolves and dumping their bodies on Cascade territory, not playing eldest son and happy family for cocktail hour.

He moved papers around and picked up the outline describing the security at the church. Scribbled across the page were Torin and Baron Kanin's notes, while at the bottom was a short message about the Timber House. Aydian had the security covered, the baron's initials authorizing the set of requested patrols. The church was becoming a security nightmare. As word spread about the wedding, and those of the non-human world attending, it had taken on celebrity status, and the promise there were going to be reporters present. There was no way to control the crowds when it sat in the center of Trinity. He was going to have to talk to the baron. Out of the corner of his eye, he saw his phone light up with Kory's number. It stared at him. She had called him once an hour all day. *The shit storm was beginning.* Irritation raced through him biting at his patience, Rutger did what he always did … he hit ignore.

Rutger had finalized the priorities, and with the baron and baroness busy getting ready for the evening, there was nothing he was going to accomplish in fifteen minutes. He might as well go home, drink, and change. Thankfully the plans had changed and he wasn't going to the Langston's estate, Coal Valley. He didn't have to worry about seeing everyone look at him like the poor sad dog Jo left behind. At the restaurant, he would be in a public place surrounded by people.

Less chance of embarrassing myself, he thought.

Like now. Opening his desk, he hesitated, knowing what he was doing was stupid, and pushed a couple of notebooks to the side. Rutger didn't care. The hell, he didn't. He shoved an empty clip, an old holster, and an empty bottle of pain reliever out the way and found several pictures. He grabbed one—as if it mattered, as if it mattered which one—and took it.

His two-story house sat on two acres of lake front property, with mountains on the left side, forest around him, and the lake in front. Rutger remembered the moment and hated himself. He'd spent the day assisting the baron while he negotiated boundaries with a group of therianthropes. After the meeting, Rutger had returned home, and found Jo missing. He'd walked through the house, and after finding it empty, headed to the deck. She was sitting on a rock, the lake behind her, her hair pulled up, wearing a tank top and shorts, and her feet in the water. When he stood at the railing, she was staring up at him with her dark chocolate eyes.

Frustration moved through him. Why the hell did he care? *Because she left,* he answered himself. She fucking left.

After putting the picture back, and feeling ridiculous for having kept it, he placed everything in the drawer, and shoved it closed. Rutger sat back, and with edgy energy he couldn't control, immediately stood. He jerked his coat, which he didn't need, from the back of the chair, shoved his arms through the sleeves, and walked out of his office. Leaning into the communication room where radio traffic was monitored, he saw Mandy. "I'm leaving. If anything comes up, call me, I have my cell. You know where I'll be."

"Yes, sir," Mandy replied. She sat at a desk, notebook to the right, and tapping keys on the keyboard.

As Rutger pushed the door open and marched to his truck, the murderer and the restaurant were on his mind, distorting his thoughts. Someone was out there killing and taking what they wanted without fear. And the woman, he knew he saw her despite there being zero proof. *To humans*. The chill from her evil and the way it pushed his wolf to protect was real, he had no doubt. He did his best to explain his feelings to Detective Russell but didn't know if it was going to be enough. He approached his truck with the Cascade pack's crest glittering in the afternoon sun and opened the door. To ease his worry and give him time to recover from any altercations with Jo, if needed, Kory would take her own car. There was the chance he would need to leave. Or escape.

Rutger started the truck bringing a rumble from the diesel engine and slowly backed out of the designated space for the Director of Enforcers. He drove the one mile driveway to the main road, checked for traffic, found it clear, and turned left. Pushing Jo from his thoughts, he concentrated on the murders. All he saw were her dark eyes, swirling the way they did when she was thinking, and drawing him in, and then he heard her light laughter. Rutger's lips curved with the thought.

"Stop." He had to relax before he saw Kory and she asked

what was wrong. He was sure Jo, his brother's wedding, and the murderer had joined forces to drive him insane.

Funny, he thought, *they all belong together*.

Rather than drive through the city, Jordyn kept to the outskirts, leaving the major highway for a narrow, two-lane road, bordered by ranches and log homes. The houses, she had known her entire life, and knew year after year, they would never change. When the land opened to the valley, she turned left and drove her SUV through the expanse of wrought iron gates. Jordyn entered her parent's property, Coal Valley estate, and slowly drove down the driveway. She gradually made her way around the circle drive to the front of the house and stopped. The house was a large mansion on ten acres backed up to national forest land on the east side and a ranch on the west. When she turned the engine off, silence immediately surrounded her, and she missed the distraction from the music.

She was home. Trinity. Coal Valley. Jordyn's nerves rumbled under her skin and fed her worry. There was an upside. She didn't have to pretend to be someone else. *Something else*, she corrected.

Sitting back, she tried containing the growing anxiety threading into her nerves. She needed to smother her unease knowing her mother would sense it and interrogate her like a murder suspect. No doubt, it would lead to more personal questions—like, was she truly happy with her life, her human lover, and the choice she made when she ran. Sure, she was.

It was going to be bad enough seeing Rutger with his girlfriend, but to feel guilty about her own damn life was going to destroy her. Before Jordyn started the engine and tried to escape, she got out and scanned the property. Facing the valley, she inhaled, and prayed she didn't make a fool of herself.

"I'm glad you arrived safely, daughter," Mia greeted as she walked down the tumbled stone stairs.

Jordyn noticed the tone and already wished there was some way she could have stayed in Butterfly Valley. "It's great to be here," she responded as she closed the car door.

"I can tell you're lying. I can also feel you're uncomfortable." Mia walked around to the passenger side and waited.

"I'm not lying. I am, however, stressed. I'm pretty sure it's leaving the gallery for a week and the idea my little sister is old enough to be getting married," Jordyn explained as she opened the door and handed her mom the hanger with her bridesmaid's dress.

"I understand that." Mia took the hanging bag. "My baby girl."

Jordyn stopped herself from shaking her head and met Mia's eyes, and saw the accusation of failure sitting in their judgmental depths. She swallowed the instant feeling of guilt, slung her camera bag over her shoulder, and jerked her suitcase from the backseat. The black duffle bag with her extra clothing remained behind. "How's Dad?" she asked, trying to change the subject.

"Busy. As usual." Mia walked up the stairs, her heels clicking on the stone, and opened the glass and wrought iron door framed in black walnut.

Crisp, clean air met Jordyn when she entered the house, followed by a sense of ease with its familiarity. She set her suitcase and camera bag down and walked into the sitting room. The large picture window opened to the front of the house, the valley, and the mountains beyond. She could lie about a lot of things, but she couldn't deny missing Coal Valley.

"I haven't gotten a hug from you," Mia said.

Jordyn turned away from the window and faced her. They hugged, and Mia's embrace felt like cold steel had wrapped around her. *Some things never change*, she thought. A chill rushed over Jordyn and she backed away. "You don't have to worry about me."

"I'm a mom and it's my job." Her mother smiled. It didn't reach her eyes and there was more than exhaustion sitting in their dark depths.

"You look distracted."

"I am. There seems to be an endless number of things to settle before the wedding. Plus, the Highguard is sending representatives to witness the union between families." Mia sighed the word *Highguard.* She sat down on a leather wingback chair, and crossing her legs, exposed a pair of heels. She wore her caramel-colored hair down, its ends barely touching her navy blue blouse. "Sit, we'll relax, and after, you can change for the restaurant."

Jordyn sat down, finding it impossible to relax when she was heading to a public place. Maybe if she called Louis and talked to him, it would settle her nerves. Because hearing about shapeshifters was going to help? No. Just like knowing Rutger remained. Rutger, his girlfriend, the baron and his family, and the wedding, she was going to face them all.

"Amelia, would you please bring us a glass of red. There's an open bottle on the buffet," Mia instructed.

The blonde girl looked from Mia to Jordyn, and back to Mia. "Yes, ma'am," she replied and left the room.

"You hired someone?" Jordyn asked.

"Oh heavens, no. Amelia is home from college and needed a part-time job, and with the wedding, I needed the help," she answered. "You know her aunt, Mandy Jenson."

An enforcer. "Right." Jordyn watched the girl … young woman, and thought the strawberry blonde hair and crystal violet eyes should have given her family lineage away. She nearly laughed with the thought. If she dared mentioned anything about linage to Louis, he would have looked at her like she was from another planet. Nope, just a werewolf. Humans didn't pay attention to the ancestry of a family the way pack members did.

Amelia returned and handed the first crystal goblet to Mia.

"How is your aunt?" Jordyn asked.

"Well," Amelia answered.

Their eyes met, and Jordyn saw the distance in them and felt the cold edge of her anger. It was Rutger. There was no telling what had been said about her when she left the eldest son of the alpha. What did she expect?

Jordyn smiled, took the glass, and sipped her wine. The spiced chocolate and plum liquid tasted like heaven as it slid down her throat.

"Lady Langston, will that be all?" Amelia asked.

"Yes, dear. Tell your mother I said hello."

"Yes, ma'am." She turned, gave Jordyn narrowed eyes, and left.

Yep, the Timber House was going to be a blast.

CHAPTER FOUR

Rutger turned right off Mill Creek Road, drove two miles, and turned right on Collins Way. After a right and briefly enjoying the views of the lake, he followed the asphalt driveway. Lined by mature pine, oak, and fir trees it ended at the only house, his two-story log home. It wasn't the sprawling Foxwood Estate of his family, and that's the way he liked it. Sitting on Nakoma Lake, the two wooded acres gave him the privacy he craved, especially after stepping down and taking the position as director. When he built the house, he wanted to have the freedom to shapeshift and run anytime he pleased. After his runs, he would swim, maybe spend time on the deck, looking at the lake and mountains, and enjoying the sunset.

His daydream of sunsets, and mixed thoughts concerning everything from shapeshifting to Detective Russell, crashed when he saw Kory's car. He parked, killed the engine, signed off his laptop, and leaving his gear in the truck, walked up the stairs. Rutger gripped the wrought iron handle, heard it groan, and turned it before he broke it. Inside, he hung his coat on the rack, unbuckled his thigh holster, and took his belt and hung it beside his coat. Without waiting to find out what Kory was doing, and why she was there, he went to the left—his bar—and poured a hefty glass of bourbon.

"Hey, you. I tried calling you today," Kory said as she slid her arms around his middle. "What's going on?"

"Work," he answered and took a sip. The tawny liquid slid

down his throat like he swallowed a glowing ember. After a day packed with questions, reports, and security details, all he wanted was some quiet before the storm. "I thought we were meeting at the restaurant?"

Kory let him go, backed away, and met his stare. "I thought we could go together."

"Separate vehicles. I have to be able to leave if there's a problem," Rutger answered. *I told her.*

"Sorry." It sounded flippant, like she was dismissing him. Korey gave a shielded gaze, walked over to the table, and grabbed her glass of white wine. "Not a big deal. I'll follow you."

He was not going to start an argument. "Fine." After taking another drink, he set the glass on the wood bar top, left the room, and entered the living room. He glanced at the lake and honey glow from the sunset, before walking over to the fireplace. Red glowed at the bottom, and shoving the charred pieces of wood over with the stoker, flames climbed and died down. A thread of anger wove through him at the sight. She could have added wood. Rutger fed the dying fire, stoked it, and getting weak flames waited for them to wrap around and flare. He added another piece, hoping it lasted, and he wouldn't come home to a cold house. Spring was dying and summer was amping up but it didn't stop the cold mornings. Sometimes Mother Nature didn't play by the rules, and threw a quick storm into the mix.

"Is this about her?" Kory asked with her hand on her hip, her blue eyes narrowed on him.

Rutger straightened. "What? About who?" Passing Kory, he left the living room, and headed back to the bar and his bourbon.

Kory's hard footsteps gave away her impatience. "Your silence. Jordyn Langston."

"No." He sounded tired and felt exhaustion's needles stabbing at his thoughts. Rutger rubbed the back of his neck, and drew his fingers through his hair.

"We're going to see her and she needs to know what she did. She's the reason you're not in line to the alpha. How much more of your life are you willing to give up to someone who chose a human over you?" Kory wasn't holding her glass, but he knew by her accusations she had been working herself up and had a couple of glasses of courage prior to him getting home.

He ignored the comment about Jo and how she chose a human. He had to. "I have two murders. Two John Does. No suspects." He left the details of missing body parts out. "My attention isn't on one person or what *I* have given up. There is a wedding, important guests arriving, and I have security details to finalize," Rutger explained calmly. Bringing the murders into the argument was a low blow, somewhat dishonest, and was being used as a distraction. He wasn't going to continue down the path she was clearly heading. And he wasn't going to start criticizing Jo. Swallowing the remaining bourbon, he turned around and poured another. "What Miss Langston does is none of my business."

"Really? None of your business? And what is this? You're playing director of the enforcers, and hiding behind security details and investigations someone else could easily take care of," she accused. Red webbed her blue eyes. The show of heartache didn't match the anger threading through her. "You take orders, like a pup. You should be the one giving them."

"Did you not hear me? There are two dead men. Murdered." He almost growled the words. *I'm not hiding.*

"I'm sorry. I'm sorry." Kory took her glass and finished off her wine. "I've let the wedding and the Langston family get to me. She does no wrong in their eyes. She waltzes into town like she owns it, and everything is perfect."

Rutger drank his bourbon, met the anger in her eyes, and

knew what Kory said wasn't true. Jo visited every Christmas and never left Coal Valley. This would be her first public appearance in three years. He tried to see her the first year only to have the baron forbid him, and Lord Langston refuse him. The Langston family, Lady Langston being the loudest voice, made sure everyone knew how they felt about her leaving. They were the hardest on her and probably reminded her of her choices every chance they got. Bravo for them.

"Forgive me. I'm being protective of my wolf." An edge of contempt laced her words. Setting her empty glass on the bar, she met his gaze and sauntered over to him. Kory rested her right hand on his hip, and with her left hand, she feathered her fingers up his muscled chest, over the embroidered Cascade patch, one fingertip following his name. "Please?"

Wolf. Don't. He wanted her to stop. He smiled, which felt fake, and bent down to kiss her. She tasted like jealousy, citrus, and alcohol. "Everyone is stressed." He took her wrists and turned out of her hold. He had to get away from her. With glass in hand, he left her standing by the bar and headed to the fireplace. Setting his bourbon on the hearth, he glanced up at the sunset photograph framed in black matte, Jo's photo, and then turned his gaze to the smoldering wood. He had time for one more drink if he timed it right. *Damn, that's a bad sign.*

"I brought my things. I'm going to start getting ready."

"Sure," he mumbled absently. Was this how it was going to be, drinking and pretending it didn't matter? No. It did matter. She mattered. He could feel her in his head, on his skin, her voice in his ears. He could taste her wine on her lips. Rutger growled, his wolf sweeping its energy through him, changing his eyes. He had to forget her. With every glass ... hell, every bottle, he prayed the alcohol would numb the weight of her memories and free him from their caress. It didn't. It weakened his resolve and gave them life.

Rutger took another drink. He couldn't continue living detached from life and with the undefined future he was drifting in, it was going to kill him. He watched the flames consume the wood like her memory was consuming his thoughts. It needed to end. They were going to see each other and the truth—their relationship was over—would set him free. He didn't need to know 'why' after three years, he didn't give a shit, and he didn't need to be haunted by the 'what ifs'. He needed a solid 'no'. Jo had to face him, end her silence, and tell him to go to hell. That's what he needed.

Fucking closure.

"I asked you if you would pour me another glass."

"Yeah." Rutger knew he sounded lost in thought and acted preoccupied, and no doubt, it was going to make things worse.

"Tell me this isn't about her?" Kory demanded. She glared at him, her apparent tears twisting into jealousy. With her hands on her hips, and her stance ready for a fight, she repeated, "Tell me."

Making things worse. "I thought you were going to get ready." He faced her with his wolf's feel crawling over him.

"Tell me."

Rutger met her gaze and fury whipped through him. "If this is happening and we haven't left the house, we are going to have problems."

"Is it about her?" Kory's eyes quickly webbed with red. "It's always about her."

"Don't. I'm not taking the bait." Meeting her gaze, Rutger realized he wanted her to leave. He didn't love her. Hell, he didn't like her. He'd created a mess.

"She's here all week," Kory confessed. "A week."

"She is part of the bride's family," he shot back. She? Jo.

"At the women's meeting, your mother informed us she will

be running with us."

Laurel, his mother, and baroness took the tradition of the women's run seriously. The pack wouldn't risk depending on someone who wasn't loyal to them. It was about proving they could band together, stand their ground, and protect the pack if necessary. The uninvited stayed behind as examples of weakness. To have the baroness tell them Jo was running spoke volumes.

"Your mother is planning something."

Probably. "I doubt she's planning anything. She and Mia have a history going back to when they were in the encampments." He held up his hand to stop Kory from interrupting. "She saw the pain and hurt Jo caused when she left. My mother is trying to mend those hearts. She is the alpha's mate, Baroness of the Cascade pack, and has obligations."

"Jo? What happened to Miss Langston?"

He could have referred to her by her pet name. Babe. "Stop."

"It doesn't matter. Whatever the hell you want to call her, she deserves to be banished." Kory continued like she didn't hear him. Her voice had taken on a jealous, bitter tone. "She deserves to be a rogue."

"She's pack."

"You're defending her?"

"I'm defending my brother's future mother-in-law and my sister-in-law's family. Not to mention the strength of the entire pack." He let his frustration corrupt his words. They sounded rough and tired. The pack came first. A marriage between purebloods, the Kanin family and the Langston family was guaranteeing the pack's power base and the family would become a foundation of strength. The Highguard would recognize them, set them apart, and they would have status. "I'm not in charge, as you pointed out, the baron is. He kept her as pack. If you want to argue with someone, argue with him. I'm sure he would love to hear your reasons."

"You know that's impossible. He likes her, always has, regardless of future relations." Kory's shoulders rose with her words while her jealousy spread out like a cancer.

In one swallow, he finished his bourbon. "We need to get ready so we can get this shit show over with." Rutger walked past the large picture window and saw the setting sun cast its colors on the lake as he went to the kitchen. Placing his glass in the sink, he stood for a minute thinking about their conversation. After Kory left, he sank into his thoughts, and wondered why the baron kept her as pack. Jo was running with the women. Why? Because she is a powerful werewolf, a strong, independent woman, and protected those she loved. He inhaled. Jo embraced power and passion and turned them into a force. Which was why he had fallen in love with her.

"I promise to let it go. Would you come with me?" Kory asked. "I'm sorry. Please, come with me."

Rutger didn't believe Kory. Jo would be there between them the entire evening. Without responding, he left the kitchen and followed Kory up the stairs, across the open loft, and to his bedroom. When they stood at the end of the pine framed bed, he saw a button-down shirt.

"Well?" Kory asked. She slipped her left arm around him and leaned on him. "Do you like it?"

No. "It's nice," he replied.

"I like you in blue and it was too gorgeous to pass up."

"Gorgeous," he mumbled.

Having never cared about fashion, preferring running shoes, jeans, and T-shirts over heels and dresses, Jordyn was aware her mother was waiting at the bottom of the stairs. *Inspection time,* she thought dryly. She wasn't without a sense of style. Shows at the gallery and dinner parties gave her a reason to indulge and dress up. Jordyn changed into a pair of dark denim skinny jeans, red heels, a black sleeveless silk shirt, completed by a black leather jacket. She hadn't done anything with her raven hair, leaving it straight. She did add mascara, black eyeliner, and smoky chocolate brown eyeshadow. "Well?"

"Well what?" Mia asked. Her hair was up; soft curls sat at her neck and ears, leaving her pearl drop earrings glittering. A soft violet blouse, black slacks, and black heels finished her look. Controlled grace.

"Do I pass?" It was no secret her move and absence had created a divide between Mia and herself. The pin pricks of energy touching her confirmed the divide had a life of its own. With Mia's focus on Bailey and the wedding, Jordyn's presence had become a check mark on the 'to do' list.

"You look—" Mia started.

"You're a famous photographer who has their own gallery and you're going out on the town," Ethan interrupted before Mia could complete her answer. "With an extremely handsome gentleman."

"Dad." Jordyn smiled, walked to her dad, and gave him a hug. His embrace felt secure, strong, and his power drifted around them. The energy had her wolf rising to bathe in its safety and strength. He met her gaze with dark chocolate eyes, his black hair a relaxed style hinting at lazy curls.

"I suggest we leave. It won't look good if the bride's family is late." With her hand on her hip, her impatience drifting around her, Mia waited by the open door.

"Yes, dear," Ethan replied with a smile. He winked at Jordyn, turned, and followed Mia out of the house.

Closing the door behind her, Jordyn took her time before going down the stairs, and at the car door stopped. "Hold on." She hurried back inside the house to grab her camera bag, and back at the car sat down. "I'm ready."

"You need your camera? What are you going to take pictures of tonight?" Mia asked.

"I never leave home without it. Anyway, there are photographs everywhere," Jordyn answered. She settled in her seat, the instant silence feeding her anxiety.

A forced quiet ate most of the drive to the restaurant. Every couple of minutes, doing her duty, Mia asked how everyone was doing and tried too hard to start a conversation. It went from one subject to another, and Jordyn knew she had a stash of topics for the next time she asked. Jordyn didn't mind the silence, didn't answer the questions, and spent the time staring out the window.

"They're gathering," Sister Andrea mumbled. "Tell Savior the important lycans are together and security is concentrating on them. Their underlings are exposed."

"Yes, Sister," Brother William replied and took his cell phone from his pocket.

Sister Andrea sat behind the wheel of the older, compact car watching the members of the Cascade pack park their vehicles and enter the restaurant. She felt the guard's senses reaching out like light drops of power on her skin. They wouldn't find them. Savior made sure the sacrifice served its purpose, allowing them to go unnoticed.

"Savior said to watch for the pendulum," Brother William relayed. He shoved the cell phone back into his jacket pocket. "Then, we can go."

"Understood." Sister Andrea tucked loose strands of red hair behind her ear, sat back, and waited for Miss Langston.

Too busy scanning the parking lot of the Timber House for Rutger's Jeep, Jordyn ignored the sun as it made its decline behind the mountains, casting the sky in sweeps of pinks and straw. The Timber House, a non-human hangout—also a favorite for Rutger and his friends—sat off the road, its bulk shielded by a canopy of pine, cedar, and weeping willows. So far, she didn't have to see anyone. No Rutger. No Kory. She would sneak in, find a dark corner, sit and hide for the rest of the evening. Her nerves jumped under her skin, with the lie she was trying to tell herself.

The covered porch and weathered log exterior gave way to light pine inside. Large framed pictures of wolves and mountain landscapes decorated the walls while a mix of industrial light fixtures gave off a soft glow, adding to the relaxed ambience. Reclaimed wood gave the tables a rustic yet comfortable feel, and matching benches and chairs made up the seating. Jordyn followed her parents, remaining behind them and trying to hide. A vibration travelled her spine in a pulse of power created by shapeshifters and magic born. Closing her eyes, Jordyn soaked in its feel as if it might be the last time she felt her pack. She seldom felt power in Butterfly Valley, so to feel it drift freely felt strange. Yes, she visited every Christmas, but she never left the property. Along with never feeling her home and power, no one saw her. No one knew she was there.

"We've reserved the banquet room for the night." Mia half turned and pointed to the back of the restaurant where a couple of staff members were opening a set of double pine doors.

"For drinks?" Jordyn asked, her eyes widening. When the doors stood open, she saw Baron Healey and the Baroness Laurel sitting at a table. An empty panic fell from her stomach to her feet and she understood there was more going on. "Who else is coming?"

"Just family," Mia insisted.

"What does that mean?" Jordyn mumbled. They were a pack. It made them family. Everyone.

Mia waved to a group of people as she walked toward the banquet room. Trying not to attract attention, Jordyn stuck to her mother like a shadow. Several bar height tables sat to one side, near a bank of windows, while standard height tables, decorated with flowers and candles, had been placed end to end for the bride and groom's families.

"Healey. Laurel," Mia said in greeting.

"Mia," Laurel replied. "Where's Ethan?"

"Making sure we have the appropriate staff."

"Jordyn," Healey greeted. His deep voice like restrained thunder matched the feel of his power. The first two buttons of his crimson dress shirt were left open, and the black points of his tattoo peeked out. Starting at his right shoulder it stopped at the Cascade pack's crest and continued to his left shoulder. The tribal ink marked him as alpha and baron. "It's good to have you back for the ceremonies."

"Thank you, Baron, I appreciate it," Jordyn responded.

"You're looking well," Laurel commented. Red highlighted her shoulder-length, sandy blonde hair, and her light makeup accentuated her velvety brown eyes. Jordyn couldn't help but see Rutger's dark mahogany eyes, dark walnut hair, and strong features and think he was a perfect combination of his parents.

Shut up, Jo. She shuddered and changed her line of thinking.

"Thank you," Jordyn replied softly.

"How's the gallery?" Laurel asked.

"It's slow this time of year, but I'm looking forward to the summer."

"I'm sure you are," Healey remarked. "With the tourist population growing and the shapeshifters ever expanding, it's sure to bring in new business. Especially when one of their own is a success."

"Yes." Jordyn wanted to run and hide. No one knew she was a werewolf. There was no 'one of their own'.

"You'll have to make plans to visit during the summer to take pictures. I would love to join you," Laurel proposed.

Mia's attention focused on Laurel, as if unable to comprehend why the baroness would talk to Jordyn. Slowly Mia's hardened gaze shifted to her. Jordyn felt Mia's stare like an oncoming semitruck. Refusing to act as if Mia was bothering her, Jordyn stared at the baroness, frozen with panic and nothing to say.

"We'll definitely have to consider something," Healey assured. "I'm sure you have a lot of visiting to make up for, Jordyn."

Dismissed. "Yes, if you'll excuse me." She took a step away from them and was grateful when her mother started talking about staff, flowers, and the church.

Jordyn picked a bar height table, next to the windows with views of the building they used to smoke meat, and freedom. It was the perfect distance from her parents, the baron and baroness, and the bride and groom. Now all she had to do was disappear. With her purse on the table, she took her cell and saw Louis had sent three messages, each one making her smile, at the same time they had her nerves on edge. A human. As a pureblood, she threatened to weaken the bloodline by being with him. *I'm not marrying the man.* It didn't stop the slithering fear someone might see his messages and question her. The nervous energy flowed in her veins as she stared at the screen. She needed a drink.

"Hey, girl."

Jordyn clicked her screen, turning it black, and looked up to meet hazel eyes lined with green eyeliner. "Claudia, how are you?"

"Umm, if you visited, you would know," she replied. Grinning, she sat down. "I'm good. How the hell are you?"

"Great." Jordyn looked around, watching other guests enter the room, greet people, and take their seats. Believing everyone would see her as a submissive, she didn't think anyone would talk to her let alone care she was back for the wedding. Right then she was grateful for Claudia's company.

"I'm sure your public appearance is going exactly how you thought it would. I know what will help, let's get a glass of wine." Claudia stood and waited. She watched Jordyn's eyes dart around the room like she was being hunted. "No one cares you're here. Your sister is getting hitched, making the Langston/Kanin family a ruling power. You're invisible."

Jordyn's shoulders relaxed and she laughed. Damn, she hoped so. Following Claudia, staying with the idea no one would notice her, they left the banquet room and walked to the bar.

"What'll it be, ladies?"

"Red wine, two," Claudia answered.

"I want the bottle with the bear on the label," Jordyn said before he left. She watched the others at the bar, laughing, talking, and felt the pain of regret, and at the same time feeling like she was … *home*.

"The bear it is. How's it going, Jo?" he asked.

"Good, Jason. How are you?"

"Well—"

"I already chewed her ass out for never visiting. Just get the wine," Claudia interrupted.

"Yes, ma'am." Jason smiled, giving Claudia a mock bow before leaving.

"I think I love him," Claudia told her.

"You two? That's great," Jordyn offered. Sadness and guilt started to move through her as her thoughts went to Rutger and the strange betrayal she felt with Louis.

"Here we are. Get you anything else?" Jason asked.

"No. Open a tab, and when we're done send it to Rutger," Claudia said and smiled.

"No. My parents are paying," Jordyn quickly insisted.

"We'll make Rutger pay. Our bar tab will be like a little surprise. Maybe a large surprise. Anyway, I'm sure he won't mind," Claudia replied.

"N-No w-way," Jordyn stammered. Panic rose from her middle and etched itself on her face. "My mother said."

"Just in time. He's right there, let's ask." Claudia took her glass, left the bar, and started in his direction.

Jordyn looked at Jason like he should stop his girlfriend and he smiled at her. Nothing. Jordyn grabbed Claudia's arm, but her fingers slipped from Claudia's lace sleeve as she increased the distance between them. Jordyn froze where she stood when she saw Rutger talking to Gavin, his middle brother, and Kory. He wore a blue button-down linen shirt, his board shoulders and chest filling it out, khaki pants, and boots. The ends of his hair grazed his ears and looked like he had combed through its thickness with his fingers. He also wore Kory, who clung to him while she searched the crowd. Before either of them spotted her, Jordyn grabbed her wine, intending on running back to her seat. She stopped. No. Bad idea. Her senses felt his wolf and slowly turning around, she watched him back away from the group and separate himself from Kory. A new crowd entered and greeted Gavin, Kory, and Rutger, who nodded in return. He didn't talk to anyone. Kory faced him, her eyes on him, and continued to talk as he looked over her. Without a reply, Kory gave up and started her search of the restaurant. Jordyn turned away, slipped into the crowd, and headed to the banquet room to hide. If she had to pay for her wine, she would do it later, much later. Maybe by mail.

Claudia laughed as she sat at the table. "You still love him.

Don't try to deny it. I heard your heartbeat, it was hard to miss."

"That wasn't love, it was panic. Not only am I not talking about him, I'm not talking about her." To change the subject, from Rutger, she could say she had a boyfriend, he's human, hates non-humans, and start that catastrophe of a conversation. An argument was better than talking about Rutger. Jordyn turned in her seat to stare out the windows so she couldn't see him and sipped her wine. It didn't stop her from hearing him; his thick rumble swept over her like silk on her skin, its rough edge threading in her head. What the hell?

"You didn't know he was going to be here?"

"My mother said we were meeting for drinks and it was going to be *family*."

"I don't feel bad anymore, you don't talk to your family either. This is the rehearsal dinner. By the way, a pack is family. He is family. He is about to be your brother-in-law. Your mother got you, girl."

"Yes, she did." Not a damn word from the woman. Facing Claudia, Jordyn took another sip of wine.

"You know you could talk to him and end the stand-off. Possibly be in the same room, acting like normal people. You know … like adults. Aw, that's right, neither of you are normal people. Which explains your three year hiatus."

Talk to him. The thought had her heart racing. She couldn't. "Leave it alone." She took a gulp and wanted another glass. She had to get a grip, she wasn't going to get drunk at her sister's party. Wouldn't that be embarrassing. Another strike against the rogue Langston daughter. "This is not the time or place."

"All right, sorry for pushing you. How's Bug Valley?" Claudia asked.

"It's good. You should visit and see the gallery," Jordyn replied, trying for casual. "There are great shops and restaurants."

 Sure there are. There was Louis, her small rental, and the lie she referred to as her life.

CHAPTER FIVE

Rutger let Gavin do the talking, only nodding when he had to, his attention and senses focused on Jo, her voice and her feel. When he risked finding her, he recognized her long, black hair, and the set of her shoulders. At the sight of her, he fidgeted with the collar of his shirt, like it was going to stop his heart from pounding and the room from getting warm. Jason, her shadow, easily smiled, his eyes on her as he laughed with her. Rutger swallowed a growl as jealousy burned through him. He stepped to the side, turning to get a better view, when Kory grabbed his arm and blocked him. She disappeared. He lost her. As usual.

Trapped between Kory and his brother, Rutger studied the crowd, the soldiers, and the enforcers present, and the way they watched everyone. He also caught the eyes of those who saw Jo and found him. Time ticked by, slowly, when Spring finally arrived, and they all made their way to the waiting families. His heart had moved to his throat while his nerves were doing flips under his skin.

"Dad. Mom," Gavin greeted.

"Baron. Baroness," Rutger greeted, and sat down at the table. Kory sat beside him, put her hand on his thigh, and squeezed. He moved but stopped the instinct to peel her fingers from his leg. "Lord Langston. Lady Langston."

"Good evening," Mia greeted with a smile.

"Rutger. Kory," Laurel replied. "How was work?"

"Busy. He didn't say much," Kory answered for him. She flipped her hair as she turned and started talking to Spring.

The baroness met Rutger's eyes with annoyance sitting in their depths. "Busy," he answered.

"Ladies and gentlemen, welcome the bride and groom," Healey announced and stood. "Can I have everyone's attention." The room grew quiet and all eyes were on Tanner and Bailey as they took their seats. "The future Mr. and Mrs. Tanner Kanin." Applause erupted, along with whistles and hollers. "I have a few words." There was another round of laughter, he raised his hands knowing he was guilty of always having more than a few words. "Only a few. I promise." Healey laughed, a joyful rumble. After clearing his throat, he started his speech.

Rutger barely listened, his concentration on the way the baron addressed his pack and guests. The baron's eyes skated across the room, pausing in places, and moving on. Rutger watched when he stopped, his eyes narrowed, and the speech continued with the security of the gathered kindred, loyalty and home. He was talking to Jo. With a lazy turn Rutger saw her holding the baron's gaze. Elders of the pack, family of the bride and groom, and friends sat and watched their alpha and the baron. He gave his son and his future daughter an oath, his kin, and his eyes moved on. It took Rutger back to the conversation with Kory. The baron protected Jo and no one knew why.

"The speech is over, it's time to drink," Gavin announced. Laugher and jokes sounded and people clinked glasses.

Standing, Ethan raised his hands to quiet the crowd. "We would like to thank everyone for coming and celebrating this wonderful joining of families. Lord Ervin, Lady Sloan, and Lord Julian, Lady Hannah, thank you for your presence. Alpha Richard, thank you, your presence at the wedding will be missed. All right, it's time to celebrate Bailey and Tanner." More laughter and chatter resonated and Ethan sat down.

Lady Sloan, a pureblood werewolf from the Highguard, stood and greeting guests made her way through the crowd and over to Jo. She placed her hand on Jo's shoulder and began talking. Rutger watched the interaction between the women and the comfortable way Jo responded—her reaction to the conversation playing on her face and brightening her eyes.

Kory squeezed his thigh, like a reminder, and leaned closer to him. "Could you get me a glass of white?"

Tearing his eyes from Jo, he stood. "Yes. I'm going to the bar, anyone want anything?" He needed to walk, burn some of the energy acting like sparks in his nerves.

"There should be waitstaff." Mia looked around the room, searching for a waitress.

"It's no problem, really," he insisted.

"We'll wait. You go ahead," the baron replied. He gave Rutger a slow grin, and proved he knew why Rutger wanted to leave the table. That's what he needed.

"Lady Sloan, I appreciate the presence of you and Lord Ervin," Bailey greeted.

"Our pleasure. It's an honor to attend your wedding, and the Highguard enjoys seeing the Cascade pack and its clansmen. Congratulations, Bailey." Lady Sloan smiled and turning, faced Jordyn. Her eyes were lined with soft kohl, hinting she might wear heavier makeup when not acting as a representative for the Highguard. Lady Sloan's raven hair ended at the center of her back, where it grazed her deep purple fitted blouse. Despite being surrounded by the pack, she held an otherworldly edge.

Jordyn plastered a smile on her face. "Lady Sloan."

"I understand your photography work is displayed in a gallery in Butterfly Valley. I would enjoy talking to you some time," Lady Sloan said, placing her hand on Jordyn's shoulder.

"I would be delighted," Jordyn replied, and tensed with her

touch. Lady Sloan's power felt like a warm breeze on her skin, teased her wolf, and stirred her power with its strength.

"We'll make plans when the wedding and festivities are over."

"Definitely," Jordyn replied.

"Perfect." Lady Sloan smiled, gave each of them one last look, and took her leave.

"Lady Sloan. Aren't you special," Claudia teased.

Jordyn met her mother's gaze and cringed. "Bailey, how are you?" Jordyn asked, and ignored Claudia. Lady Sloan. The woman was the epitome of grace and power, and with her status in the Highguard, had the authority to order the baron around. What in the world would she have to say to Jordyn? Unless she was using the gallery to question Jordyn about her absence from the pack and her human lover. Was the Highguard questioning the baron? Fear sank inside of her, and the conversation added to Jordyn's anxiety and future discussions with her mother.

"Busy. And trying to survive the details. And mom," Bailey responded with a laugh.

"It will be perfect, and you'll make a stunning bride. It's great to see you, Tanner," Jordyn greeted.

"I'm glad you're here, maybe you can calm Bailey down. Bride-zilla." Tanner smiled, waited for Bailey's reaction, and laughing, pretended she hurt him when she elbowed him in the stomach.

Rutger entered the banquet room carrying wine and bourbon, when Jo's laughter caught his attention. He couldn't stop himself from smiling and looking over at her as she drew her fingers through the ends of her hair, freeing it from her leather jacket. Jo continued laughing as she took her jacket off; her sun-bronzed skin looked darker beside her black silk top. She casually lifted the wine glass to her lips, smiled, and took a sip. The wine with the bear on the label. It was her favorite. He could swear he tasted it on his tongue.

"I saw Aydian at the door. Looks like you have everything under control," Ethan offered.

"Control? Try long hours, two murders, and a bad mood," Kory replied.

Setting her glass in front her, Rutger wished she showed more respect for Lord Langston, and wished she would stop answering for him.

"Two murders?" Ethan asked.

"Yes. Lycanthropes. The sheriff's department is investigating. I'm working with them in case it turns out to be a paranormal crime," Rutger explained.

"I'm sure they appreciate the cooperation. As Trinity continues to grow, the sheriff's department will have to increase their hiring. It would be good to see a mix of non-human and human hires. Either way, no one wants to deal with a shortage of deputies." Ethan lifted his wine glass. "Jordyn was telling us they made cutbacks to the sheriff's department in Butterfly Valley, just as tourist season is about to begin. I don't understand it." He sipped his wine, set the glass down, and smiled as people walked by.

"At least Trinity is aware of the human, paranormal population, making it possible to open hiring to non-humans. Butterfly Valley is a large city in denial about the paranormal communities. It puts them in danger," Rutger replied. "And creates the perfect environment for crime and prejudice." He felt their stares on him as a pang of guilt slid through him. Really, did he know anything about Butterfly Valley? No. Didn't matter. No one liked where Jo lived.

Alone. Rogue.

"I keep telling Rutger, he needs to quit. His place isn't with the enforcers and talking with the sheriff's department," Kory interjected, trying to change the subject.

Rutger planned to defend himself when he heard Jo and Claudia laughing. As if he was part of the conversation, he sat back, listened to the light sound, and took a drink of his bourbon.

Jordyn finished the rest of her wine and set the glass on the table. "You're crazy."

"Yeah, well, you have to be crazy knowing you'll spend your entire life in one place," Claudia began. "Not like you."

"You know, I have the gallery. As the saying goes, the grass is always greener on the other side." She was living the lie. The pressure from her mother to be perfect and Rutger cheating on her was why she left. Time slipped away and she didn't fight. Seeing him, and watching them, she knew there was no way she could watch them together for the rest of her life. Which would be an eternity.

"I guess." Claudia shrugged. "Bug Valley has the only gallery? You need to come home."

"I can't." Jordyn picked up her glass and holding the stem, twirled it between her fingers. She needed a refill. First, she needed a minute to herself. "I'm going to the restroom."

"Don't get lost," Claudia joked. "Don't run away, either. There's no escape."

Jordyn gave her a mocking laugh, and realized she had no way of leaving the restaurant without her parents.

Trapped.

Rutger listened to the baron and Lord Langston talk about their businesses, banking, the city, and the incoming guests while the baroness, Lady Langston, and Bailey talked about the wedding. Kory made small talk with Spring, but she couldn't hide her anger any time the baron or someone else mentioned Jo's name. Rutger listened halfheartedly, drank his bourbon, and hoped no one spoke to him. When his cell phone vibrated against his waist, he considered it a gift from the gods.

"Kanin." He listened to Detective Russell tell him he received the completed toxicology report. "Hold on, let me get somewhere quiet," he said as he backed his chair away from the table and stood. He held the phone against his chest. "I need to take this."

"Anything serious?" Healey questioned.

"No." Rutger hadn't lied, and figured if the baron sensed the difference, he knew it was for the best.

Dismissed by the baron, Rutger left the banquet room in a hurry. If there was evidence, he would have a place to start. Weaving through the congested bar area, he focused on the doors in front of him, and tried for a straight line toward the outside. A chime sounded, and with a quick look at the screen of his phone, Rutger saw he had a message from Ansel. *Please be good news*, he prayed. With a surprised yelp, the woman stumbled backwards. He quickly grabbed her by the waist, and her nails dug into his arm as she clung to him trying to save herself from falling. When they stopped, he held Jo close to his body, his fingers on her hip, his eyes lit up with his wolf, and his power spreading over him.

Jordyn's senses focused on Rutger, his wolf, and his scent of the woods as it wrapped around her. At the same time his power sank into her skin, its pulse calling her wolf. She met his gold gaze and knew her eyes gleamed bronze. Every bit of control turned to ash. She felt lost and exposed and like the entire restaurant stopped to stare at them.

"I'm sorry," Jordyn stammered, embarrassed; her voice

sounded throaty. "I didn't see you."

See him. She was playing the hiding game.

"No, I'm sorry. My fault," Rutger replied. Her black-lined eyes pulled him in, as her vanilla scent tangled with the wine on her lips. He let her go, his fingers slipping over her hip. "I have to take this." He sounded like an idiot. He needed to confront her.

Make her end this.

Did she miss his touch? Cringing, she backed away from him and grappled for restraint over her wolf and power. Kory. The combination quickly died. "Of course." *Pack business.* She wasn't going to stop him, she didn't want to have anything to do with him.

"My apologies," he mumbled, as his eyes dimmed and his power faded.

Jordyn barely saw the phone he clutched. His hand made the usually large cell look small, and even smaller against his wide chest. He worked out. Jordyn didn't care—she gave him a polite smile, turned, and focused on getting to her table. *You're sorry. I'm going to get questioned about this.* No, interrogated. Jordyn needed to sit down, act casual, like nothing happened. Sure.

His heart stopped its assault in his chest as he watched her walk away. Why didn't he stop her? He couldn't. Rutger exhaled and stormed outside, marched across the deck area, and headed to his truck. Jo's scent clung to him and her wolf eyes haunted him. He didn't need that. That was not the 'go to hell' he desperately wanted; instead, it was a twisted, corrupted attraction. Its heat sat in his middle and toyed with his resolve. He yanked the door open and sat in the driver's seat. "Tell me there's good news."

His bicep had felt like stone under her hand. *Stop.* Jordyn sat down and stared at her empty glass wishing she had a bottle.

"Nothing like close encounters. I think Kory might explode." Claudia's smile gave away the humor she saw in the situation.

"What did you see?" Jordyn asked. If she knew what they saw, she could diffuse the situation. Her mind raced with reasons, excuses, and what she was going to tell her mother. Hell, anyone asking what happened.

"You ran into each other and he would have sent you to the floor, if his arm hadn't gone around your waist and saved you. Then the two of you stared at each other. Very magical."

"Not funny," Jordyn replied, defensively. She could handle this. Easy. No one saw her eyes had lit up with her wolf. Or sensed her body going into overdrive from his touch.

"Here you are." Jason set a glass down.

"I didn't order this," Jordyn snapped. Like she was going to turn it away. Not a chance. But the room had its own staff. Why was the bartender delivering her wine? *Paranoid much.*

"I have orders to personally make sure you have everything you need," Jason answered. His cobalt eyes splintered, a bright white filling the slices as he stared at Jordyn.

"Why?" Jordyn demanded. "Who?"

Jason laughed and his eyes lit up. "I thought you might need it after … the run-in." Jason gave her a flirting grin, waited a second, and left them staring at his back.

"I hope someone wants you happy," Claudia started. "Cheers to that." She raised her glass and waited for Jordyn.

"This place is like the twilight zone." Jordyn swore as they clinked glasses.

"It is, for you. Bug Valley is easy because no one is there. You don't have to acknowledge the pack and your past and you don't have to explain yourself. You answer to no one. It's kinda the weak way out. Why the hell did you leave?" Claudia asked.

She wasn't joking. Her eyes narrowed and Jordyn could feel her anger.

"I'm not talking about it."

"No one is," Claudia fired back.

"Understand it's my cross to bear." The conversation turned serious and she couldn't afford to entertain Claudia. Jordyn met her emerald eyes, found understanding despite the way they glimmered, and knew she said more than she should have. Jordyn would face her mother, the baron, and playing maid of honor at the wedding was ahead of her. Whatever control she was clutching onto was slipping out of her hands. Jordyn took her glass and drank her wine. She wanted to go home. To Bug Valley.

CHAPTER SIX

Jordyn changed out of her jeans and into a pair of lounge pants, tank top, and light zip-up sweatshirt. With a glass of wine, she sat in one of the three wingback chairs, her legs under her, and watched the flames scale the wood and reach into the chimney. Her hand gripped the stem, twisting the glass, stopping, starting over, and repeating the procedure. Her mind raced around Rutger, the affect he had on her—like she couldn't breathe—and the fear she wasn't going to keep it together. Mixed in the chaos was Louis and the unanswered calls. *How did I get here?*

"You make yourself a spectacle," Mia accused as she sat down. Her pale pink silk top with silk covered buttons and matching pants looked expensive.

Closing her eyes, Jordyn gripped the fragile stem and internally groaned. She had been positive her mother had gone to bed. "I didn't do anything," she countered, not bothering to meet Mia's gaze.

"You laugh, he looks. You stand, he looks. And I know you didn't pay for your wine, and neither did I. Who did?"

"I don't know who did. Jason said he was under orders from someone, and he was probably joking. Maybe I'll get a bill. Rutger does what Rutger wants, always has, you can't blame me for his actions." Jordyn turned, looked at her mom, and saw her usual crystal blue eyes held an icy edge laced with anger.

"I can. I will. You're the one who left."

I ran. "He— Never mind. Doesn't matter. In four days, I'll be gone and your perfect world will return."

"Don't be a martyr, it's contemptable even for you. How do you want me to act when you don't tell me anything? Rutger hasn't said anything where you're concerned, and it has everyone wondering what happened. Since the baron gave you permission, we've had to accept your absence."

"I don't live here, why is it hard to accept?" Rising, she walked over to the fireplace. She took a sip, lowered the glass, and tried to get control. "I can't believe you're turning this around on me."

"You left." Mia nearly screamed the words.

"I didn't *leave* you. I didn't leave Trinity. I moved to a different city after receiving a partnership at an established gallery. I'm successful."

"You call that success? You're with a human lover. You're living a lie." The callousness of her words, like saying them gave her pleasure, dulled the fire's warmth.

"I do call it success. Other parents would be proud," she argued. Jordyn was never going to win. "Who I spend my time with is my business."

"You are a pureblood from the Langston lineage. It makes it my business. Does he understand the importance? Does he know he's with a werewolf? Or do you call yourself a lycan?"

"Don't. I haven't told him anything." Turning around, Jordyn met her mother's glare. "I would never betray the pack."

"Very selfless of you. I'm sure Healey will see it as noble." Her mother's tone turned cold. "When he finds out what you are, he will leave you. The same way you left Trinity. Fitting, I think."

Jordyn didn't have a reply or a defense. She didn't have anything. Time had become fragile. Not like a flower you want to keep forever. But a bomb. Lying to Louis was tearing her apart from the inside out and the thought of trying to continue the lies was killing her. She hadn't called him. Hadn't text him, because she didn't want to add more lies. Her thoughts shifted gears to the rules. Yes, you may visit your family during your sister's wedding. No, you may not tell anyone why you left. No, you cannot have communication with anyone in the pack. Jordyn moved to Butterfly Valley with the understanding she was going to be alone. The stresses were adding up and weaving through her muscles. They played with her thoughts and darkened her mood. "I'm not pack." Rogue.

"Your egocentricity is astounding," Mia accused, drawing out the word *astounding* to emphasize her exhaustion of having to deal with Jordyn. It was her turn to stand and pace. "You are pack. The baron reminds us at the meetings and at the gatherings, he did so tonight. The baroness is having you run with the women despite your absence. I don't have to guess, the baron paid for your drinks and made sure you had anything you wanted. He doesn't treat Bailey special. She should be the favorite, she stayed and is faithful to Tanner. You left the pack. Your family. Rutger. For a human. For a human life. That's the worst shame."

Mia was being savage with her accusations and Jordyn's heart ached with her words. Jordyn had created the situation she found herself in, and there was nothing she could do to change things. She had dug herself a hole. Grave. Jordyn set her glass on a table. "Three days. Not a day longer, and I'm leaving. I won't be back. Ever. I'm done. You can keep your world." Her throat clenched around the words and tears welled to sting her eyes. She met her mother's glare, saw the shame, and left her standing by the fire. Jordyn walked up the stairs, her eyes catching her life in the pictures decorating the wall. In her room, she closed door with controlled anger, crashed on the bed, and swore she wasn't going to cry as tears slipped down her cheeks.

Rutger sat at his desk looking over the toxicology report on the first victim. No drugs. It hadn't been an overdose. The cause of death had been asphyxiation. The victim's lungs collapsed, suffocating him. How did chamomile, nettle leaf, and valerian root kill him? He was pretty sure the baroness had a bedtime tea with the same ingredients, and she served it with honey. It didn't kill her. He moved one report, grabbed another, scanned the preliminary report from the medical examiner's office, and shook his head. Not a bruise, mark, or scratch was on the body.

He flipped both folders closed, took his cup, and sipped his coffee. There had to be more. A yawn took him as he sat back in his chair and glanced at his watch. He and Kory spent most the night arguing about his run-in with Jo. They each went back and forth, she said—he said. He explained he didn't care. Kory insisted he did. He repeated no. She asked why? Why did you stand there staring at her? Yes, you do care. Rutger gave up, slept on the couch, and after a couple of hours decided he couldn't stand it any longer and left for the office. He had to get away from her.

There was tension, so yes, people were going to notice they ran into each other. At least no one had seen their eyes. He would be damned if the feel of Jo's body against him and her hip in his hand burned through him and her wolf's eyes had his heart speeding up. It was wrong. All wrong. There should have been hate. She should have been repulsed by touching him. He actually looked at his arm to see if she left half-moon shaped wounds where her nails had been. And she did. He should hate her. Rutger jumped at the soft knock on the door and worked to recover before Mandy, continuing to work in place of CJ, peeked around the edge.

"Director, there's a Detective Russell on the phone for you."

"Thanks."

"Heard about last night."

"What are you talking about?" Rutger asked.

"Jordyn. You two together." A smile curved Mandy's lips. "Heard it was pretty intense."

Liquid bronze stared at him. "We were not together," he argued. "We didn't speak."

"Whatever you say. After you answer the call, the baroness would like to *speak* to you. She said she'll come over here if she has to."

"Fine." Just what he needed. Rutger waited for the door to close and picked up the phone.

Ten minutes later, Rutger had the name of the detective with the reginal task force, Organized Paranormal Investigations, his number, and a meeting set up. With his hand on the butt of his gun, he crossed the parking lot and the driveway wondering what the baroness wanted. How could he face murderers, detectives, the sheriff's department, and fear talking to his mom? *Easy*, he thought, *I know where I stand with them.*

The breeze surrounded him and brought the gentle scent of watered grass, the drifting fragrance of flowers, and clean air the last days of spring held. Rutger took the stairs and met Sadie, one of the baroness' personal sentinels. The ends of her rich brown hair sat even with her ears, her face kept natural, no makeup, and held the faintest bronze of a tan. The baroness hated having guards, and insisted they wear civilian clothing to keep a low profile. Sadie wore a gray V-neck shirt, jeans, boots, and a 9-millimeter tucked into a shoulder holster. "I have a meeting with the baroness."

"Affirmative, Director," Sadie confirmed. With a smile, and opened the door.

Everyone was talking about his run-in with Jo. Ignoring her,

Rutger stepped into the house and met the baroness. "Baroness."

"I'm your mother," Laurel stated, stepping to the side.

"Yes, ma'am." Rutger stood in the foyer and waited.

"Follow." She turned, her hair drifting with her motion, her T-shirt and jeans giving her a younger appearance, her flats silent on the marble flooring. "I received several calls today."

"If they aren't about the safety of the pack, the murders, threats, or pending guests, they don't have anything to do with me." *Don't be Kory.*

"Kory, for starters." The baroness led him to the living room.

Shit. He sat down in a matching chair across from the baroness. Her brown eyes, usually silken with her wolf, were hard and narrowed on him.

"While sobbing, she expressed her feeling and the fear, you no longer love her. You argued all night, and to escape answering her questions, you left." Laurel reached for a delicate porcelain cup sitting on an antique walnut table. A woman with her power and authority surrounded herself with beautiful, delicate objects.

"I don't love her. Never have. I have a job. Next."

Laurel gave an inward sigh. "Mia. She called to say when the wedding is over, Jordyn isn't staying for the women's run. And not to be surprised if she isn't present at the reception. She's leaving. 'I won't be coming back. Ever.' A quote from Mia." She watched Rutger absorb the words as if each one was a silver bullet entering his body. He sat straighter, his eyes growing dark, and his anger reaching out like it needed to hurt someone. "You know Mia. Could be an exaggeration," Laurel said casually, knowing she was adding fuel to his emotions.

Yes, he did. And it might. Still, it wasn't hard to guess what happened. Lady Langston thought Bailey should be the star of every show. His heartbeat raced with his anger. "I know Jo, too." She was going to run, again. He. Didn't. Care.

That's a lie.

"You believe the threat?"

"I do. She has everything in Butterfly Valley." He admitted too much.

"What does she have?"

"Freedom from her parents."

"And?" Laurel pushed. Her head slanted to the right, her eyes tracking him like she could read his thoughts.

Her passion is her photography. Jo has her gallery. "Her job." He wouldn't admit to knowing about the human.

"Is that all?" Laurel asked.

"I guess." Rutger shrugged, indifferent; he wasn't giving up any more information.

"Is there anything here?"

His patience crumbled. "What? When she's here, she doesn't leave Coal Valley, doesn't have *any* connection to the pack, eliminating all relationships and any reason to stay. Once she's gone, there's zero reason for her to come back. She cut everyone out."

"You keep up with her whereabouts?"

He felt like he was being interrogated. "I haven't seen her in three years. What information I know, I've been told."

"Of course." Laurel sipped her coffee.

"Did Lady Langston try to apologize?"

"Apologize? For what?" she asked. Laurel watched Rutger consider her, his power surrounding him like a protective barrier. She hated its distant feel.

"It's Lady Langston. She accused Jo of something." Rutger's wolf rose, inciting his protective instinct. No. No. No. Regardless of his attempts, it kicked in and demanded he find Jo and make sure she was all right. He saw her one time and his walls, denials, and the defense he spent three years creating went to hell.

"No. She asked me to talk to Jordyn." Laurel set her cup on the table.

"Are you?"

"No, I am not. I'm not doing Mia's work for her." Her voice rose, giving away her irritation.

"What does this have to do with me?"

"Everyone saw the two of you last night and how you acted around one another. Reacted to one another."

"I didn't talk to her. I didn't do anything. Hell, I was answering a call about a murder investigation, and I ran into her. Nearly knocked her on her ass. Damn it. Nothing happened. I didn't do anything." *Rambling my defense.* If the baroness sensed his lie, and he knew she had to, she let him have it.

"You didn't notice Jordyn. You don't love Kory?" Ignoring his foul language and his denial, Laurel turned to the table, and picking up her cup, took a sip. She didn't look at him, letting him think about what she said.

Rutger stood, ready to walk out of the room. "No. And no, I don't. I didn't. I don't know how this happened." He sat down, his hand on his arm where her nails had been.

"My advice, son, don't say anything to Kory until after the wedding and Jordyn has left. You need to be honest with her, and if you do it now, she'll think it's because of Jordyn. Once Jordyn is back in Butterfly Valley, you might consider telling her how you feel."

He wasn't telling Jo anything. She could leave. He was better off without her. He reminded himself she had a human boyfriend. Human. Lover. The human's hands had touched her. He inhaled, snuffing his instant jealousy.

It was one time.

Rutger touched her, felt her body against his, and she tore through his world with the violence of a storm. "I'll wait. Not because of Miss Langston, but because I don't need the

distraction. The wedding and security of the pack take priority."
Rutger rose, his anger eating at him. He was finished talking
about Kory and Jo, and in silence, walked to the entrance of the
room and turned around. "Miss Langston hasn't been a part of
my life for years and is a ghost to the pack." He sounded like
Kory and it pissed him off.

Laurel struggled with her motherly instincts to tell her son
what to do, and how to save himself from getting hurt. Some
lessons were painful. Laurel felt it as if it was her own. "If you
don't have any feelings toward *Miss Langston*, then you're free
of any distractions. You're free to do your job."

"I'm free." Rutger turned to leave, hesitated, and faced his
mom. The baroness.

"I won't tell your father we had this little meeting and I was
right." She smiled and it softened her hard glare.

"About?" Rutger asked.

"You, my son." She took her cup, decorated with purple
pansies and green leaves, and sipped her coffee while keeping
her eyes on him over the thin porcelain rim.

Rutger didn't know what the baroness was talking about and
wasn't going to ask. After leaving Sadie behind him, he stopped,
and looking at the mountains, the office, and his truck, he
wondered what he was going to do. *Never coming back.* That
was Jo, running again. Did he want her to leave? No. Damn it, he
wanted closure. And for her to end her infuriating silence. Rutger
couldn't wait for the wedding to be over. He needed his life and
his work schedule to return to normal. Whatever that was going
to be.

It took less than a minute to cross the property to the
Enforcer's building, which was not enough time to burn off his
frustration. Seeing the gym, he longed to take his anger out on
the punching bag. In his office, he picked up the phone and

called Detective Watt with the Organized Paranormal Investigations, or OPI. Several questions later, he hung up and sat back in his chair. The second victim, besides missing his entire torso, showed no signs of a struggle. The only connection to the first murder was the presence of herbs found at his waist and stuck to his skin. Why would there be herbs? When he asked if they were any closer to knowing the identities of either man, Detective Watt explained the second victim had a tattoo on his right thigh—an image of a dragonfly, red, with what resembled Viking runes. He didn't think it was common. The report had been amended and reentered with a picture of the tattoo and tagged with both the Citizen Base, National Crime Log, and he was going to resubmit it to the UF. The explanation was a solid no. They weren't any closer to knowing who the victims were.

Mandy's footsteps sounded on the tile floor right before her soft knock. She peeked around the edge and said, "I'm headed to the church, Ansel and Luke are doing the walk through."

"All right. Afterwards, tell Ansel I need to speak to him," Rutger ordered.

"Yes, sir," Mandy answered. "Luca is taking my place."

"Noted." Rutger watched her close the door and seconds later she greeted and talked to another. Rutger recognized Tracy's throaty voice and waited. As one of Torin's soldiers, and his mate, he put her in charge of the guest list and the families arriving from out of town.

"What's going on?" Rutger asked.

Tracy stood in the entrance, one foot in his office the other foot in hallway. Her dark brown hair touched her red blouse, and her jeans ended in running shoes, like she was ready to hit the trail. "The first guests have arrived. Alpha James, his wife, and their son. They are having cocktails and hors d'oeuvre with the baroness. Would you greet them? The baron is with Torin and won't be able to return for another hour."

"Is Gavin at the house?"

"No, sir. The baron wouldn't have asked you, knowing you're busy with security and the case."

"Yes. Find out where Gavin is," Rutger ordered.

"Yes, sir," Tracy replied and waited for him.

Rutger stood, not wanting to be stuck in a room having small talk with an alpha and his family. Scanning the papers, pictures, and the itineraries littering his desk, he begrudgingly grabbed his phone, and headed out of his office with Tracy in tow. They stopped at the reception area where Luca sat looking at a computer monitor and listening to radio chatter. "I'm going to the house. If Detective Watt calls, please notify me immediately. If Ansel returns within the hour, call me."

"Yes, sir," Luca replied.

Tracy stayed behind with Luca, and he could hear them talking as he walked out the door.

"I just had a conversation with Howard about turning the formal dining room into an office. Lord knows he needs a proper office and we don't use the room. The next day while I was shopping, a member approaches me and repeats what I said. Then goes on to say she disagrees with me. I couldn't believe it." Tabitha laughed, smiled, and crossed her legs, her skirt making a whisper.

"We have to keep our conversations at home and not at pack meetings," Alpha Howard added. He watched his wife for a moment and turned. "You want to be part of the pack, but an alpha never is. There's the alpha and there are the members."

"Howard. Really," Tabitha exclaimed. "Without members, you wouldn't be an alpha."

Alpha Howard chuckled an arrogant sound, dismissing his

wife's comment. "Jordyn, how's your visit going? I can't help but notice how well the gallery is doing."

"It's slow right now. I'm looking forward to summer." Repeating her standard reply, Jordyn ignored the question about her visit. It would have been a lie, and she wasn't going to add speculation and let him create assumptions. Clearly the wedding invitation and the time spent visiting served as a thank you for allowing her to live in Butterfly Valley, without a rogue status.

"I enjoy the downtime from October to June. It gives us time to breathe and have a little freedom before tourist season starts." He gave her a narrowed look. "I'm sure for a business it's different."

"Would either of you like something to drink? I have coffee, tea, water, wine, or liquor," Mia offered as she stood. She smoothed her hands down her black skirt and surveyed the room. "We have a couple of hours before dinner with the baron and baroness."

"I understand this dinner is specifically for alphas and their families. No one else?" Alpha Howard questioned. His eyes rested on Mia, his authority sitting on his face.

"Correct. As a powerful pack, with increasing numbers, the elders represent the members. A show of respect," Mia answered. She waited for their answers, her posture a perfect picture of a hostess, loyal wife, mother of a bride, and pureblood werewolf. While she kept her power at a low hum, saving anyone from being uncomfortable, she wielded an edge to make sure they understood her status in the pack.

"Of course. Wouldn't expect anything less," Howard replied.

Tabitha looked at Howard and to Lady Langston. "Would love a glass of white wine."

"Scotch, please."

I have to get out of here, Jordyn thought as she watched them play with their power trips.

"Jordyn, would you fix Alpha Howard's drink?" Mia asked.

If I said no? "Of course." Jordyn stood. "Alpha Howard, ice?"

"Neat, please."

"Yes, sir," Jordyn replied.

Her mother left the room as Jordyn walked to the liquor cabinet. She wasn't expecting company, and choosing comfy clothes, Jordyn wore a white tank top, broke in but comfortable jeans, and walked around in her bare feet. Much to her mother's disappointment. Trying not to destroy the shreds left of their relationship, Jordyn fixed her hair, makeup, and put on running shoes. She could be presentable.

At the bar, she took a cut crystal highball glass, with the letter L etched on its side, and set it on the marble top. She scanned through the decanters, found the scotch, and poured a little more than she should have. Jordyn set the decanter down and recognized two bottles of wine. Seeing a grizzly bear on the labels, her heart stopped. She set the glass down and stared at the bottles.

"Here you are." Mia handed Tabitha the glass, its bowl already wet with condensation. "Jordyn, do you have Alpha Howard's drink?"

"Please, call me Howard. I hear alpha so often, I think it's my name." Howard's gruff laugh fell in the silence of the room.

"If you like," Mia responded with a tight smile.

Jordyn turned away from the wine and approached Alpha Howard. When she handed him the tumbler, his hand covered hers, and she buried her wolf and the simmering power that never left as if Louis was touching her. He stilled for several seconds. Long enough she felt his power on her skin, his senses searching, and long enough both women saw him. His fingers slipped from her as he took the scotch and sat back. Jordyn's heart pounded in her chest at the same time heat crawled up her throat to stain her cheeks.

"My apologies. I didn't mean to make you uncomfortable. I've been ordered to keep you safe, which means my guards secure your safety. Why would Baron Healey risk his reputation by letting you leave the pack, and personally protecting you?" Alpha Howard's eyes remained on her, their depths giving away his wolf.

"The baron understands her desire to be a photographer. One day, maybe she'll come home and open her own gallery," Mia responded before Jordyn could reply. "We're very proud."

Jordyn tore her eyes away from Alpha Howard and faced her mother as if she were looking at a stranger. With their confrontation not forgotten, she wasn't going to trust anything Mia said. Jordyn sent her senses to feel the lies in her mother's words. There were none. The woman had either lied really well or was telling the truth.

"Is this true?" Howard asked, turning his attention to Jordyn.

"He understands my needs and has graciously allowed me the time. I'm in his debt." Everything she said was true. He wasn't going to catch her in a lie.

"I see." Howard lifted the glass to his lips, as silence moved in, and took a sip. "My apologies, again. I did not mean to darken the mood. My curiosity will forever be my downfall."

"It comes with the territory, I'm sure, Alpha. I hope your curiosity has been quenched," Mia quipped. She sat down, wine in hand, and meet his gaze. Her blue eyes darkened to cobalt.

"Quenched, Lady Langston." He bowed his head with the understanding he'd questioned a prominent family member, and an elder of the Cascade pack.

Good God. Jordyn stopped herself from rolling her eyes at the display. She should have figured the local alpha would question her absence. The desperate need to run drummed through her veins. She needed to go outside for air, and away from their conversation. Making her way to the entrance of the living room, she saw her escape.

"Jordyn, the baroness gifted you a couple of bottles of your favorite wine. Pour yourself a glass and have a seat," Mia insisted.

Jordyn stopped, closed her eyes, inhaled, and turned to face her mother. Mia's smile died on her lips, her motherly moment over. Jordyn realized her mother considered it a sport and planned on winning. The youngest daughter was marrying the baron's son, and the baroness was giving gifts to the oldest daughter regardless of the shame of having left her eldest son and the pack.

A twisted world.

Mia sat with her power and influence surrounding her like it was her tiara. She hadn't defended Jordyn, and she wasn't proud … no, she saved the family from embarrassment. Jordyn ran. Like a submissive trying to escape responsibility.

I'm going to do it again. But this time, I'm never coming back. Ever. Fuck werewolves. Fuck Trinity. Jordyn walked to the bar, poured a glass of wine, took several sips, and poured more. With a full glass, she crossed the room and took her place beside her mother.

CHAPTER SEVEN

The breeze blew through the tree limbs bringing a gentle melody from the chimes. He closed his eyes, listened, and opening them met green eyes. "Did you see her?"

"Yes. Like you said, she was at the lycan's restaurant."

"Is she a rogue?"

"No. The pack will protect her."

"I need more information. Why she is in Trinity? Why will they protect her?"

"Yes, Savior."

"Until I know more, we'll wait for her to return to Butterfly Valley. We can't take the chance of the Wolf Enforcer and the law getting too close. The wolf already saw you," Flint accused, his eyes narrowing.

"My apologies, Savior." Andrea lowered her eyes.

"You put our charge at risk. And having Brother Morgan use his strength to save you, put his life at risk. He could have captured both of you. We are dealing with lycans, not humans," Flint scolded. She lifted her eyes, their dullness staring at him through her lashes. Cowering under his glare, he had to control the urge to punish her. Flint inhaled, turning from Sister Andrea to look at his Advent Calendar. Death, blood, and pain clung to the unneeded parts of the sacrifices giving him strength. Flint crossed the room to stand in front of it. For him it meant power. For the others, it was a reminder their time for revenge was coming with the full moon.

"Please, forgive me," Sister Andrea begged. Her eyes darted over the room, the calendar, and back to Savior. "Please."

"Prove yourself worthy and all will be forgiven," Flint replied absently.

"Yes, Savior."

"The third sacrifice has been cleansed with the herb fusion and is ready," Brother William reported.

The herbs used to purify the dead enhanced the depth of their essence and gave their spirits over to the gods. Flint's eye's skated over Sister Andrea and her weakness, to Brother William. "Excellent. Assemble the coven for the ceremony."

"Yes, Savior." Brother William's eyes narrowed on Sister Andrea before he bowed, took two steps backwards, and turning, walked up the stairs.

Flint remained where he stood with Sister Andrea waiting for his orders. He checked the cell and the bars. If he was going to kidnap and hold a lycan as powerful as Miss Langston, the cell needed to be strong.

Your sister sits in your miserable shadow, Mia accused.

"My shadow," Jordyn seethed. She was looking out the window at the valley with the night before sitting on her like a weight. Jordyn wanted to yell her threats, repeating she wasn't returning to Trinity a thousand times, but knew it was pointless. Mia considered her retreat a win.

"Your sister and I are going to the church. She needs time to dress, spend time with her bridesmaids, and observe the canons," Mia taunted. There was a glimmer of deceit playing in her eyes.

"All right," Jordyn responded. Like she cared.

"Don't you want to know why you aren't coming with us?" Mia asked.

"No." It could be a million things.

"If you're curious, you can ask the baron." Mia's voice held the pleasure in saying those simple words as if she had been waiting all morning.

Jordyn remained silent and watched Bailey walk into the room wearing a smile and a shadow in her eyes. "Jo, I'll see you at the church."

"Yes, you will." Jordyn met her sister and gave her a hug. "It's your day."

"I'm nervous. I'm excited. I'm nervous." Bailey giggled and shook her head.

"We need to leave, Bailey," Mia insisted from behind her.

"I'll see you." Cupping her younger sister's cheek, Jordyn smiled. "I'll be there." Her sins added to her sister's fears and made her feel worse. If that was possible.

Bailey smiled, touched Jordyn's hand, and after turning away, grabbed her things and walked to the door where Mia waited. Jordyn listened for the door to close and walked across the wood floor, the area rug, to the window, and retraced her steps. As she repeated her steps back toward the window her cell phone came to life with a song. Jordyn checked the screen, saw Louis' face, and considered not answering. After deciding to tell him the truth, which would lead to them breaking up, she didn't want to talk to him. If she ignored him, he would know there was something wrong.

"Hello." Jordyn stood at the window staring beyond the valley, the woods, and the mountains as if they weren't there, while Louis talked. He needed to hear her voice and couldn't wait to have her in his arms, and he promised her all of the Italian food and red wine she could handle. Jordyn cringed. She needed to end the charade. "I can't wait to be home. You know, you talk like that and it'll get you in trouble. I love you." Jordyn ended the call. *I'm a liar.* She turned from the window when she sensed her father.

Ethan stood behind her, his tailored, crisp black tuxedo and silver vest glittering in the light as he met her by the windows. "I love it here. I didn't think I would after spending most of my life in the encampment, but I do. I love seeing the mountains and watching the sun as it crests their peaks to climb toward the sky. Like freedom. Do you know why I named this Coal Valley?"

"No. I guess I never thought about it," Jordyn answered. She watched the past darken his eyes.

"When I was in the encampment, the nights were black, pure black, as if they had stolen the stars, and given us perpetual darkness. Those years used to haunt me. When we were released, the sky opened and the darkness ended. Coal Valley was a way to describe those days and not describe them."

"Dad, I had no idea." She watched him stare out the window, his wolf shadowing his eyes, his power a low hum.

"You shouldn't." Gathering himself, Ethan faced Jordyn. "I heard you talking to Louis and I know about the conversation with your mother. I want you to reconsider," he stated. "This is your home."

"Not anymore. The visits have been getting worse. This time, the things she said … I'm done, Dad. I can't fix Mia's problems when I don't know what they are," Jordyn replied. Her chest felt like there were metal bands holding her lungs.

"I understand. Think about it when you're back in Butterfly Valley." He met her gaze and his eyes flashed bright with his wolf. "Please."

"I will, I promise." She was going to hug him, needing to feel his strength, but he walked out of the room, leaving her alone. *I can't do this anymore.*

Jordyn looked out the window at the mountains and tried to imagine what it must have been like before the Cascade pack.

Before Coal Valley. She wanted to remember the feeling of being home before Mia had stolen it from her.

Absently she smoothed the front of her silver dress. The strapless A-line fit perfectly, hugging her curves, and would have felt beautiful had she not been trying to stop herself from crying. Jordyn was leaving her home, her family, and worried about facing the pack and Rutger all while maintaining her composure. It was going to break her.

Following the canons, Bailey and the bridesmaids were in a room with an elder, a woman named Isadora. Together they would pray for Bailey and Tanner and their future family. Pregnancies and werewolves rarely worked. The moon demanding the shift, the wolf demanding freedom, and the human body fighting both, kept baby and mother in constant danger. The couple relied on the alpha and the pack for strength. It was another ritual Jordyn hadn't been invited to and it left her waiting in the foyer. Alone.

With a fake smile plastered on her face, and feeling embarrassed about having to wait be herself, Jordyn watched ushers greet and then escort guests inside of the sanctuary where they would be seated. Thirty minutes of chatter and laughter moved like a slow stream feeding Jordyn's anxiety. She walked, turned, walked, and turned. A sliver of regret cut through her resolve. Jordyn was giving up her life as a pack member and werewolf, and would never know the nervous excitement of a wedding or hear the prayers offered by the pack for a family. Caught up in her thoughts, Jordyn dimly realized the foyer sat empty and silent.

"Ladies, when it's your turn, you will link arms with the correct groomsman, and walk down the aisle at a moderate pace," Janet, the wedding coordinator, stressed as she opened the oak door. "Do you understand? Moderate." Her graying hair feathered the material of her lilac dress. Janet held the door, inspecting the women as they walked by, their silver heels clicking on the marble floor.

"Yes, we understand," Claudia mumbled. She walked over to Jordyn and rolled her eyes. "This your bouquet."

"Thanks." Silver ribbon matching their dresses held lavender, sweet annie, purple and white annual statice, and white star flowers.

"Where are the groomsmen?" Janet asked.

In answer, across the large foyer a matching oak door opened. "Proud of you, brother," Rutger professed as he walked out of the room.

"Ah, perfect. Jordyn and Rutger, please come here," Janet ordered.

Jordyn gave Claudia a dark gaze, exhaled, inhaled, and held her breath when Rutger walked over to her. His tailored tuxedo showed off his toned arms, chest, and legs. His dark hair had been styled and combed back, leaving his face open, accentuating his cheekbones and dark mahogany eyes. *Don't stare.*

"As the eldest siblings, and the maid of honor and best man, you two will lead. Once at the front, Jordyn, you will go to the left. Rutger, you will go to the right. Before you go to your sides, you will each pay tribute to the opposite set of parents. This will close the circle of the family and will show, as the elders, you're accepting the bride and the groom as a brother and a sister and their parents as your own. Do you understand?"

"Yes," Jordyn whispered. Rutger's arm feathered her bare skin and heat raced over her. *Keep it together.*

"Yes," Rutger managed to say. He was thankful his voice held firm and he didn't embarrass himself by sounding rough and throaty.

"We're set then. Everyone, take your places." Janet eyed the two of them for a second longer before leaving to give the other couples instructions.

Rutger held his bent elbow out for Jo and struggled to stop himself from staring at her. She slipped her hand into the bend, her fingers holding his arm, her power like silk on his skin, and the skirt of her dress brushing his leg. She wore her raven hair up in a twist of curls, while pins decorated with diamonds shaped like crescent moons held each curl in place. Mascara framed her eyes, shadowed in coal and chocolate brown, bringing out their natural color. She didn't wear a necklace, like the others, but in her right ear wore three onyx stones linked together with a thin silver chain to resemble the Langston family crest. He saw the intricate crest inked between her shoulder blades, under it were runes following her spine and disappearing behind silver fabric.

"The music started," Janet whispered. "Go."

Rutger inhaled, taking in her scent of vanilla and the varied smells from the bouquet, and took the first step.

Jordyn forced her concentration on matching him, making sure she looked calm, and their walk smooth. She didn't need to think about the sanctuary full of people staring at them. It didn't help. Her instincts blazed when she felt his eyes on her and his power sinking into her skin. If her flight or fight instinct kicked in, she was going to run. Far away.

The sanctuary opened before them and the guests turned to watch. Jordyn zeroed in on the array of tiny white lights, flowers, garland, and ribbons used to create a fairy tale setting. They walked down the aisle at their instructed moderate pace, whispers and soft murmurs trailing them. At the front, Jordyn slipped her hand free from Rutger's elbow and waited for him to make the first move. Facing each other, Rutger's eyes warmed to gold and shaped like his wolf's, had her heartbeat pounding, and her human eyes melted into her wolf's. *Damn*.

She didn't move when he took her face in his hands and gazed down at her. Her instincts screamed. Jordyn should be backing away from him, his touch, and whatever he was planning on doing. The smell of his skin and his cologne took her back and made her breath catch. Jordyn didn't move. She watched Rutger lean down, at the same time she closed her eyes, and he kissed her forehead.

Jordyn stopped breathing.

In their church, in front of the pack, their parents, the elders, the prominent guests, and Kory, he promised to love and protect her. He would stand beside her and act as her shield. Her protector. Always. Squeezing the bouquet, she forced herself not to run. *It doesn't matter. None of it does*, she told herself, *I'm leaving and never coming back*.

After a restless night, and a turbulent morning of questions, he realized there was the cold existence his life had become, and then there was reacquainting himself with the old Rutger. Knowing he was courting madness and possible punishment didn't change his need to make peace with his feelings for Jo. So, he trapped her in the church during his brother's wedding.

If the baron questioned him, he would answer with silence, like he had for three years. Every muscle in his body tensed; Jo hadn't given him the closure he needed, and he wasn't sure he wanted it. He was sure he couldn't go on without her knowing how he felt. Rutger met her wolf's eyes, understanding she accepted his promise, and her power drifted around him as if her wolf consented. Jo could run for as long and go as far as she wanted, but he would be there. Rutger would serve as her protector and his wolf as her strength. He held her gaze, using the precious seconds to memorize her face and the sleek bronze of her wolf's eyes. When he released her, it felt as if he was letting go for the last time.

Jordyn's head ached and her eyes stung from holding her tears back as she turned and walked to the baron. She bent and kissed him on the cheek. In reply, he gave her wolf eyes, dark and knowing. Turning, she faced the baroness, and kissed her cheek. She, too, welcomed Jordyn with wolf eyes.

Rutger kissed Lord Langston's cheek, received wolf eyes, a smile, and a hand shake, and after kissing Lady Langston's cheek, he saw her eyes were red from tears and her cheeks damp, but was denied acceptance. He didn't care. If Jo didn't want him, she knew he would never turn his back on her.

Jordyn walked to the right, joining the other bridesmaids. She met Rutger's stare and remained strong under the scrutiny of her mother and the guests.

CHAPTER EIGHT

The cleric raised his hands and announced, "They have been bound forever by their love, and standing before us, are *One-Flesh*. I give you, Mr. and Mrs. Tanner Kanin."

The serene setting folded under the eruption of whistles and hollering when the celebration echoed in the sanctuary. Together, the new couple turned and started down the aisle. Everyone stood, applauded, and gave them their congratulations.

With the warmth of his lips haunting her, Jordyn reluctantly slipped her hand in the bend of Rutger's elbow. The touch sent her heart racing with need to get away from him. They walked down the aisle, behind the bride and groom, and when it was acceptable, she wasted no time letting go and disappearing into the crowd.

Rutger's hand skimmed Jo's arm as she slipped from his hold. *Damn it.* He wasn't going to watch her escape. He made his mind up he was going after her.

"Found you," Kory said, grabbing his arm and pulling him close.

Rutger tried to keep Jo in sight but lost her as she descended into the crowd. Shaking his head, he looked at Kory.

Jordyn blended in with the guests, and hoping to disappear, made her way outside. The warm air and gentle breeze moved over her bare shoulders taking the chill from the church. Soft floral scents of honeysuckle drifted and joined the varied fragrances from her bouquet. She stood in the sun, smiling at passing people, and trying to figure out what she was going to say to her mother.

"Jordyn, over here," Bailey called and waved. Several trees created a canopy, casting Bailey in the shade. With her yell, people turned to look at Jordyn. Without a doubt, Jordyn knew they were blaming her for Rutger's actions and she could hear their accusations as if they were being broadcasted. "Come on. We're getting our picture taken," Bailey pleaded. She tilted her head, and with a teasing smile curving her lips, said *please*.

There was no saying no. Smiling back, Jordyn searched for Rutger. When she didn't see him, she swallowed her embarrassment and started across the grass. Each step matched the beat of her pulse drumming in her ears, while the weight of the guests' stares sat on her skin. Jordyn prayed the feeling wouldn't kill her. Acting like she had it all under control, she hoped she didn't trip and make things worse.

"Mrs. Kanin," Jordyn greeted as she stopped beside her sister. Rutger, the guests, couldn't take away from the pride she felt when she was with her sister. The wedding was beautiful, Bailey and Tanner made a loving couple, and the support shown by the guests added to the day.

"Jordyn, it was perfect," Bailey cooed. She switched her bouquet to her right hand and wrapped her left arm around Jordyn. "We're still the Langston sisters."

"Yes, we are."

"All right, ladies, show me some smiles," Kelly said, raising the camera.

Bailey and Jordyn posed like uncoordinated models and struggled to smile through their giggles, as Kelly snapped pictures of them. Jordyn moved to the side when Tanner walked up behind Bailey, took her by the waist, and smiled for the next shot. Jordyn watched them, and creating more space for Kelly, laughed when Tanner started clowning around.

Jordyn's laugh caught in her throat when Rutger's hands held her waist and he stood behind her. Without getting unwanted attention, she tried to get away from him, his touch, and the camera. As if giving her his protection in front of the entire pack wasn't enough to cause trouble, he wrapped his arm around her waist and drew her closer. *I'm going to die.*

"Kelly, don't take the picture if my sister isn't smiling," Bailey teased.

Jordyn did her best to smile—any curvature of the lips was enough—and ignored Rutger's tightened grip. With wide eyes, she watched the crowd grow and stare as Kelly continued to take photos.

"One, two, and three." With the last number, a series of flashes went off.

"I'm blind," Gavin mumbled. He put his hands out in front of him and stumbled over to Rutger, like he was feeling his way. Rutger moved Jordyn behind him, protecting her from Gavin's searching hands, and turned Gavin around to face the photographer.

"Gavin, stand next to Tanner. We need one more picture," Bailey ordered.

"All right. All right. Man, she's already bossy." He gave Rutger a frown and smiled at Jordyn with accusations in his eyes when she stepped around Rutger's side.

"One."

Rutger's hands went to her hips.

"Two."

Their bodies touched.

"Ready."

Hurry up. Taking a hesitant step, she moved a sliver, creating space between them. Fully thinking she had won, Rutger tightened his hold, drew her close, and kept her near him. Jordyn leaned back, feeling him against her, and liking the way his muscles tightened when he moved. *Losing it.* She exhaled as Kory stood in front of the crowd her face twisted with anger.

"Three." Another series of flashes went off.

"Are we good?" Jordyn asked. *Please.* She gripped Rutger's thick wrists, his muscles taut, and stepped out from his hold.

"Yes," Bailey answered, her eyes going between Rutger and Jordyn. "Thank you, sister."

Jordyn acted like she didn't see the combination of confusion, hope you get back together, and you have to deal with Mia look. After hugging Bailey, she drew back. "I love you."

"I love you. Thank you for being here," she whispered. "I know it isn't easy."

"It's not for you to worry about." Bailey released her, and Jordyn stepped back as the photographer started repositioning people.

"We need a picture with the groom and his brothers," Kelly said.

"Jo, wait—" Rutger started. He took two steps and reached for her arm when Kory intervened, yet again. She grabbed his hand and stood in front of him.

"Kelly, take our picture," Kory demanded. She wrapped her arm around Rutger, bringing him closer.

"The two of you?" Kelly asked. She looked at Rutger, her eyes questioning, and then they drifted to Jo, who was speed walking away from them. Meeting Kory's eyes, she smiled. "Ready?"

With guilt running freely, Jordyn hurried across the trimmed grass, its ends too short to reach the silver of her high heels. She continued in the direction of her parents, having nowhere else to go, and saw her mother's ramrod straight back. *Angry much? I'm in trouble*, she repeated as the dreaded thought turned real.

"Why aren't you over there with Rutger? I don't think you've embarrassed Kory enough today," Mia fumed. Jordyn could feel her anger coming in cold waves despite the warm afternoon sun.

"Mia, enough. This isn't the place," Ethan warned. There was a growl running through his words. Jordyn had never heard him growl, let alone at Mia.

"How many times do I have to repeat myself? I can't control what Rutger does or doesn't do," she said, trying to defend herself. Why was she always defending herself? She couldn't care less how Kory felt. Or her mother. "If you don't want a scene, march other there and tell him to leave me alone."

"Rutger showed you respect. I believe it means he has come to terms with the way things are. I think we should do the same," Ethan advised. Softly. Her dad accepted 'the way things are' … it was her mother who had problems.

"You want to blame me for everything, fine. I've taken it for three years. I shouldn't have to remind you, this is Bailey's day. If you wait until tomorrow, you can chew my ass out before I leave." Jordyn met her mother's glare, unwilling to back down.

"Jordyn Lily Langston." Mia's face twisted, her voice lowered, as she seethed Jordyn's full name.

Jordyn's anger warmed her middle, spread out, and invaded her nerves. It felt good. Too good. It felt like she was in control and not the secrets she kept and the regrets binding her to silence. The heated edge melted the restraints and she felt free. Jordyn met Mia's glare with her own and waited for the rest of the threat. "What?"

"Jordyn," Jason addressed her. His voice thick and firm. He stood a couple feet away from them. He hadn't called her Jo. The easygoing Jason was replaced with a serious side. "Why don't you ride with us to Foxwood? I drove Claudia's car."

Jordyn's eyes narrowed on Mia. Like it would have mattered if he had driven his truck and it was covered in mud and on fire. Anything would be better than riding with Mia.

"You have to ride with the wedding party. You're the maid of honor," Mia pointed out before Jordyn replied. Her hands were on her hips; her *mother of the bride* glow dimmed and the joy she might have held vanished.

"I'm not part of the wedding party. Ask the baron," Jordyn shot back, using Mia's words. Mia glared at her, and Jordyn turned away to face Jason. "Would love to." Without saying anything else, she left. When they were out of earshot of her parents, she asked, "Friend or shadow?"

"Both." Jason opened the car door, waited for her, and closed it.

The baron had been watching her. What did she expect? He sent the one person she never would have expected. Jason. She didn't care. Jordyn swept her skirt behind her legs and sat in the backseat of Claudia's car, and looked out the passenger window. She inhaled when she saw Rutger talking to his father and staring at her. He watched the entire scene with her mother. Jordyn wanted to storm over and blame him for everything.

"What the hell is going on with you two?" Claudia asked.

"My mother is having a problem with Bug Valley," Jordyn answered.

"No," Claudia started.

"Pretty simple," Jason said.

"Do tell," Claudia challenged.

Jordyn shook her head, the confrontation with her mother feeding her anxiety, while they carried on a conversation like she wasn't there.

"Rutger loves Jordyn."

"Don't say that in front of Mia, she'll have you killed,"

Jordyn warned.

"No, really."

"No, really, don't. Please God, get me the hell out of this town," Jordyn exclaimed, scooting closer to the front seat.

"He does," Jason insisted. "And if you say he doesn't, you're blind."

"I'm not blind. He doesn't love me. A wedding is a very stressful time for the family. With heightened emotions and lives changing, it's easy to get caught up in the moment." *I sound like Louis.*

"That's bullshit and you know it. He kissed you in the church and in front of the baron." Jason's eyes gleamed as he stared at her in the rearview mirror. "He made an oath."

"We have a past. His actions are meant to ease the tension between our families," Jordyn tried. Yes, of course, they were. Empty actions. She was already sounding like a human.

"I don't know what to believe. I do know, dinner is going to be a scream." Claudia didn't try to cover her laughter.

"Can't wait," Jordyn mumbled.

"Let's hope we don't have steak or something you need a knife for," Claudia mused with a half grin.

"Why?" Jordyn asked absently.

"Because Kory will use it to kill you."

CHAPTER NINE

At Foxwood, Rutger kept his nerves at a low roar, discarded his tux jacket, kept his satin silver vest on, and waited at the front of the house for Claudia's car. He watched Jo leave with Jason, her shadow, and felt her anger. He needed to talk to her. Why it was taking them longer than everyone else to arrive, he had no idea. It couldn't be good. He knew Jason would bring Jo, it was his job, but if she decided she wasn't having it, Jason wouldn't force her. He knew that, too.

And if she left town— Damn, the thought had a growl building in his chest.

"Rutger," Healey greeted with his approach. He wore his tux and held a glass of red wine, his hardened eyes seeming older.

"Baron," Rutger greeted. He kept his eyes on the driveway, not wanting to meet the baron's gaze.

"Son."

"Father." *Here we go.*

"Want to explain what happened at the church?"

"No," he answered and took a drink of his bourbon. Rutger hadn't bothered with ice. It would melt and dilute the alcohol.

"All right. Tell me what today was about," Healey ordered.

"That's pulling rank."

"Yes. I have rank, and it gets pulled."

Rutger inhaled and could swear he smelled her. When he held her, her touch made him feel healed. "It's over."

"You're lying. You could try answering the question with more than two words."

She's mine. Rutger glanced at his glass and back at the driveway, his heart trying to beat within the constraints of the past three years. "I had to do something. We share something and I wanted her to know I'm here. She belongs in Trinity. Why can't she see that?"

Fated. Few paranormals experienced the influence of having a fated mate. Saw as a curse and a blessing, those affected could search their entire lives without finding the one fated, or like Rutger and Jordyn, they found each other and denied their feelings. Healey watched Rutger's walls of anger and protection crumble. "You saw Mia and Jordyn. Mia creates discontent and is a constant negative in Jordyn's life. One would think, since passion and emotion drive Jordyn, she would fight back. But she doesn't. She needs to learn to fight for what she wants and not back down when confronted. She can't let others decide for her."

"Jo told Mia she is leaving and never coming back." Rutger met the baron's gaze. "She can't leave."

"I have already given permission."

"Don't you want her here?" Rutger questioned. He checked the drive, the parking lot, and waited for the baron to answer.

"Yes, I do."

"Why did you let her leave?" Rutger hated asking the question, it made him feel stupid. He should know why she left and why the alpha let her go. To escape the scrutiny of his father's glare, he looked back at the road and the approaching car.

"She asked and had reasons," Healey answered.

"You know why? You've known this entire time?"

"I am the baron."

Claudia's car approached. If Rutger knew the reason, it

would be easier to talk to Jo and convince her she needed to move home. He turned to ask the baron if he would tell him why, but the man disappeared. Damn it. Rutger searched the front of the house for Kory, and not finding her, watched the car stop. He used his senses and quickly felt Jo wasn't there. His heart sank and his anger burned. A second car, a red SUV stopped behind Claudia's, and after several seconds, he saw Jo. His attention focused when Claudia laughed, and the two women linked arms, and walked together leaving Jason behind them. Rutger watched Jason scan the area and use his wolf's instincts to sense any danger as he trailed his objective, Jo.

He met her chocolate eyes bright with her laughter. "Jordyn, can I talk to you?" Rutger asked. His heart was in his throat and his pulse in his ears. The two women stopped, Claudia smiled, and Jo's eyes darkened.

"I should have stopped you. I'm leaving and I'm not coming back. Ever. I shouldn't have come here." Jordyn regretted the words as soon as she said them. She should have taken the time to talk to him, to officially end whatever they had been. She should have burned any thread of a relationship, giving her the freedom to leave with no strings attached. Why didn't she? His touch and show of affection proved she didn't want to lose him. She wanted him. Selfishly, she was holding his life hostage. Damn. Knowing he was waiting meant he belonged to her. Jordyn watched raw emotion cross Rutger's face as if a lightning strike cut through him. There was no turning back, she destroyed the slim chance there might have been to explain her side. With her mother's words ringing in her ears and her voice grating on Jordyn's nerves, she let go of Claudia. Jordyn saw the lines fan out from his eyes, his defenses creating a neutral look, but his lips ... they told her the truth. She felt them on her skin. *I hate this*. And she walked away.

Rutger didn't try to stop her. He couldn't.

"Mia blames her. It's bad," Claudia mumbled.

Rutger ignored Claudia and stared at Jo's red SUV. The hope he clung to died with the meaning of her words. Never coming back. He hated Butterfly Valley. He hated the human. He downed his bourbon, handed his glass to Jason, and in silence, walked.

Jordyn entered the house and headed for a hiding place. She didn't want to face Claudia and Jason, and didn't want to hear about her mistake. Out of sight, she sat in a corner, checked her phone, and read the messages from Louis. Jordyn read them several times, each time failing to come up with a reply. "Stop," she mumbled. Jordyn was falling apart. Without responding with a lie or a vague reply, she put her cell in her purse.

The cutting regret of seeing the hurt on Rutger's face plagued her. It didn't change her problems. Jordyn couldn't move home, not with her mother, and not while half of the pack treated her like a stranger and the other expected her to move back like nothing happened. Around her everyone mingled, and when she heard Rutger, Kory, or her mother, she moved.

"Can I have your attention?" Healey's voice thundered over the chatter and laughter, and the voices faded. "Your turn," Healey turned to Laurel.

Smiling, she faced the crowd. "The wedding party and special guests will eat in the formal dining room, while everyone else is welcome to eat wherever you are comfortable. That includes the backyard where several tables have been set up."

Jordyn remained in the sitting room—with views of the front yard, enforcer's office, and mountains—and waited for the crowd to thin before making her way to the dining room. When she couldn't wait any longer, she walked down the length of the table, and found her seat, right beside her mother. After sitting, she looked at the end of the table. The baron sat at the head with the baroness to his left, and Gavin to his right. Spring sat beside him while Tanner and Bailey sat beside them and Rutger sat with Kory. Rutger should have been seated to the Alpha's right representing the second to the alpha. Not beside his youngest brother.

"That's the result of your absence." Mia leaned closer and whispered, "I don't know why he cares for you."

Neither do I. She wanted to leave. "Thank you, Mother." Jordyn tilted her head and saw Mia out of the corner of her eye. "I'm surprised you didn't tell me."

"I was forbidden to do so," Mia replied.

Figures. Jordyn watched Rutger as Kory tried talking to him. He stared forward, drank his bourbon, ignored Kory, and wouldn't look at her. Jordyn hurt him. No doubt Mia would have loved to tell Jordyn, Rutger stepped down and put her at fault.

"Mia, leave her alone," Ethan warned, his eyes shimmering with his wolf.

Ansel heard the guest's tangled voices before reaching the entrance of the dining room. Large enough to hold thirty guests and room for servers to walk around the table with trays teeming with expensive china, and gourmet food, he stood watching for a second. He inhaled before saying, "Forgive my intrusion." When Rutger put him charge, he changed from T-shirt and jeans to the enforcer's uniform of black BDUs, boots, and thigh holster. A hush swept through the room; everyone turned, making Ansel the center of attention.

"What is it, Ansel?" Healey asked.

"I need to speak with the director," he answered, his voice serious, carrying the importance of the request.

Jordyn watched Ansel, his unyielding stance as he faced the baron, members of the Highguard, and the other honored guests.

"It's time sensitive, sir,"

The director was sitting among the important guests? The silence thickened, Ansel waited, and Jordyn following the enforcer's gaze, looked at Gavin. No. He didn't respond. Curiosity had her looking around the table with the other guests. Jordyn drew a slow breath when Rutger stood and silently demanded her attention. Her words came back, their sting adding to the understanding he lost his birthright in the pack when he stepped down to work among the members.

"Director Kanin, my apologies."

Rutger ignored Ansel. He stared at Jo and waited, expecting to see the same contempt and disappointment he saw in Kory's eyes stain hers. His heart stopped, suspended in his chest, when her head tilted to the left and her dark eyes, glittering with pride, held his. *Never coming back*. He saw the old Jo and felt the woman he had loved. He loved.

Kory glanced at Jordyn and back to Rutger, and reaching up gripped his arm. To get his attention, she squeezed her fingers and stared up at him. "You can't leave me here." The words rushing from her in desperation.

"You've caused enough trouble. Leave him alone," Mia seethed in Jordyn's ear.

No. Jordyn held Rutger's stare and saw uncertainty. His position cost him more than his birthright and place in the pack. Stepping down meant weakness in the eyes of the territory, the Highguard, and the other alphas. They saw a coward. A failure. He gave up everything to take his place as director. Damn them. Director of Enforcers suited him. *Shut up*. Guilt swirled in her middle and she felt sick. She needed to leave and get back to her reality. Her fantasy life.

"Director Kanin," Ansel repeated.

Rutger shook Kory from his arm and met the eyes of the guests at the same time he stepped around his chair. "If you'll excuse me."

"Wait, Director," Healey started, his eyes on Jordyn, "what is this about?"

If Ansel interrupted the wedding reception, it was about the murders. "It's a delicate matter," Rutger answered.

"You'll explain it," Healey demanded as he stood, the eyes of his family, guests, the other alphas, and members of the Highguard on him. He exuded the expected authority of a baron.

"Ansel," Rutger ordered.

"A couple of hikers found a body. A werewolf. Detective Russell and Detective Watt have requested the Director's presence," Ansel explained.

"Why?" Healey asked.

"They suspect magic born are involved and believe our heightened senses will aid them in the investigation and the collection of evidence," Ansel replied. "And it's on Cascade territory."

With the wedding over, the guests protected and heading home, his worries were subsiding. Healey looked at his son. "You'll take Jordyn with you."

"What? No. Absolutely. Not," Rutger argued. *No way in hell.* He shot Jo a look of disgust and fear. "No. This is a murder investigation." He did not need her anywhere near him.

"No. Rutger said no. He's the director," Kory argued, her panicked gaze meeting Jordyn's.

Rutger was staring at Kory and not wanting to agree with her. "No."

"Jordyn," Healey repeated.

"I can't. I'm a photographer. I take pictures of trees. Trees." The guests watched Jordyn sit with her plate of food in front of her and stammering over her words and excuses. She couldn't go with Rutger. "Trees, mountains, some waterfalls. I don't know anything about murderers." *Please god, no.* She couldn't be alone with Rutger. Not after what she said. Her eyes darted around the table, found others staring, and met the baron's. "Please."

"Jordyn, you'll represent the Cascade pack, work with the director, and serve as the soldier you are. You're going," Healey ordered. "Director Kanin."

Rutger slowly faced Jo. "Get your gear."

"I don't have it," Jordyn answered quickly. Not her best move, lying in a room full of werewolves and magic born. Her eyes darted from Rutger to the baron.

Nice try. "You do. You always do," Rutger replied. "Ansel, I'll meet you at the office. I have to change out of this monkey suit."

Jordyn stood and waved her arms in front of her. "I'm in a dress. And heels." Her voice lost its strength. Her words falling on deaf ears. The baron had ordered her to go with Rutger. "Dress."

"Jason, get Jo's gear out of her SUV and put it in my truck. There's a duffle bag with extra clothing, bring it to her," Rutger ordered. His gaze remained on her. The sets of eyes at the table narrowed on him. Yes, he knew Jo.

"Do I need keys?" Jason asked as he stood.

"No. Both are in the backseat." She sat down and took her wine glass and finished what was left.

"I hope you're happy," Mia taunted.

Twenty minutes later Jordyn wore jeans, running shoes, a T—shirt, and zip up hoodie. In hopes Rutger would leave without her, she had taken her sweet time removing every one of the twenty pins from her hair. Then she untangled the curls, ditched her onyx earrings, and wore her hair up in a messy bun. *At least I'm comfortable*, Jordyn thought as she sat on the passenger side of Director Kanin's enforcer truck. Ignoring Rutger, she stared out of the window, one arm resting on her camera bag, as a country song played and mixed with the buzzing from the radio. Between them a laptop blinked with information. The sun was sinking behind the mountains, its last rays creating webs through the trees.

"You don't have to do this. You can stay in the truck," Rutger offered, breaking the silence. The tires on the asphalt and the radio were the only sounds since leaving Foxwood. Like he expected, she ignored him. When his phone rang and Jo jumped, he smiled. "Kanin."

Jordyn listened as another enforcer relayed information, their exact position, and the law enforcement present. Her thoughts were going around and round, trying to think of a reason she should be back at Foxwood. After a couple of minutes of questions and answers, Rutger hung up. "I don't know what I'm supposed to do," she mumbled. "I'm a landscape photographer. I don't understand why I'm here."

You're a werewolf. "That makes two of us." Rutger's attention remained on the road, the curves, the investigation, certainly not Jo. He touched the laptop screen mounted near the console, went through the menu, chose GPS, and entered the location. Rutger looked at the road, slowed down, and made the hairpin corner. It was going to take them another fifteen minutes. He glanced back at the screen, showing a map, and the estimated time of arrival. Couldn't go fast enough.

"How far?" Jordyn asked. Like it mattered.

"ETA in fifteen." Rutger reminded himself to focus on the job. Or at least tried to. Jo gazed out the window and he imagined her seeing the scenery as pictures and turning each shot in to a work of art. He made the next tight corner and the road stretched out and into another corner. Minutes sat between them feeding off the tension and adding to the silence. Beside him, to the left and right dirt roads started, their length disappearing into the shadows. Rutger checked the map, again, hoping they were close. *Finally.* The area opened and flashing lights came into view.

"Don't get out of the truck," Rutger ordered.

"Fine." Jordyn didn't care. It didn't have anything to do with her. Except she was ordered to be there. Sitting straighter, she faced Rutger. "The baron commanded me to go with you. I have to do something."

Commanded. A little dramatic. Silence. Slowing the truck, he drove to the side of the road and parked away from the other cars. "You don't have anything to contribute. This is an investigation. Not a photo op."

Silence. It was Jordyn's turn to ignore him.

Rutger stared at the side of her face and waited for a sarcastic response. When she continued to ignore him, he killed the engine. Out of the group, Detective Russell left two detectives and started toward them. "Stay here."

"Whatever," she mumbled under her breath. No way in hell was he was going to order her around.

Rutger gave her a sideways glance before opening the door and getting out. "Detective Russell," Rutger greeted.

"Kanin, and?"

Rutger turned, irritation surged through his veins when he saw Jordyn standing behind him. He was sure he'd made himself crystal clear. "This is Jordyn Langston."

"That means?"

"She's here to help." He nearly growled the words.

"Can she be trusted?" Detective Russell's hard gaze narrowed on her.

No. He had to put his own feelings to the side. *Yes.* The baron wouldn't send her to a crime scene if he thought she wasn't going to be of help. "Miss Langston serves the pack."

Miss Langston. Nice.

"Miss Langston, if you can use your senses, I'll take it," Detective Russell responded and started walking. His gait was impatient as he made his way around patrol cars, unmarked vehicles, bushes, and the rough terrain to the body. "Same as last time. Looks like they dumped him here."

"You haven't gotten a hit on either of the victims with the CB or NCL?" Rutger asked as he kept pace with Detective Russell.

"Negative. This guy has his head, maybe that'll give us a clue to who he is. I had the other's DNA tested and added to both the CB and NCL, and the UF. If either of them have been arrested in the last five years, we might get a hit."

Free to use her senses, Jordyn brought her wolf forward, felt death's fingers touching her, and shuddered. She understood why the baron ordered her to go. She wished he would have let her stay at Foxwood; this was going to push her wolf. How many days? Jordyn couldn't remember, but knew using her power to stop from shifting had weakened her. She could walk away, get in the truck, and pretend she had no idea. Lie to the baron. That would absolutely work, no question. Jordyn's instincts rose as her senses swept through the area and began giving her information and the slightest feel of power. Enforcers. When the men stopped, she stopped. Away from Rutger.

"Isn't that—" Luke started to ask.

"Don't," Rutger replied. He stopped himself from snapping at his enforcer and airing his personal feelings in front of humans.

"Any evidence the person responsible could be in the area?" Rutger asked, trying for normal. The woman had been watching them when he spotted her.

"Negative," Luke replied.

"The first deputies on scene made a large grid, giving ample space, looked all over, and found nothing," Detective Russell explained. "Detective Watt, you've met Rutger, and this is Miss Langston also of the Cascade pack."

"Yes, Kanin. Langston. I walked the grid and didn't find anything," Detective Watt reported.

"Did the same. Nothing," Luke added.

Rutger searched the area with his senses, backed them with the instincts of his wolf and tried to find the evil feel of the woman. He turned his face to the woods, searched, and his attention splintered when he saw Jo by the body—her knee in the dirt as she leaned over the yellow plastic cover. *What the hell?*

"Jo." Rutger stepped around the men; he was going to put her in the truck and lock her inside. "Jordyn."

You mean Miss Langston. "Male. They tortured him," she whispered.

"How do you know that?" Rutger asked. "The others hadn't been tortured." Hell, they hadn't fought back.

"He was aware … awake when they hurt him. I can feel him. Sense him. There's another essence. I can't place it."

"How?" Kneeling beside her, Rutger studied the side of her face. Her expression changed with her thoughts, her eyes flickering from chocolate and bronze, and her lips parted.

Jordyn exhaled, the victim's pain falling through her like shards of glass. "I can feel heightened emotions. Sadness, happiness, fear, pain, whatever is most dominate. Between the pain and torture, it left an emotional scar. Its weight takes time to dissipate. Not like his death. It was slow. He wanted death to end the pain. It left an emptiness. A void." Jordyn took a deep breath and rubbed her arms with her hands.

"I didn't know—" Rutger started. It was hurting her and had him wanting to get her out of there.

"The baron does. It's why I'm here." Rising, she wiped her hands on her jeans.

Jo faced him, and he saw hurt in her eyes. "How?" Rutger mumbled.

"Ask him. Can I move the cover?"

"Wait. You haven't seen the body?"

"No," Jordyn answered and waited.

"But you know he's male and was tortured?"

"Yes. Can I see the body?" Jordyn had been keeping her power a secret her entire life. She did not want it out in the open for the world to judge but there is was. Torturing her. Like it had when she saw Rutger with Kory.

"Absolutely," Detective Russell stepped around Rutger, bent down, and gripped the edge to slowly expose the body.

Damn, Jo was right.

Jordyn walked down its length as death and pain hovered over the corpse. She stopped at his head where sliced tendons and muscles oozed scarlet. The cooling blood slid through crevices to the ground soaking pine needles and leaves. Jordyn leaned closer, meeting a tangy iron, and held her breath. Blood from the living mixed with blood from the dead to tangle with the man's death. The corrupt feeling anchored itself inside of her head. It was going to take days for the emptiness to leave, days she didn't have. "They took his spine."

"Yes," Detective Watt answered. "They flayed his back."

"Blood Eagle. I would say they wanted something from him," Rutger began. "It would explain the torture."

"It would," Luke agreed.

"Blood Eagle, like a Norse execution?" Detective Russell

asked and looked at Rutger.

"It's been used since the Norse," Luke said casually, his statement getting the attention of Jordyn, both detectives, and a glare of warning from Rutger.

"I'm not going to ask." Detective Russell shook his head. "It's clearly torture."

Leaning down, Jordyn inhaled. "Herbs. I almost missed the scent of salt, and humans. It's different. There's another smell I can't place." Leaves, dirt, and twigs stuck to the edges of flesh, giving way to more greenery sticking out from his sides. The mass lifted his middle higher than his head and legs. Jordyn stood, and cringed when she saw his eyes were missing. *Evil.*

"He's missing his eyes. There's more going on," Rutger stated.

Detective Russell replaced the cover and stood. "More than one person, one human. If we're staying with the witch theory, you can't sense them? They're human to you."

"It depends. If they're currently using magic, my senses will pick it up. If they're weak, and this feels weak, they feel human," Jordyn explained. She watched the group consider her. *Shut up.*

"I see. Say they're witches, are they together as a coven?" Detective Watt asked. He held a small notebook and stared at Jordyn.

"Yes. For this, they're feeding off one another," Jordyn replied. The eyes. The blood. The pain.

"If they're using torture, taking body parts, I'm guessing it's some kind of ritual. Maybe for a spell? They're killing werewolves for a reason. But what they're doing with the parts, I can't imagine. I can talk to Healey Kanin, he might know someone," Rutger offered. He stood beside Jo, her power a thin haze around her.

"I hate to consider that a possibility. Rutger, any help would be appreciated. In the meantime, I'll have the task force start investigating local witch covens," Detective Watt responded.

Jordyn had to get out of there. Walking away from the body, the group of men, and the detectives working the scene, she put several yards between them. She needed clean air, space, and needed to shed the clinging claws of mortality.

Pain. Fear. Protect her. "Are you, all right?" Rutger asked. His hand rested on the butt of his gun, his other hand on his hip; his back straight, his presence wrapped in authority.

"I will be. How long?" Jordyn didn't want to talk to him but she needed the distraction. She saw the confidence he held around humans, detectives, and tried not to think about the church and her threat.

"Over three weeks, this is the third. The first, a lycanthrope, appeared to be a single death, overdose, it wasn't. The second, missing its entire torso, no struggle, no drugs, there was the presence of herbs, like this one. The missing torso got the attention of the homicide detective, and it became a serial case," Rutger explained.

"No. How long have you been the director?"

He stopped. Rutger's heart pounded when he met her trusting eyes, and for a minute, with twilight moving in, it felt right. Anger moved swiftly through him. *Never coming back.* She took it from him. "Two years."

Two years.

He waited an entire year before stepping down. It was her fault. Jordyn's senses felt as if they were wide open and waiting for her emotions to collide and for her to fall apart. She couldn't stop staring at him and tried to think of something to say. Her racing thoughts stalled under her instincts and the chill of awareness skidding down her spine. Jordyn stepped backwards, faced the woods, her senses searching, her instincts alive with information. With the dying light, her eyes adjusted, but it didn't help. She couldn't see beyond the trees and into the darkened woods.

"What is it?" Rutger asked. He tracked her movements, followed the direction of her stare, and felt her wolf. "Jo."

"Like someone is watching us. It's cold. Dark."

"Evil?"

"Yes."

"Get in my truck," he ordered, his voice sharp. Rutger took his gun from its holster. *Get in my truck.* "Luke. Detective Russell, Detective Watt," he called.

Luke responded, skidding to a stop in front of him. "Sir."

"Jordyn is going to my truck. There is a presence in the woods. It might be our witch."

"You're not sending me anywhere," Jordyn argued.

"I am." Rutger met Jo's gaze with wolf eyes warning her not to challenge him. He couldn't stop himself. The overpowering need to protect her forced his wolf to rise. Behind Jo, footsteps closed in and a detective approached them.

"I can track them," Jordyn argued.

"No."

"I'm Detective Barthol, Detective Watt sent me," he reported. His eyes darting between them.

"Take Miss Langston to my truck," Rutger ordered.

"You're going to have a human protect me?" There was an edge of disbelief and scorn in her voice. "No."

"Not good enough to protect you, but good enough fuck," Rutger growled.

Everyone froze.

Silence thick with tension moved around them, and Jordyn felt heat rise and spread across her cheeks. How long had he been holding on to that? "Yes," she shot back and started walking. *Nice. Great comeback.*

"That escalated quickly," Luke mumbled.

"Follow," Rutger ordered. *I'm an idiot*. Jo stormed away from him with the detective following. At least she was leaving.

Jordyn was stronger, faster, and knew infinitely more about witches than the detective. And Rutger. *I might be a little rusty*, she thought, as she mumbled curses. Jordyn trekked through brush, around trees, and over rocks before getting to the truck. Twilight was fading under night's darkness and soon the detective would have to have a flashlight where Jordyn's eyesight wouldn't hinder her. She cursed a string of obscenities, clenched her hands into fists, and wanted to scream at Rutger. Where the hell did he get off saying anything about Louis? What about Kory? Jordyn didn't care, she didn't want to be there anyway. Not her problem. She mumbled another string of curses, added more obscenities, Rutger's name, and grabbed the door handle. Why couldn't he ignore her the way she had been ignoring everything, including the rules by which she lived?

Arrogant. That was Rutger. Doing anything he pleased.

Jordyn turned back toward the scene and saw Rutger's thick build merge with the woodline. The detective stood several feet away from the truck, watching her, the road, and the others as they disappeared. *Screw this*, she thought, and jerked the door open. And if whatever is out there kills Rutger? *So*. The baron would blame her. Those tolerating her would join those that hated her and the entire damn pack would hang her. Not before her heart broke, again. Because of Rutger. Jordyn stared at her camera bag, Rutger's coat, the extra magazines of ammunition, the monitor giving information, and a pack of gum while the smell of his cologne and the woods drifted around her. *Leave him be*, she told herself, *he's the Director of Enforcers*. She was nothing. She fucked a human.

Five minutes. If she waited another five maybe she wouldn't care. Five more. She can ignore him. *Nope*. Jordyn slammed the door closed, her thoughts going to Louis, and walked around the back end and started toward the woodline.

"Ma'am. Miss. Ma'am."

Jordyn kept walking. Give or take a foot, fifty feet separated her from Rutger by the time she reached the wood line. She stopped, closed her eyes, and used her senses to search. Nothing came back. She tried again and this time let her wolf rise inside of her as if she was going to shift. It was there. A presence hiding behind a spell. The magic prickled her skin, drove her wolf, and cracked her weak control. Jordyn slammed it down, withdrew, put her hands on her knees, and inhaled. Straightening, she took her senses apart, focused on the spell, and started over.

"What the hell are you doing?" Rutger demanded.

"Thinking about my human." Jordyn didn't recognize her voice or the edge of fury it held.

I hate the human. "I can carry you to the truck," he threatened. "And handcuff you."

She would like to see him try. Jordyn turned her head to look at him, her challenge obvious in her glare. Consumed inside of her senses, her eyes were a tangle of her wolf's bronze mixed with her human's chocolate. "It's out there. Witch. She's watching." She breathed her words, no sound coming from her. The magic was calling her.

Jo's power touched him like flames, cool at their tips, scalding in the middle. At the same time, she called his wolf. *Focus*, he told himself. "I can't sense anything. How can you be sure?"

"She's covering herself with a spell. No, it's a charm. It's distorting her presence. Its power is trying to confuse my wolf and human, nearly forcing them to fight."

Rutger knew the feeling. The evil had pushed his wolf and he feared losing control. "How do you know that?" Rutger stared out at the trees. Night took control, turning the trees into tall sentinels whose tops reached into the sky. Jo sensed emotions and the dead and now magic. "No, let me guess, you're an evil witch. It would make sense."

Evil witch. She hated her power. "You can either take my word for it or not. I don't care." Jordyn waved him off before starting into the woods. She gave her wolf freedom, allowing it to pick her path.

"I can feel you. You're using your wolf to track it?"

"Yes. No."

That's legit, Rutger thought. There was more going on than the power of her wolf.

"I've never felt that kind of power," Luke said, joining him. "She's strong."

"Yes."

With Rutger following, Jordyn didn't choose a direction as much as she let her senses guide her. The magic grew thicker, more powerful; it teased her, summoned her, wanting her to follow. Needles of ice found her nerves and she wished she would have brought a heavier jacket. It wouldn't have mattered—the chill started on the inside and pushed outward—but mentally the weight would have made her feel better. Jordyn continued to walk, her senses and power taking her concentration and blocking out Rutger and the others.

"Jo, it's been almost an hour," Rutger said softly.

Was that doubt? A little further. *Calling me.* Jordyn stopped when the electricity faded. The ends vibrated in the air, touched her skin, and faded. "She was here," Jordyn whispered. "She was right here." The weight of magic sat around her and she drew a breath, catching the taste of human and blood. "Took me too long."

"Was?"

"Yeah, sorry. She was watching us, and whatever she saw

created an emotion. The combination has left an imprint."

"Where did she go?" Detective Watt asked.

"I don't know. The trail feels like it ends here. But her presence is everywhere," Jordyn answered. She swayed, stumbled a couple of steps, and steadied her balance.

The deputies, detectives, and Luke searched and hadn't sensed anyone. It allowed the witches freedom to come and go as they pleased. Until Jo. He hated to admit it to himself, let alone the OPI and the baron, but he needed Jo for the investigation. Rutger watched her waver, gain her balance, and pinch the bridge of her nose. "Are you all right?"

"Sure thing," Jordyn mumbled. "I'm fine." She closed her eyes, saw white dots, opened them, and took several steps and inhaled.

Rutger closed the distance, grabbed her, and held her. Her body fitted against him like it belonged. With her close to him, he lost the anger he had been holding on to. "I disagree." Strong. Fearless. Mine.

She looked up at him, her eyes soft with her wolf, and gave him a weak smile. "I have to sit down. Burning my wolf's power while keeping the animal back kicks my ass." Jordyn inhaled. "I smell herbs."

"Me, too," Rutger replied absently. He turned his face into the breeze and inhaled. Keeping his mouth open, he closed his eyes and concentrated. "By the smell, she sat here for a while. Like they're taunting us." He helped Jordyn to a fallen tree.

"Testing you," Jordyn mumbled. "Checking your senses."

Rutger met her gaze. "Agreed."

"Tape this area off and search for any indication someone has been here. Look for hair, fabric, anything. And tire tracks," Detective Watt ordered. Detective Barthol nodded and repeated the order to the arriving forensics team. "You don't sense anything else?"

"It's witchcraft. There's more than one. It takes the strength of the coven to keep the charm active," Jordyn told Detective Watt. "Might explain why her presence splintered."

"This is going to sound stupid. If you felt the charm again would you recognize it?" Detective Watt asked. His eyes searched the area and then landed on Jordyn.

"Yes," she whispered. Death magic. "I'm sorry, I'm going to go to the truck." Jordyn looked at Rutger with exhaustion in her eyes. Slowly, she stood and took an uneven step. Her head spun and her stomach rolled, as the magic pulled on her.

You're going to walk a mile? "Not without me. Detective Watt, I'll leave you to your work. If there's anything I can do let me know." Rutger held Jo close to him, and knew if she wasn't fighting him, she must be fading. "Come on."

"No. This is important, I can make it by myself," Jordyn insisted.

"I can take her," Quinn offered. An enforcer, he stood with his hand on the butt of his gun, his BDUs showing signs of having been through brush.

Mine. "You stay here with Detective Watt," Rutger ordered. Jo leaned against him. No one was going to touch her.

Helpless to stop herself, Jordyn let Rutger hold her. As they followed their path, she felt the faintest threads of the witch. She didn't want to feel the charm and energy behind it and worked to close her senses. Her weakness left her defenseless and she had to fight against reaching the breaking point. Her knees weakened, and she leaned heavier on Rutger, the feel of him seeping into her. She felt him raise his power and part of her wanted to get as close to him as possible. Jordyn didn't need this, guilt built up, around everything she said and the things she hadn't. Her thoughts chased the trail to Louis. What was she going to do when she returned to Butterfly Valley?

Even Louis couldn't change the truth.

Exhaustion was sitting heavy in her muscles and her wolf was fighting her for its freedom, but the night proved *what* she was. Using her wolf made her feel alive. The baron knew it would.

Rutger's wolf spread throughout his body, reaching for Jo and wanting to help her, protect her. *Mine*, he thought. His frustration heated. Living in the city and not being around her own kind weakened her.

She abandoned her wolf.

When Jo sank to the ground, Rutger caught her, picked her up, and carried her. At the truck, he opened the passenger door and gently placed Jo on the seat. She woke, looked at him with liquid bronze eyes, grabbed her camera bag, placed it by the center console, and used it like a pillow. She had done that more than once. "What have you been doing, Jo?" he whispered.

"Do you want me to stay here?" Luke asked.

"Yes." Rutger closed the door and turned. "Gather as much information as possible. If they have questions, they can call me. I'm going to talk to the baron about having Jo help us. Afterwards, meet me at the office. I'll expect a report."

"Yes, sir," Luke replied with a smile.

"What?"

"Nothing. Just your wolf taking possession of a woman. Jordyn. Your ex. On your brother's wedding day. At a crime scene."

"First thing tomorrow morning," Rutger responded, his voice holding his authority. He heard Jo moving and turned to check on her. She tugged her sweatshirt tighter, a soft moan leaving her, and settled back to sleep. He would find out what she had been doing for three years and where her power came from. Rutger faced Luke. "Don't."

"Yes, sir," Luke replied as he gave a mock salute.

Rutger walked around the truck to the driver's side. He sat behind the steering wheel, listened to Jo breathe, and started the engine and backed up. Turning the wheel, he passed several cars and SUVs, and headed down the dirt road. It was late, too late. Rutger remembered the heated conversation between Jo and Lady Langston and wasn't going to take Jo to Coal Valley. For her protection, and to keep her near him, they were going to Foxwood.

CHAPTER TEN

Rutger stopped the truck at the stairs of Foxwood, cut the engine, and got out. He sent his senses out to scan the area, and the parking lot of the enforcer's office, while walking around the front. At the passenger door, he looked over the truck and out at the night, the events, the body, and Jo spinning in his thoughts. Overriding the chaos was the need to protect her. He wanted to roar to the world she was his. Squeezing his eyes shut, he bowed his head. When she left, he was going to have to live with his decision.

"I'm a damn fool," he whispered.

He needed to focus on the things he could control. If he was going to sort through the evidence and talk to the baron about Jo, he needed to get some sleep. Rutger opened the passenger door and gathered Jo's limp body in his arms as if she weighed nothing. Her head resting against his chest, her breathing was a light sound, and her heartbeat a steady rhythm.

"What happened? Is she okay?" Laurel asked. Dressed in lilac top and bottoms, she met Rutger on the top step.

"She's fine, she needs to sleep."

"If you're just getting back, you both need sleep. You can't drive to your place in your condition," Healey insisted. He held the door and stepped to the side.

"Where are you going to stay?" Laurel asked.

He threw out every rule the baron set. "We're going to my

room." Rutger took the stairs. He reached the second floor, went right, and down the hall. After three doors, he reached his old room, and went inside.

The baroness had updated the decorations from twenty something male to mature adult, while keeping the room masculine. He laid Jo on the smoky gray comforter, and gently pulled the thick cover back. When there was enough room, he took her running shoes off, and covered her. She turned into him, her hand going to the back of his neck, her fingers tightening and dropping. Through the slats of the blinds, a sliver of moonlight touched her exposed throat and he leaned down and nuzzled the curve of her neck. She responded, and turning to him, their lips touched.

Rutger couldn't move—her feel like velvet against him, her taste a mix of spice, wolf, and the woods. As she searched, she kept her wolf close to the surface and its essence, a wildness, coated her lips. He wanted more of her. His body demanded more of her. He was playing with fire, if he thought could he kiss her and watch her walk away.

Never coming back. Ever.

To hell with it. He took her lips in a kiss, and without holding back, kissed her with the desperation plaguing him. Jo's hands wrapped around his neck, her fingers tightening, and brought him closer. A heated exploration of tongues, lips, and passion of their kiss stole over him. He wasn't going to be able to watch her leave. Rutger broke the kiss. Her sleep heavy eyes opened and he met chocolate streaked with bronze and black. Like a dagger to his heart, she whispered his name. Rutger kissed her forehead, her lips, lingering over her, and after standing, he backed away. He would never forget the taste of her lips, and it gave her threat more power than he possessed.

Time ticked by, and when Jo finally settled into a comfortable sleep, he took his boots off, his gun belt, and untucked his shirt. Rutger walked to the nearest chair, turned it to face Jo, and sat down. Wild with conflicting thoughts, his mind turned on him. *I can't protect myself from her*, he thought as he drifted toward sleep. He didn't move when the baron entered the bedroom, his power sweeping through the space and wrapping around them. Rutger knew the alpha was healing one of his own. He was healing Jo. Because he knew what she was. Rutger faded as deep sleep closed in on him at the same time questions about Jo and his father consumed his thoughts.

Rutger stared at Jo as he quietly dressed and then grabbed his gear. During the night, Jo had pulled the comforter up and now it hid her face, leaving the ends of her hair visible. He listened to her heartbeat, and satisfied, went downstairs. His thoughts hadn't eased with sleep; instead, resting had given them the energy they needed to torture him further. Her kiss toyed with him and her taste sat on his tongue. Rutger mumbled a prayer hoping it hadn't been a mistake and the passion they shared would change her mind about leaving.

"A word, son." Healey stood at the bottom of the stairs waiting, coffee cup in hand.

Not now. He planned on talking to the baron after he had a chance to think about things. To sort out his feelings and have solid reasons for Jo to stay without sounding like *he* needed her. "I have to get to the office. Luke is giving me an update about the investigation," Rutger explained.

"You can spare ten minutes," Healey insisted.

"Yes, sir." Rutger dropped his gear by the front door, glanced at his truck, and followed the baron to his office. Sitting down in one of two chairs facing the desk, he waited for the baron to take his seat. "I should get to the office."

"Indeed. I need to know what Jordyn did last night," Healey continued.

"You know what she did," Rutger replied. "She told me you knew she was able to feel emotions."

"Good morning, son," Laurel greeted. She handed him a cup of coffee, and placed a carafe on the desk. "Is Jordyn all right?"

"Yes." Rutger met the baroness' gaze. "She's sleeping."

"Very well." Laurel smiled.

Rutger wondered what she could be thinking as she left them in the office.

"I know what Jordyn is capable of. I need to know exactly what she did."

"Without looking at the body, she knew the victim had been tortured because of the emotional scar. She knew he was a werewolf and knew there was a witch involved. She said the witch was using a charm not a spell to distort her presence. Then Jo tracked the witch with her wolf."

"Go on." Healey sat back in his chair and drank his coffee. His request brought the slightest vibration of power from Rutger. Protecting his fated mate. "I'm not challenging you. Please, explain what happened with Jordyn."

Rutger tried to stick to the facts and put his personal feelings aside. "She brought her wolf to the surface. However, before she started to shift, she stopped, and used its power and instincts to track the witch's magic. She's powerful," Rutger explained. "How do you know about her? And why is she protected? She left. She denies her wolf and lives like a human. Jo sleeps with a human." He growled the words and stood. He was not sticking to the facts.

"Sit down," Healey ordered. "You can't judge her because she found someone to ease the loneliness and to spend her nights with. Jordyn, regardless of where she lives, is a werewolf."

Yes, he could. She shouldn't have left. Rutger sat down and

grabbed his coffee from the desk. He had the feeling the baron wasn't talking about the human, rather he threw Kory in his face. If he cared so much for Jo, why did he jump in bed with Kory? He asked himself the same question every day. And every time, he came back to the same answer—he felt sorry for himself.

"If I cannot trust you, I will not confide in you."

The feel of her body against his, twisted his anger in to fury. She is going to leave and never come back. "My apologies."

"Her power comes from being a soothsayer," Healey explained.

"You can't be serious. They aren't real," Rutger argued.

"She isn't an oracle, with visions of the future, no, and she will never be a crazy hag gnawing on bones. Jordyn didn't track the witch with her wolf. She used her wolf's power but guiding her was the power of the soothsayer. She recognizes magic, targets its feel, and is able to follow it to its strongest point."

"She followed the charm?" Rutger didn't know if he believed the baron.

"She followed the energy powering the charm."

"How is that possible?"

"Soothsayers seek power. Their purpose is to hold their pack, its collective, and harness the combined power. Jordyn doesn't have a pack, which helped her to track the witch." Healey sat straight and watched questions cross Rutger's face. "They're usually pureblood paranormals, and typically one or both parents are soothsayers. Very few are given the chance to find their powers, making them extremely rare. However, the stronger their lineage, the stronger they are, and Ethan is a powerful werewolf. Wouldn't surprise me if Jordyn's gift originated from him."

"Does he know?"

"I think he has his suspicions, and it might explain Mia's attitude toward Jordyn. We have adopted a lifestyle mirroring humans, and are happy behaving like humans. It doesn't help her superstition surrounds soothsayers. There are other *things* about ourselves we have forgotten, let die in the past," Healey replied. Watching Rutger consider him, he took a drink of his coffee, set the cup down, and met Rutger's gaze. "You said she felt the emotional scar left by torture. That's the beginning. Did she feel death?"

"Yes. She said he no longer existed, he was a void."

"Nothing about his spirit?"

"She said it was free. He wanted death."

"She has advanced on her own," Healey mumbled, lost in thought.

"How do you know about her?"

"I suspected it when she was a child. As purebloods, we have a signature gift separating us from the infected. It makes us stronger, superior. I watched this gift change as she grew up and felt it evolve when she became an adult. I could no longer feel her parents, as if she absorbed what strength they had passed on. She has grown powerful without any influence from a pack, an alpha, or training from another soothsayer. Did she weaken? You said she needed to sleep."

"We walked a mile, maybe more, when she found where the witch had been hiding. We stayed there no more than thirty minutes, and she said was going back to the truck. She made it halfway and I had to carry her." It was Rutger's turn to lose himself to his thoughts. *Was it good or bad?* He wanted to ask. What did he have to do to protect her? "What are you going to do?"

"She knows what she is. If not the meaning of the designation, she understands her power or she wouldn't be able to manipulate it. I'm going to talk to her about her place in the pack."

"Is that why you ordered her to go with me? To test her?"

Rutger asked. What else was his father planning?

"Yes. And you need her."

"If you believe I do, why did you let her leave?"

"I have my reasons."

"Stop. Tell me why she left," Rutger demanded.

"I'm not telling you. You have to figure it out for yourself. Son, put your selfishness aside and you will find the answer."

Bullshit. Selfishness wasn't his problem. He held onto anger and hurt and used them to protect himself. "I need her for the case. She's the only one who can track the witch. We're convinced this is black magic and there is a coven involved."

"I'll talk to her." Healey leaned back in his chair, held his cup, and studied Rutger. "Besides the investigation, she has no reason to stay?"

Rutger did not want to answer the baron's question. "She's leaving and never coming back, she said so. Whatever happened last night won't matter." Rutger's sharp response cut the end of his words. He couldn't hide his anger or the pain of knowing she was as good as gone.

"What happened last night?" Healey asked.

"Nothing." Rutger stood. "I have to get to the office."

"Jordyn isn't going back to her parents, she will stay here. I will talk to her about the investigation, and afterwards, we'll meet you at the office."

"We'll meet here," Rutger responded. He didn't want to see disappointment crease her face and didn't want his enforcers to look at him with pity in their eyes.

"As you wish."

That was too easy. "Are you going to tell her parents about her being a soothsayer?" Rutger didn't know what being a soothsayer meant. He didn't know what the baron was planning for Jo and the fear of the unknown was killing him.

"If I must, but I doubt I will. It all depends on Jordyn."

Rutger walked to the doorway and stopped. "If she needs me
…"

"Of course, son."

Rutger remained a minute longer, he didn't know why, like the baron might say something else. Silence took them both and Rutger left the house.

With sleep holding her, Jordyn covered her face in the bend of her elbow and felt her sweatshirt. She turned and felt her jeans. She'd slept in her clothes. The sunlight caught her in the eyes as the events and images from the night before filtered through her memory. She kissed Rutger. Wanted to kiss him. Guilt laced with dread gripped her heart and her stomach rumbled with panic, its force making her sit up. She was in his room, in his bed, and she smelled like him. "I'm an idiot," Jordyn mumbled.

Damn Claudia. Jordyn should have ditched the reception, packed, and left, like she wanted.

The embarrassment of having thrown herself at Rutger didn't end there … no, she was going to have to face his parents and after the scalding humiliation, Jordyn would face her own. She pressed her fists against her temples and waited for the pain for having denied her wolf to send spikes across her skull. There was nothing. No pain. No ache. And the usual exhaustion wasn't tormenting her. Shame remained.

Jordyn crawled from the bed, her feet touching the thick carpeting, and crossing the large room headed to the bathroom. After hitting the light paddle, she entered the room, and met pale cream walls, brushed nickel accents, and cognac and cream marble countertops. The bathroom was twice as big as the one in her rental and was nicer than her entire house. She drew a slow breath in and exhaled slowly when she saw her makeup bag sitting on the counter.

"What the hell?" Jordyn left the bathroom and went to the bedroom. Beside the closet door sat her suitcase, the duffle from her SUV, and camera bag. Out of curiosity, she opened the closet and found her clothes hanging beside several of Rutger's shirts.

They moved her to the baron's house.

Something was wrong.

CHAPTER ELEVEN

Jordyn changed out of her sweatshirt, T-shirt, and jeans, and preparing to meet the baron and baroness, put on clean clothes, brushed her teeth, washed her face, and grabbed a thicker sweatshirt. She inhaled, her hand hovering over the handle, before opening the door and heading downstairs.

The large house sat silent, her footsteps the only sounds as she wandered through the living room, sitting room, and peeked into the baron's office. Creating reasons and excuses for why she threw herself at Rutger made her anxiety spike out of control. And she would have to explain herself. With a groan, she entered the kitchen and saw the double French doors open to the backyard. The morning sun brightened the space and a cool spring breeze drifted, carrying hints of voices. Jordyn stood in the sunlight for several seconds enjoying its warmth before walking outside and to the edge of the massive the deck.

The tables and chairs used during the wedding reception had been stacked beside a waiting flatbed truck. Next to them, sat plastic totes marked decorations. Jordyn scanned the yard, to see another table where the baron and baroness sat together. *Here I go*, she thought.

"Jordyn, get some coffee and join us," Healey hollered.

"Yes, sir," she replied loud enough he heard her. Jordyn left the railing, her nerves bouncing, and looked for the coffee.

"It's over here," Gavin said. The umbrella shaded him, a

carafe, bowls of fruit, and plates and cups. "Rutger returned you to Foxwood."

"Yes." She cautiously walked over to the table.

"I'm not going to bite you, Jo, that's Rutger's job." Grinning, he sat back out of the shade, his russet eyes turning lighter in the sunshine, giving away his wolf.

She ignored his comment, wondered who else knew, and took a cup and the carafe and poured herself some coffee. "Heater?"

"Please," he replied, leaning forward. "If you're leaving, I'm not sure why he cares."

They all knew she was leaving. "That makes two of us." Jordyn poured, refused eye contact, set the carafe down, grabbed hers, and made her way to the baron.

"Good morning, Jordyn," Laurel greeted. "I hope you were comfortable."

"Yes, thank you," she replied. The baroness met her gaze and there was a combination of fear and joy in her eyes, and a tremble of both in the air.

"Have a seat." Healey waved to the chair beside him.

"I'll make more coffee," Laurel said, excusing herself.

Jordyn sat down, her heart sinking into her stomach. They all knew what happened. One visit and she couldn't stop from making a fool of herself. She set herself up for a heartache. She needed to get in her car and leave before she made it worse.

"You'll be staying here for the rest of your visit," he started.

She hadn't planned on staying. "Yes, sir. How long am I staying?"

"I'm not sure. Rutger expressed his need to have you nearby in case he needed you. For the investigation. You impressed him with your ability to sense witchcraft. As for why you're here, after you left last night, your mother became upset. Has Mia said anything to you?"

That's what she needed to do, tattle-tell. So, lie? Jordyn wasn't going to lie to the baron. "She said Bailey lives in my shadow. She resents me for leaving. She said I left her. Rutger. Trinity. She hates Louis, and thinks my gallery is a waste of my time. Mia blames me because Rutger gave up his place in the pack. She thinks I make a spectacle out of myself and it's the reason Rutger is paying attention to me."

"You haven't defended yourself or told her why you left?"

Jordyn couldn't face Mia, Rutger's rejection, and the embarrassment sure to follow. "She has never asked why I left. Anyway, I said I wouldn't and I haven't," Jordyn answered. Those were the rules.

"You take her verbal abuse and allow her to blame you?"

It sounded like an accusation not a question. "I guess I have." Jordyn sat back in the seat and placed her hands in her lap like a five year old being scolded. She was sitting in the sun, wearing a sweatshirt, and a chill managed to settle on her.

"When you first came to me, I hoped you would fight, Rutger, Kory, and prove to them what you wanted. Then, when we came to this arrangement, I thought you would argue with me and demand to be treated fairly. I thought you would blame Rutger and demand he make changes in his life. Jordyn, you didn't put up a fight. You walked away from everyone."

"Not everyone."

"You have. I understand Rutger. Your parents didn't deserve the same treatment. Your mother is hurt." Healey waited for a response but when Jordyn's eyes remained on her folded hands, he sat back, crossed his legs, and took his coffee cup. "You continue to reject your wolf. It's a pack animal and you are refusing its need to be with its own and its need for strength. You have denied its instincts to run."

"I haven't denied anything," she argued. *Lie.*

"Your eyes tell a different story. You used your wolf last

night and struggled to maintain strength. How long have you used your power to deny the shift?"

No idea. "I've been busy. I can't just walk outside and shapeshift. What do you want me to do?" she asked. Jordyn cringed with the sound of desperation her voice held. "I created a life I like. I have my gallery, it's what I worked for."

"How long?" Healey demanded.

"Maybe a month." Lie.

"Jordyn."

"Three months." She gave up.

"Three moon phases. It's dangerous."

"I can fix it," Jordyn insisted. Sure she could. Getting the hell out of Trinity was going to fix everything.

"Can you, without your human finding out the truth or worse, getting hurt? You're on the edge and you don't understand the risks you're taking." His eyes narrowed, his power increased enough she felt its edges.

"Louis isn't my human." She stared at the coffee in her cup, the reflection of the sky and clouds moving in the ripples.

"Ending a relationship with someone you love can be hard."

Jordyn met his gaze. "I don't love him, and relationship is a strong word, when I've lied to him the entire time. He considers non-humans, shapeshifters beneath him, and when he finds out what I am—" Jordyn stopped talking. She deserved Louis' criticism for betraying him and lying to him about what she was and the details in between. Then she threw herself at Rutger. With the weight of the baron's gaze on her, Jordyn turned and looked at the valley and took a sip of coffee.

"After hearing, 'you're never coming back,' I'm assuming you intend on giving up your Christmas visits?" Healey lifted his cup to his lips, sipped, and set it back on the table.

"Yes."

"By cutting your ties to Trinity, you'll be alone."

"Alone." *Always alone.* "What will happen with my status?"

"You will remain pack. When you're needed, you'll be summoned," Healey answered.

"Yes, sir."

"I need to know you understand the consequences of your decision."

"I understand," Jordyn mumbled, averting her eyes. *Crystal clear.*

"That's settled. Now, about last night … it's important I know what you did."

Jordyn inhaled, trying to calm her nerves and focus her thoughts. "I tracked the witch. She was there watching everyone. Her scent and the scent of blood lingered, like it stuck to her and stayed where she had been sitting. I didn't find her in time." The consequences and the baron's accusations dug in and were working on her attention. So, she ran. It was her choice.

"Explain how you tracked her?" Healey asked, breaking through her thoughts.

"I used my wolf." *And liked it.*

"Your wolf helped you. I need to know about the energy you call when you deny your wolf."

"That's all it is, an energy."

"It's true, but there's more," Healey pushed.

"It's always there … a part of my body, in my veins, and sits in my being," Jordyn tried to explain. She didn't think she was doing a very good job. "I don't call it, like my wolf, and it doesn't rise. It feels my need and I manipulate it any way I like."

"You learned this by yourself?"

"Of course." Jordyn's eyes glittered with her wolf.

"Do you know what having this power makes you?" Healey asked. He sat straight, his eyes narrowing on Jordyn, the alpha's instincts demanding he bind her to the pack. He waited as Jordyn considered the question. When she didn't answer, he said, "You're a soothsayer. You have a place in the pack."

"No. No." Jordyn stood, placed her cup on the table, and took a step. "That's impossible."

"It's true and you know it."

Maybe. "I can't be here," she argued.

"Why?"

"It's too much." Jordyn faced the valley. This was not happening.

"It's not up to you," Healey replied. "This is about the pack." The threats Jordyn faced as an unaligned soothsayer were mounting from all sides. The Highguard. Alpha Howard. The alpha was talking to packs instigating an uprising against him. Healey gathered his power and his wolf filled him. "I'm ordering you."

Jordyn shook her head. "No." She turned and felt the baron take control of her wolf. She felt him. "No," she whispered. Her power swept through her in defense.

"What are they doing?" Gavin asked. He stood at the railing with Laurel.

"Your father is testing our soothsayer," Laurel answered. "You can feel her power on the air."

Soothsayer? "Ours. She is leaving and not coming back."

"She hasn't left."

Acting hypnotized, Jordyn sat down, raised her hand, and inched closer to Healey.

"What are they doing now?" Gavin leaned on the railing, his wolf rushing to the surface as Jordyn's power blew through the air.

"Your father is going to give her his memories, including the nightmares haunting his past, to see if she survives. If she takes them as her own, she will prove she is strong enough to hold the pack," Laurel answered through a breath. She inhaled as tears slid down her cheeks. "If she doesn't, let's pray Rutger forgives us."

"What do you mean?" Gavin turned to look at his mother. "What do mean, Mom?"

"If she isn't strong enough, she could end up in a catatonic state, or worse, dead."

"If she does survive?"

"The baron will order her to stay." Laurel turned away, unable to stop a spike of jealousy as Jordyn placed her hand on her husband's chest. If Jordyn lived, she would be linked to the baron. Her husband. If Jordyn died, Laurel would lose Rutger. Her eldest son. As baroness it would be her responsibility to explain Jordyn's death to Ethan and Mia. She turned her head enough to see them, Healey's hand gripping Jordyn's arms, and Jordyn's hands pressed against his chest. It was enough, and she walked into the house.

Jordyn felt Healey's heartbeat against her palm as if it was summoning her. The intensity grew by the charge of energy when his power surged. In turn, her power increased, and matching his, demanded his wolf. As it traveled it threaded around him, through him, searching for his spirit. When she felt the strongest power, it dove in to its depths. She didn't want this. Didn't need it.

"I feel your doubt. You are not a submissive. Take what you want."

No. Jordyn felt it teasing her, like a thirst she would never quench. His voice echoed in her head, as a second presence wrapped around her wolf, and joining the power created the urge to drink from him.

"Jordyn," Healey whispered. He felt his wolf move through him, searching for Jordyn and wanting to give her its force.

"Baron." Her voice stung her throat and sounded foreign to

her ears. Jordyn drifted inside of his mind, hearing his thoughts, and seeing his life and the emotions clinging to them.

"Your imbibe of my wolf is your vow to me. Drink the power offered to you." Healey watched her eyes struggle between human and wolf. He held Jordyn's wrist, felt her rapid pulse, and her panic pouring from her, and feared she wasn't going to live through the exchange.

Jordyn wanted to reject him and the force tying to invade her body. Butterfly Valley. Reject him. Jordyn felt her resistance weakening and nothing else mattered but sating the thirst. She couldn't deny her wolf and the energy consuming her. "Yes, Baron." She understood and didn't have a clue to the commitment she was making. Unable to restrain herself, her power surrounded them, and she needed more.

"You have given me your oath."

"My oath," Jordyn repeated. Her body burned with the craving for his strength and her wolf rose, pushing the urge to shift.

"I have released my wolf and you are bound to me." Healey roared as he let go of his restraint.

Jordyn's head bowed, every muscle in her body tightened, and her human features faded. She inhaled as tears streamed down her cheeks, and images twisted with emotions flooded her mind.

Laurel ran outside, Healey's deep voice calling her. "She's going to fail," she cried as she gripped Gavin's arm. With orders from Healey, she fought the urge to stop him. How was she going to explain she did nothing and witnessed Jordyn's death?

"If she dies, Rutger will follow." Gavin placed his hand over his mother's as understanding of the situation became dire. "He withdrew when she left. He has tasted her and this time he'll lose his mind."

"The pack, Tanner and Bailey's marriage, and Rutger's life will be at risk. And my mate will lose part of himself. What kind of punishment will we face when the Highguard learns of our actions? The sorrow will never end."

"I understand Rutger's need to have her, he loves her. Why the hell couldn't the baron leave her alone?" Gavin's voice turned raw with emotion and anger with the refusal to call him father. How had Rutger felt when their father ordered him to call him baron?

"He wants her here. If she doesn't want to be here, she isn't going to be allowed to live."

"Why?"

"The Cascade pack protects her yet she lives without a pack. Why would the baron protect a simple woman? Those are the questions coming from the other alphas, packs, and colonies of magic born. They understand the baron would never protect a woman. He would protect a power. If an alpha found out *what* she was and associated it with the lineage she comes from, they might use her against us. Or leverage with the Highguard," Laurel answered. Simple power play. Mia had been quick to call and report Alpha Howard's interest in Jordyn. The inquiry forced Healey to act.

Jordyn felt tears slip down her cheeks and wanted to dive into the depths of her mind to escape the torrent flow of memories. The strongest point of Healey's power sat in front of her, like a radiating pulse, promising acceptance, security, and an end to the pain.

No more pain. No more fear.

Blackness surrounded her as images drifted, voices escalated into rushed whispers and cries, and emotions clawed at her insides. In the mix, she saw Rutger and tried to back away from Healey. She leaned backwards, he tightened his hold, and the force of emotions and memories continued as an explosion of chaos. She heard a low growl, his hands clenched around her wrists sending white pain snaking into her hands and the sting travelled up her arms and in to her shoulders. Closer to the pulse, the baron held her, and when he stood his power increased.

"Call your wolf."

Unable to stop herself, Jordyn sank into the darkness, death, and pain of the baron's life. She continued to struggle, wanting to get away from him, and at the same time tried to find a safe place to hide inside of herself. *Can't.* A piercing panic twisted a scream in her chest and she dreaded drowning in her fear.

"Drink."

The baron's order echoed off her skull and sent vibrations through her body. Jordyn stopped. She floated in her mind, anchored herself in her power, and trusting her wolf, gave herself over.

Slowly, she became a ghost of herself. A thick fog moved around her and Jordyn froze in the weight of his past. His life. With her resistance weakening, her chest opened, ripped apart, and his years invaded her. She drew it in, hungry and impatient, she drank it all. With her body saturated, his wolf spirit secured itself inside of her. Jordyn cried out as the baron's power, his ties to the pack, fused with her power.

"Dear God, no." Laurel watched Healey lower Jordyn's limp body to the ground. She let go of Gavin, ran across the deck, down the stairs, and to Healey's side.

Healey knelt, let go of Jordyn, and stood. She hadn't failed. She accepted his power, his life, and the first step to accepting the pack. Jordyn had become the Cascade pack's soothsayer.

The baron's power blasted across the property like an explosion. Its waves touched Rutger when he rushed out of the office and searched the property for anything—anyone responsible for the disturbance.

Rutger scanned the immediate area. The parking lot sat silent. Gavin's Scout sat silent. The house sat silent. There was no one there.

"The baron's wolf. What do you want us to do?" Ansel asked. His hand was on the butt of his gun, his eyes gleaming with his wolf.

"Take your points," Rutger ordered. "I'm going to check the house." He started across the driveway, felt Jordyn's wolf weaken, and changed directions. His senses focused on her heartbeat and he sprinted to the backyard.

"Take her into the house." Healey's voice caught and weakened. Gavin stood unmoving and staring at him. "Take her."

"You were supposed to test her," Laurel started. "Not hit her with it all at once! What if something bad had happened?"

"She possesses the purest of power. Even when she refused to accept her fate, I couldn't stop her from taking what she wanted. She guided herself." Healey slumped in his chair and felt her continuing to turn his past into power.

"Where do you want me to put her?" Gavin asked. With fisted hands, he wasn't sure he wanted to touch her.

Jordyn's limp body and his wife's accusation brought guilt to his conscience. "In the living room on the couch. She can rest, but she has to run with the women tonight. She has to shapeshift and ease the deprivation from denying her wolf." After he rested, he would use his power and strength to help her recover. "She has to complete the transition."

"Will she be all right?" Laurel asked. Her eyes were webbed with red, and she inhaled, trying to control her tears.

"She will be. And she is. Mate, why are you crying?" Healey

asked. He took his time standing, the nausea and weakness flooded his stomach and reached for his throat.

"It's been an exhausting month. The wedding. With this, I faced losing you," she whispered. Laurel placed her hand on Healey's shoulders, urging him to sit down. "I'm not losing Rutger."

"Losing me to what?" Rutger asked, his voice rough with his worry. He marched closer, his eyes skating over the scene and searching for Jo. The baron and baroness. Gavin. Gavin leaning over a body. Body. Jo. His wolf rose, his need to protect taking over, his power lashing out. "Get away from her," he growled.

"Wait." Gavin stood, raising his hands to show he wasn't going to touch her. Rutger's wolf shadowed his body, its teeth bared, as he moved in and shoved Gavin to the side.

"Explain what you have done," Rutger demanded as he knelt beside Jo. He listened to her heartbeat, its frantic beat warning him something was wrong.

A rough round of laughter sounded a second before a rifle butt hit him between the shoulder blades, sending him face down in the thick mud. Healey dug his fingers into the sludge, his legs thrashing with his fight to lift his face. He gasped for air when a boot slammed into his back, a searing pain erupting in his spine. Under the racing panic flooding him, the gray of suffocation moved into his mind, deadening the pain. The human guards continued to shove him deeper into the muck and his wolf reared, provoking the silver collar around his neck. It burned his skin, its spikes sinking into his flesh, and stopped him from shifting. Fear, pain, and rage collided in a deadly mix as he started to lose consciousness and the world turned black.

Jordyn gulped at the air, felt her lungs burning, and her heartbeat raced with terror. There was water and mud everywhere, it covered her face and hands while she drowned in the pool. With indecision gripping her, she wrestled with gripping her throat and trying to scrape the mud from her face.

"Jo. Stop. You're safe. I'm here, Jo." Her eyes wide with dread, she crawled backwards away from him and his touch. Rutger held her wrists, struggling to keep her from tearing into her face. "Jo." With more strength than he wanted to use, he yanked her closer and took mount. She twisted beneath him, her strength increasing, and he forced her arms above her head, and held her wrists together. Her sweatshirt inched up, exposing her stomach, ribs, and veins as her body began to shift. A rush of power swept around him when her wolf shadowed her, and another presence covered her like a veil.

Rutger felt her power on his thighs, its weight moving up and wrapping around his waist. The force drove his wolf, broke his control, and made his skin ripple with the transformation. Jo stared, eyes wide as power increased and he felt her reaching for him. He didn't understand what was happening when her essence absorbed his strength, and the shift faded. Gradually his human features returned, her power eased, and he gained control.

"Please, Jo."

She closed her eyes, moaned softly, and her muscles weakened.

He loosened his hold, but didn't let go, and bending down covered her lips with his. "Jo. Come back, babe."

"Can't breathe," she whispered against his mouth, the words clawing their way up her throat.

Behind him, the baron and baroness stood watching, their presence looming over him and feeding his anger. Rutger shifted to her side and moved her to his lap. "Come on, Jo, inhale," he begged, his face a sliver away from her cheek.

Jordyn grasped onto Rutger's voice and strained to ignore the panic. Fresh air rushed in, saturating her lungs, and she inhaled deeper, the air soothing the burn. Another breath, she calmed, and opened her eyes. For a split second, she saw the encampment, razor wire blocked the horizon, long buildings made up rows, and the guards wore armor and carried guns. In the air, drifting in the gun smoke, she could smell the tinge of silver.

"Rutger," Jordyn whispered.

"Babe." He embraced her, his arms wrapping around her and holding her as her body heaved with her breaths. "Someone want to explain what happened?"

"We have completed the first step to Jordyn becoming the pack's soothsayer. What she saw is part of my past," Healey answered, the fear and pain returning as if he was there in the moment.

"She didn't see it. She lived it," Rutger accused. His wolf's eyes and cold tone expressed his dislike.

Jordyn didn't want Rutger to let go of her, but she had to gather herself. She slowly crawled away from him, trying to keep as much dignity as possible, and sat in the grass. She met the baron's gaze for a moment and turned to Rutger. "I'm all right." She inhaled and exhaled, and feeling the threads of Rutger's power, her entire body calmed. "It's over. I'm all right."

He didn't believe her while her fear vibrated around him. Her eyes looked haunted, like she experienced death. Because she had. He was helpless to give his anger an outlet when the person responsible was the baron. Rutger stood, took Jo's hands, and helped her to stand. Her eyes were swollen from crying while blades of grass and leaves stuck to her hair and sweatshirt, and her jeans were wet from lying on the lawn. "Sit. Can I get you something?"

"No," she replied softly. Like he had tossed them, his tactical belt and gun sat in the grass. He shed his gear and came to her rescue.

Rutger turned on the baron. "You did this to her? You forced this on her."

"I didn't force it on her. If it wasn't meant to be, she would have rejected me."

I tried.

"What would have been the cost for her rejection? Her life?" he accused. *Yes.* His eyes blazed, his need for possession cutting his control into fragments. The force consumed him. He didn't understand. Rutger turned away from Jo, the hurt in her eyes, and raised his walls to stop sensing her. The chance to get Jo back was within his grasp, and the baron was trying to take her from him.

"Yes," Healey answered.

"You risked her life. You didn't ask her and you didn't ask me." What if he hadn't been there? She had been dying in a memory.

"Why do I need to ask you?" Healey started. "You have no authority over her. No claim to her."

Damn, if he didn't. Rutger bowed his head and mumbled curses. She was his. He bent down, and grabbing his belt put it on and snapped the straps around his thigh. "This caused an alarm and I need to tell my enforcers to stand down." Rutger lost his control, and looking at Jo would push him over the edge and he would be courting insanity. He knew he should go to her and comfort her. He couldn't. Too many questions. Rutger's anger melted in his apprehension when he left Jo sitting by herself— her eyes on him, her shaking hands clasped in her lap, and her heart pounding. He tramped through the yard, the sight of Jo's tears in front of his eyes. *Mine.*

Rutger's muscles tightened, the tension causing them to look like thick cords under the material of his clothes. Jordyn's embarrassment intensified when she watched him leave, and her body and wolf silently begging him to stay. An empty void poisoned with rejection, and the abandoned feeling of being alone saturated her emotions. She didn't want to be alone. Not anymore. Not with the memories.

"False alarm. Stand down and return to the office," Rutger announced loud enough the enforcers heard him. False alarm my ass. Jo's life nearly ended. And if she had died? *I would lose it.* With his anger flowing around him, and unable to face the baron and Jo, Rutger entered the office followed by Ansel.

"What the hell was that about?" Ansel asked.

"The baron." How was he going to explain Jo and the baron?

Mandy rushed in, stopping beside Ansel. "I'm guessing you already asked."

"The baron," Ansel answered. "It's clear."

"Right. When Torin arrives, he wants to discuss the women's run." Mandy met Rutger's gaze.

"Got it. Anything else?" Rutger's words were wrapped in his frustration.

"No." Mandy gave Ansel a look before leaving them alone.

"There's more, I'm sure."

"I'm not having this discussion," Rutger stated.

CHAPTER TWELVE

"Jordyn, if you're able, go get cleaned up. We have to talk to Rutger," Healey said.

Rutger witnessed what she had become. He didn't want to talk her. He didn't want to be around her let alone talk to her. "Yes, sir." Jordyn stood, swayed, and Gavin moved in to help her. "Don't. Touch. Me." She held her hand up to stop him. Jordyn didn't need to feel anyone else. She gave them a guarded look before slowly ambling in the direction of the house.

"You're going to talk to Rutger?" Laurel asked as she watched Jordyn.

"He's part of the problem. Tonight, she will shapeshift and interlock the pack's power with her own. I can't have him losing control and walking away from her," Healey replied. His voice hadn't gained its strength and wavered with his words.

"Why are they doing this to one another?" Laurel rested her hand on Healey's shoulder relieved he was recovering.

"They have hurt one another and neither will give up their defenses. It's worse because they're fated."

Laurel looked at Jordyn. "You're sure?"

"Positive. Rutger has fought the natural instinct of his wolf for years. With her close to him, he can't control what he feels. Add their past, Jordyn denying her wolf, and living without her pack, it has left her weak. If Rutger leaves her while she stands in front of the pack, she will feel it as denial from her mate.

Everyone else will see it as rejection."

"Fated mates are a myth," Gavin said, jealousy lacing his words.

"You know better than that, son. Something is changing, I can feel it," Healey stated.

"I feel it," Laurel quickly agreed. "I thought it was all of the excitement with the wedding. It's getting stronger if we have a soothsayer and a fated couple. Does she understand her responsibilities?" Laurel's years gathered in front of her. Life before the Crimson Years was returning. She watched Jordyn climb the stairs, her hand clinging to the rail and her steps unbalanced.

"Yes. Whatever we do from this day forward, she will know and understand."

I can hear you, Jordyn wanted to yell at them.

"If she decides to run again?" Gavin asked.

"I will send the slayers," Healey answered.

"You're risking her life and the life of our son," Laurel warned.

"The amount of power at her disposal, and the fact she hasn't linked with the pack, puts all of our lives at risk," Healey answered.

Not true. Only mine, Jordyn thought.

Rutger met the Baron's gaze trying to decide which question he wanted to ask. "Is she staying?"

"Yes. There are consequences if she doesn't."

Rutger's anger lit up as he tore his eyes from the paperwork sitting on his desk to glare at the baron. "You bind her to you against her will, and if she decides to leave you'll kill her?"

"Jordyn holds my past, and after tonight will hold the secrets and power of the pack as a collective. If she leaves, she will become a liability to our safety," Healey explained. "She will be treated like any risk. The threat will be terminated."

"As the Director of Enforcers, I'm going to ignore the death threat to a pack member. You can't murder her and make her disappear. There would be questions."

"From who?" Healey countered, his eyes holding age and a darkness Rutger didn't like. "You don't have an answer."

"This isn't the eighteenth century, there are laws," Rutger started. "People know her. They'll know she is missing, and they'll come here searching for her. Remember, she helped the sheriff department's homicide unit and the OPI last night. They know her. Her disappearance would bring unwanted attention to the pack, Trinity, and the paranormal community." He would make sure no one took her from him.

Healey couldn't stop from enjoying tightening the bands on Rutger, and snuffed his grin, before Rutger noticed. "It doesn't change things. The slayers are on stand-by, and will do their duty."

Not likely. "I talked to Kory, it's over. You already know," Rutger said, changing the subject. He was tired of talking to the baron about Jo. Out of nervous habit, he shoved papers around, and with frustration shoved a pen in a jar with a dozen others.

"No one believed your relationship with Kory was real. After you kissed Jordyn in the church, in front of witnesses, all of their assumptions were solidified. Rutger, you have to accept you and Jordyn are fated."

God, he knew it. He had been tormenting himself with the idea. Too ashamed to ask if it was possible, he did his best to forget. To ignore it.

"You knew." Healey watched Rutger's eyes and the knowledge in them.

"Yes. I didn't think it was real until Kory."

Healey stood and stepped back from the desk. "Son."

Damn it. Rutger looked up. "What?"

"If you don't want to lose control you have to accept Jordyn as your mate."

I have. "I'm worried about her."

"Claim her and ease your conflict. For her this is the beginning. Jordyn has to learn control or she'll face more nightmares and their influence on her reality will strengthen," Healey warned.

"If I knew what was going on, what it meant, I could help her. You need to tell me," Rutger demanded.

"Take your place as second," Healey countered.

"I have a murder investigation."

"The pack is coming together at the Summit after the women's run. She will be brought forward and presented as the soothsayer. You'll be there?"

Mine. "Yes. I will stand beside her." They were being pressured from all sides before and she left and it was unfair to them both. It seemed it was going to start all over again. This time, Jo wouldn't leave. With aged anger and resentment, Rutger held the baron's stare, letting a flame of challenge show in his eyes.

"As second." Healey let his wolf, his power, and his connection to Jordyn show in his glare. "Or not at all."

Live without my mate, no. "You planned this?" Rutger accused. No one could have foreseen Jo's homecoming would create the situation they were in, but if someone was going to exploit every angle it would be the baron.

"No."

"You're lying." Rutger rose, his chair skating backwards with the force of his sudden motion.

"No. I have always valued Jordyn and would never be so

selfish as to risk her life. There are questions from the other alphas. One being my weakness where she is concerned, and why she has been allowed to live apart from her pack."

"Can't be weak," Rutger shot back.

"Faced with uncertainty, you stepped down."

Failure. "Right."

"Rutger, I didn't come here to argue. I have this for you." Healey placed a folder on the desk.

"What is it?"

"I figured you would eventually come around to asking me for help. I have information. I reached out," Healey answered.

"You risked exposing a weakness?" Rutger questioned as he sat down. He ignored the statement about asking for help. He would have asked. Planned on it.

"A calculated risk when lives are in danger. Alpha Howard approached me with details of his pack. He had a newcomer request inclusion. Alpha Howard had his staff start the background process and was going to bring it to the pack for voting when the man disappeared. No trace of him. In an attempt to locate the individual, Alpha Howard contacted others."

"I'm guessing, no luck. What is his name?" Rutger grabbed the folder.

"Edward Sharp. Alpha Howard printed out his file and gave it to me. It would do good to communicate with others about this. We're being hunted and murdered. We need to warn them."

"Agreed. I'll have CJ write up a letter, and after I review it, I'll have you look it over and sign off. Do you have connections to covens in the area?" Rutger asked.

Fated. The word played over and over in his head. He had to keep his attention on the murders. Opening the folder, Rutger spread several papers out on his desk.

"I can make some calls. The letter needs to state we're taking this seriously, actively investigating, and working closely with local law enforcement."

"Of course," Rutger replied absently. He shuffled through the papers, found Edward Sharp's file, and profile picture. "There's a note saying he's a rogue. It doesn't make sense. Why would he request inclusion? Transient, maybe."

"I don't believe it. While Alpha Howard has helped, I don't think he's being completely forthcoming with all of his information. He did have a list of questions about Jordyn. I think he figured, if he helped me, I would tell him about Jordyn." Healey let his suspicions thread through his words. "In front of his wife and Mia, he tried to use his power to sense her. He held her hand."

She did what she was good at. Jo hid her power from him. "By making Jordyn the soothsayer, you've given her status in the pack. Anything Alpha Howard, or anyone says against her, will be a direct insult to the pack."

"Correct. Worthy of retaliation."

"There could have been another way," Rutger argued. *You took the one thing she coveted. Freedom.*

"It's over. Look where he was living."

"Butterfly Valley."

"Yes," Healey confirmed.

"I don't like it."

"She's here now and will stay."

Stay or die.

Groaning, Jordyn turned to her side; her arm slipped from her stomach, and hit something. Hard. The sharp pain jerked her awake and had her turning to her back. When she opened her eyes, she saw the living room and the low light of evening as the sun sank behind the mountains. It wasn't a nightmare. And she slept half the day away.

"How are you feeling?" Laurel asked.

"Like I got hit by a truck," Jordyn answered and sat up. "My head is killing me." Her eyes held her unease as her body held onto pain.

"I have pain killers and wine. I thought you might need both."

"How long have I been out?"

"Several hours."

"Did you know what he was going to do?" Jordyn met the baroness' gaze.

"Yes. No. At least not this way," Laurel replied.

"All he had to do was tell me."

"You wouldn't have listened."

It was a weak excuse. Jordyn had listened to his rules and obeyed every single one of them. "What do I do now?" She saw worry etch its lines on the baroness' face. Jordyn's senses searched, taking in the slightest sensation and zeroing in on grief and fear. The combination wafted around the woman like a hanging fog, confirming their earlier conversation. The choice to leave or stay no longer existed. The baron stripped her independence from her.

"You are welcome to stay here for as long as you wish."

"Are you keeping me in sight?" Jordyn accused.

"No. You don't have anywhere else to go." Laurel's quick words sliced through Jordyn's resentment, and Laurel felt the injustice of her words. "You need to be surrounded by people who support you."

That was code for no one else wanted a soothsayer living with them. Jordyn thought of her mother. "I can't go back to Coal Valley," she grumbled. An impression of awareness tugged at her instincts and Jordyn met the baroness' gaze. It didn't take long for her to hate her enhanced senses. *Quiet.* "You're hiding something."

The baroness looked toward the window. "I'm not." She inhaled. "I am. Healey said Rutger was the reason you left. I need to know why."

It was Jordyn's turn to avert her gaze. How was she going to tell the baroness her son cheated? "I can't."

Laurel stood. "I don't want to order you."

"We were having problems. Pressure from my parents and the pack. There's my photography." She heard Mia's voice as she repeated the same song and dance she told everyone.

"The truth," Laurel demanded.

"He cheated on me. With Kory." The words rushed out of her mouth like the past three years pushed them. Jordyn tried to stand and couldn't, her knees giving under her weight. It made her feel weaker. "I know how stupid it sounds, especially after last night."

Last night. Laurel didn't know what happened, but after seeing Rutger hold Jordyn, and kiss her, she didn't have to. "Are you sure?" Sitting beside Jordyn, Laurel handed her a glass of wine.

"I saw them. They were by the lake in front of Rutger's house. I told the baron I couldn't stay and face Rutger's rejection." Jordyn took a sip of wine and didn't know it could ease her worry. The familiar taste gave her a slice of her life not contaminated by the events surrounding her.

"That had to have been hard." Laurel stood and walked to the window. "Do you think he loves you?"

"No. If he really loved me, he wouldn't have cheated on me." Jordyn squeezed her eyes closed and pinched the bridge of her nose. *Do I love him?* She hated the affect he had on her. "I believe he loves the past. He doesn't love me, he has Kory." Saying it out loud made her head hurt worse. Why did she care?

Given the opportunity, she didn't confront him. Nope, she kissed him.

She stood. "No, he doesn't. Kory ended their relationship. In denying him before Healey, the representatives of the Highguard, and the elders, she severed all ties with him. The witnesses carry weight. They also witnessed Rutger kissing you in the church. He did so as the son of the Baron of Paradise County and the Alpha of the Cascade pack. The eldest claimed his mate. He used an old tradition and changed the direction of the pack. The Highguard's representatives, Lord Ervin and Lady Sloan, have reported the two of you are together."

"And it starts all over."

"I won't let it happen." Laurel met Jordyn's gaze, saw the haunted darkness, and the fear sitting on her face. "I'm not sure Rutger understands the commitment you have made to the pack." Laurel watched Jordyn and her reaction.

"Honestly, I'm not sure I understand. I feel the pack. It sits out of my reach, waiting for me."

"Do you remember making the oath you would stay? I know you have your gallery and it's important to you, but what else is there in Butterfly Valley?" Laurel asked. She turned away from the window, leaving the hazy light sitting against her back.

Independence. "I sacrificed to have the gallery and my work is my life. It includes Louis. I have to tell him it's over. I have to be honest with him at least once."

"And then what?" Laurel hated pushing her; she could feel Jordyn's senses getting stronger.

"I don't know. I feel like I've become a creature out of a fantasy novel, and I should live in a cave or something. And there's my parents. My mother is not going to be happy." Jordyn drank her wine and the spice and chocolate teased her tongue while the alcohol took the edge off her nerves. Relaxing dropped the guards she had in place to control the wave of memories and the feel of the baron. One rift, and the razor blade feel of the baron's past cut through her. She set the glass down and held her head in her hands. "Why did he do this? Why couldn't he leave me alone?"

Laurel watched for any signs Jordyn was going to slip into one of Healey's memories. "Your kind are rare. Over the years many have denied their true calling." Was she going to explain her husband's actions? She had to. "While imprisoned, Healey grew up listening to the stories of old from his parents. He held onto those tales, wanting to have the same thing as if it would make his parents proud while keeping them near him. The pack would be what it once was when humans didn't dictate how we lived." She stood and gazed at the house. "Look what we've collected. We have houses, cars, and social standing in a city built on blood and fear from encampments. Our accomplishments have given us a self-righteous attitude. We feel superior for showing the humans they couldn't beat us, and we proved as shapeshifters we could be as successful as they. That kind of arrogance has a consequence. First, you left, Rutger stepped down, and no matter how hard Healey punished the both of you, the pack saw it as a weakness. They wanted an excuse to forget the old ways and live as humans with humans, and they used the failing baron. For the last two years my son hasn't been allowed in this house without an invitation from the baron. He refers to me as baroness. I'm his mom."

Jordyn lowered her hands and met the baroness' gaze. *He walked away from me.* "It sounds easy. Move back, and we'll pick up where we left off. It doesn't work like that. I have a house, my job, and a boyfriend," she argued. There was three years of hurt sitting between them.

"I'm not saying it's going to be easy, but you have us, and we'll do everything in our power to help. You're the soothsayer to the Cascade pack and are part of them. As time passes your connection will grow stronger." Laurel paced the living room. "You have to acknowledge your place." *Or face the slayers.*

Jordyn held her face in her hands. She didn't want this. She played her part and attended the wedding and should have gone home. Damn reception. She should be in Butterfly Valley and at her gallery. Jordyn mumbled curses. The visit was a fucking nightmare.

"This is our lives. The lives of werewolves. Purebloods. We can't stop the circumstances surrounding us. Jordyn. Healey, is waiting for you at the enforcer's office."

Jordyn looked up. The pressure from the baron's past was pushing on her thoughts and trying to break through her resolve. One wrong moment, and she feared one of the blades would strike and she would be fighting for her life. To die inside of a nightmare.

She cursed.

Both men stopped when Jordyn's voice drifted to the office. Rutger's heart pounded as he placed the papers back in the folder. He closed his eyes, silently praying CJ told her to leave. He wanted to see her at the house not in his office. Being reminded of his failure as the oldest son had its weight sitting on his shoulders and consuming his thoughts. If he saw disappointment in Jo's eyes, he was finished.

Rutger's shoulders sank when Jo's light laughter told another story. Together, the women walked down the hall, talking, chatting, and CJ asked how things were going. How were things? The conflict raging inside of him gained strength after seeing her struggle through a nightmare. *I left her alone. I deserted my mate.* Looking up, he met the baron's gaze. Was that humor?

CJ stopped at the closed door, the name plate telling visitors Director of Enforcers Rutger Kanin was inside. "Here you are."

Jordyn looked at his title and name. "Thank you."

After smiling, CJ walked away. When she was out of sight, Jordyn inhaled, and felt the tension in the room as if it was a warning. Like hooks it reached out, threatening her hold on reality, her nerves, and the memories she was holding back. Jordyn inhaled, slow exhale, straightened, and knocked on the door.

Healey met Rutger's gaze, his thoughts creasing his forehead as he walked to the door and opened it. "Jordyn, I hope you rested well?"

"Yes, thank you, sir," she replied. "I didn't mean to intrude. I was told you were waiting for me."

"No, you didn't intrude. Jordyn, you're about to become an important part of the pack. Your status will give you authority. You're allowed to call me Healey."

Status. That's what she needed. "Yes, sir," Jordyn responded automatically, and then shook her head. "Sorry."

Healey placed his hand on her shoulder. "You've been through a lot today and the run is ahead, so I'll talk to you later. Right now, Rutger would like to speak to you."

"Yes, sir." The nervous energy hit her skin like a million needles. Jordyn shoved her hands in her pockets as the feel of intruding came back, making her feel out of place.

"Jordyn." He stopped and collected his thoughts. "Detective Watt would like you to help with the investigation. Your ability might assist them in identifying the witches." Rutger needed her to stay. Her unease matched the concern in her eyes and he had no idea if it was his position as director or the chaos of the day.

All she had was time. "If I can help, I will," Jordyn replied.

Rutger felt distant, like there was a cold wall between them. The sight of him walking away from her after the fall into the baron's past added to her discomfort. What kind of mess had she become? Jordyn stared at him, wanting to believe their lives would survive what was ahead. But his eyes told another story. The tension held his worry … and anger.

"Jo." Her eyes searched him. She didn't wear makeup, her hair was in a loose ponytail, and she changed her hoodie for a pale pink tank top, and her jeans ended in running shoes. He stood, his fingers lingering on his desk, and unsure of himself, remained behind the desk. Rutger needed to protect her. He wanted to take her to his house, confess his feelings, and block the world out. Fated be damned. He wouldn't. Couldn't. It was happening too fast and Jo would run. The slayers would track her and take her from him. "I'll see you tonight." Rutger watched her eyes darken and the slight smile she wore when she entered the office dissolved.

"Of course," Jordyn replied. Laurel lied to her. "Was that all, the case?"

"Yes. I'll tell him. Detective Watt." Rutger sat down, his elbows on his desk.

"We have to go," Healey urged.

Jordyn nodded, like it was all she had the sense for. His cold front stole her words. Her world had taken a turn and she wasn't sure if it was for the good. She was sure it was going to destroy her.

CHAPTER THIRTEEN

After Jordyn left Rutger's office, she took a shower, applied makeup, dressed, and tried for normal. She worked through the motions, determined to leave the room when hesitation gripped her. Normal felt like a lie, and she didn't want to face the baron, baroness, and Gavin. She felt them, their presence crawling over and around her as if searching for their soothsayer. Like she was hiding from them, Jordyn sat in one of two chairs in Rutger's bedroom staring at the walls, pictures, furniture, and decorations as obscure blurs.

I'm trapped.

Jordyn looked at the door when her senses alerted her to the baroness' approach. The baroness stood on other side, hesitating several seconds before knocking. "Come in."

Laurel entered the room wearing a gray linen shirt with matching pants, and navy blue slip-on flats. Her steps were silent on the plush carpeting as she walked across the bedroom and sat on the upholstered bench at the end of the bed. "How do you feel?"

"Lost," Jordyn answered. She had plenty of time to think about what she had done and what she failed to do. "I feel stupid for having this happen to me ... I just walked into it." She stood and started pacing. "Like a lamb to slaughter. Because I didn't say anything ... I didn't defend myself ... I wanted to believe I could come and go and no one would notice. A foolish thought, because now I'm trapped here."

"You have acted like a submissive, when you aren't, and you have fought your natural instincts. Jordyn, you've never been invisible. You're beautiful and strong. Rutger saw it, everyone saw it. You were born with the gift of a soothsayer, and the alpha recognized you. You're hardly trapped," Laurel said softly, her gentle tone a weak attempt to prevent an argument. "You have authority."

"Really? If I leave, right now, how long before the slayers come for me?" she countered. She felt her eyes burn with her wolf. "Are they on standby as we speak? Yes." Jordyn shook her head as the walls closed in. "I'm dead if I leave and trapped if I stay. I'm trying to decide which is worse."

"You have status in the pack, and it gives you the freedom you crave. There's no reason why you can't have everything you want. You can have your gallery here." Laurel stopped and felt Jordyn's power drift, its edges laced with uncontrolled force. "Not only have you become an important part of the pack, but Rutger loves you."

Not likely. "Been there, done that." Jordyn's voice held a cold edge as Rutger's anger came back full force, and she felt him shut her out. He didn't need her. She didn't need him. *Bullshit.* She needed him.

"You're grasping for reasons to be miserable," Laurel countered and stood.

"No. I'm venting. I'm an adult. Have you noticed? I haven't made a decision since I've been here. None. Can't imagine why I left." Jordyn faced the baroness with the past, hurt, and power sitting in her eyes.

"I know this is sudden and you're scared, and yes, your life has changed. You have been given an incredible gift. It doesn't change your future." Laurel couldn't look at her and gave Jordyn her back. "The run is in a half-hour and you're taking your place as a soldier. Afterwards, the men will join us at the Summit and you will be brought forward as the soothsayer. Do you understand the ritual as the baron explained it?" Laurel hesitated to say anything else as she faced Jordyn.

Was anyone listening to her? "I understand." Alone with the pack.

"Rutger is going to stand by your side," Laurel assured.

Jordyn didn't trust Rutger. A chill caressed her skin, sank to her bones, causing Jordyn to stop and meet Laurel's gaze. There was more. *Leave it, there's truth*, she told herself. Her instincts plowed through, demanding her attention. "What are you scared of?"

"What?" A shadow passed through Laurel's eyes; she looked to the open bedroom door and back at Jordyn. "I don't understand?"

"That's a lie."

"Prepare for the run."

Jordyn couldn't stop her instincts, the conversations, or the sensations of fear, lies, and worry. *Focus.* "You fear … me? No. The baron?" Closing her eyes, Jordyn concentrated on Laurel's emotions. She was protecting herself but couldn't cover the betrayal sitting in her depths. "Betrayal. You fear our relationship."

"Jordyn."

"Beautiful. Strong. Everyone noticed. A polite way of saying the baron noticed," Jordyn accused. She wanted to laugh. "You're unbelievable. The both of you did this, and you're jealous of the relationship I will have with *your* husband," Jordyn charged. "You should have thought of that beforehand." Knowledge sat at the edges of her thoughts, and grasping at it, Jordyn had the feeling her mother knew about her *gift* all along and it drove her anger. No, fear. No one understood what it meant, the truth buried under myth and superstition, and no one knew what she was going to turn into. Besides a *thing*.

She was better off alone in Butterfly Valley.

"Yes. You will share things with him I will never understand. The pack will be part of you as he is, and we're on the outside." Jordyn's presence felt the same as Healey and was feeding jealousy's monster.

"As he made me," Jordyn shot back. "Rutger. What does he fear?"

"Fear?" Laurel's laugh sounded edgy and sad. She covered her mouth with the back of her hand, and unable to lie, sat down in defeat. "Rutger doesn't fear anything. When you left, he changed from the warm, caring man I raised, to cold and distant." His fated mate left. How either of them survived, Laurel had no idea.

"And Gavin?"

What is she going through? "Is angry with all of us, and I'm thankful Tanner is out of the country."

"The baron placed the pack on my shoulders. It's not my problem the great Kanin family is falling apart at the seams. Wait, it has always been falling apart." Jordyn turned on Laurel and saw the truth in her eyes. "You said the pack saw the baron as weak … he couldn't keep Rutger in line, how would he keep Trinity from slipping from his grasp? He allowed me to leave with the condition I wouldn't have contact with anyone. He knew I would have seen the truth and I wouldn't have blindly obeyed his orders." Jordyn's mind raced. The baron used her feelings to manipulate her. "Damn it, Claudia." She knew Jason had his place, but Claudia …

"Jordyn, please," Laurel requested softly, as if it was going to calm her anger.

There was a small flame of fury smoldering in her middle. "I'm not going to invade your marriage, baroness. The great baron, with all of his wisdom, is yours. I have my own problems."

Your own mate. Your fated mate. Laurel reminded herself she was the baroness, the alpha's mate, and raised her head. "You will not deny Rutger when he takes his place by your side. Healey wants him to reclaim his place as second, and you know he won't if you aren't with him."

"Don't give me orders," Jordyn snapped. Her wolf surged, forcing her to raise her walls and drive the spirits back down.

"Your power and anger are flooding the room." Laurel gasped and held her breath.

"Get used to the feel," Jordyn growled. Her eyes stung, her control slipped, and inhaling, she fought to calm down. She felt the baroness' distress in the air and almost laughed out loud, but there was fear in what it might sound like.

One. Two. Three. She counted to ten and swallowed her anger. The evening and her part hadn't started, and lashing out at the baroness wasn't going to solve anything. "Rutger hasn't done anything but shut me out. You want him to take his place, fine, I won't deny him. For some fucked up reason, the pack takes priority." Her senses were working overtime, giving her impressions of what she should do without a solid reason why. It was going to drive her crazy.

"You gave him silence. It would be easier if you admitted you love him." Laurel's pride and anger faded with the feel of Jordyn's uncertainty. "We need to leave." She met Jordyn's stare, and saw raw power working her eyes as if it was another entity. Before turning away, Laurel watched Jordyn's eyes waver between human and wolf … and there was another power there. The obsidian flakes, which were eating her natural chocolate and crowding the bronze of her wolf, glittered. Dark. Blood power. What had they done?

"Thank you for the file." Detective Watt began thumbing through the pages. "I had no idea there were this many missing shapeshifters. No one is reporting the disappearances?"

"The majority of non-humans believe law enforcement, humans won't do anything about them," Rutger replied. The baron's statement about Jo came rushing back. If she went missing, there would be a missing person's report, but who would investigate? No one. One less lycan to worry about.

"I'll enter the names, cities, and packs into the CB, and the NCL."

"Thank you," Rutger replied. "Wish there was more I could do."

"You've done more than I expected." Detective Watt turned the page and studied the names. "The first victim didn't have a clan, so I'm going to tag him as a rogue in the CB and see what comes up. How does Mr. Kanin know if a lycan doesn't have a clan?" Detective Watt asked.

"Do you really want to know?" Rutger countered. He would explain every pack had spies, and those spies kept track of every shapeshifter and paranormal in the territory. The baron received reports on the packs and their families within a three hundred mile radius of Trinity. Rogues were harder to trace, due to their transient habits, and usually kept to themselves, while living in sparsely populated areas. Harder didn't mean they weren't tracked.

"No." He turned another page and looked at another face. "Pretend I didn't ask."

"Sure thing." Rutger sat back in the chair.

"I've made a list of the places where the bodies were found, and any information associated with them. Canyon Flats was the site of a mining town. Years later a logging company set up camp and renamed it Stoddard Mills. It was abandoned when fifteen loggers lost their lives in a forest fire. It says the terrain was too difficult to get them out, the fire trapped them and they died. The families sued the logging company, and it went to court. While being questioned, the owner testified they had been attacked by wolves. Lycanthropes."

"You think the witches are purposely placing the bodies where lycans have killed humans? But why?"

"Why the specific areas, no idea. But it's a place to start. The victims have been lycanthropes, not therianthropes, or any other non-human for that matter."

Purposely on Cascade territory. "True." Rutger took the list and scanned the locations. "If they're hand picking the locations, all on Cascade territory, to dump the bodies, the same could be said about their victims." The idea there was a coven of witches targeting werewolves to mutilate their bodies changed the threat level. Up to that point, the victims have been transients, rogues, and Rutger feared it was a matter of time before they moved on.

Jo. She had been in Butterfly Valley at the same time as the last victim.

"I have consulted other detectives in the OPI and we agree the mutilated bodies resemble ritual killings. It usually indicates there's an event coming up. It's June, and the only one I know of is the Summer Solstice," Detective Watt said. "I'm not a scholar when it comes to rituals or dates concerning witches."

"That makes two of us. The Summer Solstice in the US is not the same as it is overseas. I don't know of any sacrifices associated with the day, let alone human sacrifices."

"Lycanthrope sacrifices," Detective Watt corrected. "There is a full moon. The OPI has connections with some pro-paranormal groups, a detective is currently checking to see if they'll help. What about Miss Langston?" Detective Watt asked.

She's mine. "She said she'll help with the investigation," Rutger replied. Oblivious of the correction.

"Would she be able to go to the morgue and check the bodies?"

"I can ask her." Rutger stood, the list in hand and his face neutral, to not give away his worry and the evening ahead of him. "If you get a confirmation on one of the victims, please let me know."

"I will." Detective Watt stood. "Thank you for your cooperation. The few times I've worked with a clan, it hasn't been this easy."

Rutger shook Detective Watt's hand. "We are all at risk. Human and non-human."

When he was on the highway and headed in the direction of his house, his thoughts went to Jo, the witches, and the night ahead. Damn, he had to keep his attention focused on the case. Rutger glanced at the list, considered who needed a copy, and decided he would give one to the baron. If anyone knew the history of the area it would be him.

CHAPTER FOURTEEN

Jordyn sat in the passenger seat of Laurel's luxury SUV, the heater humming, and her elbow smashed against the window. She watched the city, her hometown, a place she hadn't expected to return to, pass with every mile. She would be living there. Forever. Surrounded by judging eyes, just like before. Only it was going to be worse. She was a living superstition from the past.

Laurel turned off the highway, drove down the tree-lined road, and stopped in front of a cyclone gate with razor wire strung across the top. Several 'Do Not Trespass', 'Trespassers Will Be Prosecuted', 'Warning Lycanthropes', and 'Cascade Pack Territory' signs glittered in the dying light of the sun and the headlights of the SUV. Laurel pushed the code into the keypad, it beeped, a second ticked by, and the gate jerked into motion. When its smooth movement had tucked it behind trees planted to help hinder anyone from seeing inside of the Summit parking lot, Laurel drove through.

The Cascade pack purchased the Summit to have a safe environment to run in their wolf forms, as well as serving as their meeting place and sacred ground. Considered a wildlife preserve, it covered one hundred acres of land, and contained two rivers, a pond, and thick forest. Growing up, Jordyn loved the freedom of running. Butterflies tickled her stomach with the as time ticked by.

Laurel continued down the two lane road in silence, turned into the parking lot, and drove toward the front. Slowly passing parking spots reserved for the baron, Director of Enforcers, and Kanin family, she found the one reserved for the baroness and parked. Behind them, Abigail parked, then she and Sadie got out and waited for Laurel. Farther down, the Langston family's parking spots waited. In less than twenty minutes, Jordyn's mother would be there, and after the run she would have to face her father. Jordyn wasn't excited.

"You have company," Laurel warned, lowering her head in the direction of the Summit.

Jordyn looked up and saw Kory waiting at the entrance. She wasn't supposed to be there, no one was. Not yet anyway. "This just keeps getting better," Jordyn mumbled.

"Don't hurt her."

"If I was going to hurt anyone, I would have done it when I saw them together," Jordyn replied.

"I can only empathize with your current situation and the stress we have created, so I'm not trying to pick a fight with you." Laurel felt like she was walking on egg shells around Jordyn. Her confidence wavered with her need to protect her husband, son, and the pack while splitting her loyalty. "I know my son did something wrong, and when pushed Rutger didn't fight for you. But, Jordyn, you didn't fight for him either. You didn't give him a chance to defend himself and he was devastated after you left. I know, I watched. It's not an excuse for moving Kory in, but you left without a word, and let three years of silence take your place." Laurel turned in the seat to face Jordyn, the side of her face lit up by the neon green LED light from the dash. "He stopped living."

"I know," Jordyn admitted. She figured it was a matter of time before the world she created came crashing down. She didn't meet Laurel's gaze, rather stared at Kory. She should have fought for him. She should have kicked Kory's ass when she saw them, and afterwards, kicked Rutger's. It was easier to use Rutger as an excuse to escape the pressures from the pack. To escape her hurt. Her regrets were adding up and leading her to the question, how different would things have been if she had stayed?

"I guess we all fucked up," Laurel said and opened the door. She stood in the triangle, staring at Jordyn and waiting for a response. Jordyn didn't face her; she sat silent in the passenger seat with anxiety gripping her and doubt bleeding from her.

Basically. Jordyn waited for Laurel to close the door and walk away, guards following, before opening her door. Outside the air touched her like it knew why she was there, and at the same time the threads from the land reached up, trying to find her. Their wolves. She felt them as if she could put her hands out and touch them. And she hadn't been linked to the pack. A chill slid down her spine, under her skin, to settle in her hips, its bite continuing into her legs. Jordyn closed the door, leaned against its side, and waited for the strongest pressure to pass. Out of the corner of her eye, she watched Kory walk over. *Why?*

"Jordyn."

"Kory." Jordyn didn't want to look at her, didn't want to hear her voice. "What do you want?"

"Me?" Kory grunted, flipped her hair away from her face, and placed her hands on her hips. "From you, nothing. I'm telling you this because I care about the pack. Not you. It's over between Rutger and I."

Jordyn met her glare. "How considerate."

"Whatever." Kory's hair drifted on the wind as she gave Jordyn her back and started walking.

Jordyn exhaled the breath she had been holding as she watched Kory. Then Kory stopped. *What now?*

With an indifferent turn, she faced Jordyn. "I should let you figure this out for yourself but I doubt you ever would. Rutger had nothing to do with what happened. I mean, I knew your perfect relationship was in trouble, everyone did. I became a performer and he nearly fell for it." Kory closed her eyes, giggled a weak, anxious sound, and when she opened them, they narrowed on Jordyn. "I was jealous of you. You had Rutger. You had the chance to be the next baroness. But one kiss and you ran from him like you didn't give a shit. I couldn't believe you disappeared. I thought you would have fought me or something." Another nervous giggle. "But you didn't. It was my turn then, and after you left, I believed he would feel betrayed and hate you. I prayed he would see what a coward you really were and love me. I didn't love him. I guess, I loved having him because of his status, that he gave up because of you. Whatever it was, there were times I convinced myself, when he smiled, he was smiling at me, and he loved me. It didn't take away the hurt in his eyes, the coldness he embraced instead of anyone in his life. I would watch him and knew he was thinking about you. He didn't want anything to do with me. It was always you."

Jordyn knew the day. It was hard to forget when the emotions never died, and with Kory's confession, they came roaring back. Jordyn had sensed them, saw them, felt them, the sensations surrounding them, and the intimacy had dug into her. How could she have been wrong? Did she witness a lie? A lie that pushed her to leave her home and pack. She had been a coward. A submissive grasping onto the heartache, and she allowed it to rule her life. The sadness she carried around for three years crumbled, its heavy cloak fell, faded, and left her alone. "Why?"

"That's the question, isn't it? I suggest you ask your mother." Kory looked in the direction of the parking lot and the headlights of approaching cars. "We shared jealousy." Without another word, Kory walked away, her shoulders a little straighter from confessing a sin she'd held onto for three years.

Anger wasn't a new feeling, and the conversation with Kory sent a surge of heat to the embers she was nursing. The combination of cold and hot had her instincts questioning her actions, and Jordyn didn't know what to do. Damn it, she knew what to do. The first step was accepting her life as the Cascade pack's soothsayer. Once she took her place, she would talk to Rutger. When the chaos settled, Jordyn would deal with Mia. The night was going to be long and she wasn't sure how she was going to stop herself from confronting her.

It doesn't matter, she thought, *one step at a time.* Jordyn would face her mother later. Much later. She had a responsibility to the baron and the pack. As a soothsayer. And then she had to talk to Rutger.

Jordyn gathered herself, shoved her fears down, and walked through the entrance. With the nice weather they would use the outside seating area. She remained at the back where the soldiers and enforcers' stations sat and watched the stage. Aisles separated three rows of pews, enough to accommodate three hundred plus members. Large street lights sat at the corners of the seating area, while industrial lights crisscrossed above the pews and the stone stage. She chose a seat, set her backpack on the chair, and watched women enter. They created circles, and casually talked as they waited. The baroness stood in the center of the stage, flanked by her personal guards, and with a practiced air, smiled and nodded when anyone greeted her. Every couple of minutes, her chestnut eyes would narrow on Jordyn, she would smile, nod, and turn her attention back to the gathering crowd.

Jordyn kept her senses open, searching the area for intruders, or witches—her wolf skimming her skin, its feel sending an energy over her.

"Look at you taking your place as a soldier," Claudia teased as she joined her. "Word is you spent the night at Foxwood, with Rutger."

Jordyn looked at Claudia and wasn't sure if she trusted her. Did she have any more secrets? Nope. "We didn't get home until this morning," Jordyn replied.

"After you left, Kory officially broke up with him. And she made it *official*. Have you seen her?"

"Yeah, she told me she ended it" Jordyn answered, watching several women find their seats.

"For the good of the pack, no doubt. Not because Rutger loves you and the two of you belong together." Claudia laughed.

Jordyn didn't laugh; she met Claudia's gaze with the weight of the evening on her shoulders. "What would you know about that?"

Claudia's laugh died with her carefree demeanor. "I felt him close himself off and watched him stop living. He touched you, for a second, and it tore his heart open. Even if he didn't want it to. The same way yours did."

"What do mean? You felt it?" Jordyn figured her for a spy but had no idea what else was going on.

"My parents aren't purebloods. My mom is half fairy, and I have her blood in my veins. The combination of wolf and fairy gave me the ability to sense someone's power and the strength of their wolf. In your case, I can sense the force that makes you a soothsayer," Claudia explained. "You're strong. It's impressive."

"You knew about me the entire time?"

"Yes," Claudia answered.

"What else ..."

"I'm going to say something that'll sound like I'm losing it."

"Claudia, look at me."

"Right. You and Rutger. I believe you're *fated.*" Claudia raised her hand to stop Jordyn from interrupting. "I know how it sounds. But I believe it's true. I felt you, girl, you have to have him."

Fated. Some dark age myth. Like a soothsayer. Jordyn sighed, she couldn't deny the effect he had on her. "Yeah, well, it didn't work out so well the first time. It can't be true."

"Says your broken heart?" Claudia met her gaze.

"Something like that."

"You can't run this time. You'll have to face the past."

Perfect. "Is your gift the reason you work for the baron?" Jordyn asked trying to change the subject.

"It does. He employs those with powers. Like you." Claudia looked at the gathering crowd. Two women craned their necks to look at them as they walked by. Claudia and Jordyn watched them before facing each other. "I'm sorry, I know how it looks. We were friends before you moved, and with your public appearance, I had to talk to you. Not because of my talent, and not the baron. He saw us and asked questions."

"I don't blame you. Look where I'm at. Is that why you're with Jason? He can handle your gift?" She thought of Rutger. He hadn't run, exactly, when he found out what she was.

"Bingo," Claudia answered. "I love him, he loves me. He serves the baron as his personal sentinel and sometimes my gift comes in handy. We balance each other. Look, I gotta go, and sit with my mom. If you want to talk, vent, drink wine and pass out, call me."

Jordyn laughed this time. Not an easy going sound, but a sad, damn that's true sound. If that was possible. "Thanks." She wished drinking and passing out would get rid of the stress, but she doubted it would do anything other than give her a headache.

CHAPTER FIFTEEN

Rutger unlocked his door, turned the handle, and noticed the difference immediately. No Kory. Her stuff. Her scent. Her presence.

Her absence lifted like a weight from his shoulders. It wasn't because Kory had done anything. As soon as she declared it was over between them, the baroness quickly ordered someone to clean his house. There were new bottles of liquor, wine in the wine rack—red, Jo's favorite—and they rearranged the glasses. He knew if he checked his fridge, freezer, and pantry there would be enough food to feed the entire pack. He felt as if his parents set the entire thing in motion, and he and Jo were their playing pieces. Only he didn't know if Jo was going to play.

Rutger took his gun belt off, set it on the couch, shed his shirt, and while untucking his undershirt from his BDUs walked into the bar. The sun was sinking behind the mountains, the last of its gold and scarlet glow reflecting on the lake. The night ahead was going to either bring Jo to him or push her further away. The deciding moment would be when he stood beside her. If she refused him in front of the entire pack, he was going to live with her decision. He poured a healthy amount of bourbon, its smoke and toasted honey scent drifting in the room. He set the bottle down, took the glass, and made his way up the stairs, down the hall, and through a set of double doors.

His room and bathroom had been cleaned—sanitized if the heavy smell of cleanser rising above the air freshener was an indication. The bed had been changed and made, the shirt he tossed to a chair gone, as were a pair of boots. They eliminated Kory's existence from the premises. His imagination had him wondering if they had the house cleaned or the pack's specialized cleaner team had paid him a visit. He set the glass on the newly dusted dresser, pulled his T-shirt over his head, and carrying it to the bathroom dropped it in the empty dirty clothes basket. The counter and mirror gleamed in the hazy sunshine from the skylights casting the room in a gilded glow. Hanging on heated bars beside the walk-in shower were four thick towels. *Four?* Consumed with his thoughts, Rutger turned back to stare at his room. What would he do if she denied him? Could she deny him if they were fated? If someone could resist fate, it would be Jo.

He, without a doubt, could not continue to live the way he had been for three years. *Isn't going to happen*, he thought. Taking the glass from the dresser, he sipped the bourbon, cut the day loose, unbuckled his belt, and got ready to have a shower.

"Tonight, the women of the Cascade pack gather together. We claim this evening and use it to establish the backbone for our pack. We are here as the counselors, mothers, sisters, lovers, and mates. We are here as kin. Our station giving us over as we gather as a family. As one," Laurel began, her eyes glowing with her wolf.

Energy rose from the crowd, and like a cloud sitting above them, its ends flowed over Jordyn's skin. Her heart sped up with the baroness' words and the power building in the group. She felt their excitement and their wolves rising. It called to her power, triggering the anchor the baron drove inside of her and making it act like a lightning rod.

"Tonight, we run on land saturated by the bloodshed of our

own. We prove our strength, our loyalty, and our love for one another by overcoming the suffering of our past and looking to our future. The future made stronger with the union of Tanner and Bailey Kanin. Bailey's presence will be felt as she and my son, third in line to alpha, begin their lives. We dedicate our run to Bailey, my daughter. Your sister."

Jordyn closed her eyes and her stomach fluttered with the baroness' admission. Rutger had taken his place as second. Applause erupted, Claudia whistled, and Laurel's eyes narrowed on a single person. Jordyn felt Mia, before she closed the distance between them and stopped beside her.

"Jordyn."

"I don't have the time." Jordyn cut her off before Mia could continue.

"You've taken your place as a soldier?"

"Clearly," she answered. Her focus remained on the perimeter, the women, and the baroness. "You should go sit down."

"First, you're helping Rutger with an investigation, and now you're taking your place as a soldier. Wouldn't have thought you cared for the trivial things within the pack," Mia mused. "Since you're leaving and never coming back."

"You thought wrong."

"If you are leaving, why have you moved to Foxwood?" Her voice weakened, the last word quivering. *Insecure*?

Jordyn turned and met her gaze, and Kory's words played. She didn't have to use her senses to know Mia was fishing for information and any waver in confidence was to manipulate Jordyn. Who she was asking about ... Kory, Rutger, or the baron, she didn't know. And didn't care. "My plans have changed."

"And Rutger?" Mia continued.

"That's none of your business." Jordyn let a sliver of power fill her eyes. Her wolf hovered around her, and she watched Mia take a small step backwards. When she turned to face the stage, the baroness was staring at her.

"I am your mother, but I guess it isn't. You have procured the blessing of the baron and baroness?" Her voice sounded edgy and laced with bitterness.

Procured. Seriously? "Yes," Jordyn replied. "Go sit down. It's disrespectful to the baroness."

"Laurel won't mind if I'm talking to *my* daughter."

"Go. Sit. Down."

Mia waited a second, staring at the side of Jordyn's face. In a low voice she said, "You've changed."

Yes, I have. Without responding, Jordyn let silence stretch out between them. The baroness' voice rose when she told the group it was their job to live as an example to young girls and young women, and they would, as one, protect the pack. Mia remained, her presence like a burden, tension building between them. Seconds ticked by; the baroness' speech began winding down, and Mia turned and walked away.

Damn it. They cloaked the night in lies, half-truths, and betrayal, and Jordyn was in the middle of it all. Caught like a bug in a web. Jordyn watched Mia walk to a pew, her back straight as she carried her status with her. Kory's stare quickly found her, but Jordyn ignored her and continued to scan the area and met the baroness' questioning gaze. Jordyn didn't give anything away, keeping her face neutral, and waited for the damn speech to end.

"Women, let us run," Laurel announced.

The younger women, Claudia included, raised their faces to the sky and howled. Jordyn couldn't stop from getting caught up in the moment, her excitement rising with the combined power, and a smile from curving her lips. One by one the women disrobed, put their clothing on the pew, and began shifting into their wolves. Jordyn waited, her wolf howling in her ears, and her power growing. Abigail and Sadie shapeshifted, and circled the baroness while she shifted.

Jordyn set her hoodie on the seat, took her tank top and bra off, and then worked on her shoes and jeans. When she wore nothing, she drew on her power and slipped from the human world and into the world of her wolf. The energy from shifting purged the internal fight to keep the memories back and the denial of her wolf. The fight between her wolf spirit and her human side eased, its push fading. Inching out from her middle was the power of the soothsayer and it was coming for her. When it came time, the baron would make sure the barrier keeping it at bay, broke down.

The baroness howled, leapt from the stage, and loped into the woods with Abigail and Sadie. One by one, the rows emptied, the wolves disappearing into the dark, leaving Jordyn behind. Scanning the assembly area with her senses, she skimmed over the energy from the women, and the spell from the land.

Satisfied there was no one there, Jordyn followed the group, watched them jump and chase each other, while keeping her senses open and searching. Did she think someone would trespass? No. No one would risk challenging werewolves, let alone one hundred wolves belonging to the Cascade pack. It didn't change the warning creeping its way into her nerves. The image of the mutilated werewolf sat in her head, joining the witches' ability to go unseen with magic. Why was she worried about that? It had nothing to do with her or the pack.

The woods wrapped around her, taking Butterfly Valley, Louis, and her lies and throwing them into the wind. Jordyn lost herself in the exhilaration of running, the freedom, and the energy of being with her own. There was a sense of belonging, home, and it created a comfortable sensation of family. Deep in its richness, she wanted to remain in the easy feel of the run, and having cast off her constraints, wanted to be her true self. In a breath, the safety of the night felt like someone reached out and stripped it from her. A blaring warning pulsed in her head.

Jordyn needed to end the run.

The other soldiers and the baroness' guards continued running, unhindered by the crisis eating at Jordyn. She hesitated. She could be wrong. The same way she had been wrong about Rutger. No. She saw him. Felt them. Misunderstood the intent. The fear of losing control and slipping into the baron's past added to her doubt. Jordyn needed to decide if it was her imagination or if it was real. How? She couldn't stop her senses from overwhelming her.

Someone was there.

Before she tried convincing the baroness to stop, Jordyn repeated her search. Ahead of her, the pack raced through the night, and the thick woods pushed Jordyn's instincts into overdrive. Nothing. She cursed. The farther they ran, the farther they were from the assembly area, the distance putting them at risk. With the image of the dead wolf in her eyes, Jordyn couldn't ignore the warning any longer.

The run needed to end, and Jordyn had to reach the baroness. Seconds. Minutes. Time was wasting. They ran deeper into the woods.

Linked to the baron was the beginning of completing the circle. Tonight, she would hold the pack's power, memories, and their essences as if they were her own. Jordyn wasn't without a way to search for one of the pack. One of her own. With her strength increasing, she sought the baroness' feel. Like a sky burdened with a million threads, she navigated the drifting powers. Bold, weak, and sophisticated reached out. Prepared to give up and use force to stop the baroness, a trace of power, confident, tempered and holding a familiar vibration touched her thoughts. Jordyn traveled the thread, created a link, and absorbed the distance between them. With a solid connection to the baroness, Jordyn held onto her core, and prayed the baroness wouldn't reject her demand.

The baroness' sharp barks echoed, and Jordyn knew she received her warning. There was a wave of words from the baroness in the shape of a question. Jordyn responded. *No, she wasn't positive about the threat, but wasn't going to put their lives in danger. They were safer at the stage. Together as a group where the light would allow them to see the enemy.* Minutes felt like hours, turning Jordyn's doubt to fear. They had to return to the assembly area.

The group came to a stop, the silver veil of the crescent moon casting spider webs through the tree limbs. The baroness hopped on a fallen tree, waited for everyone to gather around, and raising her head, howled. The women joined their baroness in her ballad, its high-pitched melody resonating through the air. Swallowing her fear, Jordyn remained silent, and paced the perimeter while searching and wanting to leave.

With the melody of the women's howls echoing from the woods, Rutger found Jo's clothing and placed the robe she would wear beside the stack. The smell of her skin and her body spray, a mixture of spice and vanilla, held the air. He resisted the urge to bring her hoodie to his nose. Instead, with nervous energy he folded them and set them back on the seat. He wondered if the baron had warned her he was going to announce them. And if he had, what was she going to do? His distrust came roaring back to set fire to his failure. Rutger needed her. He looked toward the tree line, listened, and with his anxiety forcing him to move, began pacing.

"It's true?" A deep voice stopped Rutger's fourth pass by the chair.

If the instructor for the combatants was questioning him, it wasn't going to be a casual conversation. "What?" Rutger asked. He tried looking as if nothing was going on and he wasn't waiting for Jo. Rutger met the narrowed icy jade gaze of Leo, turned, took five steps, turned again, and couldn't stop himself from glancing at the woodline.

"You. Jordyn." His head turned, tracking Rutger with each pass, his attention split between watching the soldiers take their positions and Rutger's pacing.

Rutger stopped and faced him, the man's light brown curls barely controlled with the short haircut. He didn't know if he should say yes, and look like a fool, or say no, and look like a liar. "Yes."

"It's complicated," Leo stated.

Understatement. "Yes," Rutger confirmed, and started walking toward the woodline like he was being pulled.

"Leave it."

"What?" Rutger turned, his nerves churning into anger.

"Stand down. She is a soldier. Leave her be," Leo ordered.

Rutger stopped and spun around. "She took her place as a soldier?" Why hadn't anyone told him? He was going to talk to the baron.

"Affirmative. And if you're waiting for her, it makes her look weak. There is a lot riding on her conduct this night."

"The baron did this?" Rutger asked. *Unbelievable.* He saw her fighting the baron's past and the tears she shed from the pain.

"No. Torin and I agreed she would serve. She is good at what she does, and I wouldn't let a weaker wolf guard the baroness," Leo explained. "Plus, her instincts are stronger than the others."

"You don't know—" Rutger started. No one did. They were toying with ancient powers and had no idea what was going to happen. The energy he felt convinced him, he had no idea what was going to happen to Jo.

"I do know," Leo countered and scanned the perimeter of the Summit. He wore a shoulder holster with a .45 Ruger, tucked inside, and unseen, a knife at his calf. "The baron explained what was happening this evening, and the preparations have been made. There are sufficient soldiers." There was a dozen of them.

With the witches a threat, Jo becoming the pack's soothsayer, and the gathering of the pack, Rutger decided he needed his enforcers. Most of the enforcer group was present and added to the number of soldiers. The total expanse was a confirmation of the significance of the evening, the baron's power, and a display of the strength of those serving. By the end of the night, Jo would take her place and become as important as the baron and the baroness.

Leo watched Rutger look at the stack of hastily folded clothing like they would speak to him, the seating area, and the few men entering the area. Cocking his head, Leo turned when the sounds of wolves caught his attention. "They're returning."

A group of wolves emerged from the woodline and into the light. Rutger recognized the leader, a tan and dark brown wolf, as the baroness. She glanced at the area, Sadie and Abigail following, and ran to the stage where the baron waited. The others dispersed, each going to their clothing and waiting family.

Rutger stilled and watched. With his heart in his throat and his pulse hammering his in his ears, he stared at the woodline for Jo. Each minute kept pace with his heartbeat, when the woodline remained empty, its void pushing his worry to panic. *Come on, Jo.* Unable to stop himself, he took two steps, and stopped. A wolf, fur the color of dark chocolate, its throat a tawny red feathering to her sides, loped from the shadows, causing his heart to pound harder.

Jordyn ran up the left side of the pews, passing soldiers and enforcers, her senses scrutinizing the information her instincts were giving her. She went around the back, checked in with the baron and baroness, saw Jason, Sousa, Abigail, and Sadie, and continued down the right side. If they pressed her about needing to end the run, she would explain as best she could.

"I told you, she's good at what she does." Leo's narrowed gaze held Rutger's for a solid minute. "Let her be." With the last word, Leo walked toward Torin and Tracy.

Jo made her rounds and slowing, walked in his direction. If he didn't get his spiking emotions under control his heart was going to explode. With her approach, his father's words tangled in his head. *'If you put your feelings aside, you'll find the answer.'*

He watched Jo and tried to figure out what forced her to run and what created three years of dead silence. He knew and he didn't know. *She sensed emotions.* Jo closed the distance between them and he saw the lake, the beach, and Kory. He was sitting by the water when Kory found him. He wasn't expecting her and hadn't wanted to talk to her. With his mind racing, Rutger watched Jo hesitantly approach and stop in front him, her bronze eyes gauging him.

She saw Kory. She saw him. He betrayed her and she ran.

Rutger knelt on one knee, his lungs begging for air, his outstretched hand shaking as he wavered with indecision. When she didn't move, he slowly drew his hand down Jo's back and throat. Something changed between them. She let him touch her. Jo remained, staring at him with her shadowed wolf eyes, her power swirling around her like her personal wind, and her fear threading through it all. When he straightened, she shifted and stood in front of him. Her athletic body, shimmering with sweat, caused his wolf to rise with lust, while the power she held and the ease of her shift brought a streak of pride. *Mine.*

"My clothes?" Jordyn asked as she met his gaze. The itching feeling of eyes sat on her and she knew the entire pack was staring at them. Being seen together after the run was another win for the baron. They were playing their roles.

"Sorry." Rutger lifted the royal blue silk robe—the color representing loyalty, wisdom, faith, and trust—which would be the only clothing Jo would wear when she faced the pack. Her nakedness and the eyes on them drove a jealous fury through him like a flash.

Jo turned away from him, and lifting her hair exposed the line of runes representing the Cascade pack, the crest representing her pureblood family, of a wolf's head, its right ear decorated with onyx stones linked by a silver chain, and under it were more runes. He would have to look them up to understand their meaning, and the story they told. Regardless, it didn't change the obvious … she kept the pack close to her.

His eyes followed the line, down to her hips. "You've added some," Rutger said softly, his voice rough with his need.

Without answering him, she faced him. "Why don't I have my clothes?" Despite the lack of air in her lungs and the unease feeding her anxiety, her voice held.

He watched her tie the belt and fix the collar. "When you go forward as the soothsayer, you'll drop your robe, proving you're exposed to the pack. The baron said when you shapeshift, the magic inside of the shift will bind you and you'll hold the collective. When it's over, you can get dressed."

She knew that. Part of it anyway. The baron didn't say anything about the naked part. "And you? You walked away today."

I was losing control. "I know." He stopped and looked at the entrance of the assembly area like it was going to widen under his stare. He wouldn't dare look in the direction of the stage and the pews to see the judging eyes of the pack. They were falling into the same roles.

"You don't have to do this. You can leave," she lied. He would surely sense it, and when he closed his eyes, Jordyn figured he did. Rutger's chest expanded with his deep inhale tightening his T-shirt around his muscles. Fated. Was it real? Old power. Jordyn watched his eyelids twitch. He inhaled, and when he opened them, she stared at gold flakes. Knowing what the baroness said, and Kory's confession, she wanted to tell him she was sorry, and stupid, and her mother may be evil. Nothing came out.

"I'm not leaving. I'll be by your side." The words rushed from him, taking the oxygen from his lungs.

"We have to talk," she replied. Jordyn's attention went to the woodline and the night and the explaining she was going to have to do.

Rutger met her dark eyes, grasping onto the shape of her wolf. "Later. Let's get through this."

"Agreed." Jordyn nodded and directed her gaze at the ground, trying to smother her anxiety.

Rutger saw her visibly shake. "Are you going to be all right?"

No. "I don't look forward to being naked in front of everyone, and binding myself to them is scary as hell, but sure, I'm great."

"The baron won't hurt you," Rutger assured. He was going to be by her side and wouldn't let anyone hurt her.

"We'll see." She wasn't convinced. The last couple of days had proven otherwise.

"Jordyn Langston, please approach." The baron's deep voice thundered over the crowd, followed by the sound of dozens of people turning around.

Her stomach began a flurry of flips, and her skin warmed with embarrassment with having to stand in front of the entire pack, naked.

"I'm with you," Rutger promised. "I won't walk away." He took her chin and lifted her face. "With you." Leaning down, he kissed her lips.

Rutger's power flowed over her, caressing her, and calming her. Jordyn smiled; it didn't reach her eyes, and she knew it did little to convince Rutger she was telling the truth. She turned, walked away from him, and made her way down the aisle. The eyes of the crowd drilled into her, their weight flowing around her. At the stone steps, her bare feet were silent on the rough surface, and the baron nodded and his wolf reached out. At the top, she turned, gasped at the sets of eyes on her, and a sinking fear spread out as she took her place beside the baron.

"Rutger Kanin, second in line to the alpha, approach," Healey commanded.

Second in line. Drawing a slow breath, Rutger tasted her wolf on his lips and her scent in the air. He struggled to convince himself her acceptance of his kiss meant she wasn't going to deny him. 'We have to talk' could mean anything and he had walked away from her. It didn't help his confidence level had tanked, it's presence somewhere in the depths of his body where he figured it would never crawl out from. It wasn't confidence making him take the first steps.

There was nothing he could do to protect himself from her.

With his heart ripped open, Rutger started down the aisle, saw Gavin, Spring, Lord and Lady Langston, and fear snaked through him. Meeting Jo's gaze, he half expected to see doubt, but only saw her fear. On either side of him, the rush of energy from the pack carried questions, worries, and alarm, not the confidence of a run, like he expected. Rutger crested the last step and standing beside Jo, the baron and baroness greeted him with wolf eyes.

"Ladies and gentlemen of the Cascade pack, we are together

to celebrate the women's run and the observance of the union between Tanner and Bailey." As if holding back, because they knew there was more, only a few soft murmurs of those agreeing were offered from the crowd. "Tonight brings another special event. Please welcome Jordyn back into the embrace of her kith and kin."

Their questions sat in their silence. Jordyn didn't meet anyone's eyes. As the stillness stretched out, she stared at the back, toward the gate, at freedom.

"The Cascade pack has been given a gift from the ancients. It will bind our collective with an old power. Clansmen, you have been brought here to witness the absolute strength of our numbers. You are here to witness the amalgamate of Jordyn Langston as your soothsayer." The crowd erupted in whispers, and Jordyn saw her father grab her mother's wrists and hold her in place. "Before your pack, your kith and kin, Jordyn Langston, pureblood, and daughter to the elders, Lord and Lady Langston, do you willfully submit your wolf, and your life, to those within?"

Jordyn focused on Rutger's presence as he moved from her right side to stand behind her, his hands resting on her shoulders. "Yes," Jordyn answered, and loosening the tie, the ends slipped from her shaking hands and fingers.

"You have worn blue to represent your oath and your loyalty to the pack. It's time to shed your cover and stand unadorned. As you are stripped of your cover before them, their lives will be exposed to you." Healey ended and nodded his head.

Jordyn felt Rutger's light touch as his fingers freed the robe, creating a shard of ice skating over her skin. The whispers continued when she turned to face the baron. He reached out, his fingers threading through her hair to hold the back of her neck and draw her closer. Her resolve began cracking when she imagined the baroness staring at them while the entire pack blamed her for causing the baroness embarrassment. Then there was her mother. What was she going to say? What kind of accusations would be thrown at her like daggers?

Healey lowered his head, touched Jordyn's cheek with his own, leaving his lips feathering her ear. "Hear your alpha, respond to my wolf, and obey my call."

Jordyn's thoughts and worries ceased. Without her consent her neck flexed in his palm, and every muscle in her body constricted. She'd never had her wolf pulled from her and understood how it could be used as a punishment. Uncontrolled chaos. Her human features melted away, and giving into her wolf, fur replaced human flesh.

Healey continued to hold Jordyn while he slowly drew her wolf out from its nadirs. "It is time for *you* to free your wolf," he whispered. Healey drew power from the pack, it flowed over and around them, and like a warm wind, it charged the spaces between them and glided over her skin.

Jordyn let go of the pain and sank into her wolf, releasing her hold on its power, and giving it what it wanted. The power offered by the pack. She cried out as fire scrawled her right thigh, and her skin shrank from her muscles.

"Shift, Soothsayer!" Healey let go of her, then took several steps backward to stand beside Laurel. "Show your pack your absolute self."

Jordyn watched their eyes widen as her power increased, spread out, its intensity burning as she gave into the shift. Between worlds, Jordyn saw herself, a sharper imitation of the woman, the wolf, and the soothsayer. If she ever doubted it, she changed her mind. Her sight blurred, the flame continued etching her skin, at the same time a spike of darkness drove through her. Talons ripped in to her insides as it secured itself in her middle and began spreading through her mind, veins, and soul. Jordyn tried to inhale as her heart pounded and her wolf merged with the darkness. She struggled to concentrate on the shift when fear sucked the air from her lungs.

Jordyn devoured the combination of the baron's and the pack's energy, the lifeforce of the soothsayer drinking it in to feed her wolf. When she had taken what the baron offered, she pushed the shift. Jordyn stood beside the baron, staring at the crowd through wolf eyes. Inside of her, the darkness weaved around the essence of the pack, her wolf, and into her being. It wasn't right. It felt wrong. Her eyes skated over the crowd, not focusing on anyone, and she found her father. He knew what was happening to her, it was on his face and in his eyes, and she saw his fear in their darkened depths. It sent a cold wave to her heart and she wondered if the baron knew what accesses he had opened.

Jordyn's ear flicked when the Baron leaned down, his face grazing her fur. "Return," he demanded. Jordyn closed her eyes, lowered her head, and in a blur stood straight.

Her body moved with a liquid smoothness, and if it hadn't been for his wolf's sight, he never would have seen Jo shapeshift. Rutger quickly wrapped the robe around her, his body touching her. "Impressive. No one doubts you and no one will challenge you."

"No," Jordyn whispered. No one wanted her job. No one would challenge a soothsayer for status. Not when superstition ruled. She shook like chills gripped her, but it was the coldness of the shifting shadow within her. It wrapped around her wolf, merged, and changing her vision, she saw the pack through a hue of magic, their wolves like heat signatures in the night. Jordyn heard their voices, soft murmurs, and their thoughts as if the collective were speaking aloud.

"Cascade pack, I give you your soothsayer," Healey

announced.

They remained silent. Unmoving.

Some held hands, their faces drawn in a blank canvas as to not give away their emotions, while their eyes focused on her, and their thoughts penetrated her. Jordyn stood strong, staring back, while the sorcery absorbed their essence.

"I have another announcement to make," Healey started.

Rutger turned and met the baron's gaze. He couldn't protect himself from her. It was all or nothing. He nodded, giving his approval to the baron.

"Rutger has reclaimed his status as second and has given Jordyn his faithfulness." Healey's voice boomed over the crowd, his satisfaction carrying on the wind.

His faithfulness. No one talked to her. No one asked her.

Uncertainty was trying to paralyze him as Rutger faced Jo, her gaze locked on his, her eyes a tangle of wolf and human, and her body remained unmoving, like stone. The kind of frozen vampires were capable of. He raised his hand, and cupping her cheek kissed her. His doubt screamed at him as he waited for Jo's response. He feared he lost her. Riddled with lies and the unknown, he doubted they could leave their past behind them. He should have never turned his back on her. Whispers from the crowd flourished, their doubt in every hushed word. His hope gave way to his humiliation, and he prepared to step away from her.

Jordyn sank into her mind, her fear playing with the overwhelming weight from the pack, and her need to control it all. Her lips moved against Rutger's in a silent laugh as she knew she lost control the moment she crossed over into Paradise County. Trinity and the Cascade pack took what they wanted.

Jordyn was going to take what she wanted.

She wrapped her fingers around his wrist, squeezed, and returned his kiss. She let her passion intertwine with her power as her wolf sought his. In a swirl of heightened power, desire, and with their wolves shadowing their human bodies, they held onto one another.

His pulse beat in his ears, blocking out the crowd, as he devoured Jo's wolf, taking in her essence. When their wolves intertwined, tremors started in Rutger's chest and skidded down to his legs. He moved his hand to her hip and held her close as he kissed her with desperation. Jo held him as if he might disappear and wrapped her power around him.

Mine. Rutger growled, broke the kiss, held her cheek, their eyes meeting and reflecting their wolves. He slid his arm around her waist in possession and they turned to face the pack.

"The century old traditional union between werewolves has been performed. They have honored each other's path. By the blood within their veins, and the wolf spirits in their bodies, they have given their commitment. From this day forward, witnessed by their kith and kin, Rutger and Jordyn will be recognized as *One-Flesh*. The Scared Writ shall be recognized by the Highguard," Healey announced.

Jordyn felt heat radiate from her middle and burst out from her skin to race up and scald her cheeks. *In front of everyone.*

"We have honored our ancestors. As a pack, we have paid tribute to the rites they held with fervor. We, the clansmen of the Cascade pack, the men and women providing their strength and creating a pack, have made this night possible. We reclaim the traditions of the ancients, giving them new life, and we cast off the customs of humans." Healey's eyes glowed with his wolf as its low rumble threaded through his words.

"Together," Laurel added. Healey stood next to her, his hand on her shoulder, and together they gazed at the staring group.

Healey drew his wolf and power inside of himself, and calmed his nerves. "I have surprised you enough this evening.

Our next gathering will take place the night of the full moon. We will run as a pack," Healey stated. "You all have a goodnight." He hoped they would start leaving. He understood there were going to be questions, but they would have to wait. First, he would face the Highguard and their inquiries.

Jordyn waited. No one moved. Gripping the front of the robe, the silk crinkling in her fists, she took a small step. She had to get out of there. The crowd hadn't moved, hadn't made a sound— they stared at her.

Rutger felt Jo's anxiety eating the air around her. They were the spectacle of the evening, and it was finally time to end the show and get the hell out there. Pulling her closer, he leaned down and whispered into her ear, "We're leaving."

Jo nodded in response, her hair moving against his mouth, and she reached for his hand.

Jordyn watched Rutger, the second in line to the alpha, and her mate, and followed him to the stairs. The burden of what she had become, what she had done in a moment, plowed through her thoughts, mixing them up and creating madness. *Simple thoughts*, she told herself. She wanted her clothing and wanted out of the line of fire. What she needed was a break. Since shapeshifting, she felt the pack like the gathering eruption of a storm. It drove through her, sinking into her bones, and there it ached. In her soul and in her head with the darkness. Their voices and their wolves attached themselves to her thoughts and memories. Where there had been conversations, there was emotion and power. Rutger's broad back didn't give in under their publicized commitment. Lost in thought, Jordyn nearly ran into him when he stopped in front of the chair where her clothing sat.

"Are you all right?" Rutger asked. He let go of Jo and placed his fingers in the pockets of his jeans.

"Not sure," Jordyn answered. She had to sit down before she

collapsed. "It's overwhelming."

"Yes. Do you want me to take you to Foxwood? Do you need to talk to the Baron?" Rutger needed her with him. Needed her.

Jordyn met his eyes. His usual dark mahogany faded to cinnamon and there were gold flakes floating as if his wolf was catching glimpses of her. "No."

"I can't breathe," he whispered through a laugh. "Get your clothes and let's get out of here."

Jordyn stood, slung her bag over her shoulder, and gathered her clothing in her arms. Rutger stood staring at her, not moving. "Lead the way."

With a weak smile he whispered, "Sorry."

Together they walked out of the assembly area and to the parking lot. At his truck, he opened the door and stepped back, letting Jo set her clothing on the seat. He watched her with his heart in his throat and his nerves jumping under his skin. Waiting, he stood behind her, attempting to guard her from the few passing people. The robe fell to the ground and he picked it up as she pulled her hoodie over her head. Then, taking her underwear, she hurriedly pulled them up her legs.

"Are you sure you don't want to go back to Foxwood? A lot has happened." Rutger prayed she said no.

"I don't want to see your parents, and I don't want to see mine. I want to go with you," Jordyn replied softly as she faced him. "The Baron announced we were *one*."

CHAPTER SIXTEEN

Rutger struggled to control the fire warming his middle and sinking into his arms and legs. He kissed her, the taste of wolf coating her lips, and stepping back, held the door open. "Get in," he said through a breath. He waited as Jo climbed inside, wearing nothing but a hoodie and her pink, pinstriped underwear, the symbol marking her right thigh glittering in the muted light, and closed the door.

"Have a nice night," Claudia teased. With her mom, they walked between two cars, around a truck, and Rutger lost sight of them.

He forgot about the crowd, Jo's mark, and made his way around the front end to the driver's side. Sitting behind the wheel, he stared at nothing while silence sat between them. "There are years between us." Rutger started the engine.

"And lies." Jordyn watched people go to their cars. "I talked to Kory."

"It's over."

"Not about you … well, about you. But not about the two of you." Jordyn tried to pick her words to explain but her thoughts raced. Where did she start? She arrived in Trinity and within days this is where they were.

Rutger backed out of the parking spot, turned, and drove out of the lot. Around them people stopped and stared. Ignoring them, Jordyn focused on what she had to say. Rutger stopped at the main road, checked traffic, it felt like a minute too long, and drove away from the Summit. "She said—"

"What? What did she say?" Rutger asked. He turned and gave her a quick look, his eyes narrowing, before turning back to the road. Lined with streetlights and trees, it stretched out in front of him, threatening to take his opportunity to explain himself. He didn't know what Kory said, and didn't trust her to tell the truth. He knew he needed to tell his side before he lost the chance. "Kory found me waiting for you by the shore. She explained you received the offer of a partnership at a gallery and were planning to leave the pack. She said you were going to break it off with me. My life, as second, and the work I did with the pack wasn't for you … you wanted to get out from under the scrutiny of being with me. I prayed I would see you, but she kept talking, and talking. I didn't believe her. I knew I needed to talk you. Kory laughed and said you were leaving me behind."

"I saw you. You didn't stop her," Jordyn whispered. Her eyes watched the fog line on the road as if it might keep her emotions from getting away from her.

"No." His heart sank into the guilt he had been coveting. "Touching her was like touching nothing. My wolf felt nothing. No passion. No need. No risk. She would never leave hurt behind. It had been tempting. I didn't know what was happening between us. The urge I felt to have you made me crazy," Rutger confessed. "One mistake and you left town and gave me three years of silence. Since you wouldn't talk to me, I gave up my place in the pack, in hopes you would find out. It was proof I needed you and would do anything to get you back. I wanted to talk to you so I could explain."

It's making me crazy. "I watched her with you. The emotions coming from you were proof enough *you* didn't need *me*." Jordyn looked out the window at the passing city. "I assumed I had caused what was happening and you were tired of the pressure from your parents. You had the pack, your job, and didn't love me. It was better to leave than stay and watch the two of you."

"Those weren't my true feelings. I was there looking for you." His rough voice was barely heard. "I made Kory leave and waited. I don't know how long I was there, before I tried calling you. Nothing. I didn't understand why you wouldn't talk to me, and when I went to your house, you were already gone. With the baron's blessing."

Guilt moved in and grew. She should have fought for him. Mia knew Jordyn wouldn't because she never fought for anything. It was easier to play the submissive and let it go than to fight. Easier to run. "I think it was my mother, but I'm not sure, and I'm not sure, it matters anymore."

"You think your mother broke us up?" Rutger asked.

"Not the force behind it, but the nudge pushing me over the edge. Kory told me to ask my mom."

"Why?"

"I don't know. I always figured her snippets of criticism were her way of keeping me from believing I would succeed. But I never thought she would want us to break up, not when she was angry when I left," Jordyn answered. Turning in the seat to face Rutger, her muddled thoughts twisted her face and hurt sat in her eyes. "She blames me for everything. The gallery, when you stepped down, and your attention. Why on Earth would she break us up?" Jordyn stopped talking. *She knew I was a soothsayer, and like the old ones, held onto superstition*. No, Jordyn stopped herself from continuing and making it worse by guessing. "I don't know." The past was sitting between them like a starving lifeforce waiting for them to feed its existence. She looked at the side of Rutger's face, his jaw, the lines fanning out and creasing his cheek, and the way his hair rested on the collar of his shirt.

She missed him. *The truth is coming*, she thought, *we're going to face our past.* There was no way around it. *What about Louis?* her conscience screamed at her. *You have a mate and a boyfriend.*

This isn't the time, he told himself. Jordyn was facing being a soothsayer, a spectacle in the pack, he didn't need to add to her stress. *One-Flesh.* "Your parents didn't know. My parents didn't know. No one knew about us. No one knows. I never wanted anyone to interfere with *us*," Rutger assured. "I held onto the belief you were going to come back. When you didn't, I let it go and didn't say anything … just like, I didn't change. I'm not changing. I convinced myself, when I saw you at the Timber House, I was going to get the closure I desperately needed. It didn't happen. That night confirmed no one could stop what we have. Jo, we never stopped loving each other."

Fated. His confession sent an ache to her heart. "I can't erase three years of hurt and resentment, and neither can you. And this, all of this, is out of control. I have a life in Butterfly Valley and being here doesn't change that."

"You mean you have to go back to your human? Louis," Rutger shot back, jealousy marking his words and making them sound sharp.

Rutger's voice wrapped around Louis' name, creating new guilt from having mentioned Butterfly Valley. The way he said it had accusation dripping from every word and surrounded her human boyfriend. Without responding, Jordyn directed her gaze out the window. One second, lovers united, and the next … betrayal moved on in. "Yes, I have to talk to Louis, and there's the gallery. I have responsibilities. I have a life. *Had.* What are you going to do if you're forced to step down as director?"

"I have taken my place as second and you're my mate. The baron might ask me to step down. I can't. I'm not going to,"

Rutger answered. His frustration and his fragmented feelings were plain to hear. He wouldn't create another divide between them. "I don't like you leaving, but I understand your reason."

Jordyn glanced down at her hands; he didn't have to do anything. "You don't have to change. I'm done. I'm forced to give up the gallery. It gave me a place, an independent success no one could take away. I thought."

"I'm sorry." He whispered the words. "Your success is yours."

Maybe. Jordyn didn't have the energy to hold onto her anger, the injustice of giving up her life, and the future she faced without her consent. She leaned back in the seat as the scenery leisurely gave way from city scape to rural, and the mountains rose up, blocking the first quarter moon's ashen light. With the lake beside them, and minutes from Rutger's house, Jordyn rolled the window down, leaned closer, and inhaled. The breeze coming off the water, filtered through pine and cedar trees, eased some of the tension tightening her shoulders. The wind tangled her hair and caressed her face. Despite trying to ignore it, she felt the loss of everything she spent her life working for. Did it matter? She didn't know. She did understand, if she was going to have an honest conversation with Rutger, she needed to let go of the night and her mother's betrayal.

"Continue your career here," Rutger suggest as he turned down his road. "It's your passion." He couldn't stop his heart from pounding in his chest as the images of Jo's body glistening with sweat sat in front of him. There was no way he could control the outright pleasure knowing she was home.

Jordyn tried to imagine herself working in Trinity and couldn't concentrate with Rutger's feel. "I can feel you. Your heartbeat drums in my head," she whispered.

"S-sorry." Rutger stammered. He clenched his teeth, gripped the steering wheel, and fought to control himself.

"Don't be. Mine is keeping pace." She looked at him and wanted the regret, the lies, and hurt to show in her eyes. She wanted to escape the constraints created over the last couple of days with him, if just for a little while. With his silence, her heart slowed and fear seeped in. He stared forward, his jaw set, as he drove the truck down the dark road. A forced quiet took the place of his heartbeat, and she feared their broken past, the painful betrayal, and the manipulation from her mother and the baron were too much for either of them to handle.

With their approach, flood lights came on, their glare gleaming off the hood of Jo's SUV. Rutger realized someone made sure her car was at his house. So … she could leave. Rutger stopped the truck and killed the engine, his knuckles white as he gripped the steering wheel. "When you left the world forgot I was alive. I forgot I was alive. I lived with the feeling until now. You're here. Jo. Jordyn, the baron can't force us into a relationship. They tried before and it nearly broke us. What I'm trying to say … you don't have to say you'll stay. You don't have to say you forgive me. You don't have to say anything. I need you tonight. I need to feel you."

The hoodie felt tight around her neck and chest as his words took shape and stripped her emotions down to raw nerves. She was going to lose control. She was slipping. Jordyn couldn't fall into the trap of a nightmare and embarrass herself. He walked away once, would he do it again. She didn't have a choice. Jordyn remained silent, with the seatbelt buckled, and her hands squeezing her clothing. She grasped at his words, and with determination, stared at the garage door. *I need to feel him.* Jordyn needed him to know she wasn't going to run, again. She couldn't. The baron's threat came back. *Not that I have a choice.* She unclenched her fists, unbuckled the seatbelt, and faced Rutger. "I'm sorry." Two words, and his exposed feel and aroused passion surrounding him made her stop.

Rutger opened the door, got out, and slammed it closed, the force rocking the truck and making the equipment grind against each other. His anger spread out, whipping in the air, and Jordyn hesitated. She sat for second, confused, and tried calming her nerves before gathering her clothes, shoes, and bag. She slid from the seat to the ground, her car a glaring reminder of escape, and promising to take her from Rutger, his anger, her need, and the mess she created. Frozen by apprehension and fear, she stopped, going no farther than the front tire.

"What are you sorry for?" Rutger demanded and took his keys from his pocket. He opened his heart, bared his feelings, risked rejection in front of the pack, and felt as if she had taken a knife and flayed his very being. He had to know what she was going to do. Stay. Run. Leave him. Go back to the human and her life. *She could try*, he reminded himself. Leo activated the slayers and they knew what she was and what to do if she ran. No mercy. And if she didn't run? If she stayed in Trinity and he had to watch her life pass him by? Damn it. "What is it, Jo? Fucking tell me."

She didn't have anything to tell. In every word and every second, they saw the past. Three years of lies. Jordyn stared down at her things clutched to her chest. "Rutger."

"Fuck, Jo. Just say it." He stood at the edge of the rock walkway, his hands on his hips, his T-shirt tightening around his chest with his inhales, and his face in the shadows. His eyes shimmered with his wolf like he was fighting to stay in control.

Jordyn wasn't going to get mad. Wasn't going to get mad. No, she was furious. "Fuck you, Rutger, you broke my heart." She inhaled. Damn it, she hated confessions. "I came here to go to my sister's wedding and leave, that's it. I didn't come here to resolve anything with you, or ... or ... be the baron's idea of a soothsayer. I most definitely didn't come back to be linked to the pack." She took three steps forward, the pavement of the driveway cold on the bottom of her feet. She felt tears coming— not from being sad, but from the heated fury, and the pressure was making her head pound. *If I start crying, I'm never going to stop.* "I didn't want to see you with her so I left. I was told to stay away, and I did. I was told not to talk to anyone, and you know what, I did that, too. I'm sorry for hurting you. I'm sorry for running away when I should have fought for you. I'm fucking sorry for believing a lie. I'm sorry for being weak." The tears forced their way out and her words sounded messy and weak. Weak. It made her sick. "Is that what you wanted to hear? All of my mistakes."

What did he do? "No," Rutger whispered to himself. *This is killing me*, he thought as he shoved the keys back in his pocket and walked toward her. "I'm sorry. I'm sorry." He stopped messing up his apology, and his need to explain, and picked her up. With her in his arms, he kissed her lips, her cheek, and with the taste of her tears on his tongue, he carried her to the house. When he got to the door, he looked at the wrought iron handle and kissed her again. "I need my keys," he mumbled. Jo turned into him, her face in the curve of his neck, her lips against his skin, and laughed through her tears. "What?"

"You lock your door?" she asked. Rutger eased her to the ground and she wiped her cheeks. "A werewolf. Director of Enforcers. Locks his door."

"Some nights I don't come home," Rutger replied as the lock clicked. Jo giggled a weak sound, like music to his ears, and he opened the door. He clung to his control as he pushed it farther and fought harder when her arm brushed him.

Jordyn stopped, the bite from the slate floor adding to the chill from outside. She stood in the entrance and felt a possessive feeling steal over her. This was her home. Not Coal Valley, not

Foxwood, Rutger's house. To the left, the bar sat dark, while in front of her the room opened, and through the floor to ceiling windows the moon's light highlighted trees and cast shadows on the pine floor and furniture. She took three steps from slate to wood and stared at the living room. Three years.

Three years stolen from them.

Time slid through her emotions, taking the pieces and burning them into her. She saw Rutger having drinks on the deck, and together they watched the sunset with the water splashing against the rocks. Jordyn walked into the room, the pine floor, fireplace, her sunset photo sitting on the mantle, and the couch with a throw tossed over one side, brought back her past. She didn't think it was going to affect her, but it was. The regret of having missed her home rushed back, creating another surge of tears.

"I hate to see you cry," Rutger said softly.

She hated crying. Jordyn inhaled, tried to stop the tears, clutched her stuff with her left arm to her chest, and wiped her eyes and cheeks with the sleeve of her sweatshirt. Mascara and black and brown eyeshadow smeared the gray material, and seeing the mess added to her grief. Every detail sat in front of her, making her feel ridiculous for standing in Rutger's house in her underwear, stained sweatshirt, and stained face. What the hell had she become?

Jordyn inhaled and wiped the smeared makeup from her cheeks. For days, fearing what her mother was going to say, she acted and reacted, and worked to control herself and the situation. With her tight grip on everything, nothing helped getting rid of the turmoil sitting around her. Louis hadn't stopped calling or texting. And ignoring him was creating questions and making things worse than if she answered. How many times did she ask herself, why is this happening?

Too damn many.

CHAPTER SEVENTEEN

Rutger felt her unease charge the room like a low rumble of electricity and he didn't like it. He had to make it end. "Let me." He took her arm full of clothing, and put them in the nearest chair. "Come here. I have your wine."

Without switching a light on, it left Jordyn watching the way he moved, the way his feelings were passing over his face, and the way he held her hand in the muted glow of the moon. "My wine?" she asked.

"The moment we stayed at Foxwood together, my mother sent a team over." Rutger smiled, attempting to lighten the mood. "Like having your car here. There's no reason for either of us to leave."

She didn't have a reply, at least not one she wanted to share. The feeling they were pawns came back, stealing the easy feel of Rutger's touch. Stealing the fantasy of being fated. When he stopped in front of an overstuffed chair, she took the hint and sat down. Before leaving, he grabbed a throw from the back of the couch, unfolded it, and draped it over her bare legs. Jordyn sat back and tucked the soft fabric under her. It may have been the first time she sat down and relaxed. Between the cozy blanket and the soft chair, sleep began tugging at her.

Rutger walked to the bar, his wants and desires like flames to his skin. When he stood alone in the dark, he flattened his palms on the wood top and bowed his head, the muscles in his back screaming with tension. His worries about Jo were becoming outright fears, and he didn't know how to fix them. He straightened and stared like he could see her through the wall. He was her protector. He needed to protect her. But her silence was going to be the end of him. He had to get her talking. After grabbing a wine glass and a highball glass, he filled each one.

"Here you are." His low voice broke through the quiet thickening in the room.

"Thank you." Jordyn took the glass by the stem and could smell the plum and chocolate. "My favorite. At the bar, it took me back." *To us*, she wanted to add.

"Do you want to talk?" Rutger felt her hesitation and wondered how she was dealing with everything. He sat on the edge of the chair across from her, his glass held firmly in his hands, the bourbon untouched.

Jordyn looked down at the plum-colored liquid and saw her glittering eyes staring back. They didn't hold her exhaustion or her worry. They held a collective. She closed her eyes. No, she didn't want to talk. She didn't want to think.

"You're consumed." Rutger watched her eyes, saw through her worry and straight to their depths. She went on and on, forever. "Please talk to me." *Ease some of your fear*.

No. No more confessing. Jordyn sipped her wine and felt the damn on her feelings crumble. "All day, and at the Summit, I thought about leaving. I wanted to be pissed and hate the baron and the baroness for doing this to me. I want to hate my parents. Hell, I want hate this damn territory. But I can't. Somehow, I have accepted what I am and my place. This is *my* territory." Stopping, she took a sip of wine. "I don't know why you kissed me in the church, but you couldn't have known what it was going to start. And knowing the baron used me to threaten you makes it worse." She saw everyone staring at them as Rutger stood beside her. "I am forever bound to the pack as their soothsayer. I can't change that. Like you said, you have the enforcers, and I don't want to trap you." Jordyn wanted to touch the side of her leg, to run her fingers over the mark burned in her skin like it would console her. Pushing the need away, she sipped her wine. Jordyn prayed the distraction would be enough if Rutger rejected her. "I want you to know, I won't force you to stay with me. I won't trap you."

Trapped?

"I kissed you knowing you couldn't run out of the church. I trapped *you*." Nothing was going to stop him from expressing the feelings he kept like dirty secrets. "You needed to know I was here. Waiting. After the restaurant, I had to take my chances." Now he hesitated. "Does being a soothsayer change you? You're powerful. I don't understand what it means, but I'm willing to learn. It doesn't change who you are to me. I love you, Jo. You're the same woman I asked to marry me." She carried around more fear and worries than he could imagine and he was investigating a serial killer.

"I needed to hear you say it." With tears slipping down her cheeks, she met his gaze. "I needed to know you wanted to be with me. With what I've become."

Rutger set his bourbon on the side table, left the chair, and wrapped his fingers around her hand. Taking her glass, he placed it next to his. He bent down in front of the chair, meeting her gaze, and in silence, slipped the blanket from her legs. When her eyes simmered with her wolf, he didn't hesitate to hold her hips and pull her closer. He drew his fingertips down the side of her right thigh, across the image, to her knee, and slowly continued to her calve.

"I've thought about this," he whispered. While holding her gaze, he lightly kissed her, and closing his eyes rested his forehead on her knee.

Jordyn inhaled, didn't say anything, and stared down at him. Her body warmed with Rutger's touch, the sensation turning and bringing images of Louis to her eyes. Betrayal sank in to her conscience and the voice embracing fear pushed her to run. Not this time. Her body wanted Rutger. Her wolf rose, meeting Rutger's, and fought her doubt. She needed Rutger and his strength. She craved his wolf and being free. Jordyn scooted to the edge of the seat, took his face in her hands, and met his wolf eyes.

"I thought about you and wondered what your life was like. If you were thinking about me."

"You were always with me," she whispered, her eyes lingering on his lips.

Rutger held her wrist, kissed the inside, and his lips feathered her skin. "I need you."

"I'm here." She didn't say it out loud. Her lips moved around the words as if giving them sound would add years to their hurt.

"I hate the reason we're here, but I'll take it. I want you to know how I feel and I don't want any more doubt between us." Rutger stood and backed away. "Come with me."

Jordyn looked at his outstretched hand, knowing if she wanted to be truly free, and eliminate the doubt between them, she had to end it with Louis. She needed to set them both free from her lies. Meeting Rutger's gaze she saw what she wanted. Needed.

One night.

Jordyn placed her hand in his, and with his touch, felt his desire sweep over her in a violent rush. It wasn't her power as a soothsayer giving her his feel, it was Rutger's need matching her own. Unique to them. Jordyn stood, the blanket falling to the floor, the image branded on her thigh, and her guilt forgotten as Rutger led her to the staircase. She followed, her fingers intertwined with his, and staring at his broad back. She watched him move, his gait giving away the tension in his muscles, and the tremors giving away his crumbling control.

Rutger felt her power growing and mixing with the heat of her passion. There was an undercurrent weaving around him, them, creating a circle and tightening its hold. Like a physical entity escaping her. He inhaled when he reached the top stair; her vanilla and wolf quickly taken by her strength. He faced her, picked her up, and started down the hallway, the moon peeking in from the windows.

"I hope you don't need keys," she teased.

"Funny girl." Rutger rumbled the words. At the double doors, he kicked the right side and the door swung open.

"Keyless." With her tears spent and tired, her laugh sounded light and honest.

Rutger walked to the side of his bed, and lowering Jo, she left his arms and sat on the thick light brown comforter. With her knees to her chest, her cocoa eyes darkened.

"You're thinking." Rutger sat in the chair across from her and worked on taking his boots off. The fireplace glowed with low flames, its golds twisting in amber.

"I'm watching you." The steely light from the moon cast her in a shadow and like it knew her, embraced her.

My girl. Rutger stood, his gaze resting on her, and dropped his T-shirt. The knotwork-style ink started at his right shoulder, covering the muscle in black, curved under his collarbone to the center of his chest where its edges met the Kanin family's crest of a wolf's head. The right side of the tattoo depicted a wolf with a gold eye, Rutger's wolf, the left side was a wolf's skull. In the skull's empty eye socket were two interlocked silver rings. She found the old tradition in an even older tome and Rutger agreed to mark their union permanently on his skin next to his heart. If Jordyn had to guess, Kory never noticed. The idea of possession fed the pleasure pulsing through her. The tattoo stopped with the skull. When Rutger became baron, the knotwork would continue to his left shoulder and around his back. Jordyn watched his chest flex, his muscles looking as if they were carved into his sun-bronzed skin.

Rutger held the edge, the button next to his finger, and tugged. It slipped free. "Still watching?"

"Yes," Jordyn whispered, and shivers cascaded down her spine. She never confided her wants and desires to Louis. *You didn't love him.* Jordyn shook herself as the flames danced on his skin, highlighting the dark hair starting at the center of his ribs, and following an imaginary line sank below the waist of his jeans.

"My girl." His lips curved with his grin.

Jordyn rose to her knees, pulled the hoodie over her head, and dropped it to the floor. Her onyx hair fell around her bare shoulders, the ends feathering her breasts. She kept her eyes on Rutger as she sat down and slowly slipped her fingers to the waist of her underwear.

"Stop," his husky voice demanded. *Control.* "Stop." Rutger slid his jeans down his thighs, his skin turning sensitive, and farther, stepped out. With the glow from the fire on his back and the silver of the moon on his bare skin, he walked to the bed. "Stand up."

Jordyn imagined the time they spent apart, amid lies, would create hesitation, the way they saw one another, and erase the once easy way they had been. She had no idea it would change their attraction. It became infectious, but cautious, a mature need, while luring them to one another. It held a fragile edge—made from glass and capable of shattering.

Jordyn stood, her desire spreading out and warming her skin with each of his touches. He feathered her back and down to her waist where his fingers slid under the seam and pushed them from her hips and down her legs.

"I missed the way your skin feels under my hand," Rutger whispered against her stomach. "And tasted."

With his breath on her, his lips grazing her, and his arms holding her, Jordyn ran her fingers through his hair, and down his neck. Her light traces brought a low rumble of a growl as Rutger's muscles flexed under her palms. She couldn't stop thinking about Rutger's strength and confidence compared to Louis' unease and hesitation. Werewolf and human. She was where she belonged. With Rutger. A werewolf.

Rutger inhaled her scent, relished her taste, and touching her, memorized the feel of her skin. Jo shivered when he took her by the waist, lifted her and gliding her body down the length of his, set her on the floor. He wrapped his arms around her, held her close, and kissed her. Fire erupted where she touched him, while lust he hadn't felt in years worked on the barriers crafted from anger and hurt. He held her as he walked forward, backing Jo closer to the bed.

"Jo?" Rutger stopped when Jo's hands flattened on his chest.

Her eyes slipped from human to wolf to liquid coal and narrowed. Jordyn stepped backwards, stopping when her legs touched the comforter. "I want to see you. All of you."

He was going to lose himself. His muscles contracted, and tensed with his breathing. "You. Make. Me. Crazy." His growl twisted his whispered words. When gold bled through his mahogany eyes, his wolf shadowed him, and his power found her as if it needed to taste her.

Rutger wrapped his arms around her, and when he lifted her, she linked her legs around his waist. He held her bottom as she intertwined her fingers at his neck. Kissing his lips and neck as he turned, he took two steps backwards, his legs touching the bed, and sat down. Shifting to straddle him, Jordyn sat on his thighs, her palms flat on his chest, and leisurely licked his bottom lip.

Rutger fought to keep his eyes open, and saw Jo staring at him, as she drew her tongue over his top lip. "Babe."

Jordyn watched a small flame smolder in his eyes. "Wolf." The breath left her mouth without moving her lips. Caught up with the feel of his wolf, Jordyn slid her hands over him, needing to touch every part of him.

Wolf. The sensation of her touch had his wolf rising to bathe in the attention. Holding her gaze, Rutger gripped her thighs as he scooted them farther on the bed. When he could watch her, his hands feathered her sides, slid to her upper arms, and Jo pressed her hands flat on his chest. His breaths came in measured inhales and exhales, as he tried to hold onto his crumbling control. With the pale light on her throat, Rutger's instincts demanded he mark her. *No. Wrong.* Fighting his instincts, the urge dominated him and he tightened his grip, his fingers digging into her hips. He would dig through muscles and tendons and ligaments to grip her bones if it meant making sure she would never leave.

The little pieces of stillness they shared to look at one another, to remember who they were, and to indulge in the sensual pleasure of watching one another, ended. Jordyn sucked in a breath as his fingers created a combination of pain, while his conflict heightened her pleasure. Consumed by their past, she sensed his frantic desperation, the sharp edge of anger, and the inability to contain its need for revenge. Revenge. He was going to hurt her for her part in the deception. Pain and passion weaved between them, corrupting their touches, and feeling his fury, she knew he saw her silence as betrayal.

Rutger clamped his hands on her as if she were fighting to get away, and the pain swept through her hips. It didn't stop a low moan from escaping her. Jordyn met his heated wolf eyes and gave a silent challenge. She wasn't human. She was a pureblood werewolf. If he was going to punish her with his touch, then she wanted him to push the boundaries. Jordyn almost relaxed when his hands released their grip, then his right held her neck, his thumb pressed against her jaw, his left feathering her side, hips, and urging her to open for him.

"You're mine," he growled.

With one hand against her throat, Rutger's teeth ached to plunge into her skin, his wolf demanding he take her. *Don't hurt her. Not again.* Turning his touches from hard to gentle, he teased her, and watched desire soften Jo's body. Her challenge weakened, and her eyes swirled with bronze and onyx. As if he was molding her, Jo fully yielded to his touch, and he felt her desire mix with her need and power. A roguish smile curved his lips, and he felt his wolf move under his skin.

"You are wicked," Jordyn whispered.

He knew he was. She wouldn't think about Butterfly Valley and the human, ever. "I want to feel you." He knew his lips moved, they were wet from her kisses, but unsure if he said the words out loud. Jo moved with him, and guiding her, she leisurely, with an erotic edge, lowered herself down. "Who's being wicked now?"

"Fair play, Wolf." Jordyn inhaled, caught the scent of his desire, and placed her palms on his chest, his muscles contracting with her touch.

Her breath felt like it was being pulled from her when his fingers found her hips. His fury caught him in its coil, constricting him in its bands as he tightened his grip on her flesh. Tearing into her. He growled, and she felt the rumble against her palms. She opened her eyes—bronze stared at him—his hold eased, and urging her, they kept an uneasy rhythm with one another.

"You're trying to bury your power."

"You're fighting the past."

"Don't hide from me." A growl vibrated in his chest with his demand. He would give anything to release the past from his present. Jo moved her hips, her warm skin grinding against him. He growled, his lips parted, and swallowing a roar, stopped her. "Don't."

Jordyn inhaled, sat straighter, and warned, "You don't understand." Three years was a long time to hide her wolf. Jordyn wasn't going to explain what it was like to have sex with a human and the fear associated with a life of lies.

Rutger pushed on her hips and she rolled backwards. "Show me." Rutger stopped her ... them. His body trembled beneath her. His fingers sank into her, his hands increased their hold and nearly pinched her skin to her bones. Gold slivers gleamed in the moonlight as his eyes narrowed on her.

Jordyn didn't need to hear him say he wasn't human. The accusation in his tone and in the strength he was using to hold her served as proof. Restraining was as natural as breathing, but not her only problem. As her body reacted to Rutger and she sank deeper into the desire, the darkness stalking her threatened to expose its true self. "You don't know what it means."

"I'm not scared of you." Rutger raised his hips and pushed her backwards. When she responded, he stopped her from moving. *I'm not human.* "I want *you*."

"You're playing with fire." Despite her protest, his words sat in her thoughts. She couldn't hide forever. Jordyn bowed her head and inhaled. "I'm sorry." And she released the hold on her power.

Rutger growled, his back arched off the pillows, and his grip tightened when her energy surged over him like a heated wave. The current he felt earlier turned into an undertow, threatening to drag him under. The wave eased, as if teasing him with its gentle caress, and then it flared, like a blast, and her wolf rose above her. A silver hue veiled her and he drank it in, nearly intoxicated by their combined strength. Wrapped in passion their gazes locked, their bodies beaded with sweat gave in, and swept them into their desire.

Jordyn shook as the power streamed through her, its energy like silk threads wrapping around her arms and legs. Inhaling, she leaned down, touched Rutger's lips with barely there kisses, and kept rhythm with him. When the shadow lurking in her depths tangled in the energy, she tried forcing it down. Rutger growled, breaking her concentration, and in a breath she wasn't going to catch, enveloped her wolf and dove into the power of the soothsayer. Inside of the exhilaration, Jordyn leaned backwards, her back bowed, and placing one hand on his thigh, rolled her hips. With greedy touches, his hands explored her body adding another spike of passion to the heightened mix flowing through her.

"Babe." His rough whisper rumbled, his eyes glowed with his wolf, and his growl thundered between them. Drowning in pleasure and fearing losing control, Rutger grabbed her waist and turned her to her back. His canines grazed the soft flesh of her shoulder, teasing him, as he moved between her thighs and dove deep. Her body clenched around him with every stroke, spilling pleasure into his veins and spiraling through his nerves.

Without her restraints, Jordyn opened herself to him, leaving herself exposed. She wasn't hiding anymore. They were complete with one another. The reality added to the freedom she felt and created a new sense of indulgence. Rutger responded to her silent abandon, his pace slowed, his anger released, and his thrusts turned slow and sensual. Their combined passion was enthralling them as their bodies moved together in slow, gentle caressing of flesh.

"Wolf," she whimpered. With her arms under his, her hands

on his shoulders, and her fingers by his collarbone, she held onto him. A force was building. She wasn't going to be able to stop it. *What the hell?* "Rutger."

"Jo," Rutger whispered by her ear. He rose on his elbows and held her face in his hands, peppering light kisses over her cheeks, eyes, and neck. *Mark her.* "I'm right here."

Jordyn's muscles tensed, she drew her nails down Rutger's back while he continued his deliberate, seductive thrusts. "Kiss me." Rutger's teeth raked from her collarbone to her neck, and moving, he lightly caught her earlobe between his teeth. "Kiss me."

Rutger took her lips. Moaning, she arched her back, her breasts touching his chest, and she exhaled hot power into him. Tasting as dark as her wine, he swallowed and felt it hit his insides, and his wolf raged. *Mark her.*

The energy eased, her power mellowed, and she opened her eyes to Rutger's wolf. As he stared at her, he drew his thrusts into long, slow movements as if feeling every inch of her. Jordyn's hips rose to meet him, her back arching; when their eyes met, the bright gold dimmed.

"Lost in you," Rutger grated. The flare warming him and the hum in his ears settled, giving him Jo's heartbeat.

Jordyn didn't respond. She was far too gone to formulate words. She moaned, he thrust harder; she grabbed his hips, he thrust harder.

Her breathing turned to quick gasps of air tangled in soft whispered moans and he lost himself. With the taste of her on his tongue, he drove as deep as she allowed and roared a low, rough sound. Jo's nails raked his flesh, stopping at his hips when his release took him … them over the edge.

Jordyn's voice lowered with her breathless whimpers as pleasure cascaded through her. She held Rutger while tender quivers held her, and she met Rutger's wolf eyes.

"Mine." Rutger's voice rumbled in his chest. He stared at Jo's half-closed eyes, their colors changing with her emotions. With her smile, he rolled to his left—sweat gleamed in the moonlight—and taking Jo with him, wrapped his arms around her. "What did you do? Can you do it again?"

Jordyn's lips and cheek were damp from his gleaming skin. She listened to his quick heartbeat keep pace with hers and didn't know if she understood what had happened. "I think I shared my power with you."

Rutger didn't say anything, his hand doing slow circles on her back. Jordyn didn't move. She wanted to stay where she was—safe, happy, and satisfied. Jordyn knew better. She needed to clean up her life and take care of her lies. Even those thoughts couldn't dampen the thrill of knowing she let go of her control and hadn't turned it into a bigger mess.

"You're thinking." Rutger nudged her, and she reluctantly faced him.

"I am." After days of feeling tugged in every direction, she felt at peace. Even if it was fleeting.

In the light of the weakening fire, the flames cast dashing shadows over her skin. Rutger watched her feelings pass behind her eyes while they reflected her wolf. "You look exhausted."

Laughing, Jordyn rested her head on his chest. "You don't look any better, Director." She sat up, her thoughts getting the better of her, and crawled away from him.

He released his hold, his hands falling from her hips, and the absence of his touch like a look into the future. She sat on the side of the bed trying to keep the pleasure from fading and searched for her clothes.

"They brought your suitcase and things," Rutger said as he left the bed. Without getting dressed, he walked to the fireplace, and stabbed at the crumbling coals with the stoker. He added wood, watched the fire gain strength, its warmth on his bare skin, and went to his dresser. After choosing a pair of shorts, he stared at his clothes for a second, then grabbed a T-shirt from the drawer. "Here."

Jordyn wore her underwear and dropped her hoodie to the floor. She met Rutger's heated gaze, saw the edge of possession, and took the smoke gray T-shirt. Cascade pack was written across the front, its crest on the back. The soft cotton felt good on her tender skin and matched the rich scent of Rutger and his wolf. "What will happen tomorrow?" Taking a throw, she walked to a chair beside the fire and sat down.

Rutger sat across from Jo, his lack of confidence playing in his thoughts. Damn, he dreaded having the conversation. "I have to go to the office and check in with Ansel. If Detective Watt has new information, I need to talk to the baron about the missing werewolves. Detective Watt would like you to look at the other bodies in case they missed something," he rambled. *She isn't going run. Calm down.* "Are you asking about us?"

"A little of both." The fire popped, its flames climbing, while its heat did little to ease the worry over what she had to do. *Act human and break up with my boyfriend.* "I have to go to Butterfly Valley."

He watched the fire, wanted to demand she stay, and turned to meet her gaze. "Can you wait? I want to go with you. I'll be in the area and I won't interfere. I promise."

Right. "You know I have to do this alone. I have to talk to Louis." With her senses open, it exaggerated the threads of his anger as they reached out. The feel caused her to look at the fire rather than Rutger.

"Jo, look at me. I hate it, but I understand. Will you take someone with you? It doesn't have to be an enforcer. A soldier. Maybe Skylar?" Rutger asked. He tried to keep his jealousy, worry, and frustration out of his voice. He didn't want her going there alone. Why? Because there was a group killing werewolves. No. There was a human.

"I'll consider it."

Rutger heard her yawn, and the smile in her words. *Consider it, okay, babe?* "Let's get some sleep."

CHAPTER EIGHTEEN

The fire popped, its sound nudging Jordyn from her light sleep. She rolled to her side, out of Rutger's hold, and looked at the dying flames. Hazy light of early morning filtered through the window, giving away the rising sun and the time. She didn't want to be awake. She closed her eyes, wanting to sleep until Rutger forced her to wake up and they faced the day.

Together.

Thoughts about Louis and her parents drifted, whispers of what she might say, should say, glided unhindered. "Sleep," she prayed. Her eyes opened with the sound of her cell phone, its shrill ring taking her attention and forcing her from the bed.

Jordyn checked on Rutger and found him sleeping. She hesitated, taking the seconds to admire his body and letting the feel of the night return. Another round of rings sounded, and picking her steps, she made it across the room. After closing the door behind her, she ran down the hall, down the stairs, and to the living room. The ringing ended and replaced with several chimes of a notification. *It's a message, I'm going to ignore*, she thought.

Jordyn searched her bag, found her cell, turned the sound off, and saw several missed calls, a voicemail, and his messages. Her heart pounded, her stomach clenched in panic, and the strength in her legs drained into the floor. The throw from the night before lay at her feet as she sat heavy on the edge of the chair and glared at the picture in his message. Jordyn swore as Rutger, dressed in his tux, gazed down at her, his arm around her waist. The wedding. She read the message, again, trying to decide how she was going to respond. She didn't have any options. She needed to leave. Jordyn quickly typed a reply, begging Louis to stay at her house. She would explain in person. She had to explain. "Please, let me explain."

No way was she going to risk getting clothes from Rutger's room from fear of waking him. She rummaged through the pile sitting on the chair, grabbed her jeans, socks, and running shoes, and quickly dressed. Leaving everything else on the chair, she took her purse and headed out of the house, to her SUV. Jordyn gripped the wheel with shaking hands, and let her tears fall freely. She knew it was coming and knew she had to tell him the truth. She prayed it would be on her terms. *Selfish.*

"Please, be there," she said out loud.

The sounds and images from the night sat in his dreams, Jo's scent in his head, and her feel on his skin, and he sank into her presence. With his eyes closed and his body and wolf resting between sleep and awake, a low rumble of a contented growl left his lips and he leisurely rolled to his side. Rutger extended his arm, his hand searching for her and his mind expecting to touch her warm skin. He needed to feel his mate.

Mine. Another growl rumbled and stopped when the cold sheet stole his thoughts and her absence fell on him like a weight. With sharp fury taking its place, he sat up. *Please*, he thought as he used his senses. "Jo," he mumbled.

Nothing.

She ran.

He threw the covers off, left the bed, and went to his closet, bathroom, and with anxiety riddling his nerves and inventing reasons why she left, he searched his room. Jo's things were exactly where they had been the night before. She didn't take anything. She hadn't taken her camera bag. "Why?" he asked the empty room. The instant anger faded as he headed downstairs. He saw her backpack, its forgotten contents haphazard on the chair, and headed toward it. Her clothes and purse were gone.

Rutger walked to the window and gazed at the lake colored by the warm glow of the morning sun. He wasn't going to chase her. Damn, if she was going to make a fool of him. Again. His hands rested on the waist of his shorts. Jo left wearing his T-shirt. If she was going to leave him and run, she would have changed. She would have taken her things. He turned back to the open backpack, which looked as if she had riffled through it in a hurry. Jo left knowing he would have stopped her. And he would have stopped her. Her camera remained, like a blaring confession she hadn't run. Rutger shoved his beaten pride back, letting his instincts tell him something was wrong. Very wrong. Pushing them aside, he forced himself to calm down and think.

If Jo hadn't run, would the baron take his word for it? Damn the slayers. No. Because of the murders, the baron was already fielding threats from the Highguard, other alphas, and the pack. Making Jo the soothsayer without consulting the Highguard, and her disappearance would pressure him to act. The slayers would be deployed to ensure the baron's show of power and serve as a warning, he would kill one of his own if they disobeyed. Even the soothsayer.

Rutger took his cell and dialed Jo's number, two seconds and her voice told him to leave a message. He told himself she hadn't run, she had gone to Butterfly Valley, to face Louis and the life she was giving up. It didn't explain why she left in a hurry. Torn between going to Foxwood and Butterfly Valley, Rutger took the stairs two at a time, guilt and fear riding his thoughts. He quickly dressed in his black tactical BDU pants, black, long-sleeved shirt with the Cascade pack's emblem on the left side, boots, and after grabbing his gun headed back downstairs.

At the door, he secured his tactical belt and holstered his gun, and headed out of the house to his truck. He would go to Foxwood. He needed to talk to the baron first. Then he was going to Butterfly Valley and getting Jo. On the road, Rutger called Jo several more times, and each time heard her voice.

It took her less than three hours, pushing the speed limit, to drive to Butterfly Valley. With every mile, every minute, she hoped Louis was waiting for her. No matter how many times she messaged him or called, he wouldn't reply. His silence had her mind racing with guilt, regret, and her many lies. Jordyn figured he wasn't going to wait and she couldn't blame him, but then she saw his car in the driveway.

With her heart pounding, Jordyn entered the house and stopped in the living room. Louis stood in front of her, his body taut with his fury and his eyes cold with hate. "I was going to tell you."

"No. You. Weren't." He paced the small room, going from the couch to the kitchen and back. "Was anything you said true? Forget it, I don't want to know."

Hesitantly, Jordyn took four steps. "I didn't lie about us."

He stopped at the kitchen counter and spun around. "Us? I don't think you know what the word means."

"Louis—"

"Is that his shirt? Your ex-boyfriend? Cascade pack? You were really in Trinity." Louis' voice calmed, turned cold, like it was a matter of time before he erupted.

Her heart sped up as her life continued to spiral out of control. Regret turned to sadness—not for losing Louis, for not being able to be honest with him from the beginning. "Louis, there are things."

"Things? Things? I'll tell you a *thing* ... your career is over when everyone finds out *what* you are."

"I didn't lie to hurt you."

"Don't." He inhaled, his chest rising. "It explains why you didn't answer my messages," he mumbled softly and turned away from her, like he couldn't stand the sight of her. "I really thought you were busy with your sister's wedding. I felt guilty, I might be bothering you." He looked at the floor for several seconds, and back to her. "You are a fraud, a liar, and a lycan. You are nothing but an animal." His voice continued to rise with his anger. "Don't insult me by looking hurt. Fucking lycans. It would figure you couldn't control yourself around your own damn kind. Like a damn dog in heat."

"I'm sorry." Jordyn held his stare and saw his anger growing.

"I'm sure. You've made me look like a fool. Who in their right mind would fuck a lycan? Looking at you makes me sick." He turned, his back rigid, and his inhales coming in quick inhales. "Fetch." He turned, threw an envelope at her without making eye contact, and marched to the door.

It landed on the floor at her feet. Jordyn looked at it and back to Louis. "I'm sorry. I wish there was something I could say."

With his back to her, he bowed his head. "No, you don't, or you would have. You weren't going to tell me the truth. You should have left me alone." He walked out and slammed the door.

Jordyn remained in the living room, his verbal attack playing in her ears and the stench of his anger drifting through the house. With slumped shoulders, she stared at the door, expecting him to come back. When the sound of his car faded, she turned and looked at her house. It felt unfamiliar.

From the floor, the manila envelope stared at her. Absently she bent down and picked it up knowing what was inside. With little attention, she walked to the couch, her hands trembling, and sat down. Jordyn carefully flipped the tab back and took the stack of photos. The Timber House. The church. Foxwood. At the Summit, she was wearing her robe. *I sensed them.* But who was it? Who would take pictures of her? Was it blackmail? Were they going to try to destroy her career in Butterfly Valley? An uneasy laugh left her lips. Her career was already over. Someone was targeting her and she needed to tell Rutger where she was and about the pictures.

Jordyn set the photos and envelope on the table and took her cell phone from her pocket and the screen lit up. *Rutger.* Ignoring his messages, she hesitated for a breath before entering the passcode. Jordyn stared at the main screen trying to decide what she was going to say ... what excuse she was going to tell. She left Trinity without an explanation, knowing the baron would send the slayers after their soothsayer. If they found her sitting on the couch and doing nothing would they open fire on her? No, she was sure they would take her back to Trinity, lock her up in a cell, and make an example out of her. As many times as the baron deemed necessary. Of course, only after she healed from the wounds. After running, would they add silver to her wounds so the world knew she had been punished? What would Rutger do?

If she wanted to stop the slayers and live through the day, she needed to call Rutger and the baron. "More explaining," she mumbled.

Sitting back, Jordyn stared at the screen, her thoughts racing around what happened and what she was going to say. "I ran away, to explain my lies to my human. But he dumped me first 'cause I'm a dog in heat," Jordyn said to her phone. She inhaled and tossed the phone to the couch. The only thing left in

Butterfly Valley was the gallery. And someone was trying to take it away from her. A human. Another photographer. Maybe a friend of Louis' found out and wanted to protect him. Mia. She laughed and felt the drive, excitement, and adrenaline purge from her body. She had to call Rutger and explain.

Later. She needed some peace and quiet before the storm.

Jordyn's heart felt like it jumped from her chest with the rapping on the door. She sat up, and staring, figured the slayers would have broken it down, guns blazing. If it was the baron or Rutger, they would have walked right in, not knocked, which meant it might be Louis. On the way to the door, she wondered what he wanted and if he was back for more name calling.

"Jordyn," he greeted with a smile. "You like the pictures? Louis did not."

"Who the hell are you?"

"An admirer."

"What?" Confused, Jordyn held the edge of the door.

"The name is Flint. You'll soon know me by my title."

Right. Her patience crashed and anger moved in; she was going to kick his ass. Threats strung along with curse words touched her lips, when a breeze carrying varied smells of herbs and blood drifted from him and in to the house. She recognized the smell, and taking a deeper breath, knew it from the woods. The body. Herbs. Death. Witch.

"What do you want?" she asked, trying for calm.

His brown eyes, faded as if the sun had bleached them, narrowed. His face held a grimace of shock, like he couldn't believe she questioned him. His dyed, shoulder-length white hair showed an inch of dirty brown roots, giving away its real color. He took a step, trying to get his boot in the door.

"What do you want?" she repeated. Jordyn gripped the edge, held it firm, and easily out powering him forced him to take a step backward.

"You," Flint answered casually. "I know what you are, Soothsayer. And have sensed the darkness inside of you."

"You're a murderer." She was a werewolf, she could take care of one human. Witch or not.

"Yes and no." Smiling, he shoved his hands in the pockets of his jeans and took another step backward.

His feel saturated the air one minute and vanished the next. Jordyn couldn't sense him and he was standing right in front of her. She was staring at him. Her instincts went in to overload when a dark warning pressed on her wolf. Evil. Magic. The charm he was using reached out, feathering her reflexes. She wasn't going to risk fighting him when she wasn't sure what she was fighting. And trying to save a shred of dignity, she wasn't going to risk shapeshifting when her neighbors might see her. Jordyn had to get to her phone and get the hell out of the house. She should have called Rutger.

Jordyn slammed the door closed, locked it, ran to the couch, grabbed her phone, and headed to the back door. Regret chided her for not calling Rutger, its bitterness playing in her uncertainty. Her wolf skimmed the surface, the slightest vibration of power imbedding itself in her nerves, and with her heart in her throat, she searched for others. Nothing. *Doesn't mean they aren't there.* If they were waiting, she was going to bully her way through. She was a trained soldier with the pack, she could take on humans. She opened the door, scanned the yard, and finding it clear made for the side of the house. Jordyn skidded to a stop, the grass covering the toes of her running shoes, and stared at the four men.

"I looked forward to you running. Your blood rushing through your veins. Your heart pounding. The monster inside of you and your power rising to the fight. I can feel your energy reaching out as we speak." His voice hung in the air. "As a soldier, I believe you could take us all. But you won't."

They knew her position in the pack. He had been watching and knew no one was going to save her.

"Can't."

"Don't bet on it." She wasn't a lycan pretending to be human. If her neighbors were going to judge her for being a werewolf, well, that's just the way it went. She was moving anyway. Jordyn needed to shift into her wolf form. It meant losing her phone but worth the risk. She pressed the home button on her cell, and another. "What do you want with me?" she asked, stalling for time. Jordyn watched them as she let her cell slip from her hand. It landed in the grass beside her shoe, the screen glittering in the sun.

"You're my pendulum. You're going to give life to our god."

The image of the corpse filled her eyes as its pain sank inside of her. "No."

"Yes, Soothsayer. Your dark power will be the elixir he needs to live." Flint smiled, his lips drew back from his teeth.

No one moved. They waited and watched her like she was a wild animal.

Jordyn took three uneasy steps backwards at the same time she fought to bring her wolf to the surface. Quickly denied, its strength and power slipped from her grasp. "You're insane." Her voice felt frail, her words sounding slow and weak.

"Breathe deep, Soothsayer."

"No." Jordyn shook her head, trying to clear the fog. "You aren't going to take me." Her words slurred.

His mocking laugh echoed. "I will. It may take a minute. With you maybe a minute and a half," Flint boasted. "But I will take you. Just like the others."

They waited. And watched.

Threads of gray invaded her mind, confusing her while

slivers of thoughts slipped from her. Grasping for focus, Jordyn tried to call her wolf. Her wolf spirit weakened as fatigue invaded her muscles, nausea sat in her stomach, and the gray turned black. As if the earth had been pulled out from under her and the air was holding her, she felt weightless. For a breath. It came crashing down, and she hit the ground. The grass, damp with dew, cradled her while its green blades blurred her vision.

"The mighty soothsayer has fallen. Get her," Flint ordered. "We have to get out of here."

"Yes, Savior," Brother William answered. He rushed forward at the same time he took a handful of zip ties from his back pocket. "She'll be out until we get to Belle Ridge?"

"Yes," Flint confirmed.

"What about her phone?" Brother Ben asked as he joined Brother William.

"I want the Wolf Enforcer to find it." Flint knelt beside Jordyn and brushed her hair from her face. "You're mine now."

"Go to hell, Flint." She hated that she slurred the words.

"There is no hell. There's this world. And the world belonging to the gods. You're going to the gods."

Jordyn barely heard him over the pain gripping her wolf, and tearing at her insides. "Hurts," she whispered and curled into a ball.

"Yes, it does," Flint replied.

His voice faded as Rutger and his presence, like a weak breeze, drifted around her and weakened her wolf. He would find her corpse in a field covered in herbs and missing body parts. Jordyn felt the pressure of tears, and struggling to stay focused, tried crawling away from the approaching men.

"Crawling. Your strength is incredible but not enough," Flint taunted.

Hands were on her and they jerked her backward. Shadows surrounded her, and after binding her hands and ankles, turned her to her back. They lifted her and through tree limbs, she watched the cerulean sky. Jordyn blinked, blue, black, blue, black. Black.

"I'm telling you there's something wrong." Rutger paced to burn nervous energy, while his voice was nearing a yell. "She won't answer her phone."

"Control yourself, son. I have no other choice but to send the slayers. She is a risk to the pack," Healey said through a breath. "If she went to Butterfly Valley, Alpha Howard will make sure he speaks to her. I can't let him. Damn, I can't believe she ran."

"She didn't. Last night she said she had to talk to Louis, alone. It was something she had to do."

"Jordyn left without telling you. Without clean clothes? Those actions prove it was desperation. She ran," Healey challenged.

The night came back as Rutger turned and stormed over to the baron. "She didn't take her camera, and is wearing the same clothes she did yesterday." *My T-shirt.* "Something happened. Let me go."

"You have obligations here. Remember, there's a serial killer to find," Healey countered.

"She's mine," Rutger growled out.

"You were intimate last night?"

"What?" Rutger looked at the baron.

"If you were intimate, did you mark her?" Healey met Rutger's gold gaze.

Failure. "No. That hasn't been done in decades and is seen as barbaric," Rutger explained.

"But you wanted to. It was there, the instinct."

"Yes. I can't deny it, not anymore."

"You denied your wolf?" Healey pushed.

"I thought becoming the soothsayer and having her future in Butterfly Valley ripped from her was enough for one day," Rutger seethed. She had been scared to death to face her power and allow her wolf freedom. He wasn't going to add an irrelevant custom to the mix. And he wasn't going to hurt her.

Healey's worries lessened. He prepared to explain the connection Rutger shared with Jordyn, as a fated pair. If Jordyn ran, she would face the slayers, and they would bring her back for punishment. When her pain and blood saturated the air, Rutger would feel her, and the taste of her agony would sit in his head. Rutger saved himself from hearing her cries by not marking her. "Son." Healey stopped, and both men watched Laurel enter the office, worry on her face, and her fear out for them to feel.

"She knew the risk. Jordyn wouldn't run," she offered. Laurel walked to Rutger, took his arm, and met his gaze. "If she was going to run, she wouldn't have stayed with you. Son, you need to go."

"And if she denies you?"

"If she denies me—" Rutger stopped, images of her and the sounds of her breathless moans in his head. "When I bring her back, she'll deserve whatever punishment your slayers can think of," Rutger answered.

Laurel squeezed his arm, before letting go to stand beside his father. A united front.

"Go, son." Healey prayed Rutger was right as he wrapped his arm around Laurel.

Without another word, Rutger walked out of the office, heading down the hall and toward the front door when his cell sounded. Ignoring it, he left the house and got in his truck. It rang again and he answered, "Kanin."

CJ explained Detective Watt called, that he and his team were checking into witch covens, the Crimson Years, and the history of Paradise County, Trinity, and Butterfly Valley. If they were looking for a coven of witches, maybe there was something connecting them to the cities. She added the report on the body, stating there was hemlock, henbane, coriander, and liquor of black poppy stuffed where his spine should have been. "I don't know what some of those things are," she mumbled.

Rutger listened but wasn't listening. He muttered vague responses and agreed when required.

"Rutger, there was wolf's bane injected into his bloodstream. It paralyzed him. He was alive when they started cutting him up. They're using werewolf weaknesses against their victims. It explains the lack of resistance," CJ said.

No shit. "Has Detective Watt had any luck with the list?" Rutger asked.

"Yes, he'll have confirmation later today. Said he would meet up with you."

"I'm headed to Butterfly Valley, I'll be back this evening. I'll meet with him then," Rutger explained. Of course, the investigation was moving forward. If Jo denied him, he wouldn't be meeting up with Watt, he would be staring at Jo as she sat in a cell and waited for her punishment.

"Butterfly Valley?"

"Don't." Rutger ended the call.

Outside Trinity city limits, his mind took apart the night before and he saw each moment and felt each touch as if they would tell him what she was thinking when she left. "I know you didn't run."

"Soothsayer." The grumbled voice sounded distant. "Let me introduce myself. I'm Savior."

Jordyn opened her eyes to a dimly lit room. Gradually coming into focus, the walls were a combination of dirt and stone, and smelled damp, musty, and there was an underlying scent she didn't want to accept. Its potent stench wove around her and made her gag. Jordyn turned to her side; the movement induced a coughing fit, its force tightening her diaphragm and her hands held her chest. When it stopped, and she could breathe, her cheek rested on soft dirt and the smell of werewolves thickened around her.

"While wolf's bane stops you from shifting, the lack of strength hurts your human body. It took several attempts, and failures, but I mastered its use," Flint explained. He stood outside of the cell, thick bars making up walls and separating them. His fake white hair was held back by a rubber band, and he traded his flannel shirt and jeans for a dirty blue cotton top and matching pants. It looked like something from a hospital.

"Wolf's bane," she mumbled. The human world learned the ridiculous legend was true and exploited it as a weapon. Like silver. Wolf's bane held the wolf in trace, in a drugged state, while the human body remained conscious and weak. It made shapeshifting and healing impossible and left the werewolf defenseless. It explained the all over itching and pain in her joints.

"You'll be here for a couple of days. For the safety of my brethren, you'll be drugged."

"Savior. The next sacrifice has been prepared." A woman's voice rang inside of the room.

"Very well, Sister Mary. I will join you shortly," Flint responded.

Jordyn remained silent. She didn't care to acknowledge the man, and didn't want to think about the next victim. She concentrated on working through the drugs and getting off the floor. The sour stench of blood and death pushed her fear, creating panic. When she thought she could move without getting ill, she got her knees under her, and slowly, got to her feet. Jordyn stood, a small victory, looked at Flint, and down at her clothing. Nausea quickly rose to her throat and dizziness gripped her head as hot embarrassment, disgrace, and humiliation swallowed her. They took her clothes. The cotton shirt hung on her shoulders and matching pants had been cinched around her waist to keep them from falling. Dried blood circled both wrists, covering the cuts where the zip ties dug into her skin, and dirt dusted her hands, feet, and ankles. Jordyn swayed, stumbled backwards, fell onto an old cot, and hit her head on the wall. A spray of white dots blazed in front of her.

"Careful," Flint warned, approaching the cell. "I have moved among your pack unnoticed and have taken the sacrifice from your numbers. He will serve as the heart as you will serve as the soul."

No. No. Jordyn tried protesting. She sank down, slid to her right side, and gazed at Flint's blurred form.

"I won't fill your veins with wolf's bane, I want your mind active and your nightmares free to haunt you," Flint explained. "I want wolf's bane burning around the clock in here," Flint ordered Sister Mary.

"Yes, Savior."

The questions and their grumbled voices faded, and Jordyn didn't know who was talking or if it was her mind. Fear moved through her as she descended into the drugs and the pain ate away at her insides. Each minute felt like a thousand knives being shoved into her body. *Rutger will find me*, she told herself.

How? Savior's voice asked.

She squeezed her eyes shut, trying to stop herself from crying. *He loves me.*

Not good enough, he mocked.

"Go to sleep, Soothsayer. It'll make the time pass easier." Flint's deep voice waned as she fell into the abyss.

CHAPTER NINETEEN

Rutger made it back to Foxwood when evening had taken the day. Parking his truck, his heart stopped when he saw a silver luxury SUV. Lord and Lady Langston. They knew Jo had run and he had chased after her. Hanging his head, he gripped the steering wheel, not wanting to have to face Jo's parents. He closed his eyes, saw Jo sitting on his bed, and knew he was wasting time—time he couldn't afford. Her image faded when he looked at the SUV. After several more seconds, he killed the engine, got out, and made his way to the house.

In silence, Sousa and Abigail sat by as he entered the house, and in the hall Jason and Sadie watched him stand in the entrance of the living room. He couldn't go any farther. As Director of Enforcers, he faced pack members, advised discipline, and stood as witness to the slayers. He never considered he would be telling Jo's parents she had been kidnapped.

"Where is she?" Healey asked. He stood, and with questions in his eyes, he searched Rutger's face.

"Jo." Stopping, he directed his gaze out the window, unable to look at them. "Jordyn."

"What?" Ethan asked. He stood, took three steps, and stopped. "Did you leave her in Butterfly Valley? Her life is at risk. The slayers will be deployed."

"What would make you think she would come back here?" Mia quipped. "She doesn't care about anyone here."

Healey met the accusations in Mia's eyes. "Son, did Jordyn deny you?"

"No." God no. Rutger inhaled, exhaled, and inhaled again, struggling to focus. "No."

"Rutger," Healey pushed.

"Jo has been kidnapped."

"What?" Ethan asked. His eyes narrowed, their natural color draining. "Not possible."

"Who would kidnap Jordyn?" Healey asked. If they knew about her, anyone could have.

"I don't know," Rutger answered, feeling helpless. It was tempting to tell them the first twenty-four hours were the most critical, that there were deputies looking for her, and the sheriff's department along with the California Highway patrol had issued an amber alert. But part of him knew they wouldn't buy his false enthusiasm and reciting the speech wasn't going to be good enough. "I have her cell phone. They aren't going to break into it until they have more information. Detective Watt talked to local law enforcement, and they let me have it. In case I can access her information. If anything happens to her, they need it back. It's been fingerprinted, and the prints entered in to the Citizen Base and the National Criminal Log."

"Son, we're adults, not children. If we know the details, we might be able to help."

Rutger considered the baron. While he didn't want to discuss the case with them, the baron would be able to help. Maybe Lord Langston. He hesitated to say anything and worry Lady Langston or the baroness any more than necessary. And, the case was out of their territory, making his involvement tougher. "I think her kidnapping is connected to my investigation."

"You mean the murders?" Laurel asked hesitantly.

"Yes." Rutger drew the word out, his voice a rough whisper. Bowing his head, he stared at the carpet like the floor would open and swallow him.

"Wait. The murder cases?" Ethan asked. "She went with you?" His body tensed, his shoulders absorbing every ounce of stress and worked to hold onto it.

"I said I think. I could be wrong. They're doing their investigation. I have to talk to the detective in charge. Like I said, I have her cell phone." He tried to distract them from the murders and didn't want the baron bringing up witches.

"I don't know what good it'll do, it's protected by a passcode. All phones are," Ethan stated, his facts coming from him wrapped in nervous energy. He took several steps, stopped and turned, his eyes searched Rutger, his senses out to feel any emotion coming from him.

"I know. I was hoping one of you might have an idea." Rutger slowly took it out of the evidence bag and hit the side button to turn it on. After a second, he saw ten missed calls and three voice messages. His strength drained away. They were all from him.

"She didn't talk to us. We lost her when she left," Mia admitted. "The phone is a waste of time."

Rutger found a chair and sat down when he recognized the picture in the background. "Jo," he whispered.

"What is it?" Ethan asked. He took a step forward and stopped. "What?"

"Rutger." Healey approached him. His power swirling in the room. "Son."

"It's Klamath Falls," he mumbled. Old oak trees stood tall, their leaves bright green in the slices of sunlight, and he could feel her excitement.

"And?" Mia asked. She turned in her seat to face the men and crossed her legs. "What does that mean? She was always taking pictures of everything."

"She kept it." Rutger closed his eyes as the day played. Her eyes lit up, liquid bronze, and her heartbeat sounded in his ears like a rhythm created only for him.

"Explain," Healey demanded.

The melody faded and Rutger stood, his anger flowing through him, replacing the toxic mix of fear, worry, and the panic wanting to have its way. They had been torn apart and thrown back together. Now he was going to lose her. "Klamath Falls. It's where I asked her to marry me. She said yes." His voice rose as he stared at the picture.

Ethan approached Rutger. "What did you say?"

Rutger met Lord Langston's glare, his anger burning in his eyes. "I asked her to marry me. She said yes."

"No," Ethan protested. His daughter would have told him. "Not possible."

Rutger set the phone down, and tugging on the left sleeve of his shirt, pulled his arm free. "Yes. Our rings are here." Everyone saw the linked silver and the truth. Knowing what he had to do next, Rutger fixed his shirt and grabbed the phone. "When she left, we had already promised ourselves to one another." The screen changed and he touched the numbers reflecting the date. It opened to a picture of a sunset.

"I don't understand why she didn't tell us." Ethan's disbelief in his words. "She left and kept it a secret for three years."

"She received the partnership with the gallery. Jordyn abandoned Rutger to hang pictures," Mia seethed. She twisted her hands, making her skin turn white.

"No. I'm not saying we didn't have our problems but it wasn't the gallery. Jo saw us. Kory and I on the beach. Kory started hanging on me, kissing me, I didn't stop her. When I pushed her away, she told me Jo was going to end our relationship. Kory insisted Jo thought my position in the pack was the reason everyone was coming down on us, and she hated being trapped in Trinity. I didn't believe Kory. We were going to be married. I kept looking for her, but never saw her. Last night, Jo said she felt Kory's emotions, my emotions, and believed I betrayed her. Jo thought the burden to be perfect and our problems were too much for us to deal with. I didn't know about the partnership, and when I asked the baron, he said she was free to leave. I didn't understand." Rutger continued to stare at her phone.

"We all are to blame," Laurel whispered.

"Your little soothsayer," Mia mumbled as she stared at Ethan. "She should have stayed in Butterfly Valley."

"After three years of her silence and living day to day, I wanted closure. I thought the night we were at the Timber House, she would confront me. I wanted Jo to tell me it was over and I could move on. Then we ran into each other. Her eyes blazed with her wolf, and I felt her as if she never left. That was why I kissed her at the church. Whatever drove her to leave, wasn't because she didn't love me." Rutger felt like he was rambling, but he had to get it out. *Fated.*

"Son, I feel for you," Laurel said softly. He had been holding onto the pain for three years.

"You knew. Jordyn wanted to leave and you let her. You let her walk away when you could have stopped her," Ethan accused, his narrowed gaze landing hard on Healey.

Rutger looked at the baron. "You knew about her and wanted her separated from the pack. You let my mate leave."

"I did. Us, the pack, the pressure was getting worse. When Jordyn asked to leave, she used you and the partnership as an excuse, and yes, I let her move. I hoped she would fight for what she wanted. Jordyn needed to be strong if the two of you were going to survive. And I waited for her to come into her power. Son, I would never put your relationship, that we all wanted, at risk," Healey explained. "I wouldn't deny you your fated mate."

"Not possible. There hasn't been a fated couple in the Cascade pack in a century," Ethan argued.

"We are fated. We both believe it," Rutger insisted. "Kory told Jo to ask you. They talked the night of the women's run." Rutger turned to Lady Langston.

Ethan turned his glare to his wife. "Ask you about what?"

"The pack wasn't tearing them apart. Her selfish need to be a photographer was tearing them apart. It was a matter of time before she left the pack behind," Mia answered. "Just like she did. It's proof there is no such thing as fated."

"No. At the reception, we watched Jordyn when she found out Rutger stepped down. She didn't care. She would stand with him if he chose to live in a cardboard box. Hating his status sounds like something you would say, Mia. Seeing Kory and Rutger together pushed her. What did you do?" Ethan demanded.

Mia wouldn't crumble under their scrutiny despite her lies coming back to haunt her. As she tried to keep herself from falling apart, and keeping their past in the past, Mia couldn't stop her tears from slipping down her cheeks. She continued twisting her hands and inhaled, exhaled, attempting to control her breathing. Ethan remained by the window, watching her, accusations running in his eyes, and she knew he wasn't going to comfort her. *Fine.* "Jordyn left the pack. She left Rutger. Bailey is my focus. My daughter would never deceive the pack the way Jordyn has." She laughed a nervous fake sound and met each set of eyes narrowed on her.

"What did you do?" Ethan demanded.

"Jordyn told me about the partnership and said she was going to tell Rutger. I knew she was going to sacrifice their relationship. Kory wouldn't. She would be there for Rutger and the pack. I sent Kory to his house to tell him as much and made sure Jordyn saw them." Mia stood, her back straight, her defiance becoming part of her. "Rutger admitted he didn't push Kory away. He knew what was coming."

"No," Rutger shot back. "When I touched Kory, there was a numbness. With Jo, it's like an obsession."

Laurel tore her gaze away from Rutger and faced Mia. *How could you destroy your child? My child?* "Why would you purposely hurt her?"

"Laurel, you don't know her. Jordyn isn't like us. I don't have to explain myself, when you made her the pack's soothsayer. She was better off gone," Mia countered.

"Jordyn had a dream and because you didn't like it, you drove *our* daughter away and made sure you destroyed her relationship. You created a lie and blamed Jordyn. She's been living like a rogue and taking your verbal abuse for three years." Ethan's anger was draining under the absurdity.

"Jordyn stopped taking your abuse when she decided she was leaving and never coming back. You pushed her, and she would have left the pack and lived like a rouge," Rutger accused. He would have lost her.

"Healey wouldn't allow her to live as a rogue. All of you know it. It doesn't change the embarrassment she brought to the family when she left," Mia said weakly and sat down.

"Mia, you embarrass me." Laurel swore.

"Baroness." Healey's voice lowered. By referring to his wife by her title, he was giving her a subtle warning. When she turned away, he knew she understood not to press further. "No, I wouldn't. I had protectors for her, and an arrangement with Alpha Howard. She would never hold the title of rogue. I didn't know the extent of Mia's interference or I would have taken different steps."

Rutger stopped listening to the chatter and read through Jo's messages. His jealousy spiking as his heart began to pound. "*I know what you are. I know everything,"* Rutger said loud enough, everyone stopped arguing and listened. *"It'll take a couple of hours. Please, stay. I can explain. Wait for a lycan. I might be here. I might not.* Along with the messages, she tried to call him several times. Louis sent her a picture of us together at the church. The detectives found an envelope with other photos. The church, the restaurant, Foxwood, and the Summit. Someone gave them to Louis, told him she was a werewolf, and threw our relationship in his face. They have been watching her."

"How do you know?" Ethan asked.

"The sheriff's department showed me the pictures. Like a warning, I'm a potential victim. Louis reported he went back to talk to her but she was already gone. He called the authorities when he found the house empty and her phone in the backyard. While I was there, the sergeant in charge determined it was an abduction and called a detective with the Butterfly Valley crime unit. I called Detective Watt and explained the situation."

"I cancelled the shadows when I thought she would stay." Healey shook his head.

"I don't think it would have mattered. Knowing they couldn't get to her while she was here, they used the pictures as bait. Jo drove to Butterfly Valley, alone, and they grabbed her." Rutger growled the words.

"A picture of her at the Summit. During the women's run she expressed the need to end it and head back. I did. I didn't question her. She didn't say what it was, but a feeling," Laurel added.

"During the run?" Rutger looked at the baroness, her kiss of heated power coming back to him.

"Yes. After shapeshifting we headed toward the creek, when Jordyn— Wait." She stopped talking. "She sent me a message, not words. It was a feeling, conveyed through thought. I didn't think to tell you."

"She reached you with thought?" Healey asked.

"Yes. And I responded," Laurel answered. She looked at Healey, wanting answers to a question she wasn't sure she could define, and at Rutger through the eyes of a mother.

"I can try to reach her," Healey stated.

"How? No one knows how she created the link." Rutger wasn't getting his hopes up. He needed solid evidence.

"Her power … feel, essence, felt like you," Laurel said to Healey.

He held his wife's gaze, unable to admit his nightmares and the triggers haunting him had disappeared when Jordyn absorbed them. "We are linked with the pack. If I use the power it might be enough to learn she is all right," Healey explained, and turned away from Laurel.

"I'm not confident with her power, but anything is worth a try. In the meantime, what do we do? What's the next step?" Ethan looked at Rutger.

"If her abduction is connected to the cases I've been working, then the Organized Paranormal Investigations and Detective Watt will be in charge. The OPI is already in charge of investigating the murders here in Trinity and I'm talking with the detective," Rutger explained.

"We have to find her." Ethan clenched his hands into fists. "I feel helpless."

"As a soldier for the pack, she should have been able to beat humans," Mia said from the couch.

Knowing the truth about the case, and there was a chance witches were involved, Healey growled as he turned to face Mia. Her callousness was getting the better of him. "You don't know what you're talking about."

"Enough," Rutger growled through gritted teeth. Tension traced across his shoulders, its fire settling at the base of his neck.

"Son, you're not going to like this, but if the witches kidnapped her, they know what she is," Healey said.

"Witches?" Ethan asked.

"Yes. Witches. They could be anywhere." Rutger growled.

"Witches have your soothsayer," Mia said, looking at Healey. "You brought this to our door."

"Enough, Mia. They were watching her. They planned on her reaction," Ethan mumbled.

"You need to explain yourself," Healey ordered.

"No one in Butterfly Valley knew she was a werewolf, and I'm guessing she wouldn't risk shifting. In human form and scared, her wolf's instincts would push her. It provokes the power and causes her to open herself to them. Untrained, her senses, would be like exposed nerve endings and would try to isolate their power. Jordyn could have used their power to strengthen her wolf," Ethan stated.

"How do you know?" Healey asked.

"I never accepted my craft. But my mother—"

"Your mother died in the encampment with mine," Healey interrupted.

"No. No. When the Crimson Years were coming to an end and they started rounding up magic born and the paranormal, my mother fled, leaving us alone. The woman in the encampment was my aunt," Ethan corrected. "After we were released, I heard rumors my mother was alive and hiding with the fairies around the Mount Shasta area. Those were rumors and no one, including myself was going to find out. We had freedom, a life, were planning to have children. I wasn't going to risk losing my place in the pack because of her."

"Why would lose everything?" Healey pushed.

"Everything changed. The world we once knew ceased to exist. I didn't want my mother, a creature from the past, around my family. Not when there was a lot of superstition surrounding her."

"Superstition," Mia repeated and huffed. "She was dark."

Ethan walked to the window. "It was said she was dark. No one knew for sure. But fear is fear."

"If she was dark … wait, was?" Healey asked. Understanding and the reason for Ethan's fear sunk in. "You didn't accept your craft for fear you would be dark. You think Jordyn is dark?"

Ethan looked at Mia, Rutger, and back to Healey. "When Jordyn was hours old, her eyes glowed with her power and she shifted into her wolf form. I held a pup with bronze eyes. Minutes later, my mother appeared and passed her powers onto Jordyn. I'm sorry, Rutger." With slumped shoulders, he walked back to the couch and sat down beside Mia. Guilt rested on him like a concrete blanket. Mia started the betrayal and he nailed Jordyn inside of a coffin she would never escape. He should have been honest with her. "I guess we all have our secrets. I believed by not telling her, she wouldn't accept her power. I never would have guessed you would push her the way you did."

"Healey, your need to take us all back to the forgotten ages is what caused this. The Crimson Years are in the past like those ridiculous traditions. The Highguard's representatives were here, and it's a matter of time before they find out what you have done. The pack will pay the consequences," Mia accused.

"Wife," Ethan growled. He turned to Rutger. "I have to know, what happened after the ceremony?"

"Rutger wait, before you answer. What happened to your mother, Ethan?" Healey asked, ignoring Mia.

"She died."

"Before or after Jordyn shapeshifted?" Healey continued.

"Jordyn shapeshifted before, on her own, like I said, and after my mother passed." He leaned forward, his elbows on his thighs, his face in his hands, his fingers pushing through his hair, and his memories haunting him. "My mother ... I tell you, it was at the same time. Exactly at the same time. Jordyn has always been a soothsayer and I did nothing to help her."

"Jordyn absorbed your mother's powers as an infant. Naturally. She has been using it for years. When I approached her, she was scared but didn't back down, didn't question me, she took everything I was and it fed her power. At the Summit, she absorbed the pack's collective, and found her place. Jordyn knew by instinct she needed a pack." Healey looked at Rutger. "What happened between the two of you?"

"I felt her at the Summit. If I'm right, she wears a mark," Ethan interrupted as he sat up. He watched Rutger's indecision, and the shadow passing behind his eyes with his memories.

Rutger's mind raced. Words were useless. He couldn't explain what happened between them. He tried to tell himself it wasn't because she was a soothsayer, it was them. Their need. Their passion. "We talked, and she didn't show any signs of, damn it, anything. She can conceal her power, her wolf, anything giving away her true self. When she let go of her control, her power flowed through her as freely as the blood in her veins. And together—" He stopped and saw the tangle of obsidian, bronze, and chocolate of her eyes. "She does wear a mark. It's like fire burned it in her skin."

"What is it?" Ethan asked, and with his curiosity, he stood.

Rutger set the phone on the table and took a pen and small notebook from his pocket. He flipped through the tattered pages dark with his writing and found a clean sheet. He met Ethan's eyes for a second and started drawing. The scratching sound of pen to paper was the only noise. When he finished, he handed it to Ethan.

"This is an old rune. My family's history has several. When a soothsayer is enshrined in the power of their alpha, each wears a symbol of possession. It gives them an identity and warns others they are taken. It also hints at their power. The X means territory, she belongs to the Cascade pack, and the box in its middle means dragon. It was my great, great grandfather's crest. Jordyn has a territory and wears one of the oldest runes. Jordyn holds the dragon." Ethan stopped himself from going on.

"Is it light or dark?" Rutger asked. A simple mark would determine Jo's life. Dropping his notebook and pen, he grabbed the phone, its contents a comfort.

"It means she's marked by the ancients and is powerful. Her crafts could be limitless. Like talking to Laurel. There's no light or dark. I can't believe it. I've spent my life listening to lies and worrying about her." Ethan released a breath as if he had been holding it for a lifetime.

"Anything I can do to help?" Gavin asked. He placed his hand on Rutger's shoulder and took the cell phone from him. "She has a voice message here."

"I left three of them," Rutger replied absently, his mind racing with the truth about Jo.

"I see that. I meant, she has a voice memo. It's time stamped eight this morning," Gavin explained.

"Let me see." Rutger took the phone and looked. Preoccupied with Jo, the pictures, and his memories, he hadn't noticed the memo. He fumbled with the phone, his hands shaking as he tried to hit the correct button. What was he going to hear? Maybe a simple reminder. He would hear her voice and it troubled him while it made him anxious.

"Easy, brother, let me." Gavin waited for Rutger to hand it to him. He wasn't going to risk taking it from him. Rutger met his stare, his eyes showing his wolf, and grudgingly gave it up. Gavin touched the screen and voices came alive.

Silence stole over the room, and they all froze as Jo's voice sounded. A man threatened her, and turning light, mocked her and her wolf.

"Breathe deep, soothsayer."

Jo's slurred speech etched its sadness in the room. *"You're not going to take me."* They waited and heard her hit the ground.

"The mighty soothsayer has fallen. You're mine now."

"Go to hell, Flint," Jordyn mumbled.

"Crawling," the voice mocked.

Rutger moved toward the phone as if he could reach in and pull her free. If he could reach in and kill the man responsible for hurting her. Jo's whispers died under footsteps and the conversations taking place. The pain in her words and the sound she made as she fell, destroyed the strength he was using to stay in control.

"They know she's a soothsayer," Healey said, regret heavy in his tone.

"I never want to hear that again," Laurel mumbled. She met Healey, wrapped her arms around him, and rested her forehead on his chest. She wanted to soak in his strength, his calm, and wanted to stop the fear.

Ethan watched Laurel and felt her pain. Hate and jealousy besieged him. "They call him savior, but she said Flint. Play it again," Ethan demanded.

"No. Please, don't," Mia pleaded.

"Don't pretend to care. Play it again," Ethan insisted, the icy edge in his words a slap in Mia's face.

Gavin looked at Rutger, searching his eyes, face, and his reaction to the recording. Embodying strength and confidence, Rutger seemed shaken. His dark eyes battled between showing his fear and burying it. His broad shoulders, slumped enough to prove he wasn't the unbreakable wolf, second to the alpha, he wanted everyone to think he was. Gavin saw the slightest nod and touched the arrow. Jo's voice echoed off the tension in the room.

"They took her believing she's dark," Healey whispered.

Ethan met Healey's gaze. "The others are talking." He closed his eyes and concentrated on the differences. "I think they mentioned they're going to ... Belle Ridge. I don't recognize the name."

"With a name like savior, it sounds more like a cult than a coven," Gavin said.

"Cult or coven, I'll play devil's advocate ... and say Flint and Belle Ridge are both false names. They didn't worry about saying them because neither will give away their plans," Healey added. The enforcers, soldiers, and slayers were all told to use fake names if confronted.

Rutger lost her once and wasn't going to again. "Flint might be a long shot. But Belle Ridge could be an old name. They left one of the victims at Canyon Flats. Through its history, the name changed." Rutger was letting hope and all its cruelness push out his fear.

"Jordyn made sure she said his name. Flint is real," Gavin said.

"Agreed. She started the voice memo and knew what she was doing," Ethan insisted.

"I'm siding with Healey and using caution. This isn't the first time they've done this. They could have several fake names. Why would they say who they are and where they're going, when they know the Wolf Enforcer will search for her?" Laurel asked. "They kidnapped his mate." Her forehead creased with worry as her velvet eyes met Rutger's.

"They can cloak their presence from us. There have been three murders, and at each scene there has been a witch. No one sensed her, except Jo. They have the only person capable of sensing them. Flint doesn't fear saying anything, because in his mind, he has gotten away with the crimes. He might believe he's untouchable," Rutger explained. There was more. There was going to be another murder and the witches would prove their strength and mock his weakness.

"His confidence will be the end of him." Healey growled.

"What is it, Rutger? You're thinking something," Ethan asked. He watched Rutger with dark eyes streaked with pain.

"They mutilated the bodies," Rutger confessed.

"Dear God," Laurel whispered.

Rutger met the baroness' eyes for a heartbeat, forced control, and met the baron's. "We believe they're using the body parts for a spell, an incantation, a ritual, and they know I'm second to the alpha and the soothsayer's mate. The baron announced us at the Summit, the same time the picture was taken. They want me to find her." His heart felt like it was seizing in his chest. Rutger walked away from the group to look out the window. The feel of evil dwelling inside of the witches crawled over his skin.

"Why?" Ethan asked.

"They tortured the victims before cutting them up. Using their pain for their magic," Rutger responded without turning around.

"What does that have to do with you?" Laurel asked.

The ultimate power. "They want me to watch. Pain. Suffering. Death." His words were virtually tearing him apart. The weight of their truth induced images of the victims, their bodies, and their loss, he didn't want to see. "Our suffering will be part of the ritual."

Healey wrapped his arms around Laurel, held her close, and looked at his son's back. "This is blood magic. You have to explain the murders to me, in detail."

CHAPTER TWENTY

Jordyn slowly sat up, the comforter falling from her to the lush bed, and swung her legs off the side. Back in Rutger's room, she stood and started toward the double doors leading to the balcony. Rutger was there, on the other side, waiting. She needed to warn him. She needed to tell him something evil was coming.

"Soothsayer." The name scrawled its path through her thoughts like the devil. Its primal needs brought her past and future together in a whirl of emotions. With her hand on the brushed silver handle, she stopped, unable to go any farther. "Soothsayer."

Her breath left her lungs, her body ached with emptiness, and her mind fought to break through the murkiness of her imagination. She jerked her hand back from the handle when an electrical shockwave set her skin on fire. With panic drowning her, she tried leaving the room.

Flint sat on the edge of the cot, his hand on her stomach, and watched her dream. "Two days and you will leave this weak body." He scooted closer, moved onyx strands of hair away from her face, and drew his finger down her cheek to her chin. Tilting her head, her eyelids moved, her lips parted, and he bent down, leaving a sliver of space between them.

"Savior, sorry for the interruption."

"What is it?" Flint remained, watching her chest rise with her breathing, and her face twist with her dream. The simple herbs he used to keep her sedated were hallucinogens. By giving them to her, he trapped her in her own head. As she drifted into the chaos, he imagined what a soothsayer would be seeing and wondered what images Jordyn was seeing. Slowly, he feathered his hand over her face and felt her warm breath on his palm.

"Savior, the collection has bathed the heart's ewer and Brother Miles is ready to put it to rest," Sister Andrea reported. Her bright red hair sat on her shoulders, her green eyes, once like emeralds but deadened by her past, narrowed on him. Above them the chimes came to life. The harmony intertwined with the wind to rush through the trees and forest to fall from the sky to their ears. Its chorus pacifying her heart and adding to Savior's power and promises.

Brother Miles. The name invaded Jordyn's nightmare, creating men's faces where there had been blank areas. They stalked closer, their steps eating the distance, and their evil radiating from them. She needed to leave. Jordyn rushed to the door and reached for the handle, the shiny silver glaring at her as her hand passed through.

Flint stood, taking in Jordyn's ability to sense him, before leaving her alone. "The sacrifice will rest at his home. At Foxwood."

Rutger spent the night in his office in hopes Detective Watt or someone from the Butterfly Valley sheriff's department called him with news. There were no calls.

The next morning, he sent a recording of Jo's voice message along with her pictures to Detective Watt in hopes they would help. Watt assured they were doing everything they could and when they had a lead, he would let Rutger know. The standard line to appease Rutger's questions and to get him off the phone. With the helpless feeling getting the better of him, he worked through his paperwork, sent several enforcers to patrol Trinity's city limits, and busied his mind with work.

At the end of the day, he had to get out of his office. He walked to the main house; the sun had set, its golds and pinks staining the sky and highlighting the gathering clouds. Dressed in his uniform and gun, he sat at the baron's desk, tapping on computer keys and searching for anything relating to Belle Ridge, old or new. His attempts with every page, every bit of information turning up nothing pushed his frustration to spiral out of control.

"I have contacted a coven, and their mistress is willing to help us." Healey stood behind Rutger, rested his hands on his son's shoulders, and squeezed. "We'll find her."

"They planned her abduction. I think they plan on keeping her until the summer solstice, which is in two days. Two. What will they do to her in that time?" Rutger asked.

"Why do you suspect the summer solstice?"

"There's nothing else. Do you know what kind of traditions there are for the solstice?"

"Nothing in modern times. Like many Pagan traditions they have been forgotten … practicing fakes not included." Healey held his cell, and after a second, leaned against the edge of the desk. "There will be a full moon, strawberry moon, on the summer solstice. That might happen every sixty years, if that. It's also called the hot moon, representing summer, as well as the rose moon. It can't be a coincidence. I would preach that you should have stayed in contact with the paranormal, and not closed yourself off. Someone would have approached you and perhaps your questions might have been answered," Healey began. "Son, look at me."

Rutger stared at the screen, the lack of information, while the interruption pushed his anger. Knowing there was a lecture coming, he folded his arms across his chest, and turning the chair, faced the baron. "What?"

"You're doing everything within your power to find her. And you will find her."

"Not good enough. I have no idea where to begin." Rutger's mind trudged through the articles, myths, legends, whatever he could find about the solstice, witches, and soothsayers. There was nothing. Most of the information had been taken from movies. "I have no idea how to find her. Don't we, the paranormal, have books or something about this? Soothsayers, witches, blood magic."

"Most were destroyed during the Crimson Years, and those remaining are closely guarded by the Highguard. My information about soothsayers comes from my parents, and their parents. It's memory. No one could afford the humans getting the information when they take, exploit, and twist meanings to incriminate us."

"We have a problem," Jason reported as he entered the office.

"What?" Healey's voice sounded impatient and angry as he rounded on his personal guard.

"There's a body by the gate." Without backing down from the baron's anger, he looked at the baron, and risking leaving the baron's gaze looked at Rutger. "What's going on?"

Don't let it be Jo, Rutger prayed. "What does the body look like?" Male. Female. He dreaded the answer.

"Its top is naked and there is white material wrapped around its middle. I can't see its face. I can't get a read on it, it's like it's not really there." He stared at both men, the tension crawling over him and altering his instincts. "It's the murders, isn't it?"

"Male or female?" Rutger demanded.

"Male. I think," Jason answered.

"You have to call the authorities," Rutger ordered.

"Yes, sir," Jason replied.

"Jason, never mind. I'll call Detective Watt." Rutger stood, his anger in his muscles. "They're mocking us. He can't get a read on it because of their damn witchcraft," Rutger fumed.

"I didn't sense them. They were on Foxwood. My territory, and I didn't sense them." Healey held his son's worried gaze before turning and leaving the room.

"Jason, you'll need to give a statement."

"Yes, sir." Jason followed Rutger from the house to their trucks. He watched the Director of Enforcers fight anxiety, while threads of his fear wafted on the air. There was only one reason Rutger would be unable to keep his feelings from emerging. Jordyn. When Rutger's headlights cut through the night, Jason started his truck, waited to see the director's rear lights, and trailed after him.

Rutger tried to use his senses to search for the witch. The woman with red hair, anyone, and in seconds was denied any indication someone was there or had been. He couldn't sense anything, except a suspended pause. Like the area was holding an empty awareness, as if life was waiting for death to exhale.

While they waited, neither of them touched anything and didn't go near the body draped over the sign with Foxwood carved into its dark wood. The light, usually shining on the last letters, lit up the front of the body.

"I can't believe they drove in, put a dead body on the sign, and drove away without anyone sensing them. The baron should have felt them," Jason said.

"One would think," Rutger replied absently. Something as drastic as death. With their senses rendered useless, he was going to install cameras. Foxwood, the enforcer's office, and his house were going to be overhauled with the latest security. He checked his watch, the time ticking by as he waited for the detectives to arrive. His worry was gaining weight with each second, while his thoughts focused on Jo and what might be happening to her.

"Where is Jordyn?" Jason asked.

Rutger inhaled, exhaled, and inhaled again, but it didn't help. He was going to have to learn a new way to relieve stress. "I want this kept between you, the enforcers, and soldiers. No one else."

"Affirmative."

"She was kidnapped this morning." He fought for his voice to stay calm and normal.

"You think it has something to do with this?"

"I know it does."

"I've been following the progress of the investigation. I received a report about the night the baron ordered Jordyn to go with you, from Luke."

"Why would Luke give you a report?" Rutger faced Jason. Luke was going to pay.

"She left with you. I'm the baron's personal sentinel, but while she's in Trinity, I'm her shadow and was unable to follow you to the scene."

Rutger could swear hours were passing instead of minutes. "You know her every move?"

"I do. I drove her car to your house and saw you. You didn't have to yell at her. But, I didn't see her leave. Once she went to your place, the baron ordered me to leave the two of you alone."

No shit. "There's a lot you don't understand." Being reminded of the night before created guilt and regret, and her abduction was ripping his resolve from him.

"Maybe not. Maybe I do. I know she came back here with zero interest in staying. I listened to her talk about her gallery, and friends. She's ordered to go with you, and the next day she's pulled in so deep the slayers are put on standby. Jordyn faced the pack as their soothsayer and wasn't afraid of their judgement."

Rutger walked to his truck, saw the image of Klamath Falls, grabbed the edge of the bed, and wanted to roar until his throat burned and bled.

"I know I've overstepped my rank, but I have to know if you're going to find her. The ritual at the Summit proves nothing. Are you're going to protect her? Do you love her?" Jason asked.

Did he love Jo? Rutger uncurled his fingers from the frame of his truck and turned around. "With everything that I am. If I lose her, I don't know what will happen to me. I crashed and burned the first time." And she was alive and well in Butterfly Valley. If she died ... if he found her in pieces, it was going to destroy him.

"When you find out who did this, we're killing them," Jason promised.

Rutger met Jason's wolf eyes. "Affirmative."

They stood staring at each other, their bodies turning into silhouettes when three vehicles approached, their headlights glaring down on them.

The dark blue SUV parked on the opposite side of the gate, following closely behind it, a heavy-duty white SUV drove between Rutger's truck and the first SUV, and parked in front of the entrance, blocking it completely. Seconds later, the county's evidence van parked behind Rutger's truck.

Finally, he thought.

"Kanin," Detective Watt greeted. "We need to stop meeting like this."

"Agreed. The body is over here." Rutger, Director Kanin, gained a sliver of restraint and started toward the sign.

"Is it a werewolf?"

"Affirmative." Before the musk of wolf had lost its primal edge, it mixed with the rough iron of blood and the combination radiated from the corpse, telling Rutger exactly what it had been.

Surrounding it were the same mingled scents of herbs, which made his stomach heave. Rutger stopped at the edge of the grass and pointed at the torso.

The detective continued onto the grass, and once at the body, tried to see its face. "He looks young," Detective Watt muttered. "You said there was a witness?" He stood and walked the same steps he had taken.

"Not a witness. He found the body. Jason, come here."

"When did you find it?" Detective Watt asked. He took a pen and notebook from his pocket and waited.

"Over an hour ago," Jason answered, meeting the detective's eyes.

"You drove in and it was there? Just like it is now?"

"Correct." Jason's stare landed on the body.

"You didn't see anyone? A car? Van? Anything out of the ordinary?" Watt asked.

"No. I didn't see anything," Jason answered.

"Do you normally visit Foxwood at this hour?" Watt asked, trying to stay on track.

"Yes. I had to talk to Mr. Kanin."

Detective Watt understood. Healey Kanin was the alpha of the pack, and one of a few barons of a territory, and probably had several of his pack members reporting to him. His curiosity nearly had him asking what position Jason held that he needed to visit regularly, and what he was reporting. Watt wouldn't, couldn't, his questions weren't part of the case. "Thank you." Detective Watt finished his notes and faced Rutger. "I appreciate you being here, after what happened. If you want to leave you can. I can take care of this."

"I would rather stay. If I sit around much longer, I'm going to go crazy," Rutger replied. Staring at the body, he heard Jo say 'he wanted death'. "Did they find anything in Butterfly Valley?" He wasn't going to refer to it as Jo's home, because it wasn't.

"There were multiple footprints, tire tracks, and they dusted the door for prints. Looks like the abductors never made it inside of the house. Mr. Myers reported he returned to her house after they had an argument and found the front door locked. He said, he broke off their relationship and became worried so he used a key to get inside and found the back door open. I think they spooked her, so she locked the door and headed to the back. No doubt they planned for her reaction, they had the house surrounded and waited for her to go to them."

They planned on her reaction. Rutger fought to concentrate on the detective.

"Detective Fillmore of the sheriff's department will be my contact, if they get a hit from the prints."

She could have shapeshifted. 'Breathe deep.' Played through his thoughts. "What about witnesses?" he asked, as he fought his anger.

"The house sits off the street and is shielded by mature trees. It's hard to see the front from the road. However, one neighbor said she saw a van, it had a logo, but couldn't remember what it was. And isn't sure if she would recognize it again. She saw men but didn't recognize them. She did say there had been visitors to the house, off and on, and again didn't recognize them. I understand Miss Langston was in a relationship with Mr. Myers. Do you know if he has connections to Trinity?"

Louis had a key to Jo's house and returned after he broke up with her. What had he said to her? Jealousy added to the combination of anger and fear swimming in his veins. With a thread of control, he wore a professional mask. "No. He didn't know Jo was from Trinity."

"Just checking. He mentioned he didn't know she was a lycan. It explains the argument." And the reason Mr. Myers broke off their relationship. His voice grew tight with the feelings he had about Miss Langston lying. "Would your father know what she had been up to?" Detective Watt asked.

"Why?" Rutger met his gaze.

"Jordyn Langston is part of the Cascade pack, yet she lived in Butterfly Valley. Even I know that's abnormal. With the report of people at her house, I need to know if she was actively social, the visitors were from the Cascade pack, or if someone was watching her," Watt explained. "I might not be a shapeshifter with enhanced senses, but I can tell you're angry. You know better than anyone the sensitive questions needing to be asked."

Rutger wanted to argue, but his thoughts remained on the detective's statement and its meaning. He knew what they were going to ask and didn't want to hear the answers.

"Detective Watt, they have the body ready to transport. And they found a note."

"Do me a favor and look at the body," Watt asked.

"All right," Rutger replied absently. Jason joined him and they walked with Detective Watt to the gurney. A red biohazard symbol warned them the body was infectious, and another warning, non-human was written under it. The words glared from the black body bag.

Wearing gloves and a mask, the medical examiner unzipped the thick bag down to the victim's knees and shoved the sides back to reveal its chest and face. "This is disturbing."

"God," Jason whispered and took three steps backwards.

Rutger swallowed. He didn't know how it could get worse, but it was. He knew he should be looking at the chest, not the open cavity his brain struggled to recognize. From the clavicle down had been cut open, and the manubrium, sternum down to the xiphoid, and the ribs were missing. They hollowed him out. Rutger stared into the crater, at the jagged saw marks on the remaining ribs, and the scapula.

"Do you recognize him?" Detective Watt asked.

Rutger hadn't looked at the face. He couldn't tear his eyes away from the leftovers of the victim's chest and failed to restrain his thoughts. His heartbeat pounded, his pulse like rushing water in his ears, kept pace with his growing fear. He wanted to say no and leave the body and the scene. Rutger's eyes moved up from the waist, chest, neck, and to the familiar face of the young man. Bloodless cheeks collapsed into the mouth while empty eye sockets stared up and at nothing. His heart felt as if it stopped and his lungs clung to the breath waiting to be exhaled. "Zachery."

"You know him?" Watt asked.

"Yes. His family is part of Cascade," Rutger answered. How long had he been missing? And why hadn't his parents called the enforcers to report his disappearance?

"I'll need to know his full name, and his parents' names and address. They have to identify the body," Detective Watt started.

"No, I'll do it. I'll tell them. Then your deputies can talk to them." Rutger was glad his voice returned. "What the hell do they need with his eyes?" He didn't ask anyone specific. His thoughts kept going back to Jo. Each body had been cut apart. Eyes, the spine, ribs, legs—was it for death magic or to humiliate the victim? Both. They were proving they were stronger, better, and it wasn't going to end. Rutger inhaled to try and calm his nerves when he caught a thread of vanilla. It was Jo. He shook his head wanting to dislodge the scent from his instincts. It wasn't real, he was torturing himself.

"They invaded our territory, murdered one of our own. And took another," Jason said from behind Rutger.

"Detective Watt, I have the note," a woman reported. She wore a white cotton polo with the county emblem on the right side, her name on the left, and a shoulder holster.

"I listened to the voice note. While it proves Miss Langston was kidnapped, and they believe they have a *soothsayer*, I'm not linking the crimes until I have evidence," Detective Watt said and watched Jason give a sideways glance. "Thank you, Ella. Rutger, are you going to be able to listen."

"Yes," Rutger said and growled. Not the same. Every minute spent searching for a different suspect put Jo's life at risk.

"I don't know if you want a potential victim," Ella started.

"Read the damn thing," Rutger ordered. The vanilla felt thicker, surrounding him, and threatening his control. Ella's eyes widened and she took a step backwards; her fear cut through the air like a knife. "I'm sorry."

Watt met Rutger's eyes with a glaring warning and turned to Ella. "Go ahead."

She hesitated for several seconds, her eyes narrowing on Rutger, and her fear radiating from her. Rutger took a step away to give her room and felt better when Ella calmed. Taking her flashlight, she shined it on the paper. *"Her flesh will cave to the blade. Her blood will flow to quench his thirst. He will devour her essence and rise from the depths to avenge us."* Ella stopped reading, her eyes shooting between Detective Watt, Rutger, the note, and back to Rutger. *"Wolf Enforcer, her death will set her free."*

"Do you doubt it now, Detective?" Jason questioned as he stared at the body.

"No," Detective Watt answered. He looked at Ella, prepared to tell her to take the note and give them some space.

A wave of cold rage swamped Rutger, its chill gripping his heart, saturating his middle, and making his knees weak. His discipline splintered as he gave them his back and roared—a wild tangle of human and wolf, fed by pain. He roared again, his throat clenching with his lack of control. "She's mine," he growled. Unable to stop himself from seeing Jo cut to pieces and her eyes empty and black, and the vanilla from weaving through him, he marched to his truck. His quick pace, uneven gait, gave away his fading human features.

Jason stayed with him while keeping his distance and watched. "Director."

Rutger couldn't speak. Words were useless when his body was poisoning him with his emotions and his wolf was rising. Closing his eyes, he forced control, and shoved his wolf back. He was going to kill them. Kill them all. He could taste their blood in his mouth, and feel their broken bones in his hands. With clenched fists, he growled, "Mine."

"Director Kanin, remember where we are," Jason warned.

Rutger faced the group of humans staring at him, their eyes glittering in the lights, their quick pulses sounding in his head. Fear. He crossed the line. Beyond the gate, headlights lit up the black asphalt, and the sound of a car approaching ended the silence. Someone was coming to check on him, and if his senses were telling him the truth, he would say it was the baron.

CHAPTER TWENTY-ONE

Healey stopped, listened to the roar, and felt the charged static as Rutger's power blasted into the air. In seconds Sousa and Abigail ran into the house as another roar echoed.

"Stand down. Sousa, you're with me," Healey ordered. Abigail waited at the entrance of Healey's office.

"Rutger." Laurel looked at Healey for answers. Sadie joined Abigail at the entrance, both watching the baron and baroness.

"I'm going and checking on him," Healey assured.

"He's been on edge for days," Laurel said. "Something pushed him."

"I know. I'm going. Don't think the worst." Healey thought about the body as he held Laurel by her upper arms, kissed her forehead, and left the office.

The mile-long drive felt longer as Healey drove toward the gate and the half dozen sets of lights. Unable to pass the SUV blocking the entrance, Healey stopped, put the car in park, and turned the engine off. He saw Rutger, hands clenched in fists, standing beside his truck, Jason several feet away talking to him. A detective actively waved off others, while two men passed the vehicles and headed in Rutger's direction, guns drawn.

"Son, what happened?" Healey asked gently as he approached Rutger. With his wolf close to the surface, fear, fury, and grief lashed out from Rutger like razor sharp shards of ice. Rutger didn't answer. His eyes glowing gold and his wolf hovering over his body waiting for release was enough.

"They found a note, specifically threatening Rutger with the end of Jordyn's life," Jason answered. "A string of sick fucking words."

Healey watched Rutger, making sure he didn't leave, shapeshift, or hurt someone—like one of the approaching humans. "Rutger, I order you to calm yourself." Healey put himself between the detective and Rutger and waited. Rutger took three steps backwards, nodded, and bowed his head. "Sousa, watch him." Healey faced the detective. "Can I read it?"

"I'm Detective Watt, with OPI." Watt introduced himself as he handed over the plastic evidence sleeve.

"Healey Kanin. Thank you." Healey read the note, the words a blood curdling promise. "This is proof it's blood magic. They'll use her the same way they have used the others."

"Rutger discussed this with you?" Watt asked.

"After they kidnapped Jordyn," Healey replied, handing Detective Watt the note.

"Not just others, one of our own. Zachery Oliver," Jason said before Detective Watt continued. His eyes reflected his wolf, his hurt and pain coming from him in thin threads.

"Wait. The note suggests witchcraft, they called her a soothsayer, and the belief they are doing this for a higher purpose. I'm not concerned. My team is focusing on serial killers," Watt advised. Turning back to the detectives and deputies, he met their gazes. "I need the scene processed. Now." He met Rutger's gaze, his eyes shifting from brown to gold, the back and forth unnerving Watt. "You need to leave."

"They're taunting me." Rutger's voice grated in his throat. He had to get his head back in the game.

"They're taunting our pack," Healey added. "Detective Watt, this is witchcraft. The victims are sacrifices," he insisted.

"First, if that information is leaked to the press, and the public, it will cause a panic. I don't want it to happen, and I can assume, neither do you. Second, the why will be answered when I find them. We are looking for them."

"I understand. But Jo has been gone for nearly twenty-four hours." Rutger was thankful his voice regained its human sound. The desperation tangled with his fear and was going to drown him.

"Don't fall for their smoke and mirrors," Watt replied. "You're concentrating on why, we need to find out where they are."

Smoke and mirrors? "What about the note?" Rutger continued. "The words. He will rise from the depths. What if they are using the body parts, all of the werewolves, for their fucking king witch or whatever, that will rise from the depths?"

"Could be," Healey replied. "I don't know why. The summer solstice has nothing to do with werewolves. The full moon is significant. If they are waiting for the full moon to make their final sacrifice, she'll shapeshift."

"They have wolf's bane, she won't be able to," Rutger stated. Jo would stay in wolf form while her power continued to increase and eventually drive her wolf to kill her.

"Over a long period of time wolf's bane is dangerous. I've witnessed lycans become addicts. They believe they're human," Watt said.

"Yes. The side effects vary, but with the full moon, Jordyn's wolf will try to shift, the force between the two will be deadly," Healey explained.

"What about Belle Ridge?" Rutger asked.

"I have detectives researching the name," Watt answered.

"What if it's tied to their beliefs? If what they're trying to raise is something native to the area?" Rutger asked.

"Stop. We could guess all night. Let us do our job. If you

come up with actual evidence, I'll listen. I'm not going to entertain ideas based on nothing," Watt warned. "I need all of you to leave. Once the scene is cleared, I will notify you."

Rutger met the baron's neutral gaze. They were being forced to wait. Wait. As if they had the time. The baron nodded to Rutger like he heard his thoughts, and turning away, started toward his car with Sousa. Before reaching the gate, the baron stopped.

"Rutger, you'll ride with me. Sousa, you ride with Jason. As soon as the area is cleared we'll come back for Rutger's truck," Healey said.

"Yes, sir," Sousa replied.

"Yes, sir," Jason responded.

Watt watched the lycans operate like a military team. It scared him and fascinated him. "Rutger, we're going to find her."

Rutger absently nodded while Jo's vanilla scent teased him. His stare focused on the body bag as the forensic technician zipped it closed. His thoughts were racing in a million different directions. Each of them weaving around Jo.

"Son, come on." Healey waited as Rutger stared at the scene, and after a minute walked over to him.

One foot in front of the other. Rutger needed to get to the house where there weren't humans staring at him. The baron opened the car door, waited for Rutger to be seated, closed the door, and walked around to the driver's side.

When they were driving back to the house, Rutger turned to face the baron. "I'm going to make them beg for their lives, and when their throats bleed from their screams, I'm going to tear them apart. Their blood will stain my hands." His eyes glowed with his wolf, his fingers curled into tight fists, his nails bringing blood, and every muscle in his body grew taut.

They had been invaded. One of their own killed. Another

taken. Their soothsayer and his second's mate. His son's wife. "When we find them." Healey looked at his son, felt his anger, and the emotion overriding them all, his pain. It fought to break Healey's resolve.

"Good morning, Soothsayer. After a couple of days, I thought you might be hungry," Flint said from outside the cell. He sat back on a plain wooden chair, legs crossed, hair in a braid.

Morning.

Days?

With no windows and the aged utility lights casting the room in a permanent dull yellow, she hadn't noticed the time. Jordyn floated between sleep and consciousness, not knowing which was real, not knowing when day gave into night. When she wasn't dreaming about the pack, she saw Rutger, tried to keep him near, while drifting further away from him. Moments of her thoughts touched her parents but were fleeting. Her mind wasn't her own, her body was growing weaker, and she grieved the absence of her wolf.

Flint's presence invaded the room, her grief, and getting closer, an electric current swept through and set her nerves on fire. His evil surrounded her and stole the images of Rutger she clung to. With a shallow breath, she worked to ignore him.

"You can't ignore me when you can feel me, Soothsayer," he said as he wrapped his fingers around a bar.

Jordyn turned, facing the wall. She wasn't going to give him the satisfaction of acknowledging him and would rather starve.

"Come now. You have to have your strength. I'll give you twenty minutes, after the last second dies, this room will fill with the sedative and wolf's bane. I'm going to tell you a secret. If you have a full stomach the hallucinations are less painful. Your dreams might not haunt you and make you cry." He walked out of the room, the door closing behind him, the click of metal as the locking mechanism fell into place sounding louder than it should.

They weren't hallucinations.

They were nightmares brought to life and given voices by the centuries sitting in her head. An infinite collective that would never be silent. Her body battled with her demands, and Jordyn made it to her back and stared at the ceiling. If she died, she would be free.

That's the drugs talking, she told herself. *Rutger is going to find me.* She heard a sad laugh echo off her skull. That was the drugs talking. Jordyn snuffed the conversation and picked through the images and tried to separate which were real and which were her illusions. With each one, she didn't know and didn't have the confidence to decide.

The wolf's bane sat in her joints, adding to the ache of starvation. Jordyn couldn't deny her mind was slipping and it was a matter of time before her body failed. The wolf's bane stole her wolf and strength, and her human body had become a shell. She wouldn't be able to save herself in her current condition.

Jordyn held her breath, sat up, moved her legs off the cot, and her feet flopped to the dirt floor. When she sat straight, she looked at the pieces of brown fruit sitting next to a piece of raw meat draped over a paper plate. Its congealing liquid oozed off the side, and landing, made small rust-colored puddles in the dust. Her stomach clenched in defiance as the thick smell of blood, wolf, and pain wafted up. Her own kind.

One of her pack.

The feel sank into her, twisted in her memories, and his voice drifted through her thoughts. *No. No.* She closed her eyes as its raw parts saturated the room with his death and grief branded her heart, and tears slipped down her cheeks. Her stomach heaved, and she turned away, her eyes landing on a body. No, corpse. No. She shook her head in confusion and struggled to make sense of the monstrosity perched in front of her.

How long had it been there? With her? Jordyn couldn't control the nausea rising to her throat, the dizziness swimming in her head, and she couldn't stop from losing her balance. She toppled over and off the cot to land on her side. A cloud of dust floated around her, glittering in the dense light as it fell and she stared at ... feet. Black, rotting feet.

There were no flies. Just rot.

Warm tears continued to slip across her nose and down the side of her face. *I'm going to die.* Bloody toes stuck out from darkened skin, leading to bare ankles, legs, and hips strapped with wire to a mud frame. As if the seamstress didn't care, its torso and waist were stitched together with more wire. Her eyes moved up the patchwork mass, the chest a different color than the rest, its head slanted to one side, its eye sockets open holes. Bones, muscle tissue, and hair hung from various places, as if they stuck the pieces into whatever crevice would hold them. Her stomach flipped with the sight while her skin grew cold from fear.

"You noticed your guard. These werewolves will be the last you see." Flint touched a wet cheek with the back of his fingers. "I think of him as our Advent Calendar. A countdown to your ascension," Flint boasted. Leaning closer, he stared at the carved face. "They say the eyes are the windows to the soul. If I were to look in to yours, what would I see in your soul?"

With her hands in the soft dirt, Jordyn frantically pushed backwards, struggling to scoot away from her pack mate, Flint, and whatever the thing was.

"Don't be scared, after sacrificing their lives, they have begun their journey. As you will. It has been written." Flint's voice gained its intensity. He sat on the same chair and studied her. "I didn't believe it, not at first. I saw you in the woods, and I watched you take your pictures, and the way you absorbed the peace. I couldn't stop myself when you began to undress, and I stood in trance when I felt your power as you shifted into your wolf form. A rogue with power. It was intoxicating. I knew then I had to have you. I knew I had to set you free."

Jordyn hit the wall and hugged her knees to her chest. With every word, her days became shorter. Her head swam, her ears rang with the end of her life, and her heart beat in a slow rhythm as if it was giving up. *Not giving up.* She was awake and wouldn't waste the time. Think. Her mind raced. Where had she been? The light humming in her head eased back as she tried to focus her thoughts. Jordyn risked shapeshifting and running close to Trinity, one time. Where? She had been at ... near grade, something grade. Took her hours to get there and she feared the enforcers would see her and the baron would find out she disobeyed his orders. *Where was I?*

"I started watching you, thinking I would use you as one of the sacrifices. A rogue. I didn't know you were a kept and protected member of the Cascade pack. I asked myself, why? Why would a baron as arrogant and prideful as Kanin, allow you to live outside of the pack, and protect you? I prayed for an answer, and as if Wodan manipulated the events himself, he gave me the ultimate sacrifice. A powerful soothsayer and mate to the second."

Rutger. Focus. Willow Grade. She had been at Willow Grade. No, Butte Springs. The name felt empty and she doubted her memory. Butte Springs. Belle Ridge. Tears welled as her smile of victory tried to curve her lips, but failed. She had snuck away, camera in hand, and headed toward Trinity where she could feel the power of her territory. She didn't risk getting too close, the baron's threat always playing in her thoughts. The first dirt road she found, she followed, and after finding herself surrounded by tall pines and oak trees, she stopped. She saw it in front of her as if she were there and felt the wind on her fur as if she had shifted. A dark cloud inched toward her, promising to steal her clarity and replace it with nightmares. "Butte Springs," she slurred. *I'm at Butte Springs.* Hope seeped its eternal energy into her veins with the idea she knew where they were keeping her.

"The power you hold inside will pass from you to Wodan, and he will rise from the bones and take us into battle. We will rule the way we did before the Crimson Years swept us up in its chaos and killed our brothers and sisters. When the war is over and we reign again, you will greet Wodan and he will become your master and you will serve as his priestess. He will serve us through your sacrifice." Flint's hands gripped the bars, his erratic exhilaration hovering around him.

The threads of victory died, Jordyn's strength slipped from her, and leaning to the left, she sank to the floor and a ghost stole her energy.

"Your twenty minutes are up. Sweet dreams, Soothsayer."

Flint's voice faded as images of Butte Springs rose up through the gray to play in the mess inside of her head. She repeated the name, hoping it would anchor her in reality and stop her from drifting in the pack's sea of memories. If she could reach out to Rutger, he would find her. She smiled, her cheek grazing the dirt, the fine dust coating her lips, its granules sticking to her teeth. The darkness lapped at her thoughts and erased Butte Springs and Rutger.

CHAPTER TWENTY-TWO

Rutger refused to go back to his house and ordered everyone to stay the hell away from it. With Jo's belongings and her scent inside, he wanted to keep everything the way it had been. He spent the night in his room at Foxwood, dozing for minutes at a time. When the easy feel of sleep took him, he saw Jo and Zachery with his empty sockets, each memory bringing the scent of vanilla and herbs. He woke with panic gripping him and his heart pounding. There were smells that haunted him, blood, burning flesh, and dead shapeshifters. He added herbs to the list.

He stared at the ceiling, the fan sending cool air to his bare chest, his left arm above his head, his right stretched out to the side, like he was going to feel Jo next to him. The sun was inching into his room through the blinds, telling him the day was passing whether he wanted to be part of it or not. The words of the note played on, and on, like a broken record. It was destroying him. Rutger growled, his weakness tasting filthy while Jo was out there trying to survive. He crawled out of bed, showered, dressed, put his gear and gun on, and went downstairs.

"Rutger, in the kitchen," Healey called.

Rutger stopped, debated ignoring the baron and heading straight to his office. His hesitation added to his indecision, and giving up, he walked to the kitchen where the baron, baroness, and Gavin waited. *Damn.*

"I tried to sense Jordyn and failed. It might be the influence of the wolf's bane," Healey explained.

"At least you tried," Rutger mumbled. Her absence was growing heavier.

"How are you, son?" Laurel asked. She took the carafe, poured coffee into a cup, and handed it to him.

"Fine." Rutger didn't want to waste his time with small talk. Taking the seat, he yanked it backwards, and then sat down.

"You look fine," Gavin teased.

It grated on Rutger's fraying patience. He stood, took the cup of coffee, and started out of the kitchen.

"Wait, Rutger, you need to eat," Laurel pleaded.

Rutger kept walking—he couldn't do small talk, coffee, food, and sitting around. He had to do something to feel like he was working and trying to find Jo and Zachery's killers, even if he had no idea where to start.

The sunshine, morning dew on the grass, and the sounds of birds had him pausing before he pressed the number code into the keypad of the enforcer's door. Another day. With a full hour before the others started arriving, it saved him from having to greet anyone. He ordered his top enforcers—Ansel, Aydian, Luke, Mandy, Clio, and Quinn—to patrol Trinity and the surrounding areas. The others were put on eight hour rotations and would work from the office monitoring the locations of the patrols.

Safe in his office, he walked to his desk, set his coffee down, took his cell from his pocket, and set it on a stack of files. With his worries consuming him, he sat heavy in the chair, bringing a squeal. Looking abandoned on his desk were reports, folders, and messages with Mandy's handwriting. Once again, CJ was taking time off while the enforcers worked the office. His concentration was on Jo, not his job.

Letting the paperwork go untouched, he opened his desk drawer, rummaged through the same forgotten junk, and took out a picture. Rutger sat back, his shaking fingers gripping the glossy paper. Jo was sitting on the railing of his deck, the lake behind her, and he stood beside her, his arm around her waist and his hand on her hip. His thoughts chased the memory, bringing it to life, with the feel of her on his skin and her vanilla scent drifting around him. "I'll get you back," he promised her image.

"Son," Healey greeted as he entered the office. His broad shoulders tightened his sweater around his chest, and before sitting, he smoothed the front of his jeans.

"You've made a habit of visiting," Rutger said, dropping the picture in the drawer.

"You can't pretend you're all right. I read the note, and your mate's life has been threatened. And your mother heard your distress last night. She's worried," Healey replied, ignoring his comment.

"My apologies, Baron." Rutger sat forward and shifted papers and folders.

"Don't baron me. We know you're scared. I understand the loss and the feeling of helplessness."

"Zachery. Do his parents understand? It's my job to protect the pack and I failed. Not once. But twice."

"It's my job to protect the pack. And that means I failed. I have soldiers, enforcers, shadows, and slayers at my disposal and it wasn't enough. As for the Olivers, they're grieving their son. We will bury Zachery at the Summit after we find Jordyn. They want her there," Healey answered.

"Why? They should be angry." Rutger wanted to stand and pace.

"Jordyn is their soothsayer and she knows their son. She will be able to tell them he accepted his death. It will give them closure." Healey watched Rutger's eyes darken with doubt. "Son, we aren't human. We don't live with the same mortality hanging over our heads. Our immortality saves us from fearing death. However, it doesn't save us from feeling mortality's hand on our hearts," Healey explained calmly. "As outsiders, we take what we need to cope and move forward."

"I'm going to kill the witches and their deaths will give them closure."

"There's that," Healey replied. "Until then."

The job. He needed to focus on the job. "If they're using the bodies as sacrifices and mutilating them is part of the ritual, what are they going to do to Jo? Time is running out." Rutger's thoughts collided. With frustration eating him, he rubbed his face with his hands, ran his fingers through his hair, and met the baron's heavy gaze. "We have a day to find her."

"I know. I've had the same thought. There has to be someone who has information."

"Besides you," Rutger accused, his voice low, jealous, and edged with fear.

"Finish what you want to say," Healey insisted.

"For three years, you've had shadows watching her." He hated his weakness. "What was her life like?"

Healey watched Rutger struggle with his anger and fear, and it pained him. "Jordyn stayed busy by working. If she left Butterfly Valley, she searched for places to take pictures, and went alone."

"Where?" Rutger leaned forward. "Where did she go?" His cell rang; Rutger looked at the number and didn't want to answer. He waited and it rang two more times. "Kanin."

"I don't want to have to call the authorities."

"Why?"

"He's been through enough."

"Lady Langston, calm down. Who are you talking about?" Rutger met the baron's narrowed gaze, and lowering his phone, hit speaker.

"Mr. Myers. Louis. He's here, raving about how it's our fault, and we did this to Jordyn." Her voice sounded strained.

"I'm on my way. Where is Lord Langston?" Rutger asked.

"Talking to him," she answered, the panicked edge dulling.

At least she wasn't alone. "It'll take me a couple of minutes." He hadn't finished when he heard the phone go silent and screen went black. "Damn it." Standing, Rutger shoved his cell in his pocket.

"Do you need me to do anything?" Healey asked.

"No. I can do this. I have to do this," Rutger replied. He walked down the hall and entered the communication room to see Mandy and Ansel. "You finished your patrols?"

"Just," Mandy replied.

"You're both with me."

"Yes, sir." Rising, Mandy grabbed her jacket.

Ansel stood. "Where are we headed?"

"The Langston's residence. Mr. Myers is there causing trouble," Rutger explained.

"That's what they need." Ansel shook his head.

"Keep me updated," Healey ordered.

"Yes, sir." Rutger watched the baron nod, then continue down the hall.

"Before you leave, I think you should take a look at this," Luke said as he entered the communication room. He raised his hand, his fingers wrapped around a newspaper.

Rutger turned; he didn't have time to waste. His frustration was quickly turning to heated anger. "I don't have the time." His eyes skated over the headline, causing him to freeze. 'Rutger Kanin, son of Healey Kanin, alpha to the Cascade clan of lycanthropes, is responsible for finding a mutilated body on Foxwood property.' *Shit*. "Did you read the article?"

"It hints at a serial killer, then goes on to say you, as a

lycanthrope, are working with law enforcement, but they haven't warned the public because of you. After a body was found on Foxwood, said to belong to the clan, you are protecting the lycanthrope community," Luke explained.

"Wolf Enforcer," Rutger mumbled. The pictures of them, Louis finding out Jo was a werewolf, and now the press. They were actively putting people against him. Keeping him busy and proving they were better. "I'll talk to Detective Watt about the press. Right now, we have to leave."

"There is a coven, humans, magic born or not, committing the murders. The public won't care about the truth, they'll blame you because you're a lycan," Luke fumed. They all knew the injustices between humans and shapeshifters. The crease in his forehead deepened, his eyes narrowed, and he crumpled the newspaper. "They don't know the truth."

The pack couldn't risk the negative publicity. They had a working relationship with humans, and destroying it would bring trouble to the baron, and those within the pack. The repercussions of the humans' fear would spread to other packs. "I understand. Right now, we have to focus on the safety of the pack. Not what the public thinks. We need to leave. I want you to stay here."

"Yes, sir," Luke replied.

Rutger walked out of the office, Mandy and Ansel following. "You two ride together."

"Yes, sir," Ansel responded and headed to his truck.

With the office in his rearview, Rutger left Foxwood, drove through town, and toward the Langston's estate without noticing the scenery, the time, or Ansel tail-gating him. Louis flooded his thoughts. He taunted Jo with the pictures and left her when he found out what she was. His jealousy grew when Louis was the last person to see her.

Rutger entered Coal Valley through the wrought iron gates

and drove the half mile drive, his hand clutching the steering wheel. Making his way around the circle, he stopped behind an expensive sedan. With his anger coming in waves of flames, he struggled to control himself. He breathed in, exhaled, looked in the rearview mirror to see Ansel and Mandy waiting for him, and killed the engine. He got out of the truck with forced control.

"If Mr. Myers tries to harm someone, remember he is human. Don't kill him," Rutger warned.

"Got it," Mandy said. He didn't have to be a werewolf to know she was lying. If Mr. Myers was going to try anything, he was going to get hurt. Very hurt.

Ansel remained silent and waited. Like the predator he was.

Rutger took the steps, stood in front of the door, and raised his hand. The door opened before he touched it. "Lady Langston."

"Please, he's in the sitting room." She moved to the side, her eyes on the floor, and waited as they passed.

Rutger heard his voice, the pitch of anger, and the thread of fear as he hammered Lord Langston with accusations. "How long has this been going on?"

"Almost an hour. I know we should have called sooner, but neither of us wanted him hurt. Obviously, we can take care of ourselves. I think he needs someone to blame. What he learned can't be easy."

Rutger didn't care. "Where is he?"

"This way." Lady Langston walked down the hall.

"Director Kanin, thank you," Ethan greeted. Louis turned to look, his face turning pale, his mouth remaining open. "This is Louis Myers."

"Mr. Myers," Rutger greeted. "I'm Director Kanin."

"No. No. I know you. I saw you. Your shirt. Damn … ex-boyfriend." His eyes widened as he spit out the word ex-boyfriend. "She t-told me about y-you. Jordyn. The l-lycan." Louis stammered over his words and took a step backwards.

Not her ex-boyfriend. Jordyn wore his T-shirt and their relationship had been exposed. He had no idea why it bothered him. Under normal circumstances it wouldn't have. Right then it was an added strike to his fragile control. Like not marking her. "Yes, Jordyn is a lycan. She is also missing," Rutger said calmly. He remained several feet from Louis, not wanting to scare him or push him to act out. "We need to help her."

"I won't help you!" Louis screeched. "It's your fault."

"You can save her." Rutger hoped by convincing Louis he was in control, the man would help them.

"No. No. I won't help her. Not a lycan," Louis mumbled and shook his head. "Not a lycan. Not a dog."

Rutger's anger burned through him. She had been with him? "Jordyn is in danger."

"Louis, will you help me?" The familiar voice twisted Rutger around to see an unfamiliar face. "Please."

Jo's voice rang in his ears and he took a step, raised his hands, ready to stop the woman from continuing. No more, he couldn't take her voice while the face wearing it was all wrong. Wrong. In the air, there was a quiver of power, it touched him as if made from feathers, and tried to enter his thoughts. The baron grabbed his arm, his strength seeping into Rutger to help clear his head. The woman ignored him, entered the room, and walked toward Louis.

"Jordyn?" Louis asked. He took a step forward. "Jordyn, they kidnapped you."

"Where am I?" Her power grew, creating a soft vibration on the air and sending tremors across their skin. "Please, help me."

"I can't. I can't." He grabbed handfuls of hair, tugged on the strawberry blond strands, and began mumbling. When he looked up, red blotches stained his cheeks, tears slipped down, and his eyes grew haunted. "Jordyn, it's you. Your damn drives into the middle of nowhere. It's your pictures. It's your fucking pictures!" Louis yelled through tears as he stared forward, at nothing. "You lied. You. Lied." Spit slid down his chin, his chest heaved with his inhale, and his eyes glazed over with his mumbles. The woman stretched her hand out, palm up in request, and continued her approach. Louis watched her, his eyes narrowing. Suddenly, he wavered and fell. He hit the floor with a heavy thump and silence took the room.

"His memories are locked by a spell. He couldn't tell you. He said as much as he was able," she explained. With her skirt flowing behind her, she crossed the room, and knelt beside Louis. She turned him and put her hand on his forehead as if checking his temperature. Everyone waited and watched. "He's alive. Louis fought the image he saw with the knowledge Jordyn is gone. We're lucky it didn't destroy his mind. Humans don't handle such spells well."

"The coven?" Rutger asked softly.

"Yes. I thought she might be able to help," Healey replied. "I would like you to meet Mistress Rosslyn."

"Rosslyn is fine," she replied. Rosslyn kept her attention on Louis and didn't turn to look at anyone.

"How was he able to get here?" Rutger asked.

"I'm going to assume he planned on trying to find you and the spell made his anger his focus. The witch, and I'm not sure if that's what he or she is, may not know he's here. They might have thought you would go to him and question him so they cast the spell as a precaution. By his dread and angst, he knows where Jordyn is and what they're going to do," Rosslyn answered.

"How long will the spell last?" Rutger's heart raced. There might be a chance. "Can you break it?"

"You won't have the answers you seek in time. As long as

their power holds true, I cannot get through to him. I have spoken to the baron and agree, this is part of the hot moon." She sat beside Louis and closed her eyes. "He's unconscious. Deep sleep has rescued him from his current reality. You can take him home and put him to bed. He'll think it was a nightmare and won't remember physically being here."

"I will have my men take care of him," Healey stated.

"Be careful, they could be waiting for you," Rosslyn advised.

Healey nodded in agreement. "Of course. I'll call Alpha Howard and warn them of the situation."

"Why the hot moon?" Rutger asked.

"The convergence of the moon and the solstice make it the moon with the greatest power. The werewolf, your soothsayer will feed on it. She'll become a catalyst," Rosslyn replied.

"For their god." It made Rutger sick. "You said you weren't sure if he was a witch. Why?" Rutger asked. What the hell was he?

"This is a spell cast with the strength of another. He does not have his own power. He isn't magic born," Rosslyn answered.

"Jo will feed off the moon, and he'll feed off Jo," Rutger mumbled.

"Louis talked about her pictures," Ethan blurted out. Standing by the fireplace, his shoulders sank in, and his face tightened with worry.

Rutger faced Lord Langston. "What pictures? From the gallery? Her phone? Her camera? She's a photographer. Her entire life is made up of pictures." After finding Zachery, the note, and Rosslyn's comment, Rutger felt himself drowning in helplessness.

"You have her phone. Did you see a place, something out of the ordinary? A place we know?" Ethan pushed.

"No. There were pictures of the wedding, Claudia, Jason. Places in Trinity." He paced the room, ignoring Louis' unconscious body lying on the floor, and the muted moans coming from him. "She was banned from returning to Trinity without permission. Jo could have gone anywhere in the Butterfly Valley area." Rutger felt his voice failing him.

"You banned my daughter from returning to Trinity? To her home?" Ethan asked.

"Yes. She wanted to leave, there were rules," Healey answered.

Mia met Rutger's gaze. "Since her camera isn't here, I'm guessing you have it. Unless she took it with her."

Rutger sensed the hostility coming from Lady Langston and wanted to yell at her. "It's at *our* house." Like all of her things. "I'll get the camera and we can go through the pictures."

"Do you think it will help?" Healey asked.

"It can't hurt," Rutger replied. He had to keep his thoughts focused and his fear under control.

"Then we'll met at Foxwood," Healey confirmed.

"If they did this to Louis, what are they doing to Jordyn?" Mia interrupted.

"Don't," Ethan mumbled. With tension gripping him, he walked across the room, and sat down. "I can't take this."

"I can give you something to relax," Rosslyn offered.

"No. I would rather feel pain and worry and know I'm alive than to feel nothing." Ethan gripped his thighs, smoothed his trousers, looked around the room, and at Healey. "I can hear her. I can smell her. She was just here." Ethan stood, looked at the room, and pictured Jordyn by the fireplace.

"I know, old friend." Healey approached Ethan, extended his hand, and they gripped each other's upper arm. Healey gave Ethan wolf eyes as his promise he was going to find Jordyn. Her scent lingered in his house. "She isn't lost to us. We'll get her back." How many times was he going to say that? And who was he trying to convince?

"When? After they mess with her head? When they do to her what they did to him?" Mia pointed at Louis as two of Torin's soldiers picked him up and carried him out. Standing beside Healey, Rosslyn watched Mia. "Witches kidnapped her, they're torturing her, what will we get back? Jordyn won't be Jordyn. That's if they don't kill her."

"What does it matter? She's our daughter." Ethan looked at his wife, his eyes coloring with his wolf, and his anger striking through the air.

Rutger stepped around the baron, Ansel close behind him, and approached Lord Langston. The sharp ends of Lord Langston's anger surrounded him. "Calm down. To find her, we need to stay strong and keep our thoughts focused."

"Is that so? If you would have left her alone this never would have happened. You haven't stopped the murders, and they killed Zachery, and you can't find her, Director. Have you read the paper?" Mia's voice sank lower with her accusations. "This has put us all at risk."

She's scared and lashing out. "There are two agencies investigating. We are all doing what we can," Rutger said more to Lord Langston than to Lady Langston. He could talk to him. Lady Langston's cold front became a fortress around her.

"I know," Ethan replied. He raised his hands to show he wasn't going to do anything and trudged to the window like a broken man. "She's been gone for two nights and we're losing the day. As a soothsayer, her fear will provoke the pack's memories, their pain, and if she is pushed, her power will drive her insane."

"No. I refuse to believe it," Rutger argued. That was a threat he hadn't considered. His fear grew, becoming part of his pulse and the blood in his veins. "You don't know how strong she is."

"Agreed," Healey stated. "I have felt her strength and her

wolf. Ethan, she's a fighter."

Ethan didn't acknowledge Healey or Rutger, and he didn't turn around when his eyes blurred with tears. He agreed Jordyn was a fighter, she lived by herself, fought by herself, and never asked for his help. Ethan continued to look out at the valley, losing his mind to his guilt.

"We'll leave you. As soon as I have confirmation Mr. Myers is safe at home, I'll let you know" Healey said to Rutger. "I'll see the both of you soon."

"Yes," Ethan mumbled.

Rosslyn stopped beside Lord Langston, put her hand on his shoulder, and closed her eyes. "Your daughter will not fall to the memories." Rosslyn's eyes opened and met Lord Langston's. "She is fractured."

"What?"

"Incomplete," Rosslyn answered weakly.

"Will she come home?" Ethan didn't know what incomplete meant and didn't care. He met Rosslyn's russet eyes and saw doubt.

"I cannot say." Letting her fingers slip from him, she walked through the living room and into the hall. Healey remained for a moment, needing to console his friend, and knowing he couldn't, turned and followed Rosslyn.

"Lord Langston, I'll get the camera. If you need me, call me," Rutger said.

"We'll meet you at Foxwood," Ethan replied, straightening.

"I'm going to have Mandy and Ansel stay here. When you're ready, they'll escort you."

"Of course," Ethan replied with his back to them. He remained by the window remembering the morning he told Jordyn why he named the valley.

Rutger watched him, wishing there was more he could do

before leaving Lord and Lady Langston in silence. He walked down the hall, and out the door to his truck, dreading the trip to his house. He didn't want to go inside. He didn't want to smell Jo while looking through her things for her camera.

To distract himself from his mission, Rutger called Detective Watt. He explained what Louis told them, and about the spell, as best he could, and requested he call and explain the situation to the detectives in Butterfly Valley. He didn't want the soldiers arrested or detained because they were taking Louis home. Without asking the baron, he invited Detective Watt to Foxwood, to see the pictures from Jo's camera. Maybe there was a connection between the history of Paradise County and her pictures. With the time set, Rutger ended the call, and checked his messages. Ansel explained both Lord and Lady Langston were in the process of getting ready, and they would be on their way to Foxwood.

Rutger eased the truck to the driveway and slowly made his way to the front of the house, where he parked. As he stared at the front door, his knuckles turned white with his grip. "Get in. Get out," he whispered. Leaving the engine running, he got out and trudged to the door. Images of Jo standing on the walkway wearing nothing but underwear and a hoodie, and crying floated around him.

"In and out." Rutger unlocked the latch, opened the door, and walked inside. Her scent, vanilla and spice, hit him like a blast of pain. Rutger stumbled two steps back, waiting for its edges to dull, and walked farther into his house. Lying low, as if waiting its turn to tempt him, was the mulling smell of her half glass of wine. Rutger didn't wait. Passing the empty bar, and through the living room, he continued to the stairs with his heart in his throat. He took the steps two at a time, and reaching the top, the hallway stretched out in front of him. Each step felt like he was walking in place when he reached the door. Rutger inhaled, regretted it, pushed the door, and crossed the threshold of his bedroom. Their bedroom. Her feel snaked around him, her voice tangling with the scents of their skin and lust.

He was going to lose it.

No. There were people waiting for him.

"Damn it all to hell!" Rutger roared, his wolf's rumble saturating his words. His frustration turned to fury and fed his dread. "Where are you?" Rutger fell to his knees, and landing hard on the thick carpet, leaned forward, grabbed the comforter, and yanked it off the bed. The bulk landed on his thighs. "Where are you?"

With his emotions churning inside of him, he saw her abandoned hoodie, the unmade bed, and their conversation climbed out of the silence. *'I'm watching.' she said with her wolf glowing in her eyes.* It sank inside of him. The ache in his heart created an emptiness making him want to howl.

Rutger fisted the material and saw himself tearing it to shreds with his helplessness. His thoughts crashed when the shrill ring of his cell jerked him from drowning in his weakness. *I have to get my shit together.* He had people depending on him. Rutger took his phone from his pocket and looked at the number. The baron. He declined the call, put his cell in his pocket, and stood. The comforter fell to cover the toes of his boots.

To find her, he had to work.

Rutger backed away from the bed, turned, and after moving her duffle, grabbed her camera bag, and left the room. He marched down the hall, to the stairs, and out of their house. After locking the door, he went to his truck, climbed inside, set her bag beside him, and backed up. He needed to get Foxwood.

CHAPTER TWENTY-THREE

Like a knife being wrenched from her, and rammed back into the wound, her neck and shoulder erupted in a fiery heat. Its barbs reached into her muscles as Jordyn rolled to her back and opened her eyes. She stared up at the dirt ceiling, and the details of the bars as they entered the packed earth from the floor. Quickly forgetting about the pain, she realized she was awake. Not dreaming. She blinked several times, making sure what she saw was real. The details remained. The room held the heavy smell of wolf's bane, and a blend of herbs she didn't recognize, and didn't care to know. She was awake. How? She thought back to her dream, Foxwood, the pack, and Rutger. His pain sat on her and his fury burned between them. Did his invasion into her dreams force her awake? God, she hoped so.

"I told you she fell to the floor. She was talking and crying and wouldn't stop. I increased the wolf's bane, and she kept on," Brother Amos explained. He stood at the bars, pointing at the pendulum.

"I have eyes. She isn't crying anymore and isn't moving. Savoir said to put her on the cot," Sister Emily ordered.

"Fine. Unlock the door and I'll move her." Brother Amos' voice stretched thin with fear.

Jordyn closed her eyes and forced herself to relax her muscles. With his approach, she heard his heels dragging on the dirt floor like he was having difficulty walking. She might be awake but her muscles were trapped in the grip of the drugs. She was too weak to fight them. *It didn't matter,* she thought. Flint had enough people, she would never make it out of the room.

She was going to have to use what she could. If she held onto consciousness, she might be able to touch Rutger's thoughts.

The keys hit the bar, the lock clanged, and his feel moved over her like a blanket of nails. They were living in their incantations and charms, what was that doing to their minds? Jordyn knew. They locked her up and were planning on sacrificing her to a god. A dead god.

"Hurry up."

Jordyn felt his bony arms under her knees and at her back; the stringent sharp smell of burning leaves clung to his clothing. Her arm fell, her head lolled to the side, leaving her face against his chest as he lifted her from the floor. He held her against him and the coarse material rubbed her cheek, tearing her dry skin. With a feeble step, he bent down, extended his arms, and Jordyn rolled onto the cot. Her shoulder sank, her cheek hit the wood rail, and she stopped.

"Get out of there, Brother Amos. Savior doesn't want us near her for a long time," Sister Emily warned.

"I know," he replied as if he had said the words a thousand times. He turned and walked out of the cell, his heels leaving trails behind him.

"I'm surprised you don't hate her after what the animal did to you. You know she's one of them." The keys clanged, the lock clicked, and she was alone in her cell again.

"She isn't the one who attacked me. She's different or Savior wouldn't keep her alive." He hated them. Hated them all. The feel of its teeth as it bit into his legs, back, and throat haunted him. The tender scars reminded him every day what the monster had done to him. Stretched and slick looking, his scars told everyone what had been done. But the soothsayer was different. He felt it.

"He isn't keeping the wolf alive. She has a purpose and will die with the full moon."

Jordyn squeezed her eyes closed, attempting to fight her tears. She had to reach Rutger. When their voices waned and the final door closed and locked, she pushed off the wall and turned to her back. Jordyn drew a slow breath, calmed the chaos in her mind, and called her wolf—its essence feeling like a soft breeze. Without stopping, she called her power. Her wolf and power were weak, like ghosts living inside of her, and making it harder to keep them. With no time to waste, she dove into the deep of her mind and hoped it didn't destroy her. As if it mattered.

I'm dying with the full moon.

Rutger set the wireless connection from the camera to the TV, and turned the camera on. The screen blinked twice, turned white then black, and a blank screen glared at him and the audience. His fingers moved over the controls and his thoughts wondered what part of Jo's life he was going to see.

"Baron, Detective Watt is here," Sousa stated from the entrance of the family room. Less formal it was decorated with family pictures, heirlooms, had a large couch, the TV, and view of the backyard.

"Thank you, you can show him in," Healey replied. Standing he greeted the detective. "Detective, nice of you to make it."

"Of course," Watt replied. "Mr. Myers? I'm assuming everything went all right." Watt remained at the back of the room wanting to keep an eye on the families and Rutger. The sight of him losing control was enough to keep Watt on guard.

"Yes. He is safe in his house. I have Alpha Howard keeping an eye on him," Healey answered.

Detective Watt didn't know exactly how he felt about that. "Good. Rutger, you said you had pictures?"

"Yes. I know you've investigated the places where the bodies were left. But Mr. Myers indicated her pictures were the reason she was kidnapped."

"I—" Detective Watt started.

"Not the reason," Rutger interrupted.

"Want to share?" Ethan said.

"They knew about her, about us, and the pack. Her pictures are the reason they know about her. She went somewhere and they saw her," Rutger explained. She had been watched for weeks, if not months.

"Nothing they have done has been random," Detective Watt added. "Start the slide show."

"Right." Rutger's hesitation grew as excitement and hope clashed with his breakdown. With the feeling fresh in his mind, Rutger willed himself to stay in control as he hit the arrow button on the LED screen.

A picture of Jordyn appeared on the TV screen causing Rutger to go still. Ethan drew a measured breath and slowly let it out. She wore black pants, a white silk top, and matching black jacket. Her onyx hair had been pulled back into a ponytail, her makeup flawless with mascara and black eyeliner. Beside her, Louis, with his arm around her waist, wore a dark suit. They were at the gallery, each holding a champagne glass, and standing in front of a landscape portrait.

Silence invaded the room, its presence giving away their thoughts, worries, and fear. Rutger clicked to the next picture and the next. The Gallery. Parties. Friends. His worry turned to jealousy. Rutger clicked to the next picture and stopped. Steel bars wrapped around his heart, his wolf howled in his ears, and his legs felt weak. The right strap of her pink summer dress hung off her summer bronzed shoulder. Jo sat in a plastic lawn chair, legs crossed, the hem of her dress sitting high on her thigh, the grass covering her bare foot, and she held a glass of wine. A table, its previous life as a giant spool used for industrial wiring, held a bottle of wine, a platter, and a notebook. Rutger set the camera on the table and in three painful steps stood directly in front of the TV. Her frozen image stared back. With her head tilted, a small curve turned her lips into a grin, not a real smile; it was used to warn the photographer she didn't want her picture taken. He knew the look, which was always followed by, *put my camera down*. He couldn't stop from smiling at her. The dark liner framed her near amber eyes, which gleamed in the sunshine, and her onyx hair hung in ringlets to her shoulders.

"Dear God, Rutger, change it," Laurel whispered. Healey placed his hand on Laurel's knee and gently squeezed.

"Jordyn," Ethan mumbled. How much had he missed? Three years of her life. Not one visit. Not once had he left Trinity to see how she was doing. An occasional message only to receive a neutral response. Guilt wasn't a strong enough word for the sickness sitting like a cancer in his middle. She was gone.

"Rutger," Healey urged softly.

With the tangled voices behind him, Rutger placed his palm on the screen, on her thigh, that now wore a mark. His pain leaked into his veins like poison and aimed straight for his heart. His eyes changed to his wolf, her thoughts flooded his mind, at the same time he went to his knees, barely missing the TV stand.

"Rutger," Laurel called out, her voice reaching panic.

"Leave him. You feel his power growing? I can sense Jordyn." Healey stood. "He might have found her."

"This better not be a trick," Ethan warned.

"That's impossible," Mia insisted.

With wide eyes and his instincts warning him, Detective Watt exclaimed, "You are all impossible." Each person tore their gazes from the screen and Rutger, to look at him. Watt smiled a corked grin, he couldn't believe where he found himself. "The entire paranormal community, non-human was supposed to be myths, legends, mythology, for God's sake. But no. Here you all are. Nothing is impossible." He pinched the bridge of his nose and rubbed his eyes. He hated the case. "Hell, I have no idea why I think that."

"The fact you do will help find her," Ethan said.

"We'll see. We'll see if I keep my job after this," Watt mumbled. The newspaper article and the meeting with his lieutenant hadn't helped his career.

Blocking out the chatter behind him, Rutger placed his hands on the TV stand to stop from falling forward. With the little control he could muster, he focused on Jo. An awareness began searching and when it found him, turned into a push of physical emotion. It searched further and threading through his insides it found itself. The power she had shared blazed with energy and slowly morphed into her eyes. Through a haze he saw scenery, a road, the woods, both fading into a dirt ceiling, walls, and bars. Her cell. Jo's whispers moved through his mind, feeling like crystal threads and just as fragile. Her frail voice made worse by her weakness, and delusion, he could feel the insanity in the words. She was giving him as much as she could and still she tried to hold back the worst of her pain.

He willed himself to hold onto her when a cloud of smoke blinded him and broke their connection. Its toxic vapors choked him, while the smell of herbs acted like an undercurrent aiding to the infected air. Frantically, with time ticking by, he reached out, wanting to touch her, to question her, to tell her he was going to find her. One second, she was there, he could feel her, the next, she had been ripped away. Her presence, emotion, and whispers were gone. Like a razor across his mind, the force of the separation drove him backwards. He lost his balance and fell to the floor.

"Son."

"I felt her," Rutger mumbled. On his back, he inhaled, and slowly sat up. "Jo." The baron gripped his arm and helped him to stand. He looked at the baroness, the baron, and the Langstons, and saw desperation in their eyes.

"How was she able to find you?" Ethan asked.

"The night we were together, she shared her power. She marked me." Rutger's voice lowered. He held a part of her inside of him. She would be able to find him anywhere. His imagination ran wild, his wolf howled, and his body yearned to have her.

"As a fated couple made One-Flesh, you have taken the first step to merging your powers," Healey explained.

"Myth," Ethan argued.

"A soothsayer and you continue to believe Rutger and Jordyn are fated. Your belief in myth is ridiculous," Mia berated.

"There is something coming. It has magic born changing. I'm not the only who has sensed it," Healey replied. "Others are aware. It pushed me to link Jordyn."

"No. It's true. We are fated," Rutger began. "Jo is opening herself to all of her crafts." Rutger looked back at the TV. "We have to go through the rest of the pictures. It was an impression, not so much words, but I think she told me where she is."

"I don't doubt her power. That's what I felt at the run. It was an impression. How can she do that?" Laurel asked. She met Healey's eyes and saw a shadow in them. No one knew the extent of Jordyn's powers.

"She is part of us," Healey answered. "Sit down, Rutger, you need to take a minute."

"No." He held the camera, his hands shaking, and clicked to the next picture. After a half dozen pictures of Jo, which tortured him further, he found relief in the landscapes. Each landscape was followed by a label telling them where and when the picture had been taken. Rutger searched every picture, every detail, for something resembling what he saw.

"These are new pictures. Look at the date. And there's snow in some." Ethan considered the pictures. "If you forbade her to return to Trinity, how were these pictures taken?"

"I guess she disobeyed my order," Healey answered. He walked to the couch, and sat next to the Laurel without meeting her questioning gaze.

"The shadows would have reported her to you." Rutger faced the baron. "They did report to you. They told you she was making trips home. You let her." Jo had been there. Close to him and he had no idea. Or didn't want to admit it.

"I knew she couldn't stay away. This is her home, her land, she belongs here and it … the land calls to her. She needed to feel its power," Healey explained. "Without it, she wasn't whole."

It was too much. Healey's casual comments as if they meant nothing. The moments he should have been by her side and celebrating her accomplishments. *I'm her father*. Ethan stood, his anger lashing out in the room, his eyes slipping to his wolf's. "Why am I just finding out? You played with her life."

Healey stood, intending to subdue Ethan, not push a challenge. With his hands raised, he took two steps. "Calm down. While I don't understand your pain, as a father, I can empathize with you. We have to work together and find her."

"You should have told me," Ethan accused.

"She's your daughter. You should have asked her. Jordyn would have told you," Healey countered.

"This is getting us nowhere," Mia scoffed.

Ethan turned his heated glare to Mia. "Why didn't we ask her to come home?" Mia lowered her head, folded her hands in her lap, and remained quiet. Ethan shook himself, his anger fading, and turning into fear. "The full moon is tomorrow night." His past was coming for him, and it wasn't going to stop until it exposed all of his sins.

"Let's get through the pictures," Detective Watt suggested. "The quicker the better."

"Agreed," Rutger said. The situation was becoming volatile. He waited for Lord Langston to sit down beside his wife, and for the baron to take his seat next to the baroness. "She has labeled each picture. If Louis is telling the truth, the picture has to be here."

"I know. Go ahead," Ethan replied.

Rutger clicked to the next picture. Tall pines and oak trees shadowed a red dirt road, rock incline, and cast spiderwebs across wild purple sage. Rutger quickly clicked to the next picture, the label reading Butte Springs. He heard Jo's whispers. "I think this is it."

"You think she showed you Butte Springs?" Detective Watt asked. There was a hint of doubt in his voice as he raised his eyes.

"Yes. Farther up the road there's an abandoned mill, and past that, I believe there are more buildings." He struggled to get his hope and excitement under control. "The Forest Service used to have their ground crews stay in the buildings during the summer months. There were several cabins, a common building, and it was self-contained. I believe they called the camp Rocky Point."

"What happened to it?" Watt asked, his interest making him take a step toward Rutger.

"They moved the crews to a new facility closer to the city, and the camp was torn down. There's probably pieces from those cabins in the older houses in the Trinity area," Rutger answered.

"Have you seen it?" Watt had everyone's attention.

"No."

"You have no idea what it looks like?" Watt asked. "Or if there are any buildings or cabins?"

"I haven't been there in years," Rutger answered. "I do know it sits twenty-five miles off the main road." Rutger felt his hope fading.

"Even if one cabin is standing, it would be the perfect place for a coven," Healey said.

One cabin. Hope moved through Rutger. He already created a mental list of the enforcers and soldiers he was going to take with him.

Concealed. Hard to get to. "It would appear that way. Before you create your team, remember the article in the paper. You rush into a place with a team of lycans, nothing more than a group of vigilantes, and the public will go after you. You'll be left answering their accusations. I can't protect you from law enforcement. Let me talk to Detective Adan, who is supposed to interview Miss Bryan, the receptionist at the gallery," Detective Watt cautioned.

Rutger paced the living room, knowing Detective Watt was right, and wanting to cover Butte Springs with his team. When he found the coven, he would burn it to the ground. "Tomorrow is the full moon." A growl laced his words.

"The crimes are in the press. You're going to have to play by the rules. If nothing comes out of the interview, the department will investigate. If something comes out of the interview, the department will investigate. Do you understand?"

"I hate it. Yes." Rutger began to pace.

"Is it Cascade territory?" Watt asked.

"No," Healey answered. "It's still Forest Service."

"Your state licenses and certificates aren't worth a damn and won't protect you. You are not law enforcement. Your presence there would be trespassing and infringing on their rights and give them the opportunity to press charges against you, and the entire pack. If we find something, you will be notified," Detective Watt advised. "It's time for me to leave." He walked out of the family room, stopped under the archway, and turned around. "Rutger, you look like hell, get some sleep. You won't do her any good in the shape you're in. I'm ordering all of you—do not go up there." Not waiting for anyone to respond, he walked out, his steps heavy on the marble floor. Seconds later, Sousa opened the door, Detective Watt mumbled his thanks, the door closed, and they all heard his car.

"As much as I would love to send you to Butte Springs, you can't put the pack at risk. Old Town, and the shapeshifters and paranormals working there, are at risk for any backlash. And, we cannot face the negative press. It's bad enough one of our own was found here on Foxwood. The other alphas have seen the paper and know about the murders and have questioned the safety of Trinity. We have to play it safe," Healey explained.

"When do we do something?" Ethan demanded. His voice shook with his anger. "When will my daughter's life be worth more than politics and the public's opinion?"

"She's alive. The amount of strength it took for her to reach out to Rutger means she isn't losing." Healey stood, Laurel's hand slipping down his back, and faced Rutger. "What did you see? Did you smell anything? What did she show you?"

Rutger stopped mid step. "A room, dirt ceiling, dirt walls, like it was underground, with bars. She's in a cell of some kind. There was smoke, not from a fire, like a candle or something."

"What did it smell like?" Healey closed the distance.

"Wolf's bane. There was another, but I have no idea what it was," Rutger answered.

"They're keeping both her human side and her wolf sedated. Something must have triggered a response from her. Do you know what it was?"

Rutger continued pacing without answering. The uncontrolled feeling of hurt from his meltdown felt like it was happening all over again. Mingling within him like a growing bank of fog was their combined emotions. The pain he felt from Jo matched his own. They were hurting for one another. "She knows, she's going to die," he whispered, turning. "She tried keeping it from me. She tried protecting me."

"Knowing you're looking for her, you have given her hope. That will serve as her strength. You are her strength," Healey offered.

"It should have been *us*. Jordyn shouldn't have felt like she had face him alone. And the man's accusations. He called her a dog in heat." Ethan's emotions carried him on a roller-coaster of highs and lows. Hope and despair. They were going to find her. She was going to be taken from them. "I don't want to lose my child." He looked at Mia, wanting to see the fear he felt in her eyes.

"She will come home," Mia said softly. Raising her hand, she cupped his cheek.

"He called her what?" Rutger growled the words, his eyes blazing gold. *Mine.*

Healey move toward Rutger. "Detective Watt is right. Son, you have to get some rest. You're distracted. I'm putting Ansel in charge of the enforcers until further notice."

Rutger visibly shook himself and waved off the human's comment. "No. I can't. I can't sit around and wait," Rutger argued. He had to have a job, he needed to be active, have something to do to keep his mind from torturing him.

"With her connection to you, you may see her in your dreams," Healey explained.

Rutger turned back to the TV and the tranquil mountain scene. He couldn't pretend the thought didn't tempt him.

"I think she's dead," Sister Andrea uttered. She stood at the bars, her fingers wrapped around them, and waited for the soothsayer to breathe. Time after time, she watched the other sacrifices steadily go crazy, pray for death, and mentally jump off the sane train. They had been simple pieces. Parts of the puzzle. The true sacrifice was different. Savior needed her. Sister Andrea's mind raced with excuses why the pendulum was heading toward la-la land.

"No. I did exactly what Savior said to do," Brother Amos said in defense. "I told you, she fell off the cot and was crazy. Again."

The full moon felt too far away. Sister Andrea inhaled, her patience thinning. "She's staring at the ceiling and not breathing. Maybe she lost her mind. She wasn't great when I met her." There was a jealous edge in her tone. The wolf was getting more attention from Savior than the rest of them. His loyal brethren.

Flint stepped down the last stair, entered the room, and after several feet, turned the corner and saw Sister Andrea and Brother Amos standing at the bars of the cell. "What happened?"

"I think she's in a trance," Brother Amos answered. "Maybe it was too much wolf's bane."

Sister Andrea moved away from the cell, meeting Brother Amos' worried gaze. *Trance?*

"If you have harmed her, I'll offer you up as the lycan murderer and give you to the lycanthropes. The pack of animals will finish what their kin started. Do you understand?" Flint threatened.

"Yes, Savior." Brother Amos bowed his head, then took two uneven steps from the cell. His gaze stayed on the floor to show his submission and his shoulders sank in, making him appear weaker.

Ignoring him, Flint unlocked the door and went inside. His concern immediately grew as he approached the soothsayer. Her usual response to his presence was nothing more than a slight movement of her wide eyes. She remained stuck in her daze, staring at nothing, and barely breathing. "Soothsayer, come to me. Reach for the sound of my voice." Flint raised his right hand and held it above her chest. "Rise from your nightmares. Obey your master." Lowering his hand, he placed his palm flat on her chest, the tender area between her breasts.

Jordyn struggled to remain with Rutger while her pulse slowed and her lungs constricted. She would stay there, in the darkness. In the world between her dreams and reality to escape torture and her pending death. She would choose her end.

It was too late to fight when scarlet tips dipped from the fog, reaching farther, and turning into huge talons that grabbed her and dug into her flesh, heaved. She fought the fierce flames of pain and plunged deeper into herself. Her strength bled from her, and weakness moved through every fiber of her body as it wilted in the talons clamping around her. They lifted her and carried her away. At the edge of light, Jordyn grabbed the outstretched claw and shoved her pain into it.

With the soothsayer's hand clamped around Flint's wrist, and her nails deep in his skin, she pushed dread and panic through her touch. A shroud enveloped Flint, pushing his instincts to defend himself and get as far away as possible. By allowing her access to his thoughts, she would forever be linked to him, and it would destroy his ability to use incantations to deceive her.

He watched her face remain unmoving, unfazed by the strength she used to expel the desolation she felt. Flint couldn't stop from admiring her. After spending days sedated, her power hadn't weakened, it had grown with her nightmares, and taken on a life of its own. It took seconds for him to gather himself, ignore the fear, and absorb her strength. She was going to leave her human body behind to be with Wodan. Her link with Flint would give him greater power. Flint would have an instrument on the other side. He would have his own private window into Wodan's world. Drunk on the thought of such dominance, he stopped fighting her, wrapped his fingers around her thin wrist, and allowed her to invade his mind.

Jordyn's back arched off the cot when her connection to Rutger shredded and tore her focused thoughts apart. His hard push slammed her back to the cot, and forced the breath from her lungs. She gulped air, her lungs constricting and burning for oxygen.

Inside of her mind, she backed away from the wreckage, the pain, and seeking the steady feel of reality moved on the wave of her power. She hesitated when Flint's evil wove, searched, and sought to find her. He would never let her gain her strength, her body became a weapon used against her, ensuring she would never beat him in her physical condition. Weakness continued to eat her like the drugs were swallowing her wolf. She needed to protect herself. Quickly building walls, she buried the power of her wolf and the pack and hastily chose her weapon. Jordyn absorbed Flint's power. Armed with Rutger's fear and pain, she began her assault on Flint.

"Savior?" Sister Andrea asked cautiously.

"Leave him alone," Brother James ordered. After demanding Brother Amos to leave the room, Brother James stood at the cell door watching Savior use his power to control the soothsayer.

"There's blood. She's ripping his arm apart," Sister Andrea countered. A veil of scarlet covered the soothsayer's hand, slipped down to the top of Savior's hand, and began staining the cotton top she wore. "I'm not standing here while she hurts him." Sister Andrea entered the cell, approached Savior, and placed her hand on his shoulder.

"Do not touch me," Flint snapped. His low voice rumbled, broke, and ended. Flint closed his eyes, as she sliced through his mind with razor blade movements. He groaned with the pain, as images flooded him. Fighting back, his lips moved around a spell, its power moving in the cell. Fine dust floated in the electric-charged air.

Flint felt her retreat from his thoughts, and her grip on his arm weakened. He gently eased his arm from her grasp, her hand falling to her chest, her elbow landing with a smack on the frame. Her eyes no longer stared at nothing; for a moment, he watched life pass through the black and she closed them. "She's out," he said weakly.

"What did she do? What were you doing?" Sister Andrea asked. Her boldness might incite punishment, but she didn't care. Not after witnessing the sacrifices and the magic involved. Sister Andrea wasn't going to risk losing Savior when they were close to raising their true god.

"She will give Wodan the power he needs for the war." Flint stood, blood seeping from his forearm, down to his wrist where it dripped to the dirt floor. He wouldn't tell Sister Andrea, or any one of them, about the connection.

"Yes, Savior. Come, I'll wrap your arm," Sister Andrea offered. Her eyes moved with him, taking in his gait as she waited beside the open cell.

Jordyn lost the strength to continue the fight, her weakness forcing her to let him go. It wasn't what she wanted. The satisfaction was knowing she hurt him. An easy smile curved her lips. *I'm losing my mind.* Jordyn relaxed, listened to their footsteps, the cell door closing and the wood scraping the floor. After the locking mechanism sounded, she released the breath she had been holding, and basked in the delight he would feel the lesions when he slept. He would have a taste of the nightmares plaguing her.

CHAPTER TWENTY-FOUR

Jo hadn't made an appearance in his dreams, like the baron said she would. Instead, his mind carried on conversations without him. In the middle of the night, he gave up, drank a bottle of bourbon, and finally fell asleep. Like a corrupted slide show repeating the images from her camera, he watched her pass in front of him. Unable to touch her, he felt the passion they shared and it twisted with the helplessness to save her. His shorts, sheets, and blanket were soaked with sweat when he woke up, his heart was in his throat and his pulse in his ears. After spending hours trying to escape his nightmares, the delusion nearly choking him, and tossing and turning in the empty bed, Rutger gave up altogether. He showered, shaved, and dressed in clean clothes. He looked like himself. On the inside he felt a hollowness growing in his stomach.

Rutger stood in the living room looking out the window at the yard, coffee cup in hand, his mind racing with the summer solstice. And the full moon.

His attention on the coming moon didn't falter when Ansel's silver, four-wheel drive truck, with the Cascade pack's crest on the side, drove into the enforcer's parking lot. Rutger watched Ansel, his thoughts on Jo's location, as Ansel got out of his truck and headed to the entrance. He tucked his black enforcer shirt into his jeans, wore his thigh holster, and freshly shined combat boots. His cell phone was at his ear as he entered the security code, pressed his thumb on the pad and unlocked the door. Rutger absently looked at the grandfather clock and saw his second in command was an hour early. Forbidden to go to work, Rutger didn't mind Ansel taking his place. Ansel Skelton, at six foot, four inches tall, with hints of Native American in his veins, could intimidate an opponent, or charm a woman of his choice in the same breath. His ability to track, shoot, fight, and remain calm during a confrontation made him a strong enforcer, but his diplomacy, and ease in which he talked to people made him the perfect choice as second. Rutger depended on Ansel more all of the time. *Like now*, he thought.

"Did you sleep?" Healey asked. Entering the living room, he wore a chocolate brown, button-up shirt, the top button left undone, revealing the black edges of his tattoo, dark denim jeans, and dress shoes. He carried a coffee cup, the newspaper, and his cell phone.

"No." Rutger looked at the sky, the sun rising and casting its golden glow across the valley. With its decline, Jo's life would hang on the moon's rise. How much time did he have?

"Any word from Detective Watt?"

"No, it's too early. I'll call him in a couple of hours." Rutger sipped his coffee. The need to search for Jo was making his muscles tight and his nerves erratic.

"I talked to several other alphas, and we decided, if we don't hear from him, before the moon rises, a team will be sent to Butte Springs," Healey stated. "They will support the decision and aid us if need be."

Rutger turned around to look at the baron. "I appreciate the offer but this is about me. If I'm wrong about her location, I'll answer to the authorities. I'm not putting the others at risk."

"We are a pack. We stand together," Healey said as he approached Rutger. "She is pack as well as kith. There's playing it safe for the sake of public outcry and there's taking care of our kith and kin."

Rutger couldn't stop from disagreeing. The work, blood, sweat, and tears put into the relationship with humans, and the prosperity of Trinity and Old Town, were proof they needed to play it safe. One misstep on his part, one threat and the carefully threaded ties would unravel like frayed rope. That failure would rest on his shoulders.

"Stop thinking, Rutger. We're going to handle this." Healey's confidence wrapped around him, giving static to the air. "Your mother fixed breakfast. Let's go eat."

"Your influence had me screaming in my sleep," Flint said softly. He moved hair from Jordyn's cheek with his finger, traced her jawline, and moved his thumb against her lips. "I can't wait to see your visions when you stand beside Wodan on the other side."

"Good morning, Savior," Sister Andrea greeted. She watched his gentle touches and the intimacy they created. A quick flash of jealousy blinded her as it burned through her pride. *The soothsayer is nothing but a tool. A tool whose life will end when the moon sits high in the sky.* "Savior."

"Yes, Sister Andrea?"

"The sisters are waiting." She couldn't stop watching him. His hair fell forward, exposing the nape of his neck, and the dull web of purple scars.

"Have them bathe the soothsayer in the unguent and afterwards, I want her skin softened with lavender oil. When the preparations are complete, dress her in the linen," Flint ordered.

Sister Andrea pulled herself from her thoughts. "Yes, Savior."

"Has Brother James prepared the sanctuary?"

"They're doing so now."

Consciousness had been elusive throughout the night. Jordyn tried to regain the clarity she had when she reached out to Rutger but didn't have the strength. With exhaustion and confusion taking hold, any chance of a clear thought stayed out of her reach. She gave up. It was easier to sink into the numbness of the drugs than fight herself. Her deadened sanctuary ended when the wrong kind of awareness slithered over her and Flint entered her cell. Jordyn's skin crawled with his presence and burned when he touched her. She wanted to sink into the cot and disappear. It did bring her out of the haze. She listened to him talk, catching every other word and not understanding completely what was happening.

"Excellent. She will be presented, placed on the altar, and we will begin the ceremony." Flint kissed his finger and placed it on Jordyn's lips. "My soothsayer, the moon will call your wolf and your power will increase. Your wolf will be denied, forcing your essence to embrace the darkness within you. You will become the pendulum."

Jordyn drifted with the haze as a sensation stole over her. She wasn't dark.

"Brother Amos added wolf's bane to the mix early this morning, how much more do you require?" Sister Andrea asked.

"Another four ounces. I want her aware for the ceremony, but I need her to rest while in the sanctuary. I don't want a repeat of the trance," Flint answered.

"Yes, Savior." Sister Andrea watched him treat the pendulum with kindness. Another minute, and he bent down, leaving a sliver of space between their faces. The show of affection wore on her, and she took her leave. Jealousy and anger danced with her rising anxiety and emotions as she crested the last step and stood in the afternoon sunshine. The full moon, nearly translucent, sat at the horizon like a sign from Wodan. Above her the chimes of the sacrifices sang in the breeze. "Tonight, Soothsayer," she promised, looking up at the chimes.

"Did Savior give you instructions?" Sister Emily asked. Dressed in the custom white cotton pullover shirt and matching cotton pants, the end of her braided strawberry blonde hair sat at her waist.

"Yes. The sacrifice will be bathed in the herb unguent and her skin coated in lavender oil," Sister Andrea answered. "Once those tasks are complete, she is to be wrapped in the linen."

"And the wolf's bane?"

Sister Andrea looked at the moon, Sister Emily, and the sanctuary. "Ten ounces. He requires ten more ounces."

"Yes, Sister," Sister Emily replied.

"No. I'll try him again later." Rutger growled as he hit the end button. He turned and watched Ansel walk across the lot.

"What's that about?" Ansel asked.

"It was the sheriff's department. Detective Watt isn't answering his phone and has yet to call me. He said he would, after Detective Adan questioned the receptionist at the gallery. I haven't heard a damn thing." Rutger growled again. "The day is passing."

"If the receptionist is friends with Jordyn, she might be upset. Getting answers will take time." Ansel's hand rested on the butt of his gun, his eyes searching Rutger, and the area behind him.

A pang of envy slid through Rutger. He wanted his gun. He wanted to work. He did not want to be hanging out at his parents' house waiting for a human detective to call him. "True. I should have gone to Butterfly Valley and questioned her myself."

"You would have put yourself in the middle. After Mr. Myers, I think you should keep your distance from Butterfly

Valley."

"You're in charge one day and already giving me orders," Rutger said, meeting Ansel's stare.

"I do what I can." He smiled. "Seriously, you don't need your name in the paper again. Anyway, I hear Alpha Howard is making trouble where the article is concerned. He called other alphas and the Highguard about the serial killers. He's telling them it's a cult, not a coven. You created the story to work as a liaison with the sheriff's department. Jordyn is no different, she gave up the ways of the pack and aligned herself with humans. Alpha Howard is demanding a meeting to discuss whether the baron is capable of handling the situation. He has petitioned the Highguard for baron."

"The weak coward." Rutger marched a half dozen steps, his frustration building on his agitation. "Law enforcement is in charge. What the hell are we supposed to do when our hands are fucking tied behind our backs? Don't call attention to yourselves. Find the murderer. Detective Watt basically called the enforcers a group of vigilantes. I know it's Butte Springs, but one wrong move, and it'll be me in jail."

"Rutger."

"Over here." Rutger watched the baron take the stairs, to the driveway and close the distance between them.

"I talked to Rosslyn. We discussed the witches and the ritual. If they plan on raising a god from the dead, they'll wait for the full moon. The hot moon, represents the end of winter … death, and the beginning of summer … life. She is convinced they won't do anything until midnight. When the moon is at its peak. I understand it doesn't make the situation better, it does, however, give you time," Healey explained.

"Midnight." Rutger looked at his watch. It was four in the afternoon. He needed to call Detective Watt, again. "Have you heard Alpha Howard is demanding a meeting? And about his petition?"

"Yes. I've been informed. In a couple of days, so as not to look like it's been set up, there will be a challenge. No doubt, Alpha Howard will not continue. After learning a painful lesson, he will drift into obscurity."

"A challenger has been chosen?" Ansel asked. He gave Rutger a sideways glance, the suspicion in his eyes blatant.

"By the Highguard," Healey answered.

"How accommodating," Ansel said.

"Yes. Time will tell," Healey replied. The Highguard kept its distance unless it wanted something. To have their communal agree to help the Cascade pack, without making demands in return, made Healey question their motives. Motives he would worry about after Jordyn was home. "Rutger, if there is no word by nine, you will take your team to Butte Springs. You will get Jordyn back and deal with those responsible. I'm being watched and cannot appear weak."

"Yes, Baron." Rutger's heartbeat spiked, his rapid pulse throbbed in his veins, while the excitement of the hunt and the kill called his wolf. The baron gave him a satisfied grin, his eyes glowing with his wolf, and giving them his back, left them. "I need a team."

CHAPTER TWENTY-FIVE

Three hours later, Rutger stood at the front of the conference room, in uniform, his hand on the butt of his gun, his focus on his team. Ansel, Quinn, Clio, Aydian, he switched Luke with Kellen, and Mandy. Torin, head of the soldiers, stood with three of his crew—Charles, Alex, and Kai.

"We're treating this as a raid so you need to check your gear and ammunition. You need to keep your senses on point, because the witches are using a charm to conceal themselves. They'll be able to hide from us and I have no idea what else they're able to do. They have killed and mutilated four werewolves, and one of our own. I'm going to assume they'll fight back once they know we're there. They're using wolf's bane to sedate their victims and that means they've investigated our weaknesses. We need to be prepared for silver," Rutger explained. *Breathe deep*, drifted through his thoughts.

"What's the plan once we get there?" Aydian asked.

"I'm going to look for Jordyn. The rest of you gather as many of them as possible." Rutger raised his hands, and stopped talking when everyone, at once, voiced their disagreements. "Wait. Wait. They have committed crimes. Murders. I don't know if they have other prisoners, and we can't risk putting them in danger."

"So, we don't. Why take them into our charge?" Kai asked. Her blue-lined eyes glared at him.

"The Trinity sheriff's department will take them into custody and they will face prosecution. We will not be vigilantes. We will not put the pack at risk. This is our city, our territory, and we will continue to corporate with the authorities. Our work will keep our relationship with the human population safe."

"I hate it," Torin said.

"So do I. It has to be this way," Rutger replied. "Mandy and Clio, I want you to take the medical van. Aydian, Quinn, Kellen, and Ansel, you'll take a truck, and I will drive mine. Torin, take your SUV. I need all of you to ride together. The less presence we have the better," Rutger explained.

"When do we leave?" Torin asked.

"Twenty-one hundred. It'll take an hour to get to Butte Springs, leaving us a couple of hours before the ritual begins. I have no idea what the terrain is or how the area is set up. It puts us at risk," Rutger replied.

"Radios. Will they work?" Torin asked.

"Yes. I'm not depending on cell phones. Kellen fitted a booster in the truck. Tracy will be at the comm desk monitoring all communication. If we are over taken or lose the radios, she'll send help," Rutger answered.

"Why are we waiting?" Aydian asked. His fingers wrapped around the butt of his gun and his eyes shimmered with his wolf.

"Detective Watt and Detective Adan are going to question the receptionist about any visitors at the gallery," Rutger explained.

"Waiting is bullshit," Aydian protested.

"Agreed," Kellen added.

The tension in the room continued to increase with their questions pushing Rutger's frustration. "The more information we have, the better prepared we'll be."

"If you say so," Charles added with an air of doubt. "We can take out some humans."

"We don't know how many there are. I've had firsthand experience with their ability. They can hide their presence from shapeshifters and will try to drive your wolf with their evil," Rutger warned. "It creates a lack of control between the human and the wolf. And there's a full moon. The combination will challenge your control."

"Settle down, Charles." Torin faced Rutger. "It's understood and we'll be ready."

Rutger nodded to Torin and took his cell phone from his pocket. Nothing. He hit Detective Adan's number and waited. The detective from Butterfly Valley wasn't thrilled with talking to him, a werewolf. "Detective Adan, it's Rutger Kanin," he greeted as he walked out of the conference room and stood in the hall where it was quiet.

The call lasted two minutes. Rutger called Detective Watt and waited. Half a dozen rings later and Detective Watt's voice told Rutger to leave a message. Hitting the end button, Rutger returned to the conference room with adrenaline in his veins.

"What happened?" Ansel asked.

"Detective Adan questioned the receptionist. She confirmed a woman, red hair, had been in and questioned Jo about a print. Butte Springs. The woman referred to it as Belle Ridge." Rutger stared at the row of windows.

"We have confirmation," Ansel said.

"There was a man with the redhead, watching her. He stayed outside while she talked to Jo. There was a smell of herbs."

"Damn. And?" Torin asked.

"Detective Adan met with Detective Watt at the Butterfly Valley office and explained his findings. After they talked, Detective Watt returned to Trinity. No one has heard from him since," Rutger stated, facing Ansel. "There's something wrong."

"You think we should leave earlier?"

"Yes. I'm going to tell the baron we have confirmation Belle

Ridge is Butte Springs. And about Detective Watt."

"Do you think he headed to Butte Springs to check it out?" Torin asked.

"Like he said he would. We've lost the element of surprise. They'll expect us." Rutger left the room, and headed down the hall, passing his office, the communication room, and entered the reception area. Through the doors of the building, his pace picked up speed as he crossed the lot. His long strides had Ansel and Torin hurrying as they followed him to the house. Rutger took the stairs two at time, his thoughts pushing his fear. Sousa responded to the energy surrounding Rutger and without hesitating, opened the door. Rutger marched to the baron's office.

"What happened?" Healey asked as he stood. Rutger's eyes glowed with his wolf, his power circling him like a gale of emotions.

"Detective Adan confirmed Butte Springs and Belle Ridge are the same place and told Detective Watt. I believe Detective Watt went to investigate." The words rushed from him, and he stopped to take a breath.

"Calm down and explain."

He was going to get Jo. Rutger inhaled and exhaled. "I think the witches know about us and Detective Watt is in trouble."

"That changes things." Healey walked around his desk, concentration creasing his forehead, and his thoughts passing in his shadowed eyes. "All right. Take your team and go."

Rutger turned to leave, Ansel and Torin already out of the office and by the front door.

"Rutger. Bring her home," Healey said before Rutger left.

He stopped at the entrance, and turning his head met the baron's gaze. "Affirmative."

Tempted by the power in the lycan's pain, Flint left clues for the Wolf Enforcer in hopes he would find the coven, not the law. Someone leaked information because there was no way the Wolf Enforcer figured it out for himself. Worthless wolf. He was probably chasing his tail.

Could the spy be one of mine? No. Flint raced up the dirt road and away from the cops.

Around him, behind him, his brethren spread out to take their positions in the tree line. When he reached the sanctuary, he entered through the open door as three gunshots cracked through the air. The candles flickered in the breeze, the stringent smell of sage and wolf's bane held the air inside of his sanctuary. His heart pounded with adrenaline, his veins feeling like they were on fire as he approached the altar, and the lifeless body covered in white linen. She hadn't moved. He slowed his breathing and caught his breath. "It'll be over soon, Soothsayer."

Several more gunshots blasted outside, each one causing him to cringe as a barrage of shouts and yells, from both his people and the invading cops echoed. He feared for his people, but it wouldn't stop him. Once Wodan rose with his new body fueled by the soothsayer's power, their enemies would die.

"Savior, they're retreating," Sister Andrea reported through a breath.

"Any casualties?" His hands rested on the rough wood altar, his eyes focused on the soothsayer's pale face.

"No. Minor injuries."

"Our foes?" He wouldn't let the energy from death and the spilled blood go to waste. He would use it as an offering to Wodan. It would have to serve in place of the Wolf Enforcer.

"Unsure. They collected their wounded and drove away."

Belle Ridge sat inside of a cell phone dead zone, and he knew their radios were useless. Cut off from the outside world, they were unable to call for backup and without electronics it forced them to retreat. It didn't mean they wouldn't return. Time was slipping away from him. "Good. We must move forward and complete the ritual." Turning around, Flint faced Sister Andrea. "Gather those uninjured and ready the shrine."

"Yes, Savior," Sister Andrea replied. Her white on white clothing wore stains from blood and dirt.

"Sister Andrea, a question?" Flint asked as he took two steps toward the woman.

"Savior." She waited, her eyes going to the soothsayer's limp body, her labored breathing, and Savior's narrowed gaze. Had he found out she added to the wolf's bane?

"How did they find us?" Flint asked calmly.

"What?" *It's not about the wolf's bane.* "I don't know." She hadn't finished her answer when her eyes went to the floor.

"I think you do." He walked over to her. Flint raised his hand, she recoiled, and ignoring her, he placed his hand on her shoulder. "Soothe your worry. It's time to fulfill the ritual."

"Yes, Savior." With her head bowed and her eyes on the ground, she turned and walked out of the sanctuary.

Flint remained by the entrance watching Sister Andrea repeat his orders to his brethren. If he couldn't have the Wolf Enforcer, he would replace him with the traitor. That's what she had become in his eyes. "A sacrifice," he mumbled as he went back to the altar.

"There are lights ahead, everyone be on your guard," Rutger ordered over the radio. He slowed his truck to a crawl, rolling forward when he recognized the black vehicle and the sheriff's department seal on the side. Detective Watt had driven to Butte Springs to do a simple investigation. Without a complete team.

"Shit." Pressing the accelerator, he drove up the road, and pulled to the side. "Stop in formation. Ansel, I need backup."

"Yes, sir," Ansel replied.

Rutger put the truck in park, watched Ansel stop behind him, and they both exited. Quinn got out, walked around to the driver's side. Aydian walked around to the passenger side and got in the truck. If someone opened fire on them, they would use the truck as a shield, allowing Rutger and Ansel to jump in the bed.

Ahead of them the engine coughed, rumbled, and evened out. Its headlights beamed around the V-shape in the grill where it crashed into the tree. Its back end sat on the road, its right side high centered on a fallen tree. Smoke billowed from under the crunched hood, and the purging of engine fluids could be heard dripping into puddles.

As they walked closer to the SUV, they drew their weapons. Rutger cautiously approached the driver's side door while Ansel stood several feet away, his gun at the ready, and aimed at the windshield. Using his senses, Rutger searched the area, but found no one else—not that he could trust his senses. The witches proved they were able to hide. He drew a breath and caught the sweet tang of blood on the air. With his nerves jumping under his skin and adrenaline flowing through his veins, his wolf rose up, forcing him to swallow the pressure.

Feet separated him and SUV, and Rutger searched the road, the tree line, and crossing the distance to the door, checked underneath. Washed in highlighter green, the man's limp body rested against the steering wheel. Blood covered his left side, the seat, and dripped from the frame to the ground. The heated engine oil tangled in the fresh scent of blood and ruptured skin, but there was another smell drifting from the wounded man. Burnt gunpowder from the round that hit him, mixed with gun smoke from the weapon he fired. A damn fire fight.

Rutger holstered his gun, opened the door, and pushed the man backwards. Detective Watt's pale face cringed with the movement, his weak heart struggling to beat. "Detective Watt," Rutger mumbled.

"Repeat," Ansel requested.

"Get Clio up here, Detective Watt has been shot," Rutger ordered.

Quinn drove up the road. Behind him, Torin drove the SUV, to the right and off the road, and parked. Clio maneuvered the med van up the road and stopped beside Rutger.

"How bad?" Clio asked as she approached. She was pulling on a pair of black nitrile gloves.

"He's unconscious, his pulse is weak, gunshot wound. He couldn't have been here long, I can smell the gunpowder," Rutger replied, stepping away from the SUV.

Behind them, Mandy opened the back doors of the van, the LED lights brightening the inside and the immediate area. "What are we looking at?"

"Gunshot," she replied to Mandy. "We need to move him," Clio told Rutger. She backed away from the door, giving Rutger room.

As gently as possible, Rutger extracted Detective Watt from the SUV, and followed Clio. When there was room, Rutger stepped into the van, and kneeling, eased Detective Watt to the gurney.

"Let's see what we have." Clio sat on the narrow bench, unbuttoned Detective Watt's shirt, and examined the wound. "Mandy, gunshot wound, blood loss, he has a pulse. Looks like a ball round, small entrance, no exit. The entrance is near his collarbone, the round might have hit a bone and stopped. Let's hope it did," Clio explained. "Rutger, there's no trace of silver."

"Noted," Rutger replied. One less worry.

Mandy stood beside Clio, surveyed the equipment, and grabbed the red trauma bag specifically created to treat gunshot wounds. The set contained combat gauze to stop the bleeding, rolled gauze, a tourniquet, and fluid to keep his heart beating. She opened the bag and began taking supplies out. "Here you go. Where do you want to start?" she asked.

"We'll bandage the wound, stop the bleeding, and see if that improves his heart rate," Clio replied.

Mandy quickly pulled a pair of gloves on, took a package, and ripped it open. Tearing the top off the foil wrapper, she handed Clio the medicated combat gauze. Clio listened to his heartbeat and watched Detective Watt's reaction as she placed the bandage over the bullet wound. Contact with his skin activated the medication in the gauze, releasing a coagulate. He took a labored breath, his eyes fluttered, and he drifted.

Rutger walked to the backend of the SUV and stared into the dark. He had to get to Jo. "Torin, I want you to stay here with Clio and Mandy. The rest of you are with me." Rutger turned around and watched Alex move to the driver's seat, Kai to the passenger seat, and Charles remained in the backseat.

"Rutger, his pulse is getting weaker, we're going to have to get him out of here. I can't be sure the round hasn't done more damage," Clio said. "Mandy, we'll start an IV and get him ready to move."

Not knowing Jo's physical condition, he didn't want them leaving. But he didn't have a choice. Jo could shapeshift, and if she was too weak to do it by herself, he was there to help. Detective Watt was human, mortal, and needed medical attention. "Affirmative. Get him out of here. Torin go with them."

"I'm against this," Torin protested.

"I'm not thrilled about it myself," Rutger replied. "You'll drive them to the hospital and report the shooting. This will work in our favor."

"Understood." Torin grumbled and walked away. He stopped at the driver's side door of the medical van and faced Rutger. "Just so you know, I wanted to kill the witches. You're stealing that from me."

"Get out of here, Torin," Rutger ordered. "Everyone else, load up." Rutger walked to his truck and got in to wait for Ansel.

CHAPTER TWENTY-SIX

She wasn't awake. She wasn't asleep. Stuck somewhere in between, Jordyn felt a chill on her face and inhaled fresh air.

Outside.

The full moon's influence couldn't break the haze from the drugs. But it didn't stop her from realizing what was happening. No one found her and the time had come. A dark sadness moved through her veins to soak the hollowness Flint's torture created.

I'm going to die.

Panic bound her heart in barbed wire, and reaching out into her core it stung her lungs. *Rutger.* Jordyn wanted to cry and couldn't. She struggled to breathe, her chest heaving against the tight wrapping. Paralyzed and encased, it held her stomach, hips, legs, and tighter, it bound her ankles. Her arms, free of material, rested over her ribs, and the thick smell of lavender and herbs sat heavy around her. Like the others, they prepared her for death.

"Brothers and sisters, our days of bowing to the humans will end tonight. Our ancestor's deaths will be avenged." Flint's voice boomed over Jordyn as his increasing power saturated the area. "The sacrifices have given us strength, an authority, a soul, and a heart. Under the full moon they will fuse with the soothsayer's endowment."

Jordyn opened her eyes to tree limbs lit up by lights. The glare was like a barrier to the outside world.

"Sister Andrea, please assist me," Flint requested.

My time. She gazed out at the crowd as she walked to the altar and stopped at its edge. "Yes, Savior."

"I have a need." Flint's eyes darkened and he raised the knife.

Sister Andrea gasped, her eyes widened, and she stepped backwards. Brother William placed his hands at her back, allowing Flint to slice through the air, the sharp blade catching Sister Andrea's throat. The clean cut welled with blood, its mass splashed to the altar a second before she fell forward and collapsed on top of the collected bones and organs.

Flint raised his hands into the air and drank in the energy from the coven. "My brethren, with this fresh soul, call our God."

"Wodan. Wodan."

"Flesh unites the spiritual body. Blood unites the spiritual body with the soul. Magic bonds the spiritual body and the soul to the transcendent world of imprisoned gods."

Jordyn felt her feet leave the ground.

"Baptized in the alchemy of elements, we have nurtured the pendulum who will summon Wodan, the God of War." Flint's voice grew louder. "Raise the pendulum so she may become an amplifier to our spell."

Completely off the ground, Jordyn hung upside down over the altar, her arms hanging loose, her fingertips inches away from Sister Andrea. Scarlet covered the wood and spread out to soak the bones positioned to shape a skeleton. Sadness flooded her as the feel of the victim's torture rose up from the altar and out of their spilled blood. Her own rested below her. His whispers in her ears while his heart sat quiet.

"Wodan, hear the prayers of your loyal worshipers. Hear the accretions summons."

Flint left the altar and walked through the crowd, his white robe skating over wild grass, pine needles, leaves, and rocks. He touched his brothers and sisters, their chanting quickening, their bodies trying to contain the excitement. With a leisurely turn, he watched the soothsayer hang upside down over the altar, and act as a pendulum for Wodan. His brothers and sisters touched his robe, his hair, and he returned to the soothsayer. Their humming grew louder at the same time they created a tighter circle around him and the altar.

Flint stepped up, and grabbing Jordyn's right arm, held her. "Soothsayer, your blood will become nourishment and your essence will revive Wodan. When your wolf dies the walls separating us will vanish. Wodan shall break the chains of his prison and enter our world. It is time for you to absolve yourself from your life, your pain, and your past. Free yourself from your impure body and embrace your illuminated body."

Jordyn watched them sway and listened to them hum, their eyes empty of presence. Beside her, Flint held a knife and brought it to her face.

"Wodan will take the lives of those against us and send them to the prison that has kept him from us. Chained and tortured, it will put an end to the blood feud. We will be free," Flint yelled.

Cries and cheers sounded, and Jordyn closed her eyes as panic and fear churned inside of her. It was nothing compared the feeling of loss.

"May the power of the pendulum open the door." Flint turned his body away from the altar and faced Jordyn. He placed the knife's tip against her upper arm. "Under the full moon, release your energy." He cut into her flesh. She tried screaming from the pain, her lips unmoving as he continued to carve into her arm. Warm blood flowed from her and dripped to Sister Andrea's red hair and the fragments below. "The first drops of the pendulum's blood have touched the sacred body." Stepping down, Flint moved to her left side, stepped up, and held her arm. "Take her essence as your healing nectar."

Pain swallowed Jordyn, the intensity clearing the drug's haze. The numbness faded, and she felt her legs straining, and the stretching of muscles from hanging upside down by her ankles. Flint met her gaze, his insanity playing in his pale brown eyes, and he stuck the blade into her arm. Jordyn screamed, the force burning her throat while her lungs starved for air.

When the lights reflecting from the camp came into view, Rutger and his team parked their vehicles and walked the remaining twenty-five yards, staying to the tree line.

"He's inciting a frenzy," Kia warned.

"They're insane," Ansel remarked.

"It's giving me the creeps," Quinn added.

"While they're working themselves up, they're not going to notice us. We need to move," Rutger ordered. With Aydian, Quinn, and Ansel, Rutger took the left side. Kellen joined Charles, Alex, and Kai to take the right side.

"What are we going to do when we get to them?" Kai asked.

"Dart as many of them as you can," Rutger replied.

"Was hoping the tranq guns were a joke," Aydian growled.

"Torin notified law enforcement. They're on the way. No one will hurt the humans. It's time to move." Rutger ordered.

The dirt road divided the camp down the middle, leaving three cabins on one side and two on the left with the road continuing through. Rutger and his team took the left side while Alex and his team took the right. They would search the cabins for victims, loose ends, and to make sure no one escaped.

Raising his gun, Rutger entered the first cabin, and waited while his eyes became his wolf's and adjusted to the dark. The one-room building wore scars from neglect, weather, and those living inside. Sleeping bags, trash, and clothing littered the rough slab floor. He lowered his gun, kicked a sleeping bag to the side, and left the empty cabin.

"Left side, second cabin. Rutger, I think you need to see this," Charles reported over the radio.

"Negative," Rutger replied. "Update."

"Clear," Quinn reported.

"Clear," Alex replied.

"The place is empty, we need to get to the group," Rutger ordered. Time was running out.

"It's important," Kellen insisted. His voice cracked over the silence.

The sound of anxiety in Kellen's voice changed Rutger's mind and he stalked to the other side of the road where he met Quinn.

"Don't like the way he sounded," Quinn whispered.

"Neither do I." Rutger looked at the thick night.

They walked toward the second cabin, where Alex, Aydian, Kai, and Ansel were waiting for them.

"I'll stand guard," Aydian said. His eyes shifted over them, not meeting anyone's gaze straight on. In the distance the chanting and humming continued.

"You've been inside?" Rutger asked.

"Affirmative." His usual tone turned sharp with his clipped one-word answer. Aydian's past rode his face as he inhaled, held it, and let it go. He looked in the direction of the chanting with wolf eyes and his anger building.

If Aydian was fighting to remain in control and not let his demons take him, what the hell was inside? "Let's get this over with," Rutger growled as he entered the cabin. Passing Kellen, musty, dirty air hung inside like a poisoned fog. Torn, weather-aged furniture sat against the walls under faded wallpaper. Stains of age, weather, time, and humans colored the ragged, thin strips hanging down, their ends moving with the air.

"This way." Charles looked over his shoulder making sure Rutger followed. His steps caused the beaten wood to creak and moan. Charles stopped in front of a door, his shoulders straightening, his back rigid. He turned his head, left, right, like he was preparing himself for a fight.

"We don't have time to waste," Rutger said, his impatience playing in his words.

"She's going to need help," Charles whispered. He waited for a heartbeat and opened the door.

"Dear God," Kai uttered, and took a step backwards and stopped.

"Blood," Ansel mumbled. "Wolf's bane."

Jo's fear threaded up from the darkness, her scent wrapping around him and driving his wolf. Rutger pushed Charles, grabbed the door, and slamming it into the wall, ran down the stairs. He stopped cold, standing under a yellow light, and staring at the cell. The same cell she showed him. The image sat in his head. The brutal truth sat in front of him. His chest tightened, his anger and fear colliding in a place so deep it wrapped around his core and twisted his entire body. "Jo."

Slowly walking up to the bars, the cot, covered by a green wool blanket riddled with holes, stood out from the mud-packed wall. Scattered on the dirt floor was her jeans, bra, and underwear. White plastic zip-ties covered in dried blood sat on top of her shoe. Near the bars were several plates of meat. Werewolves. They tried feeding her, her own kind. Zachery. Held by a pain he couldn't explain, Rutger's knees felt weak, his thoughts unable to process what he was seeing. Beside him, pieces, parts—arms, legs, torso, and hair—hung from a frame. Their edges black and rotting, the blood created a puddle in the dirt, while liquid dripped from intestines. His T-shirt, the one Jo had worn was draped over the form. The stench of rot and death thickened as if it wasn't done.

"It's getting crazy out there," Kellen warned.

"The chanting is changing," Charles added.

They hurt her. "Destroy," Rutger growled. He couldn't complete his thought and say the rest of the words out loud.

"Affirmative." Kellen placed his hand on Rutger's shoulder.

Kai ran down the stairs, stopping when her boots hit the dirt. "Fuck." Her wolf howled in her ears with the sight and smells. Like a mine. They dug into the earth to create the room. Kia blew a breath out. "Hurry the hell up. Shit is getting real."

Rutger shoved his wolf down, brought his emotions under control, and focused his anger. Without waiting for Kai to urge them to leave, he turned and made his way to the stairs. Before he left, he looked over his shoulder at the cell and his T-shirt one last time. It made his blood boil in his veins, and his wolf heeding the moon's call wanted to rise. *Not yet.*

The team left the cabin. Outside, Rutger took a deep breath, trying to cleanse the poisoned air from his lungs, and its tang of rot from his mouth. "We surround them and take them out."

"You got it," Aydian responded, his excitement bouncing on the air around him.

"We'll head to the third cabin. From there we'll split up and go around the right side," Alex said.

"We'll head to the first cabin and move out from there," Rutger stated.

With nods of acknowledgment, they checked for people, and finding the way clear, crossed the road, and headed toward their targets. At the first cabin, Ansel, Quinn, and Aydian headed toward the tree line where they would split up. The need to find her changed to desperation that ate at Rutger. He would take the front of the crowd, search for Jo, and act as a distraction. If Flint wanted the wolf enforcer to witness his ritual, Rutger would oblige.

His hand rested on the butt of his gun as Rutger walked down the side of the cabin, his wolf saturated his body with its strength, and wanting freedom. At the end, he searched the area. Fragments of light filtered through the trees, outlining the crowd's bodies and turning them into shadows. The group's presence and their power flooded the area and the magic called his wolf and its power.

He didn't deny his wolf, not with the knot of fear sitting in his stomach. With his wolf close to his skin, his human features began to fade. Using his wolf's speed, he raced to the edge of the tree line. "Positions?"

"Confirmed," each team member responded, their wolves making their voices low and rough.

"Moving in." His heart leapt to his throat, his pulse pounded, his body shaking as he left the tree line and started in the direction of the chanting and the lights. He moved with stealth, controlled strength, and purpose. He didn't need to instigate retaliation from Flint. Fifteen yards and an eerie sound moved with the breeze. Like wind chimes, dull, empty, and heavy. Rutger looked up and saw bones and skulls. Dozens of them catching the silver light of the full moon, hung from the limbs. They were everywhere. Their haunted rhythm fell around him as he stared in disbelief.

This is not happening.

They created bone chimes.

CHAPTER TWENTY-SEVEN

Rutger roared. His wolf pushed harder as he tore through trees and brush following Jo's raw scream. He couldn't run fast enough when another cry sliced through the air.

"Shit." Kai's voice sounded over the radio.

"Fuck this," Aydian growled.

"Remember the objective," Ansel ordered.

Rutger ignored the team and their orders in his ear, his attention focusing on finding Jo and saving her. With the chimes playing, he burst out of the woods and into the clearing to plow through the dazed and chanting people. His features were a twist of human and wolf as he ran. His heart stopped cold in his chest, his blood froze in his veins, and he came to a halt in front of an altar. Jo hung upside down from a tree, her arms hanging and blood pouring from deep cuts. Her bloodshot eyes stared at nothing and everything.

"Wolf Enforcer, just in time," Flint's rough voice taunted. Red rimmed, his beige eyes narrowed, and his white hair, like straw, hung to his shoulders. His bloody hand held the knife at Jo's throat. "Watch your dark soothsayer give her life to Wodan."

"No," Rutger roared.

"Cage your beast," Flint ordered. Around them the chanting gained speed, becoming crazed and shrill.

"I'm going to kill you," Rutger promised. His features

melted, giving into human. It didn't stop him from feeling Flint's flesh in his hands as he ripped his limbs from his body. And his meat in his teeth after Rutger shifted and gave in to his wolf.

"No, you won't, wolf." Flint laughed.

"Open fire," Ansel ordered through the radio.

The chanting faded, turned to screams, and people began falling to the ground. The team continued to fire into the crowd and Flint's face fell, the confidence in his eyes fading, as he looked out at his dwindling followers. Rutger wasted no time— he jumped to the altar, his boots crushing bones, entrails, and kicking the woman with red hair to the side, stood ankle deep in a torso. He held his gun, pointed it at Flint, and pulled the trigger. The tranq dart hit Flint in the forehead, sank in and skidded around his skull, and fell. The jagged cut colored with blood and staining his white hair, slid down thin strands. Rutger shot him again, in the neck, the dart sticking out from his throat.

"You failed, Wolf Enforcer," Flint mumbled around the dart. "The pendulum." He wavered, turned to Jo, the knife in hand, and with the last of his strength, cut across her throat. The blade caught the right side, creating a waterfall. Scarlet blood hit the altar, splashing Rutger's boots and legs.

His need to kill Flint paled with his need to save Jo. Rutger's eyes burned with his wolf, its power covering him like a veil, and grabbing Flint, Rutger tossed him. He flew over people, through the air to crash into a group, the mass going down in an unconscious pile of bodies. Rutger holstered his gun, took a knife from the sheath on his belt, and wrapping his arm around Jo, cut the rope. Her limp body felt as if the weight was the material wrapped around her. The bones of her shoulders stuck out from ashen skin wet with sweat. *Not sweat, she's in shock.*

Men and women darted from the field to the woods, trying to escape the team and their tranq darts. Rutger watched others shuffle around the clearing yelling, sobbing, and howling. He leapt from the altar, with Jo held tight to his chest, and dodged the crazed fanatics. Clear of the unruly commotion, and the chimes overhead, Rutger sat on the ground, Jo across his legs, her head next to his chest. The seeping cut soaked his shirt.

"Jo, look at me," Rutger begged, his grief and pain in every word. Jo's skin paled, and any animation there drained away.

Jordyn didn't try to fight. She knew it wasn't real. He wasn't real. It was another nightmare wearing Rutger's voice and she didn't want to see him when the illusion wanted to destroy her. As if Flint could take more from her.

"Jo. Open your eyes."

No.

Rutger leaned closer, his cheek touching her chilled skin. "I'm here."

The lie was going to be painful. Through a sliver, Jordyn saw Rutger's face, and allowing herself to believe he was there and not part of her imagination, felt his wolf. "Rutger." Her dry, cracked lips scarcely moved.

"Babe. Stay with me." Rutger held her in his arms, her blood soaking his clothes, and turning the white linen wrapped around her a soft pink. "Stay with me."

Rutger's heat and power poured into her. Jordyn opened her eyes and saw the gold of his wolf floating in mahogany. Pain seared through her when she raised her hand to touch him. Life, warmth, and strength teased her cold skin. Jordyn stared up at him, heard familiar voices and the reports from the team. The witches were running into the woods, trying to getaway. She knew what she had to do. So much loss. "I can find them."

"No. Use your energy to shift. You have to shift," Rutger begged. "You're losing too much blood." He should have marked her. Should have shared his wolf. Her eyes darkened, her face twisted with pain, as stringent lavender drifted in the air tangled with the dull scent of her sorrow. He felt the ache and terror consuming her as she worked to increase her strength. Rutger held his rage inside and keeping his words soft, pleaded with her. "Jo, babe, you need to shift." *Shift.*

"Can't." She closed her eyes, and calling her power felt the coven's energy. She used the magic to focus, and moving through the twists of Flint's feel, found him. *I'm not going to live*, she thought and plunged into the connection. Pushing her power, she began dismantling Flint's carefully crafted charm. She saw flames, felt their heat, and in the distance heard cries of agony. She withdrew when more yells echoed, closely followed by roars, and screams.

No. No. No. "Please, don't leave me," Rutger whispered as he lowered his head. With her sweat-soaked cheek touching his, he held her closer, tighter, needing to feel her. Her weak pulse faded, the sensation sinking into him as her breathing slowed, and life drained from her body. She lost. Jo wilted, her body going limp in his arms. Her hand slipped from his neck and her arm fell to the ground. A storm of fury wrapped itself around Rutger, causing thunder to pound in his veins as heartache sliced through him like a sword and its sting saturated his entire body. He raised his face to the sky, the full moon glaring down on him, the stars witnessing the chaos, and roared.

Jordyn drifted from Rutger's arms to the darkness of her soul to embrace her death, with his unhallowed roar invading her ears and squeezing her dying heart.

Losing control. Second in line to the alpha. Director of Enforcers. His fury flared. His titles and power didn't stop him from losing Jo. *Losing. My mate.*

"Rutger, let me have her," Healey said calmly. "I can help her."

"Mine," Rutger thundered. His lips drew back, exposing his

lengthening canines, and the bones of his face moved under his skin like snakes, tightening his flesh as his wolf emerged. "Mine."

"The moon will help her. I will help her. Let me have Jordyn," Healey ordered. He sat on the ground, legs folded, and his arms out. "Hand her to me."

Rutger's growl weakened to a moan, then a bitter howl. He hugged Jo to his body, taking in her scent, her feel, and grudgingly handed her fragile body to the baron. Without her, a chill swept over him, invading his core and taking his heat. He leaned back, his face to the sky, and roared a sickly sound.

The baron cradled Jo in his arms and the sight pushed Rutger over the edge. He stood with his wolf shadowing his body, roared, and the beast became the master.

"Do it, before it's too late," Healey ordered.

The world blurred and came into focus as his wolf eyes narrowed. Rutger turned around, the smell of blood calling his wolf, and started toward the woodline, and the witches. *Kill them.* The feel of Jo's heart stopping and her limp body against him burned his skin. *Kill them.*

"Hurry," Healey demanded.

The rush of ferocity buzzed in his head, his muscles constricted, and ignoring the awareness skating over his half-shifted body, he stalked forward. Commotion raced around him trying to deter him, they wouldn't, not now, not until he tore them apart.

A sting stopped him.

Rutger turned to fight, his clawed hands in tight fists, and saw the baron lay Jo on the ground. Fresh blood welled to the surface of her neck, its thickness slipping down her pale skin. Her arms stopped bleeding. Her heart had stopped. Nothing moved. Rutger growled, stumbled back, and struggled to keep his balance. *Kill them.*

Healey watched Rutger fight the tranquilizer as he took a knife and cut the wrappings. Replacing the knife in its sheath, Healey flattened his palms on Jordyn's chest. His power, like electric spears, stole the oxygen from the air. His whispered words inflamed his power, and brought the feel of the moon as if it was reaching down and trying to caress Jordyn. "Obey your alpha and give me your wolf," Healey whispered.

Rutger held his breath when he heard the soft beat of Jo's heart, and watched her chest rise and fall with a shallow breath. *Alive. Trick.* He needed to kill.

"Rutger, listen," Healey demanded. "She lives."

He stopped and held onto the rhythm of her heart. Mesmerized by its haven, his legs weakened, his body crumbled in on itself, and he fell to his knees. He wavered, a fog wrapping around his mind and stealing his strength. Rutger gave in and hit the ground. On his side, he watched Jo's human body melt and reform as she shapeshifted.

"The wolf is primal. She obeys the moon and her alpha." Healey met Rutger's gold stare. "She isn't with us. She's deep inside of herself and using the power of the soothsayer to keep me out. Son, she embraced her death and has no desire to fight its hold."

Rutger closed his eyes, felt her absence, and didn't need it said out loud. Tears blurred his eyes, his grief becoming part of him. "Save. Her." The words passed through taut lips of his half human, half wolf.

The sounds, the blood, and the scene made him pause. "Baron." Ansel stood guard beside Rutger's body.

"Chain him. He'll go to Celestial with Jordyn," Healey ordered. He reached out, drawing his hand down the side of Jordyn's wolf form. "They stole her wolf when they drugged her and fed her whatever poison to keep her sedated. Flint tried to break her. She needs to stay in wolf form until her human body gains strength." Healey prayed, even with his wolf turned beast, Rutger was listening.

"Yes, sir," Ansel replied. He turned away from Jordyn to face Charles. "When Clio arrives, chain the director, and help load him into the ambulance."

"Yes, sir." Charles made quick glances at the bodies, the baron, and with a deep inhale, left.

Above them the beat of a helicopter's blade sliced the air and its spotlight lit the trees. Around them sirens echoed through the woods as red and blue lights cut through the night and flashed against the trees. The chaos of the raid was dying down, and a new chaos was beginning. One by one, engines died, giving way to voices, harsh orders, and the feel of humans. Rutger remained on his side, paralyzed, helpless, and felt the tugs on his arms and legs as they started to chain him. The silver burned his skin, sank in and burned his muscles, and weakened him further. The pain came in waves, only the fear for Jo taking its place. Through half closed eyes, he watched armed paramedics carrying a cage. Jo. The pain was going to eat him alive.

"The cage is ready," Clio stated. Waiting behind her were two paramedics, dressed in royal blue BDUs complete with weapons.

"Shifting may have healed her physical wounds, but it will not save her mind from the treatment she endured," Healey said as he stood. "Ansel, talk to the team, and the detectives. They'll want to know what you did and where you have the witches."

"Yes, sir. Do you need any help?" Ansel asked.

"No. We have this under control," Healey replied.

"Sir." Ansel nodded and walked away—part of him relieved he was leaving and part of him wanting to stay.

Rutger couldn't stop his raging emotions from draining from him as he watched the men lift Jo's body and place her inside of the silver-lined cage.

"Son." Healey knelt beside Rutger. "You understand, yes?"

Two men lifted his deadened bulk, as if he weighed nothing, and held him. His shoulders sank in, his knees bent, and the toes of his boots sank into the dirt. He feebly turned his head to meet the baron's amber gaze and couldn't form words.

"We're leaving," Clio reported. She waited for the baron while staring at Rutger, the powerful, strong, and serious Director of Enforcers, chained and held. "She's going to be all right. I'll make sure of it, and the other doctors will make sure of it."

Rutger could do nothing but watch in silence as they took her away from him.

CHAPTER TWENTY-EIGHT

His veins, like black wiring, stood out from his ashen skin as he beat the concrete walls with his fists. Every strike held an image and churned his hands into bloody broken meat. When he couldn't raise his arms from the pain, the blaring warning they were going to sedate him echoed in the room through hidden speakers. He yelled for Jo, the air burning his throat, her name echoing off the walls. When they denied him, he roared, his wolf encasing him, and the room fogged with drugs.

It had been hell.

Rutger shook himself, looked at his hands—healed and perfect—and tried to shake the memory loose.

Dressed in his version of the enforcer's uniform, Cascade shirt, jeans, and boots, Ansel entered the office, ignored the now constant brittle energy coming from Rutger, and sat down. "I have the names and addresses of the witches they released."

"I can't believe they released them when they're murderers. Not to mention kidnappers." Rutger felt his eyes burn with his wolf. Every day he heard Jo's cries and saw the image of her cell, and the mutilated body parts. Hate sat inside of him like a growing cancer that fed off him. *Not going to lose myself.*

"Their defense attorney said they were victims. Flint Platt used drugs to keep them from leaving and traumatized them with the mutilated bodies. The non-humans that have been described as witches are currently being held. They were directly involved in orchestrating the kidnappings, murders, prepared the poisons, and helped with the mutilation of the victims. They'll also face charges for using the victims as part of their dark magic. I heard the defense will try to say they were drugged and emotionally manipulated and fearing for their lives … and that's why they did the crimes. I call bullshit, but that's lawyers for you."

"Lawyers. They want the sheriff's department to charge each of us with obstruction of justice, trespassing, and assault with a deadly weapon. If I wanted to assault them, I would have. I don't need a weapon for that," Rutger added.

"After saving Detective Watt's life, it won't happen. We've gained friends in the department."

"Let's hope so."

"Rutger, they haven't been able to find Flint," Ansel reported. "No one has seen him, even his followers haven't heard from him."

"He left them to fend for themselves." A growl edged Rutger's words. He looked at the papers sitting on his desk and back to Ansel. He should have killed the man when he had the chance. "Jo knows he's out there. I bet money, she can sense him."

"How?"

"She used her power as a soothsayer to link with him and break the concealment charm. It's the reason you all were able to track the fleeing witches." After she burned her strength, she died in his arms. The void invaded his body like a winter's cold, leaving his heart a frozen chunk of meat and pushing him over the edge. He lost himself to the primal darkness of his wolf and turned it into a beast. He tasted the raw power, had its energy flowing through him, and wanted to sate its need with their blood.

Ansel felt the empty woods and almost stopped searching

when his senses blew up with their presence. "What are we going to do?"

"Hunt them. Kill them."

"And Flint?"

"If he knows his followers are being murdered, it might draw him out," Rutger replied.

CHAPTER TWENTY-NINE

'Jordyn's wounds are healed and she passed the physical rehabilitation and is able to shapeshift on her own. Her therapist, Doctor Carrion, would like to continue to see her.'

'Of course. Is there anything I can do?' Rutger's voice lowered.

'Be there for her. Support her. And if she needs to talk, let her talk freely, don't judge her. Don't try and fix her,' Dr. Preston answered. 'She has to accept the memories will always be there and the struggle to separate the collective from the truth will persist. Dr. Carrion will help her to acknowledge the triggers and control the affect they have on her.'

'I understand.'

'If you have any questions, do not hesitate to call me or Dr. Carrion. We're here to help the both of you,' Dr. Preston said.

Victim.

The word played over and over while Rutger's eyes narrowed on her with his pity. Jordyn waved off the memory and turned her face to the sun. The warm rays caressed her skin, but didn't stop her thoughts from bouncing from her breakdowns, late night crying, and her body betraying her. When her fear got the best of her, she hid in one of the spare rooms, and prayed the crippling feeling would take its claws out of her. Those days and nights had been long, difficult, and emotional. With Rutger's support, Jordyn fought back and they gradually ended. To help her cope, she resumed habits of her normal life and took her camera and ventured outside. She stayed around the house, not going too far, but there was a feeling of freedom. With all of her strength, she snatched fragments of her old self and greedily held onto them.

Like today, Jordyn thought. Boat engines, birds, and the soft rustling of the breeze through the trees flew in the air. Scarcely ten feet in front of her, the waves splashed against rocks. Jordyn relaxed in the Adirondack chair, a lightweight throw across her legs, her camera in her lap, and her coffee cup sitting on a rock.

Before heading to the lake, Jordyn waited for Rutger to leave. It marked the first time in three weeks Rutger left for work without a twenty minute lecture about being safe, call him if she needs him, don't leave the house, and don't talk to strangers. She laughed at the stranger danger, knowing he was trying to lighten the mood. Rutger didn't have to worry about her leaving the house, Jordyn had no interest in going out. Not yet. She smiled. The phrase 'not yet' had become her go-to line.

After the details about her kidnapping became public, and revealed their marriage plans to their parents, she hadn't wanted to face either of their families or the peering eyes of the pack and public. Rutger ordered everyone to stay away and he would tell them when she was comfortable. But Belle Ridge, the wedding that never took place, and her comfort level weren't the only reasons for her seclusion. Over the weeks, Rutger had become withdrawn, quiet, and they spent most of their time together in silence. He hadn't touched her. Hadn't gotten close enough for her to touch him. Always out of reach. Jordyn inhaled; he wouldn't go near her.

Her mind raced with what he saw at Belle Ridge, the upcoming trial for the witches, Flint's disappearance, and Louis. *Louis*. His lawyer's relentless calls and trying to set up a meeting so they could talk wore her out. While she was being held prisoner, Flint paid Louis a visit, explained his plans, and used a spell to keep the information locked in Louis' head. The spell, anger, and fear had done a number on him. Her instincts told her those reasons were a ploy to get her to meet with him. There was something going on. She didn't know what it was and had no desire to find out.

And Rutger? Her imagination was all she had. The reasons circled every thought as his secrets actively built a barrier between them.

A gust of wind whipped around her, tossing the rumble of a boat engine, and catching stray strands of her hair. Jordyn opened her eyes, the mountains, and the horizon turning from a soft blue to a hazy gray. The cerulean summer sky crumpled under the thickening clouds. Farther out, darker clouds crested the mountain tops as if welcoming a thunder storm. July was perfect for storms. If the sky opened, letting the rain loose, she was going to watch from inside of the house, ditch her coffee, and pour a glass of wine.

Another flurry of wind kicked up whitecaps on the lake, its chill landing on Jordyn and signaling it was time to head to the house. She sat up, slung her camera over her shoulder, grabbed the throw, and after draping it over her forearm, stood and took her coffee cup. Jordyn hesitated for a moment, looked at the lake, the waves crashing on the shore, and felt the slightest tremor skate down her spine. She twisted around to see the house as the energy from a stronger warning rushed through her. No.

"Flint," she whispered. *It isn't real. It's fear.* Jordyn faced the lake, closed her eyes, and forced herself to calm down. Unable to control the anxiety, a kind of failure sank inside of her and mixed with her growing frustration.

Rutger closed the door behind him and stood in the entrance

with silence surrounding him. He used his senses to search for Jo, and finding the house empty, walked into the bar, back across to the dining room, and into the kitchen. "Jo." Rutger continued his search into her studio and found an empty room. With long strides, he walked through the kitchen, through the living room, and headed up the stairs. He checked the spare rooms, searching the corners for her, found nothing, and moved on to their bedroom. His worry grew when he didn't find her and marched back down the hall. He left the stairs when the French door to the deck opened.

Seeing the dark blur from the corner of her eye, Jordyn gasped. "You scared me." Jordyn's right hand was on her chest, the throw on the floor, her camera hanging from the bend in her elbow, and she gripped the coffee cup.

He hated her fear. "Where were you?" Rutger asked. He tried to keep his voice from giving away his concern. His hand rested on the butt his gun, his other hand on his belt. "How are you?"

"Why?" Jordyn met his eyes and saw the secrets sitting in their darkened depths and the tension tightening his shoulders. She waited for him to answer when a warning slid through her, rousing her wolf and calling her power.

"I worry about you," Rutger answered.

Jordyn snuffed her senses. "I'm fine." She set her coffee cup on the table with her camera and picked up the throw.

Was that her wolf? He hadn't felt her power and had started to miss its silken caress. "Where were you?"

"The lake. Where were you?"

"Work." Rutger's senses searched her. She wasn't giving him anything. She continued to shut him out.

"There's something going on. I can feel it. It's either your lies or Flint."

"Jo—"

"Don't. Lie. To. Me." She'd had enough of his silence.

"I won't. If I tell you, it would put you in danger," he confessed.

Jordyn didn't have a response. She did have a list of questions he would never answer. All in the name of keeping her safe. Victim. They stood staring at each other, tension building on their silence while time burned seconds from the space around them. Jordyn flinched, her hands fisting the throw, and her heart pounding with the knocking on the door. "Are you expecting someone?" Her uneven voice gave away her fear.

Every damn time. Every noise scared her. "No." Rutger's eyes lingered on Jo for a breath, his guilt from lying settling in his heart, before he turned and walked to the door. Human. Damn it. He opened the door.

"Rutger Kanin?"

"Yes," Rutger answered. He thought he recognized the detective from the Trinity Sheriff's office.

"I'm Detective Cliff, homicide, with the Trinity Sheriff's department." He didn't offer his hand, rather he took a small notebook from his jacket pocket. "I have a couple of questions."

"I've given my statement," Rutger replied.

"About Belle Ridge, yes, I'm aware." He didn't make eye contact as he flipped through the pages. "Where were you on Tuesday, July twentieth, about midnight?"

"What is this about?" Rutger asked. He had taken risks when hunting and killing the witches, but covered his movements, and disposed of the bodies. He met the detective's gaze.

"Just answer the question. Where were you on Tuesday?" Detective Cliff repeated and looked up from his notebook.

He hated the cat and mouse game. "I was here," Rutger replied.

"The entire night? Do you have a witness, witnesses?"

"Yes, I spent the entire night with Jordyn." Rutger turned

around, and meeting Jo's gaze saw doubt in her eyes.

"Jordyn Langston?"

"That's correct," Jordyn answered. She met Rutger by the door and stood beside him.

"You live here?"

"Yes."

"You were both here on Tuesday?" he asked, his crystal blue eyes narrowing on them.

"Yes. I'm embarrassed to admit, knowing Flint is out there somewhere has made me a little paranoid. I haven't left the house." There was a quiver in her words, giving them a frailty. She knew what she was doing by playing the victim and hated herself. Nothing was going to stop her from protecting Rutger.

Detective Cliff considered her. "You haven't seen Mr. Platt?"

"No. Thank God," Jordyn answered. A tinge of pain skated down her arms, and to make it stop she rubbed them. The wounds healed when she shapeshifted, but the feeling of the knife in her flesh, left behind a phantom pain she couldn't shake.

"Mr. Kanin, we're investigating the disappearances of Mr. Tyler, Mr. Newman, and a Mrs. Macias. If you or one of your enforcers has information, I would like to hear from you. This is my card. Miss Langston, if you have any communication from Mr. Platt, or from the people I've mentioned, please call." He didn't wait for either of them to reply when he gave them his back and walked to his car.

Jordyn left the door with her heart in her throat, went to the living room, and sat down on the couch. She knew Rutger's secret. Hell, she knew their names.

Detective Cliff was playing with him and was hiding information. What it was, Rutger couldn't imagine. If the detective wanted a confession, he was going to have to arrest Rutger. He closed the door and turned around. "Jordyn." Rutger left the door, walked to the living room and sat down in the chair across from her and her accusations.

"You're killing the witches." Jordyn didn't look at him, couldn't look at him; she stared at her hands. *How many?*

It wasn't a question. There was no anger in her accusation. "The courts found them victims and released them."

Released. Victims. When were they were going to start telling her the truth? *When you stop hiding,* her mind threw at her. She shook the feeling loose. "You can't take the law into your own hands. They'll give you, a lycanthrope, the death sentence for killing humans." She stood, her body tight with fear, and her emotions bleeding through the broken parts of her. "I shudder to think you would chose having revenge than being here with me. Am I not enough?"

"Babe, you are everything." Rutger stood and approached Jo. He kept space between them, unable to be near her. If his touch made her flinch, it was going to crush him. Jo's eyes narrowed, gleamed for a second with her wolf, and she took a step away from him. Something was happening.

Babe. "If I was, you would touch me. You can't stand the sight of the broken person I have become. I'm not enough. You can't deny it when you easily put *us* at risk." Giving him her back, she faced the kitchen. She felt his eyes drilling into her, his presence crawling over her.

Her words struck him as if she shot him with silver. It wasn't true. His body yearned to be near her, to touch her, his wolf wanted to have her. Rutger didn't want to scare her. And he needed to finish what he started, then they would be free. "They deserve to feel every tendon, muscle, and bone being torn from their bodies and afterwards left to bleed to death. They deserve torture after what they did to those men. Zachery. I didn't … They were clean kills," Rutger explained as if it made a difference. He wouldn't let Jo change his mind. If the court system was going to spit criminals out, letting them go free while their victims paid the price, he would be damned.

"You're becoming one of the monsters. And your hate is like a fever and is poisoning you," she accused without looking at him. "I can't compete with revenge."

Jo's pain escaped her, forcing Rutger to ignore his senses. There was a plan in place and he was going to do what he had to. "I have work." He wanted to explain the pain and madness controlling him, the beast wanting its freedom, and the sight of her hanging from a tree, but couldn't find the words. Not when she doubted him. Rutger inhaled, watched her for a second, and left the room. His footsteps were heavy on the wood flooring and the slate. At the door he turned to see her, and for the first time in weeks noticed she was putting the pieces back together. She was healing. It didn't change his plan. He was going to have his revenge, and the witches were going to pay for hurting her. Thinking she might say something to him, he waited, and waited, and when she didn't acknowledge him, he opened the door and left the house.

Once in his truck he called Ansel. "A detective came by my house," Rutger explained. "I'll be at the office in twenty." He ended the call, drove away from his house and Jo, and turned onto Mill Street.

Jordyn waited for the sound of Rutger's truck to fade before sinking into the couch. Out of habit, like it would save her, she grabbed the throw and clutched it to her chest. With the pressure of tears building and threatening to fall, she buried her face. "Get your shit together."

Damn him. She was going to lose him. After having the blind faith in her ability to take care of herself stolen, along with her place at the gallery, and her independence, there was no way she could handle losing Rutger. "Revenge." Guilt ate at her resolve and she fought the coming breakdown and the feeling of helplessness.

My fault.

The wind beat against the French doors, rattling them as thunder ruptured the sky. With the throw clutched to her chest, Jordyn stood and walked to the doors. The advancing storm cast its chaos into the air, its energy feeding the whitecapped waves and grabbing smaller rocks, sent them tumbling into deeper water. In the distance, lightning blast through rain heavy clouds as if in search of the mountain tops. Like the weather knew the madness happening to her, she felt its pressure in her chest.

Jordyn bowed her head, an ache building behind her eyes, and a nervous energy flooding her veins. She needed to think, she needed to get a grip and talk to Rutger. First, she would call the baron and warn him what Rutger was doing, with the help of the other enforcers. If the detective suspected Rutger as the killer, he was going to need an alibi and maybe a lawyer. Strengthened by her resolve and having a purpose, Jordyn walked to the end table and picked up her cell phone.

It hadn't completed one ring when the baron's deep voice sounded. "Jordyn, is everything all right?"

She hated the question. "Yes. It's Rutger," Jordyn quickly answered. When the line remained silent, she explained everything. The baron didn't act surprised. "He left. I'm assuming he's headed to the office."

"Jordyn, he's parking his truck. I'll talk to him."

"Thank you." Jordyn nearly hung up when she hesitated. "Baron, could you wait?" she asked as she walked toward the front door. "Someone is here." Jordyn shook her head when the baron's gruff voice ordered her not to answer the door. *Stranger danger.* What if it was Ansel, or another enforcer looking for

Rutger. Or the detective? She didn't want to be alone with him and his questions.

Jordyn opened the door, shock keeping her from yelling into the phone. She needed help. She needed Rutger. Fear sucked the air from her lungs and stole her voice. Jordyn lowered the phone and stared at pale brown eyes. They narrowed and looked bleached in the shadowed light cast by the cloud covered sun.

"Soothsayer," Flint greeted, his dry, cracked lips moving around her name. The movement brought fresh scarlet to the surface, filling several thin cuts. Blood beaded on the curve of his mouth, and sliding down, washed his yellow teeth in red. His stringy, dirty brown hair no longer held white, and sat matted to his skull. "I've missed you." He smiled, and moving quick, slapped the phone from her hand, sending it skidding across the floor.

Jolted out of her shock, Jordyn backed farther in to the house. "Flint." She wanted to yell loud enough the baron heard her. Air left her lungs, she felt it, and knew she said his name. It wasn't enough when a thread of fear snaked down her spine with her failure. Her entire body hurt like he ripped open every wound. Jordyn felt her blood drain from her body, her heartbeat slowed, and her world dimmed. *Not real.* She didn't move. She didn't look for her phone. She didn't turn and run. Jordyn stared at Flint. Somewhere the baron's muffled roar invaded the silence. He knew. She had to believe he would get there in time.

"Your wolf is hunting my people and killing them," he hissed. When a bellow grew louder he searched the floor. "Killing them!" Flint yelled in the direction of the baron's roar.

Jordyn flinched with his anger and the shrillness of his voice. "They know you're here."

"*They* will be too late." He stalked forward, his left foot dragging. "This time, I'm killing you."

Jordyn's muscles felt like rebar wrapped tight around the

bones in her legs. Her mind turned trap flooded with fear and images of her cell. He yelled orders, walk, move, and pushed her. Jordyn remained frozen, her legs and feet foreign extensions.

CHAPTER THIRTY

"Rutger!" Healey burst out of the house, his cell phone clutched in his hand, the first drops of the summer rain dotting his dark gray T-shirt. With Sousa and Jason following, he pushed the office doors, the force sending them backwards and bouncing off the protective stoppers. Healey growled at the empty reception area and started down the hall. "Rutger."

"What? What is it?" Rutger walked out of his office, Ansel and Kellen behind him. The detective had paid the office a visit, asked questions about the enforcers and their jobs, and questioned Rutger's whereabouts.

"Jordyn called."

"It's under control," he replied in defense.

"Flint is there." Healey's voice thundered.

"What?" Rutger was focused on the detective, the murders, and their next move. He hadn't considered Flint. Damn, rather than threaten Rutger, Flint went after Jo. Again.

"He is at your house with Jordyn. He has her." Healey saw the bewildered look in Rutger's eyes and a pang of regret stuck him. So much pain. After considering the enforcers present, he said, "I want Ansel and Kellen ready to roll. Now. Where is Aydian?"

"Patrols," Kellen answered. He gave Rutger a sideways glance.

Healey watched Kellen and Rutger. "Jason and Sousa, stay

here with Charles. I want you to monitor communications."

"Yes, sir," they replied.

Rutger gathered himself. "Radio Aydian and explain to him what's going on. Ansel and Kellen, head over to my house." His words, mixed with dread and fury, rushed from him. His house. Their house. Jo was healing and returning to her old self. His darker side quickly took over, and the thought he was going to face Flint meant it was his chance to kill him.

"I'm coming with you," Healey insisted. His power saturated the room, while his rage infused the air. Rutger wasn't going to argue, anything he wanted to say would be discussed on the drive. "I suggest you call Detective Cliff. By giving him Flint, he might see you in a different light," Healey advised as he walked out of the office.

"What exactly did she tell you?"

"You're using the enforcers as your personal death squad. I'm not against it, but you haven't covered your tracks."

Rutger got behind the wheel of his truck, started the engine, his heart racing, and called Detective Cliff.

Jordyn backed into the French door, the cold glass a hard edge to the panic spreading out and snaking down her legs. Flint kept pace, matched her steps and trapped her. Her entire body began shaking as the memory of Flint's touch invaded her skin.

"The first time I saw you, a lycan with powers, I feared you. Not today. I broke you and made you mine." He laughed, his lips splitting and dripping blood.

Flint's guttural laugh stopped when he closed in, his arm behind her, his hand on the handle. His body towered over her, forcing Jordyn to turn her head as he pressed his chest against her. "I have a surprise for you." He opened the door, and the wind catching it, swung it wide.

She stumbled out of the house to the deck, the humidity in the air wrapping around her like a second skin as drops of rain landed on her head and shoulders.

Flint casually stepped out and pointed to the stairs. "Go, Soothsayer."

She had taken the same stairs, before the rain, before finding out Rutger was killing witches. Before he left her.

Jordyn walked, her steps feeling heavy, at the same time the illusion of security she felt broke into millions of shards. He invaded Rutger's house and stole her safe place. Her fear held her hostage. She couldn't save herself. Her quality of life spiraled in terror and turned into her personal prison. Stepping down the first stair, her wolf pressed on her, the opportunity to end her misery sat in front of her. Stood behind her. She could do it. Thunder erupted, and she flinched—lightning lit up the darkened sky, and she wished she had the throw to clutch. *Damn.* The gates opened, letting rain fall freely as he laughed at her fear. Loud and hard, its mocking infecting her ears.

Fat drops of rain pounded the wood, the ground, and she could hear it hitting the lake. Trees swayed in the gusts. It pushed the brush sideways, their branches touching the ground from its force. As Flint shoved her, she grabbed the wet railing, stopping herself from tumbling, and took the next step. Before she reached the last stair, Flint grabbed her by her hair and jerked, hard. Jordyn stopped, her head back, her face to the sky, her eyes closed and the rain assaulting her.

"Slowly, Soothsayer," Flint ordered. He pushed his evil into her, its feel like razors on her skin.

When she stood straight, Jordyn stepped down and her running shoes sank in the mud. Her hair whipped in the wind, making stray strands stick to her wet cheeks and forehead.

"Raise your hands," Flint ordered.

Jordyn raised her hands, embarrassment joining in with her fear when her T-shirt crawled up, exposing her waist.

"Good dog," Flint mocked and laughed. "You can lower your hands."

He was human.

She was a werewolf.

She hadn't been able to stop him before, what would make her believe she could get away from him after Belle Ridge? Jordyn's doubt bubbled in her stomach, its acid poisoning her confidence. A slight tremor cascaded through her and her wolf reacted to her fear. Jordyn ignored it and shoved it down. She hadn't used her power, hadn't trusted herself with the power of the soothsayer. She didn't want to feel Flint and his darkness. Her self-loathing didn't end. She blamed being a werewolf on why he kidnapped her and she lost everything. She didn't want to have anything to do with her wolf. She wasn't sure if she wanted anything to do with her life. It became a maze she was having trouble navigating through. Her thoughts froze and her breath caught when she heard material rustling and felt something at the back of her head.

"I heard death by silver is slow and painful. If you run, I'll find out if it's true," Flint vowed, nearly spitting the words. As if he needed to convince her further, he chambered a round, the steel on steel driven by the wind. With his free hand, he shoved her forward and they walked with the rain pelting them.

Jordyn turned her face out of the wind and rain and looked at the barrel before meeting his eyes. "Rutger is on his way. He'll kill you this time."

"I know he is," Flint replied. She didn't know if it was confidence in his voice or insanity. "He won't touch me. He'll be trying to save you. His failure will taste sweet."

He motioned, with the gun, for her to walk. Jordyn hesitated like she was going to stand her ground, gave in, and obeyed. The scent of rain-soaked trees sat in the wind, making the air heavier, thicker, more threatening. She walked through brush, oak trees, and pine trees, the thin, cinnamon-colored needles creating a thick layer on the ground. To stall, she took careful steps and moved low branches out of her way. At the same time, her instincts and wolf demanded she save herself. Can't. Weak. *He has a gun.*

She wasn't fast enough to beat a silver bullet. Reacting to her fear, her wolf whined in her ears, the power of the soothsayer teased her, and she fought to shut them down. Flint shoved the tip of the gun into her back, urging her to walk faster. Jordyn stepped over a fallen tree, the sun fighting to beat back the clouds, weakening the downpour to a drizzle. She accepted; she was helpless to save herself. Several steps and the stringent scent of death, and the rot of blood rose up around her. Human parts, small and large, wet and rotten, peppered the flooded ground.

Jordyn stopped. Days. He had been there for days, and she knew it, felt it, but thought it was her imagination. She was convinced she was drowning in the broken parts of her mind.

"I've been watching you, Soothsayer," Flint said with pride in his voice. "While he hunted and murdered my brothers and sisters, I hid right in front of him. I watched his mate." Jordyn turned to face him and he laughed a deep sound, his joker smile drawing his cracked lips back, exposing broken teeth. He inhaled and raised the gun. "I sacrificed Sister Andrea for nothing. She was my favorite. It was ruined. You ruined it. Wodan is lost to me."

Jordyn watched his jerky movements and felt her fear snaking through her. He was losing his mind.

"Walk to the tree," Flint ordered.

Jordyn tore her eyes from him but didn't move. A crude carving with half-moons, a box, and upside down cross scared the trunk of the pine tree, its pale inside stained dark crimson. Scattered around the trunk and half buried in leaves were bones.

"Move."

A hard shove and she stumbled. Losing her balance, Jordyn tripped over a branch, her knees hit the soft ground, and she put her hands out in front of her to stop herself from hitting her face. Inches from the dirt she faced bloody human remains and bones. Fresh kills. Innocent victims. With the feel of the dead invading her, trying to break her wall, Jordyn scooted backwards, away from them, and rapidly got to her feet. It had to end. She needed to end it. "You're insane," she hissed, turning. Something clicked inside of her and started a fire in her middle.

"Soothsayer, go to the tree."

"No." She wasn't going anywhere. Her wolf rose up, its energy warming her skin. With her increasing power, her senses slammed into her, telling her Rutger arrived. His fury moved through the woods like the Angel of Death searching for victims, its cold edge touching her skin like blades of ice.

The sky darkened, thunder rolled above, etching a path for lightning, and a new torrent of rain poured down on them. The storm didn't cover the feel of humans, werewolves, and the energy of their emotions.

"Go to the tree," Flint demanded. His words rushed and tangled while his eyes widened, his muscles tightened like he was getting ready to hit her. He began whispering. She couldn't make out the words with the thunder and the rain pounding the trees, ground, and shrubs.

Jordyn blinked her eyes, trying to hold his gaze despite the torrent. "Go to hell." His incantation lashed out and she fell to her knees.

"I'm not done with you." Flint took a step toward her, his lips moving around silent words.

Jo's fear called Rutger, and leaving the detective, deputies, and enforcers behind him, he loped through the woods. Her feel strengthened as her fear changed and following it, he navigated through the trees and brush. Rain pelted his face, soaked his T-shirt, and his BDU trousers. Rutger searched and saw them through the trees and slowed his run to a walk. No. No. His worst nightmare came to life. Jo was kneeling, Flint stood over her, the barrel of a gun resting against her head as if he was planning to kill her execution style.

Rutger stopped and with his hand on the butt of his gun, gauged the scene. "Get away from her."

In seconds, the baron, Detective Cliff, and three deputies stood beside Rutger. Ansel, Aydian, and Kellen moved in the woods, taking their positions and making sure Flint wouldn't escape.

Flint glared at the soothsayer for a heartbeat before turning and facing the Wolf Enforcer. "You will savor the feel of her lips as she dies. Blood will taint her kiss, its taste will sit in your head, and poison your dreams. The soothsayer's death will haunt your days and nights." Flint's rough voice turned deep, like he was seeing what he was saying. He stepped to the side, closed the distance, and touched her head with the tip of the barrel. "The earth will swallow her dark soul."

Jo stared at Rutger with her mascara sliding down her cheeks, her wet hair framing her face, and her T-shirt sticking to her thin frame. He expected to see terror in her eyes, panic saturating their depths, and her fear riding the air. There was nothing. She had erased her essence. His chest tightened as he watched her eyes turn bronze with her wolf and harden like stone. She was changing. His wolf howled in his ears, as her words, and the past days played in his thoughts. *Don't let her die*, he prayed.

Detective Cliff stepped around Rutger, his men raising their guns. "Mr. Platt, walk away from her, and we will protect you," Detective Cliff promised.

"I don't need protecting. When she is dead, I will have her power and you will be defenseless," Flint responded.

Jordyn watched Rutger's eyes gleam with his wolf, and his shoulders straighten with Flint's threat. Beside him, she saw the detective, the deputies, and the baron all staring at her, but didn't really see them. She listened to the promises of protection and safety and wanted to scream. What was there to protect? Flint was an insane serial killer who had her kneeling on the ground, a gun at her head, in a storm and surrounded by the bones of those he murdered. No way in hell was Rutger going to jail. She closed her eyes, released her power, and finding the dead and Flint's incantation, let its energy fill her wolf and her body. With Flint's magic sitting on her, she searched for its strongest point. When she found it—him—the stirring energy burned as it grew, the worse of it setting the mark on her thigh on fire. Jordyn opened her eyes and knew they changed when Rutger couldn't stop staring at her.

"I don't need protection!" Flint screamed. He kept the gun pointed at Jordyn, his free hand holding the side of his head.

"Mr. Platt, lower the weapon. Don't make us fire on you," Detective Cliff ordered.

"No." Flint hit Jordyn in the head with the barrel. "I did it."

"You did what?" Detective Cliff asked.

"I killed them." Flint laughed. Tremors gripped him and the barrel continued to hit the side of Jordyn's head. She turned away from him and stared at the remains. "I killed them all."

"Who did you kill?" Detective Cliff asked. His attention shifting from Mr. Platt to Miss Langston. She was staring at the body parts, her eyes a broken bronze.

"My brethren. The traitors. I found them and killed them for their betrayal," Flint answered as he hit the side of his head with his fist. "Spilled blood. Sacrifices."

"Lower the weapon and tell me what happened," Detective Cliff tried. *What the hell is happening?*

"Betrayal has a price." Flint's voice quivered. His eyes darted to Detective Cliff, the deputies, and the Wolf Enforcer. Flint swayed, closed his eyes, his lids stained with dirt, and started mumbling. Drops of spit and blood slipped from his mouth to his chin, and his split lips bled freely. "When she is dead," he mumbled as he looked at them, "I'll have the power to kill you."

"Mr. Platt, lower the gun. I won't tell you again," Detective Cliff warned. He raised his hand signaling the deputies to ready their guns.

His lips curved, he laughed, and shook his head. "No."

"Mr. Platt—" Detective Cliff started his warning.

Rutger held Flint's gaze and saw his insanity. No, his internal fight.

"She dies," Flint whispered. "She's the pendulum."

Thunder crashed across the sky as the gunshot echoed around them. *No. No. No.* Rutger watched mud, pine needles, and human remains give under Jo when she landed on her side.

CHAPTER THIRTY-ONE

Rutger raced to Jo's side, her muddy running shoes next to Flint's boots. *Don't lose control.* When he heard her heartbeat, he gently turned her to her back, and gathered her in his arms. "She's unconscious. I'm taking her to the house to get her out of the rain."

Detective Cliff knelt beside Flint. "Dead." He faced Rutger. "Affirmative. Deputy Garvey, call this in and get the forensic team and the medical examiner out here."

"Yes, sir," Deputy Garvey replied. He watched a minute longer, his eyes on the remains, Mr. Platt, and Mr. Kanin as he picked up Miss Langston. His radio jolted him from the grisly scene.

"Deputy Arey, go to the house and stay with Mr. Kanin and Miss Langston. If they need medical attention allow them to call," Detective Cliff ordered.

Healey watched as Ansel and the others left their positions and headed to the house. "Detective Cliff, I'll go with Deputy Arey."

"One minute, Mr. Kanin." Detective Cliff stood, his eyes on the gun and the head wound.

As if they weren't standing in the rain, Healey stopped and faced the detective. "Of course."

"Mr. Platt confessed to murders he had nothing to do with and killed himself. I'm not an expert on the paranormal, or mind control, but I do believe he was being coerced."

"By whom?"

"You."

"No. We, shapeshifters, cannot control minds or influence the thoughts of another," Healey answered.

"And Miss Langston? He kidnapped her, called her a *soothsayer*. He said he would have her power. What is she? What power does she have?"

"He also called her the pendulum, and was going to use her to raise a god from myth, Detective. To answer your question, a soothsayer is a keeper of records. Miss Langston doesn't have any special powers. I would say, those are the words of madman. A serial killer."

"That might be so. I said he had nothing to do with the murders, and you didn't disagree. You didn't defend your son," Detective Cliff continued.

"Detective, if you're implying my son had any involvement with the murders, rest assured I would not defend him. The Cascade pack has a relationship with the human population of Trinity, and we strive to live as an example to them. Like helping Detective Watt. Supporting Old Town and its success. I'm not putting our hard work in danger by having a vigilante taking the law into his own hands. Flint confessed to you. The evidence is at your feet. And unless there's *evidence* contradicting his confession, I would say you have your murderer," Healey replied. The downpour teased an end, the thick clouds not giving up their assault brought an erratic rain.

"When I became a detective, fifteen years ago, I was given one piece of advice—don't believe anything you hear and a third of what you see."

"You don't have to believe me. Believe what you see." Healey looked at Flint's body, the human remains, when sirens screamed in the distance. "Is there anything else?"

"Not at the moment," Detective Cliff answered. He looked down at the body and back to Mr. Kanin.

"Wake up, babe." Rutger realized as he held her close to him, it was the first time in weeks. Guilt raised its ugly head at the same time the feel of her wet clothes sank into him. The memory of her dying in his arms waited for him to dive in and drink it up. He wouldn't. *She isn't dying.* "Babe."

The images from Flint's mind played and played until they faded and finally stopped. Jordyn relaxed. She was free of Flint and her mind was hers once more.

With a violent jerk, resulting from her power streaking through her, Jordyn sat up straight. Rutger's hands slipped from her sides, and she met his gaze. "I'm good. I'm all right."

"I thought he shot you." Rutger's eyes darkened with the confession. Letting her stand, he watched her sway, and gain her balance. "Do you want me to help you?"

Jordyn took a step, the motion making her head swim, her wolf to howl, and her power to flare. "No." She covered her eyes with her hands and waited for her head to stop spinning.

Doesn't need me. "I'll get some towels." He stood, watched her, and in silence walked to the bathroom.

When he returned Jordyn was standing in front of the window looking out at the lake. Her shoulders held her anxiety, and he wondered what she was thinking. "Here."

Jordyn didn't talk as she wiped mud and blood from her face with a damp towel and after setting it on the table, grabbed a dry one and started on the worst of her hair. Needing to sit down, but not wanting to get the furniture wet and bloody, she left Rutger standing by the window and sat on the hearth. A chill sat on her skin from her wet clothes and she wished there was a fire.

Rutger placed the towel he used to dry his face beside Jo's, and picked up the throw from the floor. "Here. Jo."

Jordyn took it from him, without meeting his gaze, and covered her legs. "Rutger." She heard and felt the exhaustion threading through her. Denying her wolf and power meant it took more strength than she expected to capture Flint's thoughts and twist them. Still, it had been too easy, and it felt ... good.

"You made him confess. You made him kill himself." Rutger watched confidence backed by power and knowledge sit in Jo's eyes. She was strong enough to use her power to kill someone.

"Yes." Jordyn held Rutger's gaze, waiting for his challenge. The lectures of her therapist happily died with Flint. "You aren't a suspect and the bastard died by his own fucking hand, giving me my revenge." She squeezed the bridge of her nose, inhaled, and looked at Rutger. "You know something about revenge."

"Jordyn—" Rutger started, but stopped. He did know. He didn't want her to live with the dirty sorrow of having blood on her hands.

"Deputy Arey is here to ask if you need medical attention," Healey announced when he entered the house.

Jordyn looked away from Rutger and at the baron. "No, I'm all right."

"Are you sure, ma'am?" Deputy Arey asked. He remained several feet away, close to the door, his fear wafting around him.

He didn't like werewolves. "Yes, I'm sure." She imagined what she must look like. Her soaked clothing, her makeup washed from her eyes and leaving streaks on her cheeks, and covered in blood and dirt. Don't forget, scared. A victim. Jordyn looked at the colors of the throw and back to the deputy. "I'm fine."

"I'll let Detective Cliff know. If you need anything, I'll be outside," Deputy Arey replied. His radio came alive with seconds of static before voices and orders cut through. He started to leave, his pace quickening, and after closing the door answered the radio. Jordyn wanted to tell him closing the door wasn't going to stop her from hearing him.

"You've endured another attempt on your life. Are you all right?" Healey asked.

"Yes." If this was going to be another round of 'are you all right' she didn't want any part of it. Since they couldn't comprehend she was fine, she wasn't going to explain the feeling of power and control knowing she beat Flint.

"What did you do?" Healey asked.

Jordyn met the baron's narrowed eyes, his wolf sitting in the shadows and waiting to judge her. "I controlled his thoughts."

"How?"

She nearly shrugged and left the question unanswered. "My power. It came naturally."

"Our link is weak and getting weaker, and this proves you've lost your pack. Through his treatment of you, you've been forced to choose a side." Healey rested his hand on her leg, the cold saturating the blanket and sinking into his palm. His eyes felt older with a tinge of regret as he focused on her. "You used the pack and killed someone. You chose darkness."

Jordyn wanted to point out Rutger killed the witches and used the enforcers. Was he dark? "No, I didn't use the pack. I haven't lost the pack and our link is strong. I control what you feel. He tried to kill me and was denied. I took from the dead around me and gave it to him," she explained. "I didn't choose a side. There are no sides. No dark. No light." Thunder rolled, sounding as if it was right above them and its bulk was trying to get into the house. Jordyn tossed the throw to a chair, disgusted with herself, as her instincts flooded her with information and a chill skated down her spine.

"How can you be sure?" Healey asked and watched her.

Don't question me. "It would have happened at birth." *I'm pissed.* Maybe later when she wasn't tired and her senses weren't overloading, she would be able to explain. Maybe not. A slight vibration sat on her skin, and she turned to look at the door as Aydian peeked around its edge.

"Sir, there are men wanting to talk to you," he reported.

"Let them in." Rutger walked to the door, expecting to see detectives. He stopped when two men, dressed in black suits stood in the entrance. "What are you doing here?" Rutger asked.

"The Highguard sent us." The first man looked around Rutger and met Jordyn's gaze. Watching her, he reached inside of the suit coat, purple lining the inside, and took an envelope from his pocket. Crip white with scarlet lettering scrawled across its front and he handed it to Rutger. "They will be expecting your response." The man left Rutger. "Baron Kanin. You have inaugurated traditions of dark epoch by taking the scion and enshrining her as your soothsayer. You have declared the fated Rutger Kanin and Jordyn Langston as One-Flesh, yet she has not been marked. I will report this to the Prime."

"Jordyn has been through a traumatic event. She needs time to heal," Healey said in protest.

I'm right here. Jordyn glanced from the man, to Rutger, and to the baron. He wasn't a werewolf or a shapeshifter and had the ability to cover his presence. The messenger continued to stare at her. He was studying her. Making a mental report for the Prime.

"That is a dead tradition. We live in the time of humans," Rutger said, defending himself. He hadn't touched her in weeks, their relationship becoming second to her fear and his revenge. Was he contemplating marking her? His jaw clenched with the thought.

Marked. Jordyn's insides caved. She had heard the horror

stories of men losing themselves to their wolves while they marked their mates. With their fangs, they tore into the soft flesh between the neck and shoulder, then pumped the bite full of the lycanthrope virus. She would carry him in her skin and veins, and others would recognize it. There were other stories where the male poured a silver mixer into the wound and the silver would stay. Like a gruesome ravaged tattoo. Jordyn figured it was the reason the tradition was forbidden. "No." Everyone looked at her.

"Your disagreements are futile. As your erroneous assumptions will cost you. Read the letter." His emerald eyes gleamed, blazed like a spark, and dimmed. "The Prime and the Highguard are pleased you are all right, Soothsayer." His eyes held hers for a breath, before he bowed, turned, and walked to the open door. "The Prime will be waiting." With his last words, both men left as swiftly as they had come.

Jordyn stared at Rutger. "I don't understand."

Rutger didn't say anything. He read the letter, going back and rereading, and reading it again. "They're saying the baron didn't show the Highguard due diligence when he enshrined you in his power and that of the pack. They're accusing the baron of embracing an untested soothsayer. You weren't added to their books. The baron has put the collective at risk."

"It's true, I didn't go through the proper channels, I didn't think it was necessary. Jordyn is pack. Her parents gave their approval. I thought it was enough. I'm guessing they have followed the case. They understand how powerful you are," Healey explained.

"They will deny the Sacred Writ of our union, if I don't mark her. It states it needs to be excessive. Silver. What the fuck?" Rutger held the paper like it was poison and would easily sink into his palm. "I'm not scarring her."

"It's real?" Jordyn mumbled. *Silver.* She rubbed her neck. The idea of Rutger, half shifted with his teeth in her skin, made her stomach turn but despite her unease, it brought her desire to life.

"I've never heard of this. The Highguard's intrusion into pack matters doesn't make sense. Why us?" Healey paced and faced Rutger. "What else?"

Scion. "Marked. Excessive. Untested. They know more than all of us. This is my punishment," Jordyn mumbled to herself and sat straighter. Her jeans were beginning to dry, the denim getting tighter around her legs.

Rutger cast her a glance before saying, "There's more. The bodies by the tree."

"Yes." Healey watched Rutger's eyes darken. "What about them?"

Rutger inhaled. "Are the witches I killed."

"The Highguard has spies." Healey looked out the window and at the lake. "What do they want?"

"Jo," Rutger answered with a growl. "They aren't taking her."

"Why?" Jordyn asked. "Seriously, I don't understand."

Healey faced Jordyn. "They think you're untested. They don't believe you've accepted the collective. They don't know about your mark and our link. Once you have a pack, you cannot be separated from them. You understand the feeling. While you were living in Butterfly Valley, you returned to Trinity to feel your territory."

"Then tell them I have a pack," Jordyn insisted.

"I can't refute the Highguard. They'll want proof of our nexus," Healey said. "I'm not confident it exists."

Jordyn's power weaved through the room, between them, it's light feel changing when Jordyn added the weight of the pack. Voices, faces, drifted through her mind and she didn't stop them.

Jordyn let them move freely at the same time she brought her wolf forward. "I control my power," Jordyn whispered. "It does not control me."

"Jo. This is you?" Rutger asked. He felt the pack. The woods. The energy they created when they ran together under the full moon. For the first time in weeks, his teeth ached to feel her flesh. His wolf rose up and he struggled to shut it down. The memory of losing himself weaved fear around his need.

"Yes. I hated being a werewolf and refused to use my power, fearing I would feel Flint. It would act as a beacon and he would find me." Jordyn stood, laughed a sad, weak sound, and shook her head. He had been there the entire time. "Do you feel our link?"

"Yes, Jordyn. I understand. We need to make the Highguard understand," Healey replied. Fear sat as a shadow at the fringes of his mind.

"Baron, Lord and Lady Langston," Aydian reported. His wolf filled his eyes and they narrowed on Jordyn.

Jordyn cut her power and buried its feel. "I don't need this," she mumbled.

"Daughter, are you all right?" Ethan asked. Leaving Aydian at the door, he rushed to the living room. "We came as soon as we heard what happened." He grabbed Jordyn and hugged her.

"Jordyn, I'm glad to see you're all right," Mia said as she approached.

Ethan let her go and she sat down. Jordyn wanted to run up the stairs and lock herself in her room. Forever. "I'm fine."

"Fine? Your life was in danger. That man hunted you, watched you, treated you like an animal. If you weren't a soothsayer this never would have happened." Mia sat beside Jordyn. "You smell like the dead."

Meeting Mia's ice blue gaze, Jordyn let her choice of words

settle, fighting her demons and her self-loathing. No more. Jordyn looked at Rutger. He wasn't looking at her. He was watching her. Gauging her. "I can't change what I am. I can only protect myself."

"He was going to kill you. He took you from the Director of Enforcer's house. No one protected you," Mia argued.

"*Our* house. He took her from our house." Rutger swore, the low rumble of a growl playing with his words. *Control.*

"I was never in danger," Jordyn replied. Her head ached. "He was losing his mind."

"Leave her alone, Mia, it's over. She is safe and doesn't need to be reminded." Ethan stood with his back to the window, blocking the view to the lake, the steely sky, and the storm clouds.

"Son, can I have a word?" Healey asked.

Rutger wanted to say no, but there was more. "Yes, sir." He looked at Jo stuck between her parents and wanted to rescue her from them. A darker thought plagued him—he was going to have to rescue her from himself. He turned and walked with the baron to the door, opened it, and they both stepped outside. He heard Mia ask about the Highguard before he closed the door on them. His body tight with anxiety, and his face twisted with his worry, Rutger met the baron's gaze. "You have to read the rest of the letter."

Healey took it from Rutger, unfolded the parchment, and began reading. "This changes things."

"What does the Shadow Lord want with Jo?" Rutger asked. The two-thousand-year-old vampire was given the name Shadow Lord because no one had ever seen him. He existed as a shadow. The proof of his power sat with his representatives that served the Highguard. With his seat on the Highguard, he ruled his territory of Regulus, Latin for King of Serpents, through fear. Rumor said his coven numbers were close to one thousand.

"How does he know about her?"

"That is a good question. I suspected something was amiss when the Highguard agreed to remove Alpha Howard. Now this. I will contact the Prime's office. In the meantime, you have to mark Jordyn." Unless the Highguard understands powers of the magic born are changing. And it includes Jordyn.

Fear teased Rutger's wolf. He couldn't, not after losing control. "If we refuse. He has evidence." Rutger's voice lowered when the house went silent. "The bodies by the tree are a gift from him. The Shadow Lord. I'm in his debt." He needed to protect Jo.

"It won't come to that. We'll take the necessary steps to solidify Jordyn's place within the pack. Go inside, she needs you. If you need anything... anything, call me." Healey folded the letter, having no intention of giving it back to Rutger.

Any control over his emotions fractured and his energy drained from him. "Yes, sir." Rutger watched the baron leave with Ansel. With the rain easing, Kellen and Aydian stayed behind—Kellen taking his position at the back beside the French doors, while Aydian stood by the front door. At least he had his enforcers.

"Mr. Kanin, Detective Cliff is on his way, he needs to ask you some questions," Detective Arey reported.

"Aydian, let the detective in when he arrives," Rutger said, thankful his voice held.

"Yes, sir." Aydian, dressed in the enforcer's uniform of black BDUs, boots, and thigh holster, moved to stand beside the door.

Deputy Arey watched from the end of the stone walkway, his eyes taking them in, his questions hanging around him. Rutger entered the house, his own thoughts racing in his head and creating questions. After closing the door behind him, he saw Jo standing at the window, her right hand on her shoulder, and her parents sitting on the couch.

"Detective Cliff is headed our way. Are you going to be all right?" Rutger asked. He wanted to take her in his arms and hold her for an eternity.

Jordyn turned around. "Don't ever ask me that again." She had been thinking, the bronze flakes floating in her cocoa eyes giving away the conflict.

"The baron said he'll call the Prime and let us know when he finds something out. We're going to clear this up," Rutger promised. He prayed they cleared it up. He took his thigh holster off and placed it beside the door before walking to the living room.

"What are you talking about?" Ethan asked. "Why would Healey need to call the Prime?"

Jordyn didn't want to have this conversation and turned back to the window.

"Is it about the Highguard? They think you're dark?" Ethan's gaze darted from Rutger to Jordyn. "One of you could answer me."

Dark. Superstition ruled where facts were limited. "I'm untested. In their eyes, I'm not enshrined with the pack," Jordyn replied. She wasn't going to say a word about not being marked.

Mia snickered. "I warned Healey about forcing us into the past. The Highguard is proving me right." She looked at Ethan. "This is about you. I told you. I told you, your mother was dark. This is why—" Mia stopped and stood. She smoothed the front of her black slacks, trying to remove invisible wrinkles. "Bailey isn't a soothsayer."

"Enough. You can think whatever you want about me. But understand, your comparison of us will never change the relationship I have with my sister," Jordyn shot back.

"It doesn't change what you are."

"Mia, relax. I'm not dark," Jordyn interrupted. Letting go of her fear opened her to her powers and the truth in them.

"Excuse me, sir. Detective Cliff is here," Aydian reported.

"Let him in," Rutger replied and walked over to Jo.

Jordyn left the window, stepped around Rutger, headed to the hearth, and sat down. *I need a fire and wine.*

"Jordyn," Mia started, "they're human law."

"Really?" As if she hadn't been dealing with humans for weeks. Jordyn covered her legs with the throw, trying to get the chill to ease. She wanted to wash the smell of the dead off her body and get out of her clothes and change into something more comfortable. Comfortable and dry.

Aydian held the door, letting Detective Cliff enter the house. He scanned the area, saw Rutger's gun and belt, as he made his way to the living room. At the edge of the slate, just before the wood, Detective Cliff stopped, keeping them in front of him. "The forensic team is investigating the scene and the surrounding area. It will be taped off while the evidence is collected and everything is cleaned up," Detective Cliff began. "I need to ask Miss Langston some questions."

"Detective Cliff, we're her parents. We would like to stay if it's all right," Ethan requested.

"If Miss Langston agrees."

"I don't have a problem." Jordyn's heart was in her throat and her pulse beat in her head. Rutger stood beside her, his power feathering her skin like a warm caress. She needed him.

"Can you tell me what happened when Mr. Platt arrived?" Detective Cliff held a notebook and pen poised for her answers.

"He knocked on the door. I answered it, he pushed his way inside," Jordyn answered. *Frozen with fear describes what happened.*

Detective Cliff looked up from his notebook and met her gaze. "You let him in?"

"I did not let him in," Jordyn stated, slowly.

"What happened after he entered the house?"

"He said he was going to finish what he started." Jordyn stopped and inhaled. Retelling the story brought back the feel of his weight in her head. Rutger placed his hand on her shoulder and squeezed. "I backed away from him. He trapped me against the doors leading to the deck. He said I was broken and ordered me out of the house. When I followed his orders, he laughed at me."

"Did he have the gun?" Detective Cliff's eyes remained on her.

"Yes. He said he'd heard silver was painful way to die. If I ran, he would find out." Jordyn felt the tip of the barrel on the back of her head, his voice in her ears. It pissed her off.

"Did he say anything about the others? His followers?" Detective Cliff asked. This time, he didn't look up from his notebook.

"When he wasn't threatening me, he was rambling. He didn't make any sense."

"You continued to do what he said?" Detective Cliff's eyes narrowed on her over his notebook.

"I didn't want him to shoot me in the head." Jordyn's frustration was quickly turning to fury.

"How did Mr. Kanin, not Rutger, know you were in trouble?" Detective Cliff looked at her. There was a glimmer of excitement in his eyes, and his pulse quickened.

You're going to lose. "I was on the phone with Mr. Kanin when I answered the door."

"Why did you call him?" Detective Cliff asked as he stared at Rutger.

"I needed someone to talk to," Jordyn answered, her gaze dropping down to her clasped hands.

"Rutger was here. You couldn't talk to him? Or did you call

Mr. Kanin for another reason? After Rutger left. After I left. Maybe to warn him."

"There's no reason to badger her. She is the victim here," Ethan protested and stood. He looked at Jordyn. "He had a gun to your head?"

"Dad, it's all right." *I can't believe I said that.* "I didn't want to bother Rutger, again. For weeks he has listened to me. Mr. Kanin is like a father and I just wanted to vent to someone who hadn't been overwhelmed with my problems. Sharing the misery, I guess." Jordyn met Detective Cliff's narrowed gaze and knew there was victory in hers.

"What did you talk about?" His blue gaze narrowed.

Detective Cliff was chasing a case he wasn't going to win. And for what? Protecting serial killers. Or wanting to send werewolves to their death. "Nothing. Mr. Kanin answered his phone, Flint knocked on the door."

"I see." He glanced down at his notebook and back at Jordyn. "You didn't know Mr. Platt was on the property?"

"No. I don't venture out very often, and when I do, I don't go far." Jordyn physically shuddered. The sickening weight of invasion rushed through her.

"You didn't *sense* him?" Detective cliff said absently. "Rutger, you didn't know he was here? You didn't *sense* him?"

Before Jo could answer, Rutger explained, "No. As a practicing witch, he used the ability to conceal himself from our senses. And I have concentrated my senses on Jordyn." The case and Belle Ridge should have explained everything.

"You are the Director of Enforcers, and you didn't think it was important to check your own property?" Detective Cliff asked. His eyes skated over the group, a glint of superiority shining in their depths.

"I understood human law enforcement was searching for

Flint, and it meant I didn't have to worry about protecting my property," Rutger replied. No, he didn't check his own damn land. He was hunting the witches and leaving Jo alone.

Detective Cliff raised his notebook and began writing. "Rutger, you were at Mr. Kanin's house when Miss Langston called?"

"I was at our office building," Rutger corrected.

"I understand that's where the Director of Enforcer's office is. What were you doing there?"

"Working and checking in with my team. Mr. Platt's witches are out there, and we have the right to patrol our land."

"But not your own land. I see. Mr. and Mrs. Langston, is this the first time you've had contact with your daughter, Miss Langston?"

"Yes. We wanted to wait until she was ready," Ethan replied. The pain from her kidnapping and missing out on three years of her life burned through him. No. He hadn't had any contact with his daughter.

"Ready. For what?" Detective Cliff asked.

"People. Mr. Platt kidnapped my daughter, starved her, drugged her, with the intention of killing her and using her as a sacrifice. She was held prisoner by serial killers for three days. Her therapist said she needed time and we weren't going to push her." Anger laced Ethan's words.

"Forgive me. I'm the lead homicide investigator in the murders of three people associated with the coven, and there are four others missing. I came here today to question Rutger Kanin. And while Mr. Platt confessed to murdering his own followers, before taking his life, I need to make sure I'm not falling for a paranormal trick. Mr. Platt called Miss Langston a soothsayer. What does that mean?" Detective Cliff asked.

"It's a title from years past used in the name of tradition. I keep the pack's history," Jordyn answered. Her patience with the detective's questions was thinning.

"There are no powers associated with the title? Mind control?"

"No, Detective. Just mad organizational skills," Jordyn answered. "Because of Mr. Platt, I lost my place at the gallery, and Mr. Kanin gave me a job." That was how it went, right? Jordyn sat straighter, felt Rutger's eyes on her, and stared at the detective.

"I'm not a non-human, so I can't sense your lies. I have been a homicide detective for a long time. I'm not without my own instincts," Detective Cliff said. He let time pass between them, the silence settling in the room with the tension. "I'm done here. If I have further questions, I'll be in touch."

Rutger squeezed Jo's shoulder, left her side, and walked Detective Cliff to the door.

"The investigation isn't over because Mr. Platt is dead," Detective Cliff warned.

"I wouldn't have thought otherwise," Rutger replied. *You need to protect the humans.* He opened the door and waited for Detective Cliff to leave. Rutger watched him, his anxiety burning his nerve endings. Three bodies. Four missing. Also, dead. He wondered which ones were by the tree.

"You're a suspect?" Ethan asked from the living room.

Rutger closed the door, felt the effects of denying his wolf for weeks on his nerves, and turned. "This is our territory. This is our pack. They invaded it, murdered innocent werewolves, and put all of us in danger. Flint kidnapped Jo. He tried killing her. They're dead. It's over."

"Doesn't surprise me, Director of Enforcers." Mia nearly cooed the words. "You played your part quite well, Jordyn."

A little slice to her patience. Jordyn met Mia's gaze and the accusations sitting in them. "I learned from the best."

Ignoring his wife and his daughter, Ethan focused on Rutger. "Why was he asking about mind control? Werewolves don't possess the ability." With nervous energy, Ethan stood, leaving his wife, and walked over to Jordyn and met her heavy gaze. Jordyn contacted Rutger through thought. "You."

"Yes," Jordyn hesitatingly replied. She looked at her hands— innocent hands, which had held her camera, champagne glasses, and now was responsible for killing someone. Lifting her head, Jordyn faced her dad. His wolf stirred, feeling like a breeze on her mind, and she saw him inside of a ... metal box. The connection to the pack was strengthening and crowding her.

"The Highguard knows this. Daughter, I failed," Ethan confessed. "I'm responsible for the darkness inside of you." His eyes dimmed, and his grief wafted from him to her.

"No, you didn't. I'm not dark," Jordyn replied. Her voice held firm, not giving away the image of her father cowering in a corner as guards threatened him. "The gift comes naturally. It has nothing to do with sides. There are no sides. There are only actions."

"You're wrong. Soothsayers are inherently dark," Mia challenged, her eyes holding their usual condescending glare. "Magic has good and evil. This is no different."

"That's archaic. You have no idea what you're talking about." Jordyn narrowed her gaze on Mia.

"You think you know what you are?" Mia stood, her back rigid, and her power leaking into the air.

"I do." Jordyn stood, her eyes reflected her wolf as her power wrapped around her. "I'm stronger than you, Mia, watch yourself." Jordyn slipped into Mia's mind, her racing thoughts the opposite of her clam demeanor. Accusations intertwined into every thread but it was the layers of lies causing Jordyn to deepen her search. Truth sat in the depths of Mia's hate. Jordyn's anger flared, regret and loss poisoning her.

Rutger heard Lady Langston's breath catch as the air thickened and turned static from Jo's raging energy. "Jo, you've proven your point."

No, I didn't. I found the truth. Jordyn extinguished her power as if it had a switch and found all eyes were on her. "I'm done defending myself." *To you.* The Highguard will have their own accusations.

"You're safe now. I think it's best if we leave. Mia," Ethan said. He stared at Jordyn with a combination of horror and fasciation. Almost like love lost.

Rutger watched Jo sink deeper into her thoughts, her head down, a wall of violent emotion circling her, and didn't know what happened. Continuing to the door, he stopped as Aydian opened it. "Jo has been through enough. Lord Langston, if there is news, I'll contact you."

There were threats surrounding them. The pack. The Shadow Lord. The Highguard. Jo was becoming a threat to herself. He felt helpless. With his mind in turmoil, weakness sliced through him, adding to the restless feeling. He couldn't stop the thousand thorns from his wolf as it sank its power into him. The primal need to protect Jo pushed his control, opened the gates to his hurt, and released the darker side of his beast. He had no idea how the hell he was going to keep Jo safe. *Take her. Mark her. Make her mine.*

Mia ignored Jordyn and Ethan, and strode to the door. When she stood in its opening, she turned to the living room, her blue eyes gleamed like crystal. "Time will tell, Soothsayer."

Jordyn's head jerked up, her lips already moving around her accusations of lies and deceit. She stopped, her words unsaid. Rutger's wolf shadowed him; a burnt gold colored his narrowed eyes, as a wildness called her wolf.

Believing he had buried it, Ethan felt his past clawing itself from the grave, and with heartache he acknowledged what he had to do next. Jordyn needed help. Without saying good-bye, he walked out of the house and closed the door behind him. Looking at Aydian, he said, "Keep them safe."

Rutger locked the door, the click of the mechanism a warning for Aydian not to disturb them. Remaining where he stood, his muscles grew taut, his wolf moved beneath his skin, its veil covering his entire body. "You know what I'm going to do?" His low growl broke his words.

"Yes." Jordyn stood. Cast in the shade of his wolf, she saw Rutger, the man, through a haze. She had heard bits and pieces from the night Rutger found her at Belle Ridge. After rescuing her from the altar, he felt her when she chose death over life and died in his arms. The cavity death created, and the sorrow he felt, caused him to lose control over his wolf. He had become a distorted combination of human and beast.

When werewolves lose themselves to the primeval forces of their beast, the human side of morals and rational thoughts surrendered to the primal forces and instincts of the wolf. Unable to keep a true human form, and unable to fully shapeshift, the monstrosity spent its life in a cage.

While Rutger stayed at Celestial, drugged and chained, his hurt had found her more than once. It broke her heart. When she begged the baron for information, he assured her, since Rutger had witnessed her come back from the dead, he was able to dominate the beast.

The beast was gaining strength. Rutger's own sins, fear for her life, and the Highguard pushed him and tipped the scale. Jordyn saw anguish in his eyes from the pain he was going to inflict on her.

She knows I'm going to hurt her. "What did you see?" Rutger asked. *Can't hurt her.* The internal fight made him shake, and throughout his body, his muscles shuddered, uncontrolled.

"Mia isn't my mother." She didn't want to admit it, not yet. With Rutger's senses targeting her, she wasn't going to risk lying.

"Who is?"

Going to lie. "I don't know. I'm not sure." Jordyn took a hesitant step and her powers drifted. "Wolf," she soothed. Marked. She had made the first strike. Jordyn sought the power inside him and tried to calm him.

Wolf. He ignored her. "You're lying. Don't fucking lie to me." He drew his brows together, his eyes deepened with his words, and the dark veins in his neck pulsed with his heartbeat.

Rutger's wolf lashed out, she turned her face, and felt its claws on her as if he had touched her. Standing her ground, Jordyn met his unsteady gaze and touched the power she had shared. "Lady Sloan. The baron didn't know what he was doing when he started this."

Jo's voice echoed. *Wolf.* He felt her compassion and it soothed the beast. "No, he didn't. We're caught in a web that will continue to wrap around us." His voice was returning to normal, human. His features softened, his body relaxed, and he took a deep breath. "Punishments will come quick."

Secrets from her past were going to open old wounds. "The Highguard called me a scion. I'm Lady Sloan's scion and they know. Rutger, they'll force me to leave you. I won't go without your mark," Jordyn promised. Her eyes burned, and her heart hurt. She would be leaving Rutger and her home, again.

Part of him caved with her words. He wanted it. His teeth ached with the need. His body drummed with anticipation. Rutger took an uneven step, and another, forcing his stiff legs to work. *Can't hurt her.*

"God, Jo. What are we?"

"The beginning of the dark ages…"

ABOUT THE AUTHOR

M.A. Kastle is originally from Northern California, and now resides in sunny Southern California. She is the Author of Tales of Woe, A Curse Revisited, and is published in the First- Women in Horror Annual. With a notebook, pen, and camera, she enjoys traveling, camping, and hiking.

Made in the USA
Monee, IL
21 February 2023

28183763R00216